RISE OF THE GIANTS

RISE OF THE GIANTS

The Guild of Deacons, Book 1

JAMES MACGHIL

ISBN: 0996193502
ISBN-13: 9780996193504
This book is a work of fiction. Names, characters, places, and incidents either are the product of the author's imagination or are used fictitiously. Any resemblance to actual persons, living or dead, events or locales is purely coincidental.

Library of Congress Control Number: 2015904285
Stephen Gilmore, Tallahassee, FL

This book is dedicated to the lasting memory of Dean Robinson Gilmore and his unrivaled legacy of quick wit, bad jokes, and relentless sesquipedalian prose. Be thou at peace.

TABLE OF CONTENTS

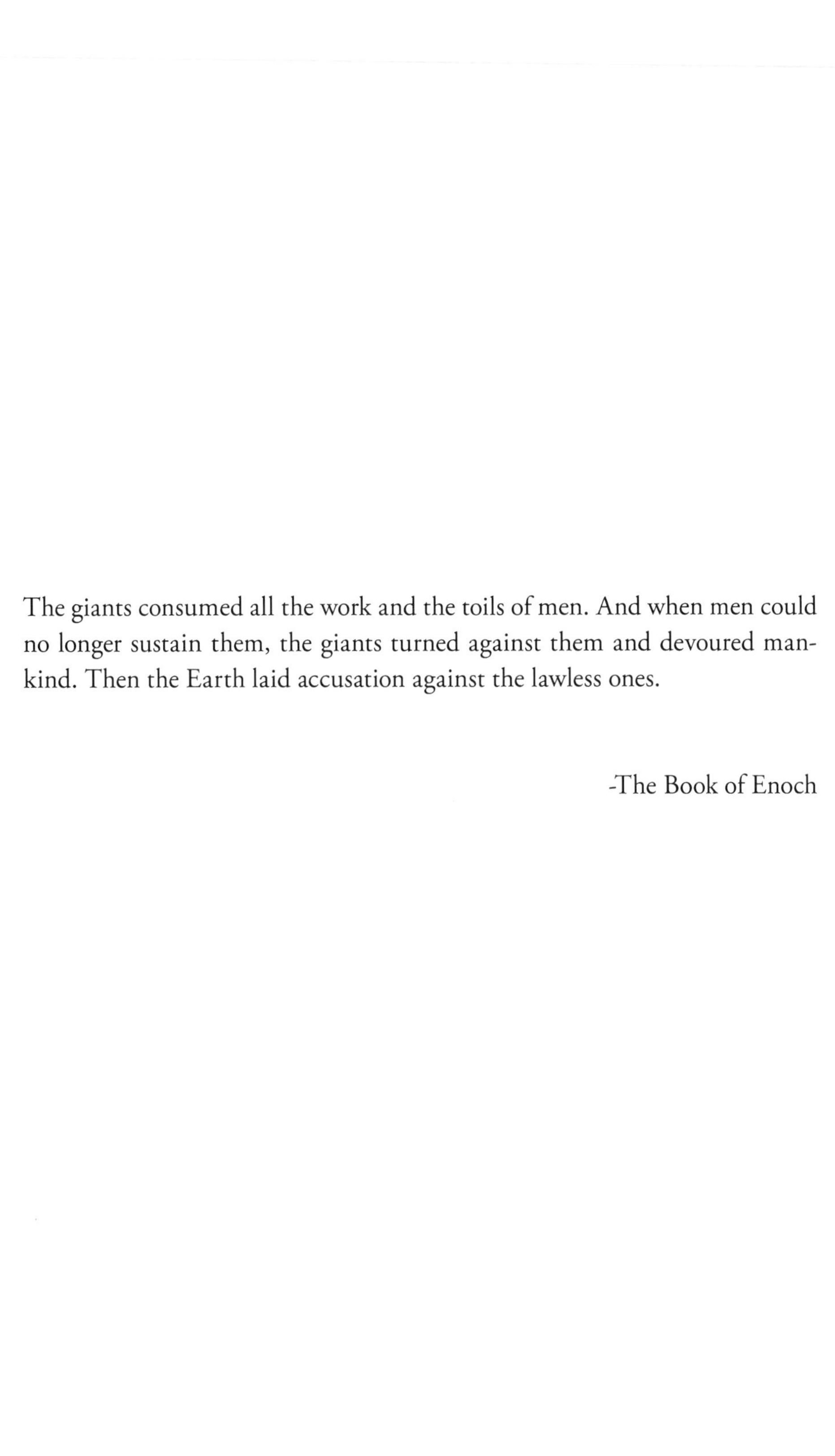

The giants consumed all the work and the toils of men. And when men could no longer sustain them, the giants turned against them and devoured mankind. Then the Earth laid accusation against the lawless ones.

-The Book of Enoch

PROLOGUE

Everybody has dreams. Some pleasant. Some not so much. Either way, dreams are truly an interesting phenomenon. The strange and unusual places your mind drifts when not tethered to the confines of reality. Subconscious manifestations of your deepest desires or darkest anxieties. An infinite possibility of surreal concepts creeping from the seldom used nether regions of your mind.

Some folks believe that dreams are visions or premonitions, possibly even messages from beyond the grave or a higher power. I, personally, know that to be complete bullshit. If dreams were any sort of glimpse into things to come, there would be beer. And women. And more beer. Preferably in that order.

It is also said that the average person has three to five dreams per night. I'm evidently far below average in that regard. I have only one. It's always the same.

I saw through his eyes. Heard through his ears. Felt through his perception of reality. It began as I watched him brutally beaten at the hands of his captors, then, without warning, I was inexplicably and unwillingly thrust into his consciousness. I equated it to riding shotgun in someone else's head.

The ultimate first person shooter experience where you had absolutely no control over what was happening, nor any idea what you were doing there in the first place. A generally unsettling way to spend your evenings, if you get my drift.

Never complete segments — more like fragments jumping between time and place completely out of context. Sort of like a badly spliced movie where the screen went blurry, and the speakers hissed with static during the poorly timed scene transitions. A highlight reel where you got just enough of what was happening to be exceedingly interested, but left thoroughly confused in the end. Frustrating as all hell.

After one hundred and seventy-seven iterations you'd think I'd have it down cold, but each time there was always a slight variation. Some small, near unnoticeable detail revealed that was previously hidden. Like a name, spoken and clearly audible where it was muffled and undecipherable in a prior iteration. Or a symbol, out of focus and seemingly insignificant but subsequently emphasized through both action and emotion.

Unlike past dreams, I remembered every detail, every moment like they were instantaneously burned into my memory. Things I could not unsee — unfeel — unlearn. Amazing things. Impossible things. Unfortunately there were no women and there was no beer — typical.

While I haven't figured out who he was nor why I was privy to his visions, I have figured out one thing — he was not to be screwed with.

My name is Dean Robinson. In life I was a soldier. An elite product of the U.S. Army. Upon death I became … well, let's just say I became something else and leave it at that for now.

There is an evil in the world of man. It's been here since the beginning. Hidden neatly within the fabric of our very existence, festering through generation upon generation — Manipulating — Corrupting — Evolving. Closer than you could ever imagine.

Conversely, there are those of us that maintain the Balance. This is how it began. For me, the tale began at the end.

Chapter 1

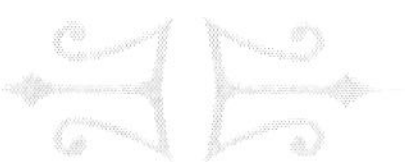

Quick Reaction Force Compound
Outskirts of the Bosnian Township of Brčko
27 December 1998 - 02:43 Hours

For some reason I could never get to sleep after a mission. My mind would race for hours. It absolutely refused to power down. Something about overstimulation from repeated exposure to hostile gunfire. Life and death situations. Blah, blah, blah.

Evidently there were numerous academic studies done on the topic. Like I gave a shit. It was part of the job. An occupational hazard. Annoyed that I had to get up again in an hour, I struggled to keep my eyes shut. Turning to my side in frustration, I adjusted my sleeping bag as my piece of shit, US Army issued, cot creaked and moaned in protest.

The fact that today was my birthday may have also been contributing to the insomnia factor. The ripe old age of thirty-three — practically a damn senior citizen in soldier years. Thinking that I'd give my kingdom for a real bed at the moment, I chuckled to myself at the thought of the ridiculous places I'd spent my birthday over the past few years. Caves, swamps, foxholes — a soldier's life was something special. No doubt.

At any rate, three more days and we'd be stateside again, at least for a short while. Real beds. Real food. Real beer.

Mesmerized by the faint swinging motion of the dim light bulb hanging from the center of my GP Medium tent, I finally felt my eyes get heavy and my thoughts start to wane. Slowly drifting into that awkward sleep state that only happened when you were completely exhausted or piss frigg'n drunk, I felt it start — the dream. The goddamn dream. Just like every other night since getting here six months ago. Too tired to resist, I felt my eyelids flicker shut and the familiar scene came into perfect focus. Goddammit — I really frigg'n hate this part.

It always started outside the towering gate of an ancient city. The time period was unclear, but my guess was sometime in the first century. It felt like Jerusalem in ancient times. Not that I had any personal experience with what Jerusalem in ancient times actually felt like, but I had seen Ben-Hur a couple times. Perhaps one time too many. Don't judge me, it's a frigg'n classic.

I stood within a crowd of people and watched as he was dragged through the gate and casually thrown to the ground by soldiers donning bronze-plated armor and sheathed swords. As the soldiers disdainfully muttered something and walked away, he remained hunched over on his knees in the center of a sand covered road. His hands were bound together and firmly pressed against the ground supporting the weight of his upper body as he halfheartedly attempted to get up.

The sun hovered directly overhead in the midday sky, which was a radiant blue and completely absent of clouds. The heat was blistering, and I saw him wince as his palms clearly burned from contact with the sand. His tattered cloak was soaked with sweat that dripped down his forehead and stung his eyes as he squinted while attempting to shake it from his face. As he slowly raised his head, sullen eyes viewed an incensed crowd that had formed around him in a semicircle. His soiled and sunburned face was that of an honest man holding no contempt toward those who persecuted him. He appeared weakened and worn. Exhausted. Defeated, yet somehow resolute.

Venomous shouts of 'blasphemy,' 'heresy,' and 'impiety' poisoned the air. He scanned the crowd to find faces twisted into vicious scowls and looks of utter revulsion. Accusing eyes filled with pure disgust, all fixed solely upon him. As the shouting grew to a thunderous level and feverous tone, the crowd parted, and seven figures dawning ornate crimson robes trimmed with golden fringe slowly emerged. With heads bowed, they strode in perfect unison and stopped directly to his front, forming a perfect line. Standing rigid in a military like manner, they made no eye contact with anyone, as if awaiting orders to perform their next action.

"*Sanhedrin*," he muttered under his breath.

Their faces were blank, devoid of emotion in every respect. While their eyes were intense they also seemed distant, as if their thoughts were not completely of their own making. As if on command, each figure simultaneously removed his ceremonious attire and handed it to a child, with unusually red hair, on the inner perimeter of the crowd who apprehensively accepted it and piled it at his feet. One by one, they stepped forward and secured a jagged stone from a carefully placed pile at the feet of a white-robed man standing to their immediate left.

As the scene began to slowly blur and the crowd faded into a background of softened obscurity, my focus shifted to the white-robed figure. Easily a head taller than anyone else in the crowd, his robe was of fine silk and the purest of white.

It flowed to just above his bare feet with a perfectly sewn hem, keeping it just above the tarnished ground. His eyes were deathly cold yet somehow burned with the ferocity of an apex predator. A vivid crimson red with tiny, calculating pupils. His stare was absolutely mesmerizing — Frigg'n terrifying. His mouth curled in a satisfying grin. He began to speak, but the sound was muffled and indiscernible.

As the inaudible words faded, the phrase "Your time has ended, *Deacon*" echoed through the crowd in a mocking tone followed by subtle paled laughter. Raising his right hand above his head, he gave the frenzied crowd a stern look. They fell perfectly silent. Instantly. The robed figure then turned to each of the seven.

"Now my brothers, return this *heretic* to the fires that await all blasphemers. Do as the Lord commands. Do it now, in His name."

As the order was given, they simultaneously raised the stones clutched dispassionately in their hands and stepped forward in unison.

Clearly drawing upon all his remaining strength, the prisoner stood upright. His hands clasped and lowered to his front, offering no resistance. As the first blow struck his face, his head violently snapped backward.

⁂

As I felt the impact of the blow slam into my forehead, I painfully realized I was no longer a casual observer in the dream. I was now an active participant — the main character in fact. In some kind of a pseudo Vulcan-mind-meld maneuver, I was sucked into his head and had a front row seat from there on out. Like it or not.

The first few times it happened I was thoroughly confused. Now, after one hundred and seventy-seven repeat performances, I just kind of go with the flow. Not much of a choice in the matter. For a reason I had yet to discern, I was hitching a ride in the body and mind of some random first century guy with anger issues and a propensity to wear cloaks.

Like the saying goes, 'You can pick your friends but you can't pick your dreams.'

So, I might have made that saying up — Frigg'n sue me. It helps me cope.

⁂

As my head slowly rocked forward, a veil of blood gradually coated my eyes. I looked down at my bound hands. They were unfamiliar to me, mainly because they weren't mine. They were his, and I was seeing through his eyes, which were actually now mine. It's all very confusing and generally unsettling. Trust me on that one.

Time slowed to a creeping halt. My head dropped in apathy. Death was imminent. I could feel the sour emotion dominate his thoughts, now my thoughts.

Drop by drop, the blood gradually tumbled from my bludgeoned face and was quickly absorbed by the thirsty sand and scorched rock waiting at my feet.

"Forgive them Father," I heard myself mutter in an unfamiliar voice, "*They know not what they do.*"

I slowly raised my head toward the placid sky as countless blows repeatedly struck me down. There was no pain, only confusion, and brief moments of fleeting clarity followed by numbness. There was peacefulness. And then, there was nothing.

As my sight faded, the sky opened and there was blinding darkness.

Like the abrupt changing of a channel, I found myself standing alone in an open field bordered by a plush forest on three sides. It was dusk, and the sun was low on the horizon. I bore no physical sign of the brutal beating I'd suffered nor did I experience any feeling of pain. My tattered clothes were replaced and a curious black cloak hung from my shoulders.

In the far distance I gazed upon the outline of a majestic city spread artfully throughout seven adjoining hills. From prior iterations of the dream, I knew the city to be ancient Rome though I was unclear as to the actual year. I'd make another Ben-Hur reference here, but I'm not sure it would be appreciated.

"*The great city of man,*" I muttered gazing remorsefully at the city. "*What evil do you nurture within your walls? How easily deceived.*"

Something was different. I felt older. Uncompromising. Wrathful.

It was the eve of a battle. Legions of soldiers were forming outside the walls of the city. Hastily built encampments littered the banks of the mighty river running to its north. There was a great stone bridge reaching from one bank to the other, and a smaller, hastily built wooden bridge running adjacent to it. My gaze followed the structure across the river and focused on the invading army that was forming rival encampments tucked in the foothills to the far north. As I pulled the hood of my cloak over my head, I sighed.

"*Here blood will spill and the path of man decided.*"

My hand reached back and tightly wrapped around the hilt of a seemingly uncommon to the era longsword sheathed and fastened to my back. Upon drawing the blade, the sword seemed to hum with power as if charged with an electric current. With the index finger of my left hand I traced the outline of a symbol boldly emblazoned in the pommel. A bold '*X*' with a prominent '*P*' struck through the middle. I turned toward the rival encampment and began to walk.

⁂

The scene blurred for a split second and day became night. The moon was bright in the evening sky, casting a distinct glow over the vast countryside. I walked, unchallenged, through cluster upon cluster of soldiers preparing for battle. Countless soldiers. Tens of thousands.

The air was charged with a nervous energy as the barking of orders, grinding of remorseless metal, and clinking of armor melded together to form the macabre sound of battle preparation. Despite the vigilant security and guarded entryways to the encampment, no one tried to stop me nor seemed to pay me any attention. I simply walked through all the commotion. A stranger, neither seen nor heard. Like a ghost.

⁂

I stood directly in front of a large tent guarded by at least a dozen soldiers bearing highly polished bronze armor and carefully honed spears. A gold staff bearing a vexillum suspended by a gold crossbar was carefully placed in the ground to the right of the entrance.

"*The mark of Constantine*," I murmured as I studied the lustrous red flag adorned with three golden circles and golden tassel.

The guards heeded me no attention as I walked directly through their formation and entered the tent. Crossing the threshold, I decisively drew the sword from its scabbard, releasing a ripple of energy into the chill air.

⁂

Standing within the sleeping chambers of the tent, I gazed upon the would be commander of the invading army as he rested in his bed. In a blur of motion, I placed both hands in a reverse grip on the hilt of the massive sword and drove the blade firmly into the ground. Standing directly behind it, I then placed both hands to my front with palms facing upward.

"*Constantine,*" I whispered with a serene voice. "*Awaken.*"

Rising from his slumber, the commander was surprisingly unalarmed by my presence. He simply stared at me in utter reverence as he rose from his bed and knelt in front of the sword. As he began to speak, white noise flooded the vision disclosing mere audible fragments of the exchange.

"Are you an angel of the Christian God? Please, tell me, what is your purpose here?"

"I am my Father's Wrath," I replied. *"My time here is brief."*

"Are you to claim my life?" He asked.

"You have found great favor with the Lord. My charge is the ruination of the bastard sons of heaven and those that foster their abhorred existence on His earth. I am to restore the Balance."

"I do not understand. Are you to command my legions? Am I to unify Rome — to defeat Maxentius?"

"Your enemy is not who you believe him to be. Maxentius is not a man. He is an angel — a heavenly Watcher — fallen from grace. A son of God who defiled himself and his brothers. His true name is Azazel. Weapons of man cannot defeat him."

"How will I combat such power? What am I to do?"

"Be strong in the Lord and the power of his might," I replied as I bent down and etched a symbol in the dirt with my index finger. It was a peculiar '*X*' with a '*P*' struck through the middle, encased in a triangle and bound within a circle. "*With this sign, you shall conquer.*"

Without any further words I turned and faded from the tent.

Like a vinyl record skipping several tracks and picking up midstream in a different song, I found myself on the edge of a woodline facing a mighty river.

It was dawn. I knelt with my head bowed and left hand placed firmly on my knee. My longsword was drawn with the mighty hilt clutched in my right hand and the blade thrust forcefully in the ground, supporting my weight. I was praying.

Although I did not understand the words as I muttered them under my breath — I got the gist. It was a soldier's prayer and I was asking for strength. Rising to my feet and pulling the hood of the dark cloak over my head, I sheathed the sword and walked determinedly toward the riverbank. Toward the bridge.

❧

I stood alone in the center of the great stone bridge. A thick layer of morning fog clung tightly to the calm waters of the river below and extended onto to the far bank like a hovering blanket. The sound of soldiers gathering in battle formations was evident to my front. In the distance, I gazed outward to see countless legions of soldiers, horses, and weapons of war carefully placed in defense around the gates to the city. Stopping to peer over my shoulder behind me, I saw the invading army assembling in an offensive formation on the edge of the horizon. The battle was imminent.

Reaching the end of the bridge, I drew the sword with my right hand and resumed the kneeling position. Bowing my head, I muttered something in a whispered voice. Slowly raising my head, my sight projected clear across the great distance separating me from the defending army. It was like looking through a powerful zoom lens rapidly honing in on its target. As it slammed to a halt in the middle of the vast formation of soldiers, a chilling armored figure mounted on a pale horse came into perfect focus.

As if he instantly knew he was being spied upon, his crimson eyes flashed with fury as he returned my gaze, looking directly at me despite the great distance. Although no words were spoken, I heard them clearly in my mind.

"Dare you cast Sight upon me?"

"The Lake of Fire thirsts for you and your bastard sons, Azazel. As He commands it, so it will be. The Balance must be restored. Your treachery has run its course."

"You!" he snarled. "Returned from the Realms after so many centuries? Father's great *champion*. He sends a *son of man* to face a Son of the Heavens. Contemptible. You exited this world as a feeble sheep. Your *martyrdom* was for not. Mankind is mine to do with as I wish. Have you not heard, *Deacon*? Crawl back to *your Father*. He has no power here. Nor do you."

As the vision blurred, the armored figure bellowed an inaudible command to his waiting soldiers and the morning turned to darkness as the sky filled with arrows.

With a single word, hundreds, if not thousands of razor tipped bolts smoothly launched from the bows of the waiting archers and blocked out all light cast from the morning sun. Without moving from my position on the bridge, I remained kneeling and looked upward to see them reach the peak of their menacing arc and begin the fatal downward plunge. Closing my eyes I felt an intense, serene focus wash over me as my concept of time changed and everything seemed to dramatically slow to a crawl. Although I knew that the immeasurable barrage of arrows was mere seconds away from impaling me, I felt no dread.

Instead, I felt powerful. Intoxicatingly powerful.

Difficult to describe, but it felt like I was drawing upon some form of energy with every breath I slowly pulled into my lungs. The source was uncertain but the sensation was unmistakable as it propagated throughout my body. I felt —indestructible.

As I stood upright and opened my eyes, an assertive grin stretched widely across my face. With my right hand still clutching the sword hilt, I confidently raised my left hand above my head and curled it into a tight fist. Boldly held in the air, it crackled with energy and pulsed with a subtle white glow. Within seconds, an ethereal gauntlet like glove manifested around my fisted hand and slowly crept along my forearm, stopping just under my elbow. In a spectral flash, it took full physical form and perfectly encased my hand in a weightless, silver-grey metal-like material. Instantly, a brilliant radiance of white flamed fire surrounded the seamless gauntlet and traveled the length of my left arm as it began to visibly shake from the raw power coursing through it.

Feeling the power reach its climax, I forcefully extended my fingers toward the sky and released a staggering shockwave of light, heat, and unadulterated power into the charged air. As the wave of throbbing energy exploded from my palm and collided with the onslaught of arrows, I watched in extreme slow motion as they instantly burst into wave upon wave of splintered wood and tiny shards of metal.

For a split second, time slammed to a complete halt. A seemingly endless cloud of debris hovered in the sky as far as the eye could see. Frozen in time, perfectly still. Casting my gaze across the battlefield, I locked gazes with the armored figure atop the pale horse and defiantly pulled my metal-clad hand into a tight fist as time resumed with a deafening boom that ripped through the air like a clap of thunder. The shattered remnants of countless arrows blew violently upward into the morning sky and incinerated into nothingness as if they were never there.

"*Our Father has bestowed great power upon me, Azazel.*"

"You know nothing of *great power*," he replied with a look of disbelief mixed with utter disdain. "My sons will quickly remind you of your *limitations*."

As his face curled into a wide grin bearing his perfectly white teeth, the ground began to quake. Through a swirling cloud of dust I saw the dark silhouettes of impossibly large figures emerge from the gates of the city. Completely dwarfing the legions of soldiers they passed through, with their raw size and bulk, they had the shape and proportion of men but easily five times larger. Giants — heavily armored and wielding oversized swords, battle-axes and spears.

"*The bastard sons*," I muttered under my breath. "*You will receive no mercy.*"

Pulling the tip of my sword from the ground, I raised it in an offensive posture, wrapping both hands firmly around the hilt. In a spectral flash, a matching argent gauntlet formed around my right hand and glistened with the fervent white fire. The flame instantly erupted from my hands and encased the mighty sword in a pulsating glow. The air rippled with waves of searing heat and a brilliant glimmer of pure white light.

As echelons of giant soldiers poured from the city and readied for the coming fight, I confidently strode toward them with a dark grin on my face.

Like I knew something they didn't.

⁂

With the blur of a fast forward sensation, I found myself in the middle of the battlefield standing opposite a hulking, manlike creature wearing various components of barbaric bronze armor. The remaining horde of giant soldiers was gathered roughly a mile in the distance, anxiously stirring like a pack of rabid animals on the verge of frenzy. Despite the great distance, I could clearly see the heaving of their massive chests and striations on their impossibly large muscular frames.

With a badly tarnished and oversized breastplate crudely strapped to his towering shoulders, a brooding twenty-foot behemoth, with eyes like pools of oil, stood directly to my front. Clutching twin battle-axes in its powerful hands, it snarled at me through double rows of deep yellow, animal like teeth. Wave after wave of rancid breath poured from its mouth. In a condescending tone, it spoke with a guttural voice that dripped of arrogance and contempt.

"Human slave," it growled. "Endless will be your suffering. The days of man are fleeting. As it was before — so shall it be again."

With inconceivable speed and agility, it then launched at me while raising both weapons high above its head. Closing the distance between us in the blink of an eye, it savagely lowered the axes in a decapitating deathblow.

As my mouth curled into a dark grin, a stiff jolt of power coursed through my body as I impossibly leapt upward and gracefully dodged both blades. In what felt like extreme slow motion, I then casually hovered above the massive creature and firmly wrapped both metal encased hands around the mighty hilt of the longsword. In a single fluid motion, I then rolled to the left and mercilessly swept the glowing blade downward across my chest. With uncanny precision, it violently lashed into the back of the giant's broad neck and surgically cleaved the massive head from its shoulders — leaving nothing but a fine mist of dark blood hanging, ominously, in the air.

The enormous severed head plummeted to the ground with a heavy thud as I nimbly landed in a crouched position. With the sword grasped in my left hand and boldly held out to my side, I slowly raised my head and glared disdainfully upon the watching legion of giants.

Daring them to advance.

Maddening howls bellowed from their gaping mouths as the headless carcass of their slain champion collapsed like a felled tree. In an uncontrolled fury, they bound toward me with inconceivable speed, brandishing all manner of weapons in their enormous hands.

The earth trembled beneath my feet.

As the vision started to distort, I thrust my longsword to the sky and muttered words in a strange language. Upon completion of my speaking, the white flames that encircled my sword instantly tripled in intensity and danced with impassioned purpose. In a blur of movement I reversed the sword and thrust it with all my power into the ground before me. As it penetrated the surface, a boundless wall of infernal white fire erupted from the earth like a raging volcano. It stretched from left to right as far as the eye could see and subsequently raced forward with unbridled speed toward the charging mob. Reaching the front of the formation, the fire mercilessly ripped through the endless throng of giant men until they were nothing more than blazing silhouettes against the morning sky. Their screams formed an inhuman sound of unthinkable pain which rung continuously through my ears as they methodically fell to the ground and were swallowed by the earth.

My final vision was that of the crimson gaze of the dark figure as he rode from the battlefield at great speed atop the pale horse. His eyes were laden with a combination of astonishment and absolute horror as he faded into the fleeting distance and melted from sight.

⁂

"*Dean, It is time to open your eyes. And See ...*"

Upon hearing my name I instantly woke up. As my eyes focused, I realized that I was lying in my shitty, olive drab cot.

I was me again.

"Lottery," I grumbled sweating and gasping for breath. "Why can't I dream about winning the fucking lottery? Big frigg'n yacht. Scantily clad women. Fruity drinks with little umbrellas. Why can't I dream about that shit?"

Chapter 2

Shaking my head in disbelief after experiencing the one hundred and seventy-seventh iteration of the same dream since arriving in Bosnia, I wiped the sweat from my forehead thankful that I'd woken up. Sitting up in the cot, I reached over to the empty ammo crate used as an improvised bedside table and grabbed my notebook and a pen. A few months ago I started keeping a journal documenting my outlandish dream experiences. Figured it was a good idea for a couple reasons.

One, I'd need it for the intense psychiatric treatment I'd require when we got stateside and my mind finally snapped, which I was fully expecting to happen at some point soon.

Two, although the dream was generally the same every night, there seemed to be small details sporadically revealed every few iterations. Things like names. Words. Symbols. In some versions they were either audibly muted or visibly blurry, but in others they were clear as day. While I had no clue as to the significance of the revelations, I found myself extremely curious.

Like I said, I had some serious therapy waiting for me down the road. There was no doubt.

Last night was interesting. I picked up on a few things I hadn't noticed before. A couple names came through loud and clear. There was also a strange symbol shown to me in two separate instances. It looked like an off set '*X*' with a '*P*' running through the middle of it. As I made the notes and wondered what it all meant I heard voices and the sound of people stirring outside my tent.

Glancing at my watch, I noted that it was almost o'five hundred. Damn. I overslept. First Sergeant Tony Coates, my second in command, usually kicked my ass out of the rack by now. He must have been feeling sorry for me this morning. Said I'd been going out on too many missions lately. Was going to burn out. Bullshit. We had three more days in this shit hole. I was doing just fine.

I command a team of specialists from an undisclosed unit of the US military. A veritable 'strike force' highly proficient in Noncombatant Extraction Operations — NEOs. Rangers, shooters, door kickers, demo experts, snipers — that's us. Loners and expendables. You wouldn't hear about us on the evening news. In fact, you wouldn't hear about us at all. We were formed in the past few years as a grand experiment to handle situations that never made it to the watching eye of society. The dirty missions that required soldiers with the darkest of skills.

We were the best of the best or the worst of the worst depending on which end of our weapons you sat. The Army wasn't concerned about what to do with us at the end of the experiment because they figured we'd all be dead. Seemed logical enough. I'd tell you the name of our unit but we didn't really have one. Seemed all the good ones were taken. Typical.

As far as the world was concerned we were part of a training battalion stationed at Eglin Air Force Base in Northwest Florida. Instructors at the infamous swamp phase of the legendary U.S. Army Ranger School.

At this very moment we should have been enjoying a day off at a beach somewhere on the Gulf of Mexico with a case of Corona and Jimmy Buffet's greatest hits. But unfortunately, we weren't.

We were holed up in a secured compound tucked into the remote, mud-laden countryside on the outskirts of the *thriving* Bosnian metropolis of Brčko. Not exactly a hopping vacation spot if you get my drift. So, how did we score such a primo assignment?

For the past five years it's been home to a multinational military task force conducting 'peace keeping' and 'stabilization' operations on the tail end of the Bosnian war. Roughly eight months ago, a dramatic, unexplained spike in civilian abductions along the Bosnian/Serbian border caught notice of the military and we got the call.

We were referred to as the Quick Reaction Force — QRF for short. Not having much contact with the larger task force, we were a bit of a mystery. Although they didn't know us, they knew why we were there. Innocents got snatched by bad guys — we got them back. It's what we did. I'd be lying if I told you we weren't good at it. There were none better.

"Morning, First Sergeant," came the chipper voice of Sergeant Willis from a few steps outside my tent. "Have you seen Captain Robinson? I have a message from Task Force for him."

Willis was a supply sergeant from the Task Force main compound in Brčko and one of the few people authorized to know our location and actually interact with us in person. He made an incognito supply run to us every two weeks. Food, water, and bullets. He occasionally showed up with a few cases of beer when he could get his hands on it. God bless him.

Despite the fact he was incredibly young, a bit green, and not a true soldier by our definition, we'd grown to like him over the past few months. Well, most of us anyway.

"What the hell's so good about this particular morning, Willis?" Abruptly answered First Sergeant Coates in his gruff morning voice. I smiled, envisioning the death grip he most likely had on his Green Bay Packers coffee mug and intense scowl plastered across his face. "And why are you here so goddamned early? Wasn't expecting you until tonight. Lucky we didn't shoot your happy ass on mere principle."

Tony was a career soldier. A genuine American hero and one hell of a good friend despite the fact I was the commanding officer and he the first sergeant. We'd been together for more than five years now and seen more shit than either one of us cared to talk about without large doses of alcohol involved. I'd put my life in his hands on more than a couple occasions. Granted, it was usually by his doing my life was in jeopardy in the first place, but what are friends for.

It kept things interesting.

"Apologies First Sergeant," Willis replied. "Got a bunch of supply runs today and had to get an early start. But I did bring some of that Italian coffee you like. Fresh brewed about an hour and a half ago. Made it right before I left."

"Well shit, Willis. Why the hell didn't you say so," Tony replied completely changing his demeanor. "Might be a good morning after all. Don't be shy with that stuff now, Sergeant."

Chuckling to myself, I envisioned Tony dumping out the shitty Army coffee in his mug and holding it up for Willis to pour him some of the good stuff from his thermos.

"Goddamn — that's good," Tony muttered as he happily slurped on the Italian goodness. "I take back all the bad shit I've been saying about you."

"I live to serve, First Sergeant," Willis snidely replied with what I imagined was a shit-eating grin.

"So what's this important message for the Captain you were spouting off about?" Tony asked. "He was on patrol last night. Not out of the rack yet and he's off limits for the next couple hours."

"Understood," Willis awkwardly replied as he realized he wouldn't be able to speak directly to me. "I — ah — wanted to let him know that Father Watson and Doc Kelly are in the vicinity and may stop in for supplies."

"That's it?" Tony scoffed. "That's the *important message* that you drove out here at the ass crack of dawn to deliver? What the fuck?"

"Actually — No, First Sergeant, I — ah — was hoping to talk to Captain Robinson about —"

"For Christ's sake Willis, Spit it out!"

"Well, it's just, I wanted to ask him if he'd be up for some sparring."

"*Sparring*?" Tony asked. "You want to *box* Captain Robinson?"

"Roger that, First Sergeant. Heard all the stories about his matches over the years. And I've been hoping to go a couple rounds with him since you guys got here six months ago. I mean — he's kind of a boxing legend."

"You're serious," Tony said skeptically.

"I am, First Sergeant. With the QRF rotating back to the states in a couple days — this may be my last chance."

Erupting in a hearty laughter, it seemed that Tony spit out all the coffee that he had in his mouth as it sprayed against the side of my tent.

"Are you shitt'n me?" He said amidst persistent chuckles. "You've heard the stories, eh? Have you ever seen the guy fight?"

"Well, No," Willis replied clearly insulted. "But I'm pretty sure I can hold my own. Golden Gloves — four years running."

"Shit, Willis. You got some serious balls. I'll give you that," Tony grumbled. "There's not a Ranger in this compound that would step into the ring with Captain Robinson without a gun pressed to their head. Not a Ranger in the whole goddamn Army that would do it if they have any sense about them. The guy's a goddamn machine — built like a brick shit house and faster than you can imagine."

"Come on, First Sergeant," Willis said clearly unconvinced. "All those stories can't be true. I mean —"

"True?" Tony scoffed. "Shit, He's the only frigg'n guy in the history of West Point they banned from competitive boxing. *Why?* Because he put too many cadets in the goddamn hospital. That's *true.* And just last year he knocked out the post champ of Fort Benning in half a round. Fight lasted all of thirty seconds — also *true* — saw the whole damn thing." Pausing for a slurp of joe, he said, "Never had a match go longer than a minute. Goddamn fact. He floats around the ring like a ghost. Hits like a fucking sledgehammer. Absolutely fearless. Never seen anything like it."

"But if he's that good, why doesn't he fight more?" Willis impatiently blurted out.

"Because it's not important to him," Tony grumbled. "Not worth the time."

"I don't get it, First Sergeant. What is?"

"The mission," he replied in a sober tone. "The mission and his men. Everything else is just noise."

Figuring Sergeant Willis had enough brow beating for the moment, I pulled on my uniform, grabbed my coffee mug, and stepped out into the chill morning air.

"Morning gents," I said pointing my mug at Willis. "Is that the good shit you got there, Sarge? Fill me up."

Clearly not expecting me to stroll out of the tent at that particular moment, a startled Willis dropped the thermos of precious high octane java and stood there, momentarily speechless, as it quickly drained into the frost-hardened mud at our feet.

"That's a damn shame," I said glancing down at the spilled liquid and holding back a smile. "You alright, Willis?"

"I'm fine, sir," he replied somewhat embarrassed. "Sorry about that."

"Well, I guess if there's no coffee to be had I'll get on with my workout," I said shaking my head while giving Tony a wink. "I haven't boxed in a couple weeks. Think I'll go a couple rounds with McCormick before I go running. Gotta stay sharp."

"Not this morning, sir. The LT's on patrol," Tony said with a shit-eating grin. "Won't be back until tonight. And I don't think he's fully recovered from the last time you *sparred* with him. Still has that twitch in his left eye. Piss'n blood. Forgets where he is every couple days. And his jaw never set quite right. Kind of droops, poor bastard."

"Shit. That's right. Hey Willis, I heard you box. You up for going a few rounds?"

"That's a great idea, sir," Tony grumbled before Willis had the opportunity to answer. "Sergeant Willis, here, is a *genuine* boxing legend. Just explaining how he's been dying to knock your sorry ass all over the ring. Golden Gloves six years running."

"Actually," Willis said starting to backpedal, "It was only four years and —"

"Ah, Hell. No need to be modest, Sergeant," Tony said with a mischievous smile. "Give'm hell. No mercy." Leaning closer to Willis, he muttered under his breath, "I'll go wake up the medics. Get a couple ice packs. Maybe a stretcher. Some of those smelling salts too. You know, just in case."

He then turned and walked toward the other side of the compound shaking his head in laughter.

"No, sir," Willis said as all the color instantly drained from his face. "That's not what I said — I mean I might have — but it's not what I meant. All I meant was —"

"It's Ok, Willis. I get it. You got skills," I said with perfect deadpan delivery. "Let's just hope I can last the first round. It's not often I get to box with someone of your caliber out here."

"I don't think this is a good idea, sir," he replied anxiously. "I mean, it's cold and I need to stretch and — I actually worked out last night so I'm pretty tired this morning — and I left my gloves back at Task Force. Another time maybe. How about next month?"

"Come on, Sarge," I replied with a wide smile. "You know we're heading stateside in a couple days. Let's do this. I'm not afraid of a good ass kicking. I'll grab some gloves and headgear. Get loosened up. Be right back."

As I turned to walk into my tent, the look of utter dread on his face was priceless. Not able to keep a straight face any longer, I started laughing and gave him a slap on the shoulder.

"I'm just screwing around, Willis. Besides, I can't have my men see you knock the shit out of me. Be bad for my image and all. We can spar some other time. Deal?"

"*Damn, sir*," he said with sigh of relief. "You had me going there for a minute. Think I'm all set. Let's forget this whole boxing discussion ever happened."

"Fair enough," I replied with a modest chuckle. Switching topics I asked, "Hey, did I hear you mention that the Padre and Doc Kelly were inbound?"

"Roger that, sir. They were loading up their hummer when I pulled out of Task Force this morning. Father Watson said to let you know they'd be stopping by en route to the Pole."

"*The Pole*?" I scoffed. "Why in the fuck would they be going to the Pole? Are you sure about that?"

"Yes, sir," he replied. "Father Watson said they received an urgent radio call for help last night. He was gassing up one of the hummers and loading it with medical supplies when I pulled out a couple hours ago."

Tony walked back to our position as Willis bent down to pick up his dirt covered thermos and began to wipe off the mud with his sleeve. As we traded intense glances as to what possible business Father Watson could have in Brezovo Polje, the radio clipped to his vest cackled to life, announcing that a Humvee was approaching the gate to the compound.

"Roger that," Tony barked into the mic. "Be right there." Turning to me, he said, "Looks like the Padre and Doc just showed up. Let's go find out what the hell's going on here."

"You're reading my mind, Big Sarge," I muttered with a mild smirk, fully realizing that the moniker of 'Big Sarge' really went up Tony's ass sideways.

"Sir," he said as irritation flickered across his weathered face, "Can I ask you something?"

"Absolutely."

"How many frigg'n times do I have to tell you to quit with that *Big Sarge* shit?"

"At least one more, First Sergeant," I smugly replied. "Two tops."

Chapter 3

Leaving Sergeant Willis to go about his business, Tony and I started across the compound to the front gate. The QRF compound, our humble home for the past six months, was not particularly large but it was built like a veritable Fort Frigg'n Knox tucked into the Bosnian countryside. Home to eighteen of America's finest at any given point in time, it was bordered by twelve foot cement walls constructed to withstand a direct blast from a 105mm howitzer and topped with a rather unfriendly triple strand of concertina wire.

The inner perimeter was lined with several GP Medium tents, a bunker where we stored ammo and weapons, and a wooden shack that served as our tactical operations center. It wasn't much but it did its job. Amidst missions and patrols, I rotated all the boys out to a secured annex on the main Task Force compound in Brčko, on three-day stints to rest up, get some real chow and enjoy a hot shower. Tony and I stayed here. Always.

As we walked past the tent where we housed our weight bench and gym equipment, I was instantly pissed at myself for oversleeping and missing my morning workout. Making the mental note to get my sorry ass to the gym later in the day at some point, I looked up to see Father Watson and Doc Kelly walk through the front gate with Sergeant First Class Lucas by their side.

"Hey sir, Look who I found probing the perimeter," Luke quipped in his signature smart-ass tone. "I thought the Swedish bikini team was in town again, but then I saw the combat boots and Red Sox cap and realized it was only Doc Kelly." Turning toward Erin with a shit-eating grin stretched across his face, he said, "Hey Doc, I think I may have pulled my groin muscle on patrol last night. You mind taking a look at it? Might need a good rub down."

"No Problem, Sergeant," Erin snidely replied, fully indoctrinated to the ill-fated Ranger sense of humor. "Let me get some tweezers and a magnifying glass. Be right with you."

As the surrounding crowd burst into laughter at Luke's expense, she said, "Funny how every time I stop by, your genitals seem to be the subject of a different medical condition. Are you having sex with animals again? That would explain the herd of cowering sheep we saw on the way in here."

Turning her attention toward me with a mischievous smile, she said, "You know Captain, you should really keep a closer eye on your men. Poor Lucas here may require another round of vaccinations. You know how he hates needles. Maybe we should just have him neutered and be done with it."

"Ok. Ok, Doc," Luke conceded realizing he was bested yet again. "Good one. As usual, always a pleasure to see you. And you too, Padre."

"Shit Lucas, You got off easy," Tony said not missing an opportunity to get in on the fun. "If the Doc beats you in arm wrestling again you'll have to hand over your Ranger tab and go work in the motor pool." Grinning at Erin ear to ear, he casually tossed in, "No offense, Doc."

"None taken, *Big Sarge*," she shot back. "Although, I seem to remember beating your sorry ass a few times. Or was that just your '*old football injury*' acting up again? Difficult to remember."

The grin instantly dropped from Tony's face.

As per her usual fiery demeanor, the Doc was on a roll. Verbally bitch-slapping Luke and Tony within thirty seconds of stepping foot in the compound was some impressive shit. I guess that's why everybody liked her.

Erin Kelly was hell on wheels. All of five foot two if wearing a pair of combat boots, which she did most always. Once you got beyond the petite frame, hypnotic brown eyes, inviting olive skin, and flowing chestnut hair most often pulled into a tight ponytail poking out the back of a baseball cap, you quickly learned she took shit from no man, woman, or beast. Despite her raw, striking beauty she could drink most Rangers under the table, beat them at arm wrestling, and out shoot all but a few.

From Boston, a renowned cardiothoracic surgeon back in the civilian world, Erin turned her back on it all a year ago and shipped out to Bosnia with the Red Cross. Her reasons for doing so were her own, and it wasn't a topic you visited with her more than once.

Whatever the reason, I couldn't care. Erin was good people — and I might be slightly infatuated with her. That's a story for another time, however. Army Rangers are bereft of feelings in a combat zone.

You know that. Everybody knows that.

"Now that the pleasantries are over," I said breaking into the conversation, "Either one of you care to explain what possible business you have in Brezovo Polje that you don't expect to end in tears?"

"And a good morning to you too, Captain," Father Watson replied stepping toward me with a somewhat amused look on his face as he placed his hand on my shoulder. "Care to offer an aging servant of the Lord a cup of that famous QRF coffee? I've been thinking about it all the way out here."

Walking right past me in the direction of the mess tent, I figured it best to follow. It seemed the Padre wanted to speak privately. He could've picked a better cover story though. Everybody knows our coffee blows.

Even the sheep.

Despite the fact we didn't do much actual cooking in the mess tent, we did keep a couple of industrial strength coffee percolators in there. Tony usually made the morning brew, which generally tasted something like turpentine mixed with — well, mixed with more turpentine. It was, however, hot as hell and had a general brownish appearance, so we drank it.

Army coffee, as a matter of practice, tasted like shit. I was convinced it was written in a regulation somewhere. That didn't keep Father Watson from grabbing a styrofoam cup and helping himself to a man-sized dose of the menacing dark liquid.

"You sure you want to go there, Padre? The First Sergeant's coffee isn't for the weak or faint hearted. The hand of God himself may not protect you from that shit."

"Thank you for the concern Dean, but I'll take my chances," he replied as his face broke into a mild grin. Taking a cautious sip, he said, "On second thought, maybe I'll let it cool for a moment — perhaps a very long moment."

Reaching into his jacket he produced a silver flask and tipped it my direction like he was proposing a toast. As he unscrewed the cap and took a healthy pull, he muttered, "Amen."

Father Watson had devoted the past five years of his life to missionary work in the Balkans. He claimed that he was summoned here to fulfill the will of God. Don't know that I agreed with him on the subject, but in many long discussions at the QRF compound I'd come to respect the hell out of the man regardless. Never been one for organized religion but the Padre was the real deal. And the guy could hold his liquor. He was alright in my book.

"Fair enough," I said amidst a chuckle. "So what's on your mind, Father? Are you serious about this venture into Brezovo Polje? If I may be so bold — That's one epically bad fucking idea. No way in hell you're going in without us. That's nonnegotiable."

The Padre raised his right hand and nodded his head in a '*Yeah OK*' type of motion. "Before we discuss that, I would like to hear about your visions. Are you still experiencing the dream?"

Despite having the patience of a saint, Father Watson was also one stubborn bastard, and it seemed he was clamming up about his motives in Brezovo Polje until we chatted about my dream. Realizing I'd have to momentarily acquiesce, I replied, "I am. Every night. Wish I could say otherwise. Always the same. Strange and unusual. No beer. No women. Satisfied?"

Father Watson was the sole confidant I entrusted with the knowledge of my recurring dream and its insane content. Figured, being of a somewhat biblical nature, he might be able to shed some light on what the hell it all meant. Or better yet, maybe convince me that I wasn't completely losing my mind. Aside from being extremely curious, he'd unfortunately not done either.

He told me to have faith. That the true meaning would be revealed in due time. As if a dream about stonings, giants, and a dude in a dark cloak with a flaming sword had any '*true meaning*' beside that of the guy conjuring the images being a total whack job. I also felt like he was holding back on me but I trusted his judgment just the same. It did, however, make me wonder what the hell was in that flask of his. Must have been some good shit.

"Not quite," he replied tucking his flask back into his jacket pocket as he fixed me with an intense glance. "Have you discerned any further details since last we spoke? Perhaps a name?"

"Matter of fact I have," I replied thinking his timing was a bit suspect. "Last night. Got a couple. The commander of the invading army. My cloaked dream avatar buddy called him Constantine."

"*Constantine*?" He gasped. "Are you certain?"

"Yep. He called him by name a couple times during the conversation in the tent. It was loud and clear this time. And the guy with the crazy eyes. He called him Hazel or Zazel - something like that. Said we he was an —"

"An angel," he said cutting me off in mid-sentence. "Azazel. One of God's chosen. Fallen from grace."

Abruptly turning and starting to pace throughout the tent, he raised a hand to his chin in thought, and muttered, "That is interesting. Was there anything else?"

"One more. The cloaked mystery man himself. Although I prefer Cloakboy, I think his name is actually Deacon. Although, that sounds more like a flannel shirt wearing country singer or a truck driver than a first century —"

"You heard him referred to as Deacon?" He said cutting me off again as his eyes lit up.

"I did," I muttered with a mildly annoyed look. "Prior to the stoning and again at the battle. This making any sense to you?"

"Deacon is not a name, Dean," the Padre replied completely ignoring my question. "It's a title."

Returning to his anxious pacing routine, he produced the flask from his pocket and helped himself to yet another healthy swig.

"A title — Like a pastor? A church deacon? That doesn't make any frigg'n sense."

"By definition, the word *deacon* simply means servant," he said stopping in mid stride as he looked directly at me. "However, in this case I believe we are talking about a church deacon. *The* church deacon. First of the original seven. Falsely accused and martyred."

"Sorry. Don't get it," I said completely confused as to where this conversation was going and why the Padre was worked up enough to start popping a cork this early in the morning. "Why is this relevant?"

"Tell me Dean, did you see this?" He asked as if he didn't hear a word I'd just said.

As he finished speaking, the Padre curled his left hand into a fist and held it outward displaying the signet ring he wore on his index finger. His hand was shaking from what I assumed was excitement. The face of the ring was etched with a perfect circle encasing a triangle that contained a prominent symbol. An '*X*' with a '*P*' struck through the center.

"Yes," I replied momentarily stunned. "It was on the hilt of his sword and he drew it in the sand after talking to the commander. How in the hell could you know that? What's that symbol?"

"It's called a Chi-Rho," he muttered in a feverish tone, paying my first few comments no attention. "It's a Christogram — or an early symbol of Christianity. Glamorized by the Roman Emperor Constantine the Great during the Battle of the Milvian Bridge in 312 A.D." Deliberately pausing, he said, "It also has another meaning. Perhaps more significant."

As my mind raced to keep up with the Padre, I dialed back some of the military history classes I mostly slept through at West Point. Vaguely remembering the Battle of the Milvian Bridge, I said, "Isn't that when Constantine liberated Rome despite being vastly outnumbered? He supposedly had a vision from God. And painted symbols on the shields of his legions."

"Yes, Yes, Dean. You are correct." Tapping the face of his ring, he added, "He painted *this* symbol. The Chi-Rho."

"Ok. So that's interesting. I'll give you that," I muttered doing my damnedest to follow the plot. "Now granted, I may have missed this small detail in the history books, but I don't remember reading about a horde of mythical giants at the battle."

"The fact it was not written does not make it any less plausible," Father Watson replied in a surprisingly sober tone.

"Come again?"

"There are many who believe that *giants* are much more than mere myth," he said. "In the early days of man there are tales of the nephilim — a cursed race of giant beings spawn of fallen angels that nearly devoured mankind. Albeit not a *history book*, their origins and subsequent demise are well documented in the apocryphal writings of the prophet, Enoch."

"You lost me," I replied. "So you're saying the giant gladiator guys in my dream were *real*?"

"I'm not sure this is the time or place for this discussion, Dean," he said pensively. "I fear you are not yet ready to hear what I believe is happening."

"Aw — for Christ's sake, Padre. Seriously? Throw me a frigg'n bone here."

With a look of apprehension strewn across his face, Father Watson began to speak and then abruptly stopped. Letting out a long sigh, he lowered his head and intently stared at the dirt floor of the mess tent. Reluctantly, he said, "What if, for argument's sake, I told you that everything you've witnessed — everything you've experienced — in your dream — is real." Raising his head and fixing me with an intent gaze, he said, "What if I told you that you've been given a repeated firsthand viewing of a series of *actual* historic events from well over two thousand years ago that, by and large, have shaped the world as we know it? The will of Heaven played out on the Earth. Divine retribution for an unspeakable treachery that occurred at the very beginning of time itself. A manifestation of the left hand of God walking amongst men."

Not quite sure how to react to the Padre's comments, I let out a sigh of my own and decided it was time to tempt fate with a dose of the First Sergeant's industrial strength coffee. What the hell. I was clearly delusional and the Padre was evidently drunk. Holding my mug under the spout, I watched the toxic steaming liquid reach the top of the brim as I contemplated what to say next.

Nope. I got nothing. I started laughing and turned to Father Watson.

"Are you fucking kidding me with this? Let me get this straight — an army of giant men roaming the streets of ancient Rome dressed up like gladiators — *That's real.* A dude in a cloak with a big-ass flaming sword that puts the beat down on said army of giant men dressed up like gladiators by shooting a wall of fire at them — *Also real.* Oh, and *Cloakboy* was monkey stomped to death by a bunch of rock swinging, robed cronies *before* he showed up and opened a fiery can of whoop ass on aforementioned giant gladiator wannabes — *Real.* Actually happened. *Frigg'n Seriously*? That's the best you got? Sounds like a bad comic book for Christ's sake. Come on, Padre."

"Yes, of course," Father Watson replied with a look of disappointment mixed with frustration. "This is clearly a discussion for another time. Your visions are a remarkable gift, and I truly feel you are very close to understanding their intent. Now, I'm afraid it is time for me to go. The Lord's business awaits the good Doctor and I in Brezovo Polje."

With that, the Padre tucked the flask back into his coat and shot me a stern look signifying that the conversation was over. Maybe I should have held back on the comic book reference. Might have gone a tad over the top there.

"Great. Thanks for that keen insight," I grumbled. "If I didn't like you so damn much I'd think you were a real asshole. What the hell's in that flask anyway?"

"Holy water," the Padre muttered with a dismissive smirk.

"Holy water my ass," I chortled.

Not sure whether to be pissed or confused by the Padre's latest commentary on my dream, I decided to let it go and change the subject.

"So, let's talk about the Pole. What the hell are you thinking? Did Petrovich contact you directly? You do realize he's a goddamn war criminal right? Not the most trust worthy of individuals."

"Yes," he replied very matter of fact. "Mr. Petrovich did contact me at Task Force last night and request emergency medical assistance. And, Yes, I am fully aware of his reputation. Before you say it — Yes, both Doc Kelly and I fully realize it's a military restricted zone." Without so much as giving me a chance to rebut, he turned and started to walk back to the main gate where the others were still gathered. "And Dean, I greatly appreciate you not giving us any shit about this. There are people in need and we all have our jobs to do."

"Damn it, Padre! We're going with you," I grumbled throwing my mug on the ground in frustration as I caught up with him.

Approaching the rest of the crew still huddled by the gate, I detected a similar conversation occurring between Tony, Doc Kelly and Luke.

"Gentlemen," Father Watson said facing the group. "Although we appreciate your concern, it is not possible for you to accompany us. Firstly, it would be viewed as an act of aggression by entering the restricted zone. Secondly, I gave my word to Mr. Petrovich that we would come alone. He has wounded soldiers, women, and children that require our help."

"But Padre," Tony said shaking his head. "This is a really fuck —"

"First Sergeant! We are not discussing this any further," Father Watson said sharply, with a look of priestly admonishment. "We are noncombatants and the Lord will protect us accordingly. We'll see you tonight for dinner. And I sincerely pray that you cook better than you make coffee."

"Don't worry boys, we'll be fine," Erin said giving me a reassuring glance. "In and out. Nothing we can't handle."

"You watch your ass, Doc," I said with a disapproving nod as I locked eyes with her. "These are dangerous people. Unstable. Any sign of trouble and you bail. We clear?"

"*Yes, sir,*" she replied mockingly. As she packed the remainder of her medical kit into the hummer and climbed into the passenger seat, she said, "See you tonight, Captain. First round is on you."

And then they pulled out and headed south into the countryside.

"I've got a bad feeling about this, sir," Sergeant Lucas said in a somber tone as the hummer finally faded from sight.

"Same here, Luke. Where's the scout team right now?"

"They're patrolling the eastern sector. Not far. Lieutenant Mac checked in about an hour ago."

"I'm on it, sir," Tony said evidently reading my mind. "I'll radio the LT. See if they can't drift south a bit and pick up the Padre's trail. Keep eyes on them for the rest of the day. Real quiet-like."

"I want a report every hour on the frigg'n hour," I grumbled.

Watching Luke head back to his position on the perimeter for morning watch, I turned to Tony and discreetly muttered, "First sign of trouble —"

"We're going in," he said completing my sentence. "I'll put a Blackhawk on standby."

Reaching down to grab the hand mic clipped to his vest, he paused and grumbled, "You know the Padre's gonna be pissed when he finds out we followed them."

"Ah hell, they say the Lord works in mysterious ways, First Sergeant. And we're some mysterious fucking people. I think we're Ok here."

Chapter 4

Brezovo Polje, Bosnia
27 December 1998 - 23:52 Hours
19 Hours Later

"Sir, You good?" Tony murmured as he adjusted the assault sling on his M4 rifle to properly seat the butt stock firmly against his right shoulder, while simultaneously casting me an intense glance.

A glance I instantly recognized. It was go time.

It's called the stack drill. Simple really. Heavily armed, highly trained soldiers stacked on a wall for the sole purpose of entering and clearing a room full of bad guys. Not to state the blatantly obvious, but the concept of 'clearing a room' is a pleasant description for the placement of two well controlled rounds, from your weapon of choice, into the chest cavity of anyone foolish enough to be standing in the room at the time providing opposition.

Every man in the stack had a job. Every man was expected to do his job and his job only. No exceptions. Bad guy in your quadrant — you shot him. Bad guy not in your quadrant — you didn't shoot him and had faith that your Ranger buddy would before aforementioned bad guy returned the favor.

Simple. Boil it all down and the stack drill was all about faith. Balls of steel and a lot of frigg'n faith. It didn't make a goddamned bit of difference how many times you'd done it, practiced it, talked about it, or even thought about it. When you're about to willingly step through a doorway where a high probability exists that bad guys are waiting to pump your sorry ass full of bullets, your mind tends to cast doubt on your ability to self preserve.

Serving under my command were the hardest men to trod with booted feet on God's green earth. And every one of them would be lying their ass off if they told you that clearing a room during a combat situation was not the single event they feared most in this life or the next. It was fear at its most basic level. Extreme fight or flight. Pure adrenaline pumping on overdrive through every kernel of your being. And yet we did it.

Why? Also simple.

Bad guys seemed to have this unbreakable habit of taking good guys against their will. Subsequently, we kicked their fucking doors in and shot them. Good guys went home. We got ready for the next mission. There was no glory. There were no thanks. There was only the next mission and the fleeting hope we were tipping the scales a bit in the right direction. For me and my men, that was enough.

Pay sucked, food sucked, coffee really frigg'n sucked, but the company was good. Most of the time anyway.

"Sir, you with me?"

The subtle yet irritated tone of First Sergeant Coates indicated he was clearly losing patience.

This particular door I was about to kick in had my mind racing a bit more than usual. Could have been the fact that it was almost midnight, unnaturally dark, raining like hell, and the middle of winter in the cozy province of Brezovo Polje — situated tactically on the not so friendly western border of Bosnia and Serbia — where two thousand Serbian refugees were supposedly dug in, after driving all the Muslim inhabitants out of town with extreme prejudice.

Some said the Muslims were still there, just no longer drawing breath. Others claimed they'd gone to ground awaiting an opportunity to strike back and reclaim their homestead. Either way it was a damn mystery, as it was a military restricted zone and we were forbidden to enter under pain of court martial. So the short story here was that my presence in 'the Pole' was neither sanctioned nor welcomed.

Could have been the fact that it was my frigg'n birthday and we were on day one hundred and seventy-seven of a one hundred and eighty day deployment to this literal hell hole where thousands of years of bloody genocide, ethnic cleansing, and unholy death seemed to emanate from every pore of its physicality like a continuous putrid sweat. You could literally feel it. Sense it.

Could have been the fact that Tony and I were huddled on the wall of an ancient church where a reported maniacal Serbian zealot had taken unwilling possession of two American humanitarians, who my men and I had become rather fond of, over the past one hundred and seventy-seven days. And I swore I was hearing the faint echoes of misshapen screams escaping from somewhere deep within the sanctuary.

Could have been the fact that the entire damn village seemed utterly devoid of any human presence, despite the regular intel we received about the inhabitants and their activities. Oh, and every dwelling within eyesight of the church was on fire. The place was a literal flaming inferno. Taking into account the biblical proportions of rain dumping from the blackened sky at the current moment, that was one hell of a feat. No pun intended.

It was our very own circle of hell. The air was suffocating and reeked of a stench potent enough to make your stomach churn with the force of a cement mixer. Sulfur. It stank of sulfur. If I didn't know better I'd swear enough napalm was dumped on this place within the past hour to erase all evidence that human life ever existed here. The town was not being destroyed — it was literally being consumed around us as the flames steadily slithered through the mud-strewn landscape toward the church. Toward us.

As my mind struggled to make sense of what I was looking at, I felt repeated waves of adrenaline surge through me. No stranger to combat, I'd personally led more than a couple NEOs and this was clearly not playing out according to script. Plans usually went to shit fairly quickly and we dealt with it as a matter of practice, but this felt — off. Like something was waiting for us to get here. Something predatory.

And for the first time in a long time, I felt like the prey.

"Sir! Goddammit — You with me?"

No longer a barely audible whisper, the 'answer me right frigg'n now or I'll rip your face off' bark of First Sergeant Coates snapped me from my place of momentary reflection back to the mission.

"I'm with you," I dryly replied with my gaze still fixated on what appeared to be the remnants of a humble farmhouse fully engulfed in vindictive flames on the far perimeter of the church courtyard. "Taking in the landscape for a moment. You take me to the nicest places, First Sergeant."

Despite the surreal setting, our current plight should have been a basic snatch and grab mission, but unfortunately it was a bit more complicated than that. It was personal.

Goran Petrovich, local mass murdering whack job and self proclaimed liberator of Brezovo Polje, had made the very unwise decision to lure two American humanitarians into his shit hole of a refugee camp and keep them against their will. The Padre and Doc Kelly were a local fixture for me and my men since we arrived in Bosnia. Good folks. Good friends.

It was unclear as to Petrovich's motives behind this baited abduction, but I can't imagine he was overdue for his flu shot or had an unyielding need for morning mass. Although highly ranked on the military threat list, we had absolutely no intel on him, not even a frigg'n picture. Believed to be the iron-fisted leader of a local faction of Serbian extremists, it was rumored that he'd personally led a series of bloody raids throughout the past year, resulting in the 'liberation' of Brezovo Polje, in which countless Muslims were executed in a heinous act of ethnic cleansing. It was also rumored that he was nearly seven feet tall and exuded the presence of a '*god*', instilling both terror and adoration in those he presided over. A regular cult icon. What a frigg'n guy.

None of which I could care any less about at the moment. He took my friends. Nobody takes my friends.

I don't have that many to spare.

According to my scouts, Father Watson and the Doc were met at the wired perimeter of the village by three of Petrovich's cronies and escorted, by way of gunpoint, to the church. That was nineteen hours ago and they had yet to resurface. Back to my earlier commentary on the unbreakable habit of bad guys taking good people against their will.

They needed help.

My help.

When I notified my superiors at Task Force command of the situation, and that we were going in to extract them, I was issued a direct order to stand down. Do not engage under any circumstances. I was given a lengthy lecture on how the civilians were duly warned to stay out of Brezovo Polje. That 'the Pole' was restricted territory and if they chose to go in, they were on their own.

Fuck that.

Against all principles of military protocol, I made a command decision. I decided to wipe my ass with that particular order and go get my friends. Tony unfortunately thought that to be a good idea so we hastily recruited two of our best shooters who shared our not so military perspective on the situation, and set out on an off the books NEO to pull the Padre and the Doc out of the frying pan. Damn the consequences.

The adrenaline rush seemed to be wearing off a bit as my body started to wake up to the coldness of the church wall I was leaning against. It appeared that the exterior walls were constructed with fieldstone. It was cold and unforgiving as I felt the course texture of unfinished rock rub against my shoulder through my soaked tactical uniform.

It was time.

Instinctively adjusting the setting on my red dot scope to close quarters and rotating the selector switch on my M4 from safe to semiautomatic, I returned Tony's steely glance with one of my own.

"What the hell happened here? Frigg'n mess," I muttered reaching back over my shoulder and quickly adjusting the faithful SPAS-15 combat shotgun slung across my back. The M4 was the best for burst fire and stand off distance but you couldn't beat the stopping power of the shotgun. I liked it so much I named it Bertha.

So what — I named my shotgun. It's a common practice.

The SPAS-15 was one of the few magazine loaded, semiautomatic tactical shotguns, which made it both sexy and functional, in my humble opinion. Bertha was one big-ass, sexy bitch. No doubt.

"You ready to do this or plan on crouching in the mud whispering to me all night?" I said giving Tony a nod.

"And here I was thinking you weren't paying attention again," he grumbled as a dark beam stretched across his face and he visibly relaxed, realizing I was ready for business.

His attention quickly turned from me to a final systematic study of the short distance from our current concealed position on the corner wall of the church to the front door, which we figured to be the only entrance.

"Lucas and the LT should be in position by now in the overwatch," Tony said peering over his left shoulder and squinting into the darkness. "Can't see shit through the rain. NODs are useless. They should be right on our 9 o'clock — 50 meters back. Assuming they didn't drown in the frigg'n mud or burst into flames getting there."

Hoping the rain hadn't turned my tactical radio into a canteen by now, I held down the transmit button clipped to my vest and murmured into the throat mic, "Luke — You set?"

Sergeant First Class Lucas and Lieutenant McCormick volunteered to be part of our hunting party. And by volunteer I mean outright demanded, to the point of veiled threats and blackmail, that they be included. I agreed on the strict condition they were on back up duty from an overwatch position. If things went south I didn't want them in the direct line of fire on a rogue mission.

For professional soldiers the only thing worse than having your life abruptly ended was having your career abruptly ended. Exposure of their participation in an unsanctioned raid into 'the Pole' would have them in civilian clothes before the ink dried on their dishonorable discharge.

A quick cackle of radio static was followed by Sergeant Lucas as he replied, "Roger sir — We're set. Got eyes on you and the Big Sarge. Clean line of sight to the OBJ. No movement observed — Anywhere."

"Roger. We're going in — 2 Minutes — Plan's in effect. Radio silence. Robinson Out."

Luke would pay for that 'Big Sarge' crack later, I thought to myself. His comment about not observing movement was Luke telling us that he and Mac shared our anxiety about the current state of affairs in 'the Pole.'

Something here wasn't right. We could all feel it.

"Roger sir. Good hunting. Radio silence."

As agreed before we left, Tony and I would only break radio silence under two conditions.

One — the church was secured. Two — it had all gone to shit.

If by an unfortunate series of events, the second condition prevailed, Luke and Mac were to return to the QRF compound and call it in to command. They were not to come in after us under any circumstance. I was pretty sure they wouldn't follow that order, but I was also pretty sure I'd be hard pressed to be pissed at them for it. We had the Ranger Creed to uphold after all. Fallen comrades were not left at the hands of the enemy — Ever.

"It's go-time Big Sarge," I said intently. "I blow the door and enter first. Cut the room in half. I go left. You go right. We should hit the vestibule first. Secondary door leads into the sanctuary. Clear the room. Restack. Same drill into the sanctuary."

"Better plan," Tony muttered giving me an irritated yet sarcastic glare. "You blow the door. I enter first. I go left. You go right. Do me a favor and try to keep up this time."

As he reached down to adjust the tac light mounted to the barrel of his M4, he casually tossed in, "And sir, Call me Big Sarge again and I'll open the goddamn door with your face."

"Fair enough," I replied realizing I wasn't going to win that argument. "You enter first. I go right. That really is a better plan. What would I ever do without you?"

I was going to throw a 'Big Sarge' at the end but thought the better of it. Tony was built like a linebacker and had the tenacity of a cage fighter. Not the most jovial of characters. I tried to avoid making him upset when at all possible.

"Ok — Let's do this," I grumbled snapping into mission mode. "Shoot anybody that gets in our way. Grab Doc and the Padre. Slap high fives — Call it a day. You good?"

"Roger that," he replied.

Sliding the selector switch to safe, I let the M4 tightly retract against my chest with the assault sling and reached back to trade it out for Bertha. Several ways to blow a door but I always preferred putting a twelve gauge slug between the doorknob and the frame, shattering any locking mechanism in the process. Aside from granting free access, it typically gave whoever was on the other side something to think about right before Tony and I flowed through and introduced ourselves.

"Where the hell are all the people?" I muttered under my breath, to no one in particular, as I made a final visual sweep of the surreal setting laid out before us.

Realizing that answer would have to wait, I pumped a round into the shotgun chamber and crept in front of the First Sergeant to start our advance to the doorway — then I heard it and stopped dead in my tracks, momentarily frozen.

A scream. A woman's scream. Erin.

Fuck.

An eruption of rage coursed through me as I instantly locked eyes with Tony.

"On Three."

With his face curled into an intense scowl, he nodded acknowledgement. Not giving a shit about concealing myself any longer, I boldly approached the door to the oldest church in the Balkans. Placing the muzzle of my shotgun squarely between the wooden frame and the doorknob, I waited the mere seconds it took for Tony to assume his assault position adjacent the threshold. Ready.

One — Two — Three.

Chapter 5

I could only describe it as a momentary suspense of time and space. A fluid consciousness of my surroundings that either propelled me into mental and physical overdrive, or conversely, reduced everyone else in close proximity to extreme slow motion. It was a sensation I'd experienced for most of my life when the fight reflex kicked in. All of my senses seemed to hyperextend to mind blowing proportions. Interestingly, since arriving in Bosnia it had increased one hundred fold, which I casually attributed to daily doses of being shot at. Seemed logical enough.

I had yet to determine the true reality of what was happening, but I had figured out one thing — it was my edge. It gave me the mere split-second advantage I needed. Having experienced it now more times than I could actively remember, I knew it was coming, and I was waiting for it. Counting on it.

As my index finger exerted pressure on the shotgun trigger, I felt myself slip into the welcoming state of calmative awareness. Almost instantly, my senses ignited and extended into the vestibule. I could hear the rapid thumping of three distinct heartbeats. They were afraid. I could smell the fear exuding from their bodies. They were not soldiers but prepared to defend the entrance to the church with their lives. Prepared to sacrifice themselves. One bad guy on the left and two on the right. Not sure how I knew it but I did.

Tony's eyes shifted from me to the breach as his momentum began to slowly carry him forward. I felt every millimeter of movement as the trigger deliberately moved backward until it abruptly stopped. Click.

With a stiff jolt, Bertha recoiled into my right shoulder as the deafening blast released an almost visible shockwave into the surrounding air. I could feel the shotgun slug as it raced down the length of the barrel and smashed into the door, sending an explosion of meticulously polished wood and disfigured metal shards into the waiting vestibule.

I watched as Tony lowered his right shoulder into the door, causing it to swing open, as he simultaneously flowed into the room, raising his rifle to a reflexive firing position just below his chin. He activated his tac light and broke to the left. The signature 'crack crack' of a two round burst radiated from his M4, accompanied by the momentary muzzle flash as the rounds exited the rifle. The fatal groan followed by a distinct thud confirmed his shots hit their target. I faintly heard Tony's voice signal, "Enemy Down."

Before the second round exited Tony's rifle I was moving through the breach directly on his heels. Clearing the threshold and breaking right, I squeezed the muzzle grip on the shotgun to activate my tac light. I easily picked up the first target right where I was expecting him, crouched behind an ornate desk, at my four o'clock. With eyes burdened of fear and indecision, he clumsily raised his weapon. As his finger approached the trigger, my shotgun barked and the first slug hit home obliterating his right shoulder, causing his arm to fall limp with an unnatural motion. His rifle tumbled to the church floor. As the shotgun barked a second time, he sagged to the floor to join his discarded weapon. Lifeless.

"Enemy Down," I grunted.

Within a fraction of a second, my head snapped left as I resumed scanning the remainder of my quadrant. My eyes instantly locked onto the second target to my one o'clock, huddled adjacent the closed double doors that presumably lead into the sanctuary. Clearly as untrained as his buddy, taking up floor space at my feet, he raised his weapon in my direction. He looked beaten. His face was worn. His hands were shaking. He didn't want to shoot me. Without hesitation or remorse I swiftly put two successive slugs into his chest, lifting him clear off his feet and slamming him into the rear wall of the vestibule. Gradually slumping down the wall leaving a telltale, red smear behind, he finally came to a halt on the floor, five feet from his partner.

"Enemy Down. I'm Clear."

"Room Clear," Tony announced. "Three down. They didn't even get a shot off."

Placing his M4 on safe while kicking the weapons away from each of the dead bad guys, he said, "All their weapons are still on safe. And I think this guy pissed himself. What the hell?"

"Worry about that later. We need to move. Same drill into the sanctuary. Restack."

Without the need for further words, Tony and I instinctively moved to the rear wall of the vestibule, to the right of the sanctuary doors, and reformed our stack. We didn't have much time to spare now that we'd made our presence known. Every bad guy in the rest of the church knew we were here and would be gunning for us. We needed to move. Now.

Taking a knee, I ejected the six round magazine from the shotgun and slammed home a fresh one. Taking a quick moment to assess our next move, I focused the beam of my tac light on the sanctuary doorway. The double doors were easily eight feet tall and appeared to be solid as hell. Mahogany. Maybe a dark oak. Hard to tell. Carefully carved into each panel were several symbols, which I faintly recognized for a reason that I couldn't quite place. It appeared they were placed there somewhat recently, as they clearly stood out from the polished finish.

As I contemplated that for a second, my eyes made a somewhat more disturbing discovery. The doors seemed to be bound together by a heavy chain secured by an oversized padlock. They were locked from the outside.

"Why would the sanctuary doors be chained from the outside?" I asked looking over my left shoulder to get Tony's attention as I held a beam of light directly on the locked chain. "The guards — Here to keep people out — or something in?"

Pointing the shotgun muzzle to the floor, I trained the light on Bad Guy Number Three lying dead by our feet. Despite being covered in blood with a large hole where his chest used to be, he was dressed in full-on hospital scrubs, complete with sterile covers on his shoes. Panning the tac light across the room on the other two bodies, I found the same obscurity. Confirming what I sensed earlier, I said, "These guys aren't soldiers. They're fucking doctors — or nurses. What the hell?"

"I have no —" Tony started to speak and stopped mid-sentence as we both picked up on the sounds permeating from the sanctuary. It was faint but undeniable and growing steadily louder. A bone chilling cacophony of high pitch crying, groaning, and whimpering. It sounded almost animal in nature. The sound of concentrated suffering. Women suffering. Several women.

"What in the fuck is that?" He asked in a subdued tone as his face went absolutely blank.

"Sounds like our goddamned invitation," I replied with clenched teeth. "Help me check these assholes for a key."

After a hasty search of the dead bad guys turned up empty, I barked, "So if these jokers don't have a key, how in the hell were they supposed to open the frigg'n door?"

With the clamor of torment and misery continuing to amplify from within the sanctuary, I was clearly losing patience. Reaching into one of my ammo pouches, I pulled out a pre-made doorknob charge. "Shotgun's not going to handle that padlock. We'll have to blow it."

A doorknob charge is a nifty little tool of the trade that consists of a molded piece of C4 wrapped in detonation cord, and primed with a fuse igniter. Simply hang it on the doorknob, pull the igniter, wait three seconds, and ta da … no more doorknob. Clearly not as cool as the shotgun breach, but just as effective.

"I'm going to set the charge," I announced. "Watch my back."

"Roger," Tony acknowledged taking a couple steps off the wall, raising his rifle to cover the front door and secure our six o'clock. At this point we weren't too concerned about anyone popping through the sanctuary doors with the medieval quality security measures in place, but more conscious of someone getting the drop up on us from behind.

Creeping along the wall to the doorway, I reached the man-sized padlock securing the two massive chains together. Somebody was really fucking serious about making sure these doors could only be opened from out here. I was nearly finished setting the charge when the sound of a booming thud echoed through the dank air, and I momentarily lost my footing as the entire floor of the church buckled. It felt as if something had shaken the foundation with the force of a goddamned earthquake.

Shifting my gaze to Tony for an explanation, he simply shrugged his shoulders in a 'No idea' fashion. It happened again, forcing me to throw my hands against the doorway to prevent my head from slamming into it. I braced myself for a repeat performance, but it didn't come. It seemed to stop as abruptly as it started. Shaking off the latest unexplainable element of this mission, I focused back on the task at hand and quickly finished rigging the charge. I signaled to Tony that it was time, and as I reached down to pull the pin on the fuse igniter, I heard it as much as I felt it.

It felt like footsteps. Big fucking footsteps. Running toward the doorway. Building up a head of steam. Shaking the floor to the point of failure.

Completely losing my balance, I fell most ungracefully toward the floor, throwing my left arm back to brace for impact. Keeping my attention locked on the doorway, I watched in utter bewilderment as the eight foot, solid hardwood doors, locked up tight with a chain — thick enough to tow a goddamn tank — blow clear off their hinges hurtling large, fractured chunks of lumber and splintered shrapnel in my direction. And here I was thinking we had the situation well under control.

Despite my best attempt to avoid the incoming onslaught of exploding door fragments, I was clearly unsuccessful. Raising my right arm to shield my face from certain disfigurement, I caught a four-foot section of door, traveling at break-neck speed, squarely across the midsection. As the pain meter spiked to new levels, I heard the distinct cracking of ribs as all the air in my lungs was instantly forced out of my mouth, leaving my chest in a perpetual heave cycle trying to replace it. The shear force of the impact hurled me clear across the vestibule and violently slammed me into the wall, adjacent to the front door. Dazed, confused, and really fucking pissed, I faintly heard Tony's voice as I raised my head enough to see him barreling toward me in a state of wild panic.

Reaching my position in a matter of seconds, Tony assumed a kneeling position placing himself squarely between me and the now gaping hole in the sanctuary wall. Instinctively raising his M4, he braced for the coming assault.

"Jesus Christ, sir, you Ok?"

"Fucking great," I painstakingly replied as the ability to breathe slowly returned. "Thanks for asking. How are you?"

Fighting through the agonizing, stabbing sensation of broken ribs, I mustered enough strength to pitch the slab of wood off my chest. Staggering to my feet and wiping the blood out of my eyes with my hand, I muttered, "Goddamn Big Sarge — didn't see that coming."

The intense throbbing sensation in my head was a clear indication that I'd evidently whacked it pretty hard on the floor, the wall, or some other immobile structure on my short but exciting trip. Subsequently, the sizable gash on my forehead was returning the favor by releasing a steady flow of blood down my face. As quickly as I was able to stand up, my knees buckled and I quickly returned to a very unsoldierlike position on the floor.

"Damn It!" I barked after trying three times with the same result. "I need a second."

Unfortunately, it seemed we didn't have a second.

"Sir! I've got movement! Stay down!"

From my temporarily compromised fighting position on the vestibule floor, I hazily watched Tony swing his M4 toward the doorway as his tac light flicked on briefly, illuminating the breach. It was deadly silent. All sounds of torment previously heard from within the sanctuary had ceased, replaced by an indistinct rustling amidst the doorway. Holding back the pain, I forced myself into a kneeling position and clumsily reached for Bertha amidst the pile of kindling surrounding me. I also pulled a flash-bang grenade from my ammo pouch.

"I'm good," I grumbled making sure Tony knew I was still in the fight. "I'll pop a flash-bang on first contact."

Tony nodded and slid the selector switch on his M4 to burst. He'd lay down a field fire while I tossed a flash-bang at whatever came through the door, temporarily disorienting them. We'd mop up with a barrage of bullets, grab Father Watson and the Doc, and call it a day. Not exactly the way we drew it up, but it would do.

Now we'd been doing this sort of shit for a good long while, and until this very moment I could have honestly told you that we'd seen it all.

Steadily emerging from the dimly lit glow of the distant sanctuary and into the focused beam of Tony's tac light came two hands. Two really frigg'n big hands that firmly grasped the very top of the empty eight foot doorframe on opposing sides. Human hands that appeared, easily, four times larger than what they should've been. Realizing that my brain was perhaps not functioning at full capacity due to recent events, I shook my head a couple times in attempt to restore clarity. Unfortunately, what followed next either confirmed that I'd hit my head much harder than I thought and was fit for a white padded room with a rubber sheeted bed, or much worse — I was seeing just fine.

Protruding from the darkness into the beam of light came the silhouette of a massive head, clearly ducking under the remains of the doorframe. As I struggled to rationalize what I was seeing, the head was followed by the colossal muscle-laden body attached to it. As the mind shattering figure cleared the threshold and stood upright, it was just barely contained within the limits of the vestibule cathedral ceiling that was easily fifteen feet in height.

It was a man. A fucking giant man. And in a bizarre fashion, it was also familiar to me.

Like a dreadful case of déjà vu, my mind flashed to the recurring dream that haunted my subconscious every night since arriving in Bosnia. In the dream I witnessed a cloaked figure slaughter an entire army of these creatures outside of ancient Rome. An army of giants. Making a mental note that I'd need some serious therapy when this was over, I focused back on the abomination at hand.

Clothed in what appeared to be the tattered uniform of a Roman soldier complete with sullied tunic, tarnished bronze breastplate, and makeshift sandals, it just stood there fixing us with an intent stare. Its eyes were a paralyzing solid black, like pools of oil, searing with uncontrolled rage. They bore a hole right through us with a sinister squint.

Watching us as if curious to see what we would do. Its mighty chest heaved up and down as rancid breath exited its furled mouth. Its head was covered in a thick black mane of disheveled hair with its chiseled face hidden well within a mangy beard, which was braided and crusted over with remnants of a recent feast. Its mouth stretched into a wicked grin, bearing ghastly double rows of canine-like teeth, dripping with a steady stream of elongated saliva or something clearly worse.

As if the goddamn shock factor of standing face to face with such a creature wasn't enough to make you shit yourself and go blind, it then did something I was completely unprepared for. It spoke.

"Centurion," its thunderous voice boomed from oversized vocal chords while looking directly at me.

Completely dismissing my injuries and associated pain, I instantly stood up with what I could only imagine was a clear look of disbelief.

"Father knew you would come," it said. "But you are too late. The children are born. It has begun."

"It has begun," the creature repeated. "Again. Like before."

Right about then I turned to a clearly confounded First Sergeant Coates and muttered, "Now. Now we've seen it all."

And opened fire.

Chapter 6

Not having the benefit of any prior experience fighting in close quarters with a fifteen foot behemoth decked out like an extra in a gladiator flick, I figured it smart to shoot low. For the record, I blame this sort of thinking on my government education. That's your tax dollars hard at work.

"Knees!" I yelled. "Take out the knees!"

Letting the flash-bang drop to the floor by my feet, I brought Bertha to my shoulder and squeezed off two slugs. Any hint of pain, resulting from my broken ribs and throbbing head, was gone. Replaced, instantly, with a turbo shot of adrenaline — driven by the desire to survive the next five minutes.

I drifted to my left as I fired an additional two more slugs, which hit home, smashing into the giant's left kneecap. Tony took his cue and starting hammering the giant's right knee with a deluge of burst fire from his M4. The sound of persistent gunfire within the confined area was deafening, but unfortunately not loud enough to drown out the laughter reverberating from our oversized foe. Without moving an inch from his original position, the menacing figure stood there and roared a hearty, ominous laugh. It was a bit unnerving, to put it mildly.

"Weapons of man cannot hurt Anak," it bellowed amidst intermittent chuckles. "You are powerless against me, Centurion."

With an unnatural speed that should not have been possible for a creature of such size and mass, it crossed the room in a fraction of a second and swatted Tony with a dominant backhanded blow, catapulting him into the sidewall of the vestibule. With its mouth curled into a wicked smile and still chortling, its eyes narrowed with focused fury as its attention turned solely on me.

"Enough play. My father will see you now, Centurion." Pointing a massive finger at Tony, it growled, "Your legionnaire will furnish my morning feast."

Realizing now that it was blood dripping from the giant's foreboding jaws, I diverted my attention to the far side of the room where Tony's body lay in a heap. I picked up slight movement. He was alive. Badly hurt, but alive. Instantly overpowered with a burning need for vengeance, I met the creature's unsettling gaze.

"Hey, Tiny! Stop fucking calling me that," I shouted as I nonchalantly reached down and picked up the flash-bang I'd discarded moments earlier. Pulling the pin, I counted to three and tossed it toward his mammoth face. "Catch."

Quickly spinning around and shielding my eyes from the imminent discharge of blinding light, I heard the pop of the grenade followed by a thunderous howl of pain. Looking up I happily watched as my oversized foe staggered throughout the room with hands clutching his face.

"Blinded Anak with sorcery!" Its voice boomed. Followed by repeated screams of, "Centurion!"

"Thought I told you to stop calling me that, asshole," I muttered feeling rather pleased as I quickly bound to Tony's position. Propping his head up with my right hand, I said, "You OK, Big Sarge?"

"Not quite dead," he answered with a pain-riddled face. "Fucking close though."

"Need to get you out of here. I'll come back for Doc and the Padre."

Sliding his left arm over my shoulder I hastily got the First Sergeant to his feet and turned toward the front door.

Unfortunately, that was as far as I got. Tiny was waiting for me. And he was pissed.

Evidently done talking, he simply grabbed the First Sergeant with one brawny hand and threw his limp body over a massive shoulder. As I heard

Tony wince in pain, I stepped backward and fumbled for another flash-bang. Before my hand reached my ammo pouch, Tiny violently grasped my tac vest and jerked me ten feet upward to eye level. With my arms and legs dangling in midair, I found myself up close and personal with the stuff of nightmares. I'm talking — no sleep for weeks — type of nightmares.

It was not pleasant.

With his teeth tightly clamped together, he was growling like a frenzied animal on the verge of tearing apart his prey. I could feel his torrid, festering breath envelope me in uncontrolled waves. The nauseating reek of copper and decayed flesh dominated the air. Images of the empty village filled my thoughts. The people didn't leave. They were eaten. He fucking ate them. Fixing me with soulless eyes, he held me there for what seemed like an eternity. Fuming.

"After father," he carefully said clearly holding back his fury with every ounce of his being. "You are mine."

Without another word he effortlessly flung me across the room. As I made my second trip of the evening headlong into a wall at a high rate of speed, I watched him casually turn and lumber into the darkness of the sanctuary with Tony slung over his shoulder, and disappear. Not good.

So Tiny clearly didn't have his heart set on damaging me much more than I already was because I was able to collect myself fairly quickly after slamming into the wall — again. With my shoulder throbbing, head pounding, and left arm now fractured I stumbled to my feet. Unfortunately for him and his aforementioned father, this was not over.

I was now officially pissed off.

Retrieving my shotgun, I dropped the magazine and popped in a fresh one. Expecting the sanctuary to be much larger than the vestibule, I slung Bertha on my back and opted for the M4 still clinging to my chest. I'd need the standoff distance and larger magazine capacity now that I was flying solo. Hastily loosening the assault sling enough to let the rifle butt seat into my shoulder, I took it off 'Safe' and muttered to myself, "So Tiny's dad wants to chat. OK, asshole, Let's chat."

With the element of surprise clearly shot in the ass, I figured the situation called for nothing less than a full on frontal assault. At this point in the mission I had nothing to lose. Approaching the entrance to the sanctuary I instinctively raised the M4 to a reflexive firing position and paused just outside the threshold along the wall.

Taking a deep breath, I buried the pain and focused on the mission. Focused on the sanctuary. Focused on Erin — Father Watson — Tony. As my mind welcomed the expected serene sensation, it poured over my broken body like warm, healing sunshine. Time crept to a transcending slowness and for a fleeting second, it stopped.

Like progressively emerging from a pool of water, my senses ignited one by one as I mentally broke the surface. I instantly picked up heartbeats. Several of them. Faint. Almost like that of a child. And there was death. Recent, unnatural death. And there was something else. An intense energy, a feeling of dread — and then there was only static. My senses instantly returned to normal. Something shut me down. I was blocked. Whether it was the intense pain I was feeling or something else entirely it mattered not. My edge was gone. I was on my own.

"Damn it!"

Dropping to a knee and bowing my head, I exhaled a long, controlled sigh. Pushing the immeasurable pain streaming through my body into a far away place in the back of my mind, I channeled the adrenaline, the fear, and the anger. I was as ready as I was going to be.

"The old fashioned way then," I muttered to myself with renewed conviction as I rose to my feet. "Fair enough."

As I broke the threshold with weapon raised, scanning for targets, I quickly realized I'd stepped into a whole new level of strange. Taking into account everything that'd happened thus far on this operation — that was really saying something.

If the smoldering town outside was a circle of hell, the church sanctuary was without a doubt its festering heart. Years upon years of training for this specific scenario could not have prepared me, in the least, for the harrowing scene laid out before my eyes. The sanctuary floor was completely cleared of pews and had the appearance of a warehouse, dimly lit by what appeared to be thousands of candles throwing malevolent shadows eerily dancing across the cathedral ceiling. To the right of the doors was a cavernous crater carefully excavated in the church floor, penetrating deep into the earth below. As I crept past the edge of the abyss, the stench of death and rotted flesh filled my nostrils. A grisly pile of discarded body parts was haphazardly strewn about the entrance.

"That's cute," I muttered cautiously squinting into the darkness. Hoping like hell Tiny hadn't taken the First Sergeant down there, I kept moving.

The entire left side of the sanctuary appeared to be a makeshift hospital ward complete with at least a dozen shoddy cots posing as hospital beds, rusted IV stands, and jury rigged lamps running off what appeared to be car batteries. The blood spattered cots were occupied by unkempt women who appeared to be in a permanent state of shock. Or dead. There were cribs. At least a dozen of them, which glowed under the direct light of the lamps.

Slowly creeping closer, I started to make out modest movement and faint whimpers. Babies. Holy shit. It was an improvised frigg'n maternity ward. The guards dressed in scrubs now made sense. Well, not exactly, because none of this made any frigg'n sense, but at least it fit within the general parameters of the overall weirdness.

"The children have come —" I muttered out loud in a state of complete bewilderment, remembering the unsettling words spoken by the giant. Lowering my weapon and peering into the first crib that I approached, I found a healthy newborn baby lying on its back.

"My God —"

The child evidently sensed my presence and slowly opened its eyes. As they fully opened and locked with mine, I nearly shat myself. They were completely black. Like the giant. Completely stunned I jumped backward three steps and raised my M4.

"What the fuck?" I blurted out despite myself. As I contemplated what to do next, the silence of the large room was broken by a barely audible, desperate voice.

"Dean? — Is that you?"

I know that voice. Snapping my head toward the far end of the grisly row of hospital beds, I located the source. Barely visible in the dim lighting was a feminine figure slumped over the motionless body of a hapless patient.

"Doc!" I exclaimed lowering my weapon.

Hastily advancing through the labyrinth of sordid furniture and medical equipment, I reached Erin just in time to catch her as she collapsed from complete exhaustion. Her usual radiant face was stricken with terror, anger, and utter depletion. Hair mussed and scrubs speckled with blood, she hung limp in my arms. A steady stream of tears flowed from her sullen eyes as she tried to speak.

"He's a monster," she murmured. "Petrovich … These poor women … Dead … All dead … Father Watson … He's … He's —"

Without the ability to say anything further, Erin burst into tears and buried her face in my chest.

"It's Ok, Doc," I said fighting back the torrent of rage that instantly swept over me as I held her tightly. "It's Ok. I'm here. Taking you home."

"No! You don't understand!" She yelled pushing off my chest with both hands. "He and that — that *creature* tortured Father Watson! Horrible things! "Fighting back the tears, her eyes filled with anger. "He made me — made me deliver all these babies. Said if I didn't he'd keep hurting him."

Pausing to catch her breath, she said, "They all died after they gave birth — every one. I tried to revive them but — they were just — dead. Petrovich laughed. Told me they weren't important. Only the children. And these babies … They're not — normal …"

As the tears returned, a now subdued Erin dropped her head despondently.

"Heard enough," I grumbled coldly. "We're leaving. Now."

As I held Erin up with my throbbing left arm, I reached down to activate my throat mic. Time to call in the cavalry. I'd hand the Doc off to Luke and Mac then come back to take care of business. And I was going to take care of business. Hell or high water I would raze this place to the ground. Getting that distinct feeling that someone was behind me, I realized we were not alone in the sanctuary.

"The infamous Captain Robinson, I presume. Legendary warrior from the western world. Fearless commander of the venerable dark soldiers. What a fortuitous surprise. How I have absolutely yearned to make your acquaintance. Welcome, Captain, to the christening of the new generation. Please join me in this grand celebration. Champagne?"

Before I could react Erin instantly jumped from my arms and backpedalled several steps.

"It's him," she whispered. And stood behind me.

Slowly turning to meet the object of my indignation, I placed both hands squarely on my M4. As I laid eyes on Goran Petrovich for the first time, I couldn't help being a bit taken back. He spoke perfect English without the slightest hint of a Serbian accent. If anything, he sounded British. The guy was every bit of six foot eight, if not taller. Seemed that urban legend got that part right.

He looked like a male model. Statuesque in appearance with meticulously styled thick, black hair that flowed to just above his broad shoulders. His eyes were utterly chilling.

A dominant, burning crimson with tiny, snakelike pupils — thoroughly soulless. I instantly recognized them for a reason I couldn't quite put my finger on. He was wearing a suit. A really fucking nice suit complete with a pristine white shirt, royal blue silk tie, and gold cuff links. His features were striking as his mouth curled into a lascivious smile bearing perfectly white teeth. In one hand he casually waved an unlit cigar in the air. In the other he held a half filled champagne glass.

At this point I made a mental note to retract my earlier comment about seeing it all.

Now. Now I'd clearly seen it all.

"You Petrovich?" I barked.

"How I do enjoy Americans," he snidely replied. "Abrupt. Straight to the point. No mincing of words. Cut to the chase."

He paused to take a modest sip of champagne and cast me an amusing glance. "Well, Captain, I've had many names and many faces through the years, but here and now, I am Goran Petrovich."

Offering a theatric bow complete with clichéd hand gesture, he quipped, "And it is my sincere pleasure to meet you."

"Trust me, handsome," I said smiling. "The pleasure's all mine."

Raising my M4 directly to his chest, I then proceeded to empty the entire fucking thirty-round magazine. Round after round pummeled his torso at point blank range, spraying a gruesome spate of flesh, bone fragments, and blood soaked snippets of his really nice clothing throughout the air behind him.

"Waste of a nice suit," I muttered, watching contently as his mangled body slid to the floor. "Should've dressed for the occasion, asshole."

I ejected the empty magazine and tossed it on his tattered corpse. Slamming in a fresh mag and chambering a round, I turned toward Erin to find her huddled in a ball against the far sanctuary wall.

"It's over, Doc. Time to get you out of here before Tiny crawls out of his pit."

If witnessing such a remorseless act of manslaughter bothered Erin she sure as hell didn't show it. Instantly rising to her feet she ran toward Petrovich's corpse and squarely planted a boot in the side of his head for good measure.

"Fucking animal! Burn in Hell!" Turning toward me with a look of pure determination, she boldly declared, "I'm not leaving without Father Watson."

And proceeded toward the rear of the sanctuary, leaving me standing there in mild astonishment.

Doc Kelly is quite the woman. No doubt.

"Ah, Ok — Sure thing. Right behind you."

Snapping the M4 back to my shoulder, I followed Erin as we cleared the remaining row of hospital beds and reached the pulpit, at the rear of the church, shrouded in darkness. As my eyes adjusted to the faint lighting provided by two small candles, I saw the silhouette of a person sprawled across the altar. Flicking on my tac light, I focused the beam and stopped dead in my tracks. Shocked and disgusted.

It was Father Watson.

Or what remained of him.

Chapter 7

Lying flat on his back, the Padre was nailed to the blood stained alter by large rusted railroad spikes pounded clean through his wrists and ankles. His nearly unrecognizable face was thoroughly battered, swollen, and coated with blood. Responding to Erin's voice as we approached, he turned his head in our direction and opened his eyes revealing empty eye sockets.

His fucking eyes were gone.

Grim trails of dried blood and burn marks streaked down the length of his cheeks and neck indicating they were crudely removed with a blunt instrument. Or something inexplicably worse.

"Padre — My God," I managed to blurt out after a prolonged moment.

There are no words for what I felt. Reaching down to grasp his hand in assurance I unknowingly wrapped my fingers around the bloody stump of an arm. Instantly jerking my hands back in utter revulsion, I realized that his left hand was brutally hacked off at the wrist and lay in a dark pool on the floor below. The signet ring he proudly wore on his left index finger eerily gleamed in the candlelight as it lay on the floor within the puddle of blood.

"Son of a Bitch! Padre, Can you speak?"

In an incredibly calm demeanor, devoid of any discomfort, Father Watson spoke as if he was greeting me under perfectly ordinary circumstances.

Looking directly at me with blackened, empty eye sockets, he said, "Hello Dean. I had faith you would come. And here you are. Just as He foretold."

"We need to go — Now! You need a hospital." Clearly shaken by the Padre's condition, I turned to Erin and said, "Doc, How the hell do we get these spikes out of him?"

"I have no intention of leaving," Father Watson declared before Erin could reply. "I am precisely where I am supposed to be. My purpose is nearly achieved."

"Purpose? What purpose?" I asked astounded. "I'm not leaving you to die like — like this. Not a fucking chance."

Frantically reaching down and clutching one of the spikes, I tried unsuccessfully to pry it loose from the alter.

"You are my purpose. You've been chosen, as have I. It is as I suspected all along," he said as his eyeless gaze diverted from me and drifted over my left shoulder. "It is time to open your eyes. And See."

Not having the faintest clue as to what Father Watson was going on about, I sensed someone behind me and spun around to find Petrovich. Large as life and clearly not as dead as I left him just minutes before. He simply stood there smiling. Wickedly. What should have been a bullet shredded corpse was now standing within spitting distance of me without so much as a scratch on him. He was perfect. Everything from celebrity grade hair to immaculate clothes.

"Neat trick," I muttered while giving him a puzzled look.

"Indeed," he smugly replied. "Did you think it would be so easy?"

When I offered no response, he said, "This is pleasant, is it not? I'm simply overjoyed that the good Priest has not yet expired. After all, I have so many more sins to confess." No longer holding the cigar nor the champagne glass, Petrovich was casually tossing my discarded M4 magazine up and down in his hand. "Oh, and Captain, I believe you dropped this. You see, I really have no need for it."

With blinding speed he struck me square in the face with the empty magazine followed by a crushing blow to my damaged rib cage. With what seemed like a single motion, he then ripped the M4 from my hands and snapped it clear in half flinging the pieces to opposite corners of the church. Hunched over and gasping for breath I realized, for the third time in this short mission, that perhaps — I had not seen it all.

"Perhaps now you will show me the proper respect," he said with a sharp edge.

Speechless, I collapsed to the base of the alter where Father Watson lay imprisoned, and helplessly watched as Erin boldly positioned herself between us and Petrovich. In a show of spirited defiance, she said, "You will not hurt them!"

"My dear Doctor, Your courage is commendable but quite unwarranted," Petrovich condescendingly replied as a patronizing grin curled across his face. "You have performed your function here well beyond my expectations. You very skillfully succeeded where your three predecessors miserably failed. You have ushered the next generation of my children into this world and I am forever in your debt. I have no reason to harm you for I will undoubtedly solicit your services again."

Taking a step toward Erin, he said, "For you see, Doctor, this is merely the beginning." Fixing her with a paralyzing stare, he casually reached up and placed his hand on her forehead. "Now please, be seated while I have a much needed chat with our friend the Captain."

Upon his touch, all emotion abruptly left Erin's face as she simply stepped backward and sat on the sanctuary floor, staring into nothingness.

"Now, Dean, alas I have a captive audience," Petrovich said cleverly as he turned his full attention toward me and strolled toward my position hunched against the alter. "We have much to discuss and unfortunately a brief time remaining, for I must see to the relocation of my children to a more discreet setting."

"Who … What are you?" I managed to awkwardly force out as I labored to stand upright despite the latest wave of agonizing pain.

"Names are not significant," he replied with a brazen smile. "Nor are my origins. I'm afraid you would not understand even if I explained. What is of significance is the proposal I would like to extend."

An ear splitting roar emanating from deep within the giant's oversized rabbit hole stopped him in mid-sentence. Shifting his gaze toward the abyss, he said, "It appears you may have damaged my son, Anak. Not an easy feat."

"Tiny? Yeah, doesn't do so well with bright light, it seems. Cute kid though. Bad teeth. Interesting taste in clothes. Bit on the eccentric side." Barely able to stand on two feet I braced myself against the altar. "So you're his father. You sure? Struggling to see the resemblance."

Completely ignoring my commentary, he said, "You'll have to forgive his temperament. He's my oldest and only surviving son from a distant past. He's never quite recovered from our betrayal in Rome, hence the attire. We were so close to achieving our goals then. Quite unfortunate. Different times. Live and learn, as the humans say."

"Where's my First Sergeant?" I sternly asked, while slowly slipping a hand into my ammo pouch and wrapping my fingers around a fragmentary grenade. At the very least it would buy me some time. Or so I thought.

"Ah Yes, First Sergeant Coates. As you can imagine it's quite difficult to sustain such a strapping young lad as Anak. His appetite is simply voracious. Like his brethren, he developed quite a taste for human flesh over the years. One of the many reasons I choose places like this for my endeavors. All the misguided butchering and bloodletting in the name of the great *God* himself make it quite challenging to keep track of all the humans. Who's to notice a few, or a few hundred, missing here and there. It reminds me of old times when the Earth was so much more — primal."

Dismissively glancing at the evidently not so subtle movement of my hand, he said, "I'm afraid your First Sergeant is destined to be Anak's morning meal. An unfitting end for such a great warrior. Which, brings me back to my proposition."

As I slowly withdrew my hand from the ammo pouch clutching the grenade, he waived a finger back and forth in a scolding fashion.

"Please, Captain, No more distractions," he chided. "It was I that gave weapons of war to mankind. They have no effect on me. What you witnessed earlier was merely theatrics. An illusion of sorts. Just a bit of fun, I'm afraid."

Despite all evidence to the contrary I was not convinced and retained a firm grasp on the grenade. At the very least, it was making me feel better.

"Fine," I grumbled. "You want to make a deal — let's hear it."

"Much better, Thank You," he said condescendingly while pulling another cigar from the breast pocket of his suit jacket. "For reasons you are not capable of understanding, I am rebuilding my family. As such, I wish your service in my — organization. A human of your particular talents and warring nature would serve me quite well. Given the proper encouragement, of course."

Producing a lighter from another pocket, he lit the cigar taking several long drags and blowing a steady plume of smoke into the still air.

"In exchange for your pledge of servitude, I will grant your First Sergeant, the good Doctor, and what remains of the addled Priest deliverance from my subjugation. Freedom to return to their lives."

"Me for them," I grumbled. "Fair enough. And if I'm not interested?"

"A most unpleasant ending in the depths of Anak's cave for the lot of you," he said with a smug grin.

"Hell of a deal, handsome," I replied forcing a grin. "You sell health insurance in a past life? Used cars? Maybe real estate?"

Lying, silent, on the altar behind me, Father Watson chose this moment to speak. He quietly began to murmur in a faint, but deliberate tone.

"And when the Lord thy God shall deliver them before thee — thou shalt smite them, and utterly destroy them — thou shall make no covenant with them, nor show mercy unto them."

"The words of Enoch," a visibly annoyed Petrovich muttered as he turned his attention toward the Padre. His eyes grew cold and focused. "Silence, Priest! Your poisoned tongue shall follow course with your deluded eyes soon enough."

"Proceed against the Bastards and the Reprobates, and against the children of fornication," Father Watson continued with his voice steadily rising. *"And destroy the children of The Watchers."* Lifting his head from the altar and looking directly at Petrovich, with barren eye cavities, he shouted, *"And to Azazel — To him ascribe all sin!"*

As the words resonated with my subconscious, I felt like I'd been struck by lightning. In a moment of clarity — It all made sense.

My dream.

The insane dream I'd lived every night, for the past six months, was a prelude to this very moment. The slaying of the army of giants at the hand of the cloaked figure. It actually happened. Father Watson tried to tell me as such but I didn't believe him. Son of a bitch. Maybe he wasn't drunk after all.

Stunned, I spun around to face Petrovich and fixated on his frigid crimson eyes. The eyes that haunted me night after night. It was unmistakable. I recognized them instantly from the dream. He was there. He was their leader. Their father. Azazel. The angel.

Holy shit.

With the newfound power of this revelation, I focused all my remaining strength, stood upright, and confidently strode toward Petrovich.

"Azazel," I muttered. "I know what you are. I've seen it. Seen you. Defeated by the cloaked warrior."

"You dare speak my name," he said in an uncharacteristic, subdued tone as his focus whirled from Father Watson back to me. I detected a fleeting but undeniable look of befuddlement, and for the briefest of seconds I saw fear. He was afraid, and deeply confused as he contemplated the meaning of my words.

"You know of the Deacon," he said pensively. "How?"

"I've seen him," I barked. "Felt his power."

"That — Is not possible," he scoffed. Pointing at Father Watson with an irritated scowl, he said, "Lies! Fed to you from this misguided *priest* no doubt. You've seen nothing."

"I saw the terror in your eyes as you ran from the battlefield while he destroyed your army. Your *children*. You ran — Like a coward."

As the words boomed from my mouth, his eyes flashed and emitted a bitter glow while his face twisted into a hellish mask. In an instant, towering flames erupted from every candle in the sanctuary and his body seemed to expand in height and width as he stalked toward me. Outraged.

"Insolent human!" He growled with a deepened voice that was painful to my ears. "You cannot begin to fathom what I am *nor* what I have sacrificed."

With a flash of movement barely perceptible to the human eye, he then ripped the shotgun from my back and thrust the butt into my chest shoving me forcefully against the altar. "And now I grow weary of your company."

Using one arm, he then proceeded to lift me a solid foot off the ground and violently hurl me into the wall to the right. Covering a ten-foot span in a fraction of a second, I slammed into the wall with the force of a tornado. I didn't even have the chance to say 'Ow' before he was standing over me again. With a satisfied grin, he forcefully jabbed the muzzle of the shotgun into my chest and methodically emptied the magazine.

Turn about is evidently fair play.

Damn.

Should have seen that one coming.

As I felt the weapon discharge six distinct times with each slug ripping through my chest, I slowly slumped to the base of the wall and rested on the floor. My perception of time came to a screeching halt as my senses steadily faded to a state of void. With the life force draining from my broken body, I couldn't help but think that the mission had now officially gone to shit. Adding insult to injury, he casually tossed Bertha on my mangled body in triumph as he stood there gloating. Right before my eyesight faded to black I was drawn to the smoke, steadily pouring out of the shotgun muzzle as the searing barrel burned my legs.

Shot with my own gun. On my frigg'n birthday. That is so goddamn wrong. I really hate that guy.

The last thing I heard was laughter. Sustained euphoric laughter. Oddly, it was coming from Father Watson.

Then it all went dark.

I was dead.

Worst birthday ever.

Chapter 8

As I felt the last breath escape my devastated lung cavity and my eyes slide shut for the last time, all I could hear was the continued ringing laughter of Father Watson echo throughout the ether. Not sure I agreed with the comedic content of getting six shotgun slugs in the chest from a psychotic fashion astute angel, but the Padre always did have a sick sense of humor. Probably why he drank so damn much.

I waited for the bright light that everybody talked about when you died but it didn't come. There was only darkness. Intense, almost painful, darkness. Felt like I was floating unbound by time and space in an endless void of unadulterated black. After the initial shock factor wore off, it actually felt kind of peaceful. For the first time in a long time I felt truly at peace. Figured. I needed to die to get some downtime.

How's that for frigg'n irony?

Just as I started to get used to the whole being dead thing, the infinite darkness instantly transitioned to a brilliant blue sky scattered with sporadic clusters of low hanging wispy, white clouds. Oddly, I was no longer floating. I was standing. In the middle of a frigg'n stream. A cold, bubbling stream of fast moving water steadily flowed just above my ankles as I stood atop the smooth pebbles and river rock, lining the bottom. And I was barefoot. What the hell?

In a panic, I instantly placed both hands on my chest and quickly realized that it wasn't riddled with holes nor was I covered in blood. In fact, I felt great. Not a scratch on me. My fractured body was completely healed, and a warm, tranquil sensation gently pulsated from the soles of my feet up through my torso and out the crown of my head. I can't begin to put words to how absolutely amazing it felt. It was like waking up from a good night's sleep knowing you had absolutely nothing to do for the rest of the day. Like watching a baseball game from behind home plate at Fenway Park on a sunny Saturday afternoon in late spring with a cold beer and a warm pretzel. Like sitting in your favorite chair by a roaring fire place on a cold winter day with a good book and some old blues on the stereo.

I wasn't anxious — or angry — or afraid. Despite the circumstances, everything seemed absolutely perfect. I had no idea why. It just did.

My disheveled uniform was gone. Instead I was wearing my favorite pair of Levis and lucky Dave Matthews Band tee shirt that I'd bought two years ago when I saw him in Nashville. Perhaps the most comfortable tee shirt on the planet. I wore it so much it had more holes than actual fabric, but there was no way in hell I was throwing it away. Sliding my hands from my chest to my face I felt the course stubble of a fledgling beard, indicating at least a week or two of not shaving. Running my hand over my head I felt the uncharacteristic wave of thick, long hair. Seeming that I'd been sporting a tight to the skull buzz cut for my entire adult life, that was also a bit unexpected.

"Interesting," I muttered awestruck and wondering what in the hell was going on. "If this were Heaven there'd be beer. So — where the hell am I?"

Slowly turning to survey my surroundings, I realized I was in the middle of what appeared to be a lavish green field of ankle-high grass tucked neatly within a series of stately rolling hills. In the remote distance, the bold silhouette of majestic mountains thrust far into the skyline, proudly defining the horizon in all directions. The stream seemed to flow directly through the center of the field stretching as far as the eye could see to my left and right.

As I stood in a state of wonderment, taking it all in, I observed no movement or signs of life in any direction. Although the picturesque clouds were slowly swirling in the sky above, there was no wind. No birds. No animals.

No people. I was completely alone. Like the *Omega Man* cruising through the deserted streets of Los Angeles in his Mustang.

So — I have a weak spot for Charlton Heston flicks. Although, that whole *Planet of the Apes* deal seriously creeped me out. And I digress …

The only sound was that of the water rushing through the shallow stream I was still standing in. As I continued to scan the horizon, I vaguely made out what appeared to be the outline of a structure of some sort to my immediate front. It stood perfectly alone, atop a modest green hill, completely out of place amidst the surreal landscape. Curious as hell and figuring I really had nothing better to do at the moment, I decided to check it out. As I slowly stepped out of the stream and planted both feet firmly on the soft grass of the surrounding field, the calming sensation I was thoroughly enjoying abruptly ended, taking my momentary euphoria with it. Thinking that was completely unacceptable, I quickly stepped back in. And it came back.

"Much better," I sheepishly muttered looking around to make sure nobody saw me do it. "Think I'll hang here for awhile."

As I stood barefoot in the water feeling pretty good about myself for some undetermined period of time, my gaze couldn't help but drift back to the peculiar structure. Although it was a fair distance from where I stood, I swore it looked like a door. A very frigg'n large door.

There was no building. Just a door.

It also appeared that the formation of clouds I noticed earlier was circling it in a steady pattern — Odd. As my curiosity began to steadily overtake my unexplained and uncharacteristic happiness, I decided it was high time to quit lounging around and figure out what the hell was going on here.

Maybe I'd get lucky and it was a door to a bar. A big bar.

And it was happy hour.

"Alright, Damn it. Time to go. What's a guy got to do for a pair of shoes in this joint anyway?"

Determinedly stepping out of the precious healing water, I momentarily paused as the cuddly feelings of rapture and bliss instantly evaporated.

Feeling like my normal, generally pissed off self again, I stretched out my arms and muttered, "Now then, that's more like it." And started walking in the direction of the mysterious building-less door in the dead center of the uncanny green field, amidst the peculiar ring of clouds, which all seemed to be in the middle of a literal nowhere.

What can I say? For some reason it seemed like the thing to do.

As I started walking, I was pleasantly surprised to find that the grass felt like a rich carpet underneath my bare feet. I was still miffed that I didn't have any damn shoes, but at the moment it wasn't slowing me down. My destination seemed to be at least a solid mile from where I stood. Maybe a little farther. Hard to gauge the distance with the vast open nature of the encompassing landscape. At any rate, it should have taken me at least fifteen minutes or so to get there. So imagine my surprise to literally take three steps and find myself at the top of the hill standing an arm's length from the peculiar doorframe. Completely befuddled, I abruptly stopped and turned quickly around to see the spot that I started from, by the stream, in the far distance down the hill.

"Didn't see that coming," I muttered to myself as I stood there wondering what the hell just happened.

Getting the unshakeable feeling that someone was behind me, I spun back around to face the rogue doorway. As I attempted to put on my best 'barefooted tough guy, wearing a ratty tee shirt' face I realized there was no one there. Only the door. The big-ass, ancient looking door that was conveniently lacking a building surrounding it.

Momentarily mesmerized by its commanding and unexplained presence, I was immediately drawn to the intricate arrangement of symbols laid masterfully throughout the weathered panels. As I stood, pensively studying the artwork, a sharp gust of wind, originating from nowhere discernible, whisked violently across my face accompanied by an unsettling whisper-like shriek. It was over in a split second but damn if it didn't scare the ever-living shit out of me. Jumping backward I instinctively threw my hands up in a defensive posture wishing like hell I still had my shotgun. Quickly regaining composure I started to slowly circle the structure looking for the source. Step by deliberate step I thoughtfully crept around the back of the door. For whatever reason, I couldn't shake the acute feeling of impending doom.

I had the unequivocal suspicion that some seriously bad shit was about to happen. The only thing missing was the frigg'n horror movie music that came on right before the poor unsuspecting dumbass got a pitchfork in the chest from the whack job in the clown costume. As I cautiously completed my circular sweep to find the only thing in back of the door was actually the back of the door, I started to relax a bit. Evidently, the general weirdness of the overall situation had me a bit on edge. Feeling somewhat satisfied that I was alone and *evil clown guy* was nowhere in the general vicinity, I affirmably muttered, "Get a grip on yourself asshole. You're already dead for Christ's sake. Quit acting like such a puss."

Figured that needed to be said.

Back where I started from, in front of the imposing doorway o'doom, I got back to my very well conceived plan of figuring out what the hell was going on here. With arms defiantly folded across my chest, I stood boldly in front of the menacing structure for a couple seconds before I came to the shocking realization that I unfortunately had no idea what to do next. The only thing left to do was open the door. And for some reason I really, really didn't want to. It seemed wrong. Like I wasn't supposed to.

Not yet.

The doorway was a thing of ominous beauty. It was easily ten feet in height. A brawny set of panels encased in a full rectangular frame of incongruous brick and mortar. The contrasting color of the assorted bricks spanned all shades of red, ranging from those of a deep crimson to others of an almost orange hue. The top section of the frame formed an ornate crown like cap into which the doors perfectly melded. At first I thought them to be made of wood, but upon further inspection, they were clearly metal covered with a solid layer of rust giving them a wood-like coloration. Iron. They were made of solid iron as I studied the bold indentations of ancient rivets and mighty hinges holding them firmly in place. The entire marvelous structure sat squarely atop a rugged threshold of what appeared to be expertly cut granite that was chipped and pitted with unfathomable age.

As my eyes scanned the breadth of the structure, I was drawn back to the artful collection of symbols inscribed throughout the massive panels. They were stunning. Intricate, flowing designs flawlessly seared directly into the unyielding iron backdrop. Coincidently, I had encountered something very similar to this, hastily carved into the wooden doors of the church sanctuary in Brezovo Polje. They were also familiar to me for another reason that I still couldn't put my finger on. The pattern seemed to repeat from left to right and vice versa in crossing diagonal bands spanning the length and width of both panels forming a large X.

As I followed one with my index finger trying to pick out the pattern, I reached the intersection of the two lines and just about shat myself. The symbol marking the junction of the two bands was a perfect circle encasing a triangle containing a bold *X* with an elongated *P* struck through the center. The symbol from my dream. The Chi-Rho.

Inadvertently taking a step or two backward, the words spoken to me by Father Watson, as he lay mutilated and bound to the altar in the forsaken church, flashed through my head.

"*You are my purpose. You have been chosen.*"

"Chosen for what you crazy drunk bastard," I muttered bowing my head and closing my eyes.

Wishing like hell I'd taken him a bit more seriously when he tried to tell me that the outlandish visions in my dream were reflections of actual events, I just knelt there stewing. If I'd only listened to him I may have a frigg'n clue as to what was going on here. Damn the bad luck.

Just as I was about to say 'to hell with it' and open the damn door, I felt a presence to my right followed by a hauntingly familiar voice.

"Dean, it is time to open your eyes. And See the evil in the world of man."

Quickly opening my eyes, I slowly rose to my feet still facing the doorway. Although I knew without a shadow of a doubt who was standing next to me, I couldn't bring myself to look at him. Was I dreaming again? That would explain quite a bit actually. But I usually woke up when he spoke my name in the dream.

Damn. This might actually be happening. I hope he didn't hear my *Cloakboy* reference. That would just be awkward.

"Any chance I'm dreaming?" I apprehensively asked with my gaze still firmly fixed straight ahead.

"I'm afraid not."

"Damn. There's not, by chance, a bar behind that door either, huh?"

"No, Dean. There is not."

"Hmm. Well, I guess you're really standing there then."

"I am."

Figuring my line of questioning was rather futile at this point and the enigmatic cloak wearing, fire throwing giant slayer was actually standing next to me, I had no choice but to turn and face him. Taking a deep breath I slowly turned to my right and locked eyes with the man I'd been vicariously living through for the past one hundred and seventy-seven nights. Although I was intimately familiar with him from the first person point of view, I wasn't exactly sure what he looked like. My only impression of his appearance was when he was beaten within an inch of his life, and deposited on the sand covered road prior to being stoned to death. At that particular moment he wasn't exactly in the best shape, if you know what I'm saying.

Well, let's just say he cleaned up pretty well. As I awkwardly stood there face to face with the infamous Deacon for the first time, I was overpowered by a feeling of modesty. It was absolutely humbling. Although not a terribly large man physically, his presence was dominating. Almost crushing. His face was flawless, with a stone-like chiseled jaw and short-cropped auburn hair. He didn't look a day over thirty yet his deep royal blue eyes were pensive and powerful. Laden with centuries of knowledge — so much so that it was difficult to maintain eye contact. In lieu of the iconic cloak, he donned an expertly cut black suit and starched black shirt with the top button opened. No cuff links. Thank God.

As I stood there nervously gawking at him, he said nothing. His eyes were intently fixed on me as the hint of a mild smirk faintly appeared on his face. Breaking the awkward silence, he simply said, "You must have several questions."

Finding myself momentarily at a loss for words, I painfully forced out, "Questions?"

"Questions," he casually replied. "You must have questions."

Reestablishing control over my ability to speak, I muttered, "Questions. Right. I do have a couple, actually."

Pausing for a second to gather my thoughts, I said, "Let's start with the obvious. Who the hell are you?"

"Interesting," he commented with a hard gaze. "*Am I dead*? is usually the first question typically followed by *Is this Heaven*? I figured you'd be different though."

Casually unbuttoning his jacket and sliding both hands in his pockets, he said, "My name is Stephen. Although I honestly thought you would have riddled that out by now. After all, you witnessed my stoning one hundred and seventy-seven times in your dream. It's rather well known as I understand it. Must be that government education you're always referring to."

My face went completely blank as I realized the meaning of what he'd just said. Not the part where he sarcastically slammed my West Point degree but the other part. The words of Father Watson, from our discussion at the compound, once more flashed through my mind.

"The first of the original seven. Falsely accused and martyred."

Stephen. Saint Stephen. The original deacon of the early church. Falsely accused of blasphemy by the Sanhedrin and stoned outside the gates of Jerusalem by an incited mob.

Damn. I can't believe I never put that together. Frigg'n government education.

"Well, in my defense I imagine stonings were an everyday thing back then, right?" I blurted out. "How the hell was I supposed to figure out you were *him*? Could have been any number of deacons … or other random heretic-like people stoned in Jerusalem. I mean in Ben —"

Stopping me in mid-sentence, Stephen casually raised his hand and said, "If you're about to make a Ben-Hur reference, I will kindly ask you to refrain."

"Right. Ok, fair enough," I muttered figuring my first impression was evidently not going so well and making the mental note that he was clearly not a Charlton Heston fan. "Well, you look pretty good for a guy that's almost two thousand years old."

"It would seem," he said amidst a modest chuckle. "You'll find that the concepts of age and time have little validity here. For example, years will pass in this particular location before a fraction of a second expires on the Earth.

The principle varies throughout the Realms and actually reverses in some of the more extreme regions."

"The Realms," I muttered as my gaze shifted from him to the vast landscape. "Where exactly are we?"

"A simple question not easily answered. For only the faithful will understand and therefore believe," he replied while gracefully taking a few steps away from the door, gazing yearningly into the open sky. "Everything you see before you is a Realm within the southern region of Third Heaven. Otherwise known as the Mercy of Paradise. A place reserved for the good and the righteous. This particular Realm is reserved for those akin to you and I."

"Third Heaven?" I intuitively asked, thoroughly confused by several things he said. "There's more than one?"

"There are ten levels of Heaven all told. Each unique. Each with a specific purpose," he said, matter of factly while lowering his arms and striding toward me. "The Realms of Third Heaven are the closest, if you will, to the earth. There are seven discrete points in which the two worlds physically touch. Subsequently, the chosen few who are graced with purity of soul and knowledge of their location, possess the ability to cross the threshold." Pausing to ensure he had my full attention, he added, "The ability to literally travel between the Heavens and the Earth."

Not completely sure how to receive such a bold revelation, I lowered my head and simply stood there in silence contemplating the implications of the statement. Gradually wrapping my head around Stephen's comments, I muttered, "So, that explains how you clandestinely returned from the grave hundreds of years after your death. But it does not explain why."

Casually placing his hands back in his pockets, Stephen simply stood there fixing me with an intense, pensive stare. He was clearly not offering anything further until I asked him and it felt more and more like he was testing me.

Why or for what purpose, however, I wasn't quite certain.

Feeling like I needed to provide some levity to the situation, I raised my head slightly to make eye contact and said, "Is this like a genie in a bottle sort of gig where I only get three questions?"

"No, Dean," he dryly replied. "It is not. And I believe a *genie* would grant wishes. Not answer questions."

"Right. Just wanted to clear that up, Steve. You don't mind if I call you Steve do you?"

"I do mind," he reproachfully replied as his eyes closed into an intense squint. "Very much so."

"Fair enough," I awkwardly said clearing my throat. "Glad we got that out of the way, Stephen. Mr. Deacon. Sir."

"Just Stephen will do."

With the mood clearly not lightened, I made the mental note that *Stephen* did not appreciate sarcasm. Or at least he did not appreciate my sarcasm.

"Moving on then," I fumbled desperately to get off the topic. "Petrovich. He's an angel."

Nodding his head in acknowledgement and seemingly thankful that I abandoned my failed attempt at levity, Stephen replied, "Yes, he is. As you previously surmised, his given name is Azazel. An angel fallen from the Father's grace. He was one of the chosen heavenly Watchers. In the early years of man he was cast into an eternal prison in the depths of Dudael. Bound and chained by the archangel Raphael. Sentenced to suffer in darkness, upon jagged rocks until the day of Judgment when he was to be cast into the fire."

"A Watcher?" I asked not quite following the plot. "What'd he do to get such a stiff rap?"

As if he knew I was going to ask that very question, he said, "Watchers were a class of angel charged with the observation of mankind during the early days of the Earth, nearly six millennia ago. Their purpose was primarily to safeguard the Father's revered creation from premature exposure to the Forbidden Knowledge."

"Forbidden knowledge?"

"Knowledge of the Realms," he quickly replied, "Concepts that mankind was destined to discover of their own accord given time and maturity. Matters such as technology, science, mathematics, metallurgy, farming, and the making of weapons — amongst many others. More arcane subjects include astrology, enchantments, and even sorcery."

He paused and studied the somewhat confused look on my face. With an understanding nod of his head, he said, "You must understand, Dean, the Father feared that premature discovery of such things would be catastrophic to mankind. As man grew strong in his faith over generations, he would gradually discover and understand such notions. At which time, it would be his uninfluenced choice to employ them for the betterment of the race, dismiss them as profane, or embrace them for selfish benefit. Regardless of the chosen path, it was to be of man's choosing and his alone. A future of piety or impiety was to be decided by the free will of the human race. Conversely, untimely revelation of such notions would undoubtedly lead man down a dark spiral of confusion, bloodshed, and an Earth devoured by its own corrupt impulses. The Watchers were to prevent this from happening. It was their purpose. Their charge."

"Understood," I said with an affirmed nod.

Returning my nod with one of his own, he said, "After centuries of honoring their responsibility, Azazel and two hundred of his angelic brothers became smitten with human women. Maddened by their insatiate lust, they gathered on the summit of Mount Hermon and entered into a treacherous pact. Amongst each other, they swore a binding oath to illicitly defect to the Earth in human form and take upon them wives. An oath that condemned each and every one of them to a path of abiding depravity. A fall from grace. For many years following, they slaked their carnal desires in irreverent acts of blasphemous infidelity with the daughters of the Earth."

"Let me guess. They had kids. Freakishly tall. Bad teeth," I said as a light bulb went off in my head.

"Correct," he replied with the ever so faint glimpse of a smirk. "The sacrilegious union of angel and human resulted in an abomination. The nephilim. A cursed collection of hybrid beings. The literal birth of a race of giants amongst other creatures of an unnatural persuasion. A scourge upon the Earth, they devoured all that man had sowed, reaped, and nurtured until nothing remained. Then they turned their appetites upon mankind itself."

Removing his hands from his pockets, he straightened his jacket and began to casually stroll to my front. Raising his hands in a lecturing gesture, he said, "Unfortunately it did not end there. The Watchers' insolent disobedience worsened as they purposefully revealed and spread all facets of the Forbidden Knowledge. All too eager to stray from the ways of the Father, mankind embraced all that the fallen ones bestowed upon them. A contagion of immorality and violence swept throughout the Earth spurned by the twisted hearts and corrupted souls of men. The Father's great creation was forever tainted. Stained in blood and smothered in turpitude."

"Where the hell were the other angels in all of this? Where was God?"

"The Father was outraged at both the Watchers and man, alike, for entering into this unspeakable transgression. His precious creation had devolved into the most unholy of sacraments at the hands of his very own sons. When mankind could no longer endure this fate they cried out to the Heavens for deliverance and the Father responded. He dispatched the archangels to restore the Balance. And he dispatched the flood to raze the Earth."

"*The flood*?" I asked. "The Great Flood?"

"Yes, the very same," he casually replied. "The Father commanded Uriel to warn Noah that the Earth was to be rid of its wickedness and the human race reborn by his seed. He commanded Gabriel to wreak havoc and confusion amongst the nephilim, thus turning them upon each other in murderous fury. He commanded Michael to bind and condemn the fallen Watchers to Tartarus where they would suffer in sadness and regret until the day of Judgment. And he commanded Raphael to bind Azazel to the solitary prison of Dudael to suffer in dark isolation, estranged from his fallen brothers."

Stopping and looking directly at me, he said, "For the sins of Azazel were of the greatest offense to the Father. To him alone, the Father ascribed all sin of man. Finally, He sent the wrathful waters to cover the Earth and wash away the iniquity, only to start anew."

Astonished by this revelation, I was still having trouble with one small detail.

"So if the Watchers and the nephilim were taken out by the archangels more than six thousand years ago, how are they still hanging around?" I asked with what I imagined was a somewhat puzzled look on my face. "And why the hell is Azazel strolling around masquerading as a Serbian extremist in a ten thousand dollar suit? He should be locked up in a cave somewhere strapped to a boulder, right?"

"And here I was thinking you weren't paying attention," he said with a coy smirk.

Why the hell does everybody think I'm not paying attention? Damn government education.

As the smirk vanished and the statue-like stoicism returned, he said, "I cannot answer that question for I honestly do not know."

"What?" I scoffed. "What the hell do you mean you don't know?"

"The means of Azazel's liberation is uncertain. What is certain is that at some point after the flood, he shed his bonds and has subsequently managed to freely roam the Earth for millennia, assuming various human identities."

Beginning to slowly pace again, he said, "In the Earth year of 1998 you know him as Goran Petrovich, however it was he that instigated my mortal death at the hand of the Sanhedrin in the year 32."

"The white robed man at the stoning," I muttered as a vision of the crimson eyes flashed through my head. "That was him."

"That is correct," Stephen replied nodding. "It was also he that ruled the Roman Empire with an iron fist from 306 to 312 as the Emperor Maxentious. Within the walls of Rome, he secretly bred an army of nephilim, which he planned to unleash once more upon mankind. Had he succeeded, the path of human history would have taken a radical divergence."

"But then you showed up."

"Then the Father sent me," he replied abruptly turning his gaze toward me. "It was the faith of Constantine — the actions of man — that ended the reign of Maxentious and liberated Rome. Not I."

"With this sign you shall conquer," I muttered under my breath, looking pensively at the Chi-Rho sitting squarely in the center of the ominous doorway. "Constantine didn't have a vision from God the night before the battle. He had a visit from you. You drew that symbol in the dirt on the floor of his tent. The Chi-Rho. The symbol of Christ."

"While mankind has assigned many meanings to the symbol, it has but one." Turning his attention from me to the doorway, he solemnly said, "Balance."

"Restore the balance," I muttered thinking out loud. Turning from Stephen and beginning to slowly pace, I said, "So, Azazel is about to monkey stomp mankind with the power of the Roman Empire backed with a new generation of giants, you show up and issue a heavenly beat-down with that whole flaming sword montage thing you do, Constantine rolls in and mops up with Chi-Rho's painted on his men's armor and bingo — Christianity is off and running. Good guys win. Balance restored."

"Horribly simplified," Stephen dryly replied pensively gazing at me. "But accurate."

"Ok, So what next?" I asked feeling rather pleased with myself. "What happened to Azazel after the smack down in Rome?"

"Rome was unfortunately just the beginning," he replied somewhat ignoring my twentieth century interpretation of the events. "It was the first of Azazel's many well conceived assaults upon mankind. Throughout history he's assumed several prominent human identities and was responsible for instigating countless acts of war and bloodshed. As quickly as he becomes visible to our Sight — he simply vanishes, only to resurface years later. Each time more powerful than the last. He is somehow warded from the all-seeing eye of the Heavens — which should not be possible. He and all those that bear his mark, the Maradim, operate under a veil of secrecy. We fear he's receiving aid from within the Realms. A traitor in Heaven."

Not sure what to say, I simply stood there speechless for a long moment, studying the intensity of Stephen's face. After a painful string of silence, he said, "The nephilim that I encountered so many years ago and those that have plagued the Earth since, are from Azazel's seed. Throughout the generations he has persisted in rebuilding the condemned race. His hatred of man is boundless. It is matched only by his hatred of the Father. He will not desist until his fallen brothers are freed and the Earth is once again plagued by the darkness that prevailed during the reign of the Watchers."

Overwhelmed, frustrated and thoroughly confused, I started shaking my head. Making direct eye contact with Stephen, I impatiently asked, "Why tell me all of this? Why the dreams? What's any of this got to do with me?"

"Come now, Dean. I believe you already possess that answer," he said as a hint of disappointment flashed across his face. "Whether or not you understand your predestination begs a greater question."

Taken aback by his response, I turned to my left and blankly stared into the vast landscape. Beginning to slowly pace back and forth, I thought hard about the inconceivable knowledge Stephen had revealed to me and replayed the various scenes from the dream in my head.

Thinking out loud, I muttered, "Bastard sons of heaven — Treachery — Restore the balance — Bestowed with great power." Abruptly stopping and quickly turning to face Stephen, I said, "You referred to yourself as the Father's wrath. Please explain."

"Ah, a proper question, he said with a nod as his mouth stretched into a stern grin. "The true reason we are here."

As he placed his hands back in his pockets, a mild iridescent glow subtly formed around his shoulders and casually flowed along the outline of his body creating a spectral silhouette. Within the blink of an eye the brilliant light gracefully faded as his suit jacket violently morphed into a menacing black cloak, forcing the surrounding air to visibly ripple with palpable energy. For a long moment he just stood there perfectly still like an ominous statue cast in a shadow of dark reverence.

Didn't see that coming. Holy shit.

"Do I get one of those?" I asked completely taken by surprise, as I took three ungainly steps backward and clumsily shielded my eyes.

Treating the whole magic cloak thing like it was no big deal, he stoically replied, "You have worn the Deacon's cloak your entire mortal life, Dean."

"I have?"

"It is as much a part of you as you are a part of it. Have you not felt its presence every time you entered combat? Every time that inexplicable sensation augmented your perception — your agility — your strength? Unfortunately, until this very moment you have not possessed the knowledge to understand its purpose nor its consequence. There are few that do."

Shifting his gaze from me, he slowly began to stroll toward the door with the signature cloak boldly flowing about his body. It elegantly shimmered with what seemed like a will and presence of its own. Reaching out with his left hand and tracing the outline of the bold symbol in the door's center, he said, "Tell me, what do you know of divine retribution — the left hand of God?"

"Ah, not so much," I awkwardly replied still wrapping my head around his cloak comment.

"Very well," he said locking eyes with mine as the steely smirk briefly appeared on his face. "From the beginning then."

As he turned from the door to face me, an ethereal gauntlet-like glove of translucent material manifested around his left hand and slowly crept up his forearm. In a spectral flash, it took full physical form and was covered in a subtle layer of white flame. Maintaining steady eye contact, he purposefully strolled toward me, and said, "It is time to See the evil in the world of man. Time to understand that which you already know but do not yet believe."

Stopping directly to my front, he carefully raised his flaming hand to my forehead and pressed his palm gently against my temple.

Now, circumstances not withstanding, I typically wouldn't be too jazzed about some dude thrusting their paw all up in my face. On fire or otherwise. But for some unexplainable reason it felt right. Like it was supposed to happen. Like perhaps it had happened before. Like I was waiting for it to happen again. As his hand graced my forehead, I instinctively closed my eyes and felt the fervent warmth of the inexplicable otherworldly flame slowly overtake my body. It didn't burn. It embraced.

Standing in a welcomed daze of euphoric wonderment, I felt the memories begin to flow into my mind like water pouring through a funnel. Slowly at first. Then, like the bursting of a dam, they slammed my subconscious. All of them.

In a transient moment of perfect clarity, my eyes forcefully flew open and it made sense.

Everything.

Chapter 9

Time was a lost concept.

Minutes — Days — Months — Years. I literally had no sense of how long I'd been here. I was never hungry. Or thirsty. Or tired. The sun never moved. Night never came. With exception of the swirling clouds diligently patrolling the blue sky and the bubbling stream steadily flowing through the center of the sweeping panorama — nothing changed.

Pensively gazing at the striking profile of the distant mountains, I stood alone atop the green hill with the doorway to my back. The millennia of forbidden knowledge infused into my mind weighed heavy. An infinite volume of uncorrelated data and obscure concepts from the beginning of time raced through my thoughts. Unfortunately, I lacked the ability to string it all together. Stephen filled in some of the blanks but left the good majority for me to work out on my own. A regular biblical Yoda that guy was.

In life I was a soldier. In death he presented me with a choice. An opportunity to continue the fight. To combat a divine treachery. To balance the scales. To wield an immeasurable power entrusted to man by God himself for he'd long ago lost confidence in angels to do his bidding. A mantle of power created for one sole purpose. To maintain the Balance between mankind and the bastard offspring of heaven — the nephilim. Hybrid beings resulting from the blasphemous breeding of angels and humans. An ancient race of giants that nearly devoured the human race. Literally.

I had two options.

Option A — I accept my mortal fate, take my rightful place in a duly appointed Realm of Heaven, and go on about the everlasting peace that apparently waited for me in the afterlife. An early retirement of sorts. He even said I'd get a pair of shoes out of the deal. Nice shoes. Very tempting.

Option B — I step up to the plate, join the cause, and accept all the potentially horrific shit that came along with eternal servitude as one of God's hit men. The Deacons. Not quite human and not quite angel. Blessed and cursed with the power of God's Wrath. Touched by the left hand. Conceived of mankind but no longer a part of it.

For most logical human beings I'd think the whole '*happily ever after in eternal happiness*' gig would win hands down. Unfortunately, that wasn't my style. I evidently still had work to do.

A duty to uphold.

A new mission.

Angels — Giants — Evil Clown Guys. Bring it.

Besides, Stephen let it slip that consuming mass quantities of beer was heavily frowned upon throughout the heavenly Realms. That, I'm afraid, was a total deal breaker.

Eternal peace … My ass.

Unfortunately, volunteering of my own free will was only the beginning. Despite the fact I was destined to perform this divine service and the path of my entire mortal life seemingly led me to this very moment, I had yet to prove worthy. There was a qualification process. Trials.

The first of which was sacrifice. I had evidently completed that one by having my head kicked in by a fallen angel and subsequently surrendering my life in protection of innocents. Arguably not my best moment but apparently good enough. Before his departure, Stephen advised me that the second trial was forthcoming. He vanished some time ago as abruptly and mysteriously as he arrived. Amidst one of our endless training barrages, in what seemed like several months ago now, I turned my back for a split second and he was gone. Just like that. The guy could seriously make an exit.

Despite the lengthy time we spent together, I still had much to learn. But not from him. He was clear about that. There were others. The Guild. He said they would find me if I was successful. He was mum on the topic of what would happen if I failed. Although he didn't tell me where I was going nor what I had to do, he said I would know when it was time to go. The Balance must be maintained.

Yet again, I found myself standing alone atop the green hill with the door to my back. Completely lost in thought, I yearningly gazed at the distant mountains. Many times throughout this period of solitude I made valiant attempts to reach them. I'd lost track of how many journeys across the landscape I'd made. Each one a distinct failure in its own right. Regardless of how far I walked, the mountains remained a mere silhouette against the sky. Taunting me. A destination I was forced to look at but could never reach. Interestingly, it only ever took three steps to get back to the hill. It was infuriating.

Although I never slept, there were distinct memory lapses where my mind seemed to slip into a state of hibernation. Not quite a total shutdown. More like sleep walking. Like I'd been awake for too long and my brain was at the point of melting down. As I stood there motionless for an undeterminable period of time, I felt the mental switch subtly flip to the off position and instantly drifted to a state of void. A vision of Stephen filled my head as his words rung in my ears.

"Again, Dean. Focus."

"I am focusing," I shot back with clear irritation in my voice. "It doesn't frigg'n work!"

"Then focus better," he simply replied equally irritated yet always the stoic. "Remember, the cloak is the source of our abilities. The literal embodiment of the Father's Wrath. To truly embrace its power you must first will it into physical being. You must call it with your mind — a clear mind."

"I don't understand," I muttered while trying to massage away a splitting headache. "How the hell do I do that exactly? Say please? Buy it a drink?"

"It is a part of you — anxiously waiting in the deep shadows of your soul to be summoned — summoned by a Deacon. Your birthright grants you this authority."

"You talk about the cloak like it's alive," I grumbled, feeling like my head was about to explode and wishing like hell I had a stiff drink.

"Not alive — aware" Stephen replied in a sober tone. "It is the dark rage of the Father removed by his very hand for he vowed never to wield it again upon mankind. Do not underestimate its influence. Summon it with anything less than a pure heart and the consequences will be dire. It seeks one purpose — to dispense the Wrath of the Heavens. It must be bridled. Focused."

"I don't know if I can do this," I muttered shaking my head.

"You must, Dean. It is our purpose. We alone possess the strength of will to control the Wrath and maintain the Balance. The fate of mankind is ours to preserve. Now, clear your mind. Focus. Again."

The sound of the stream churning in the distance broke my momentary trance and my eyes again focused on the mountaintops. "Again," I muttered to myself as I instinctively began the short walk down the hill to the streambed to continue my lonely training regimen.

⁂

Alone on the hill I stared blankly into the boundless sky as my mind wove in and out of active consciousness. I was getting close. I could summon the unimaginable power but I could not command it. Once it manifested, I was at its mercy. My will was not yet strong enough. As my thoughts continued to wander, I drifted into a not so distant memory.

Tolerantly gazing upon the apocalyptic firestorm I'd inadvertently created throughout the once green landscape, Stephen stood amidst the flame and sighed.

"Our power is from wrath," he said in a fatherly tone. "Wrath is not our power. Do you understand, Dean?"

Doubled over and gasping for breath, I willed the cloak and the ethereal gauntlets covering my hands into retreat.

"I can't control it," I forced out shaking my head in denial. "It takes over. Too powerful."

"Because you fear it," he replied firmly grasping my shoulders and helping me upright. "Control the Wrath and you will command the power."

With a casual wave of his hand, the flames subsided and the field returned to a brilliant green.

"Again."

Snapping out of the daydream, I muttered under my breath, "Control the Wrath." And began my short journey to the streambed.

Standing alone on the hilltop, I begrudgingly glared at the faraway mountain range. Why the hell couldn't I get there? What the hell was I missing? Feeling a prominent surge of anger pulse through me, I unknowingly clenched both hands into tight fists. Gritting my teeth I felt the muscles in my neck constrict to the point where veins started popping out. Overcome with rage, I inadvertently willed the cloak into being and felt it abruptly manifest around my shoulders in a spectral flash of white luminescence. Feeding off my sour emotions, it rippled and swelled about my body sending visible waves of intense heat pulsing through the air. The surrounding green grass instantly ignited and formed a sprawling circular pattern of charred earth around me.

As my hands started to shake in fury, I threw my head back and let out an ear-splitting, primal scream.

In the midst of my childlike outburst, I defiantly threw my fisted hands in the air and the gauntlets manifested in a spectral flash covering my hands and forearms in rough-hewn ashen stone. Feeling a bit foolish, I lowered my arms and admired the uncanny, weightless substance perfectly encasing my flesh as a vision of Stephen flashed through my thoughts.

"What's with the gloves?" I asked curiously mesmerized by the ethereal matter shielding Stephen's hands and forearms.

Placing his hands casually out to his front, the shimmering, translucent material morphed into what appeared to be a lustrous argent metal.

"Gauntlets, Dean. Not gloves," he replied. "Combined with the Deacon's cloak they complete our divine armor. A means to channel the forces of Heaven and smite the vile beings we seek."

"What the hell are they made from?"

"Fundamental elements of the Realms," he said in his signature stoic tone. "Ashen stone from the molten cliffs of Tartarus. Barzel, the iron of Heaven, milled in the angelic forges. Fire of Gehenna summoned from the unquenchable lake. With mastery of your bestowed abilities the gauntlets will manifest in the form of your choosing."

"Interesting," I muttered holding in a smirk. "Do they come in green?"

The thought of the stiff right to the jaw I received for that last comment instantly snapped me out of my daydream and back to the present. Let's just say that a clenched fist perfectly coated in an otherworldly metal packs a slight wallop. Trust me on that one.

Calmed down a bit and returned to a rational state of mind, I willed the cloak and gauntlets into retreat with a spectral flash and began my short walk to the streambed. I evidently had some anger issues to work through.

It felt like months had passed. My head hung low as I stood on the hilltop with my eyes closed. Although the rage coursed through my body like an uninterrupted current, I no longer feared it. I welcomed it.

Slowly opening my eyes, I focused on my left hand and willed the ethereal gauntlet into being. Instantly manifesting around my hand, it slowly crept along my forearm as the translucent material shimmered ominously in the sunlight. Turning my palm toward the sky, I very carefully opened it and called for the fire. In response, the gauntlet ignited with subtle flame and a perfect sphere of wraithlike white fire carefully formed and hovered perfectly within my open hand. Slowly rotating, it crackled and hissed with abstract heat and intangible power. Frigg'n astonished that it actually happened, I momentarily let my concentration lapse and it vanished as quickly as it appeared, in a brilliant flash.

"Son of a bitch," I muttered triumphantly exhaling deeply. "I did it."

Willing the gauntlet into retreat, I thought of Stephen and a wide smile stretched across my face as my mind drifted back to one of our first conversations.

"Why fire?" I asked mesmerized by the otherworldly flame.

"Not mere fire, Dean," he replied with no hint of emotion. "Fire of Gehenna - The unquenchable lake. The final judgment."

"What does it do exactly?"

"Upon the Earth it has the power to do many things. Heal. Cleanse. Corrupt. Wound. Ruin. However, wielded as His judgment by a Deacon it will destroy anything it is cast upon. It is a grave burden to shoulder such responsibility. Our burden."

As the weight of his last comment hit home, I muttered, "It will destroy anything."

"The judgment of Gehenna fire is absolute. Nothing remains — body nor soul. It is only to be wielded upon the enemies of Heaven. Violate that covenant and the Wrath will turn upon you."

"Understood," I somberly said nodding in affirmation.

"You will find mastery of some aspects of the fire easier than others. Regardless of how you employ it — Do not do so without reason."

I peacefully stood on the hilltop peering across the lush landscape at the majestic mountains. This time I felt different. The repeated anger I'd held on to for being denied access to them was gone. For a reason I couldn't quite put my finger on, I made peace with the fact that many things still remained outside my level of understanding. When the time was right — I would be shown the path.

Good lord, I might be all grown up. That is a damn scary thought.

Luckily I didn't have much time to dwell on it because the sun began to set for the first time since my arrival in the Realms. As I stood contemplating the meaning of that particular omen, I felt a sharp gust of wind whisk across my face accompanied by a whisper-like shriek. Although it no longer scared the shit out of me, I still had no idea where it came from. Making the mental note that I'd really like to figure that out at some point, I assumed it was probably a hint.

Apparently it was time to go.

Chapter 10

As a surge of adrenaline shot through me, I turned to face the door. Taking three bold steps I stopped at the base of the granite threshold, reached back over my right shoulder, and effortlessly sheathed my sword in the leather scabbard strapped tightly across my back. Willing it into retreat I felt its presence instantly fade.

Yes, I had a sword - a spatha to be precise. Bit smaller than Stephen's long-sword. More suited to my 'talents' as he politely put it. I made a pretty compelling argument for a shotgun but evidently that was currently an unsupported weapon in the divine armory.

Typical.

Although, after dragging me through what seemed like an eternity of training sessions, I think Stephen was going to try and pull some strings. I wasn't exactly Connor MacLeod if you know what I'm saying.

Intently gazing at the door, I focused on the inlaid symbols, which I now knew to be angelic glyphs. Reaching out with my left hand, I placed it squarely upon the Chi-Rho exquisitely cast in the center. As my hand firmly set upon the symbol, I closed my eyes and muttered the phrase required to activate the gateway. The words instinctively flowed from my mouth in a strange language, like it was second nature. A strange language that I now spoke. The language of angels. Enochian.

As the final syllable exited my mouth, the glyphs immediately responded by systematically illuminating in a steady pattern. In a precise sequence throughout the doorway, each glyph answered, in turn, by emitting a bluish white glow. As soon as one completed, the next one started. The sequence fluidly continued until the coordinates to my destination were completed, and the gateway established. With the lighting of the final glyph, the door's impregnable locking mechanism disengaged as distinct whirring, clicking, and sliding sounds were evident from somewhere deep within the mighty panels. An ominous thud echoed throughout the still air indicating it was unlocked. Reaching back I pulled the dark hood of the cloak over my head, and mentally prepared myself for the journey. Releasing my hand from the Chi-Rho, I securely grasped the ironclad handles and threw open the massive doors.

I was ready.

Glaring fearlessly into the boundless, swirling vortex of time and space, I confidently stepped across the threshold and felt a surge of determination course through my body as my mouth stretched into a confident grin. It was time to fulfill my purpose. Prove my mettle. A new mission.

As I pierced the veil between the worlds, I quickly came to the realization that, tragically, I might not have been quite as ready as I recently thought to be. Damn it. I knew I should have paid more attention to Cloakboy when he was explaining the whole threshold thing. Instantly paralyzed by complete and utter sensory overload, I flawlessly executed a full bodied belly flop brilliantly capped off with a nose splitting face plant. Epic fail. That is *so* leaving a mark.

Right before I blacked out I couldn't help but wonder if this happened to Stephen the first time. Gotta be a common occurrence. That first step's a real bitch. Somebody should paint it yellow. Maybe put a sign up.

⁂

I was coaxed back into consciousness by the sound of laughter. Wave after wave of hearty, celebratory laughter. A sound I'd heard before. Carefully opening my eyes, I painfully squinted and blinked a couple times as the blurred scene slowly came into focus. I was sitting on a wood floor with my back to the wall. My head hung limply with my chin resting firmly on my chest. As my eyes fully adjusted, and my torso and legs came into focus, I realized that I was dressed in my tactical uniform. Or at least what remained of my uniform. It was shredded and covered in blood.

Slowly raising my head, I saw a shotgun draped across my feet. My shotgun. Bertha! The muzzle was warm against my legs, and a thin layer of smoke hung in the air that reeked of expended gunpowder. Six empty shells were scattered about my feet. With the unexplainable laughter starting to wane, I raised my head fully upright and was hit with a surge of adrenaline as I confirmed what I'd suspected. I was at the church. Son of a bitch. I was back.

The second trial. Petrovich. Azazel. Whatever the hell his name is. Should've seen that coming. Amazingly, it appeared I'd returned only mere seconds after making my not so glorious departure. Evidently, the whole Heaven versus Earth time disparity deal was no joke. With my eyes now functioning at full capacity, I carefully panned my head to the right and found the alter where Father Watson lay imprisoned, and still softly laughing. His eyeless gaze was fixed firmly on me like he was anticipating my return. Huddled in the corner to the right of the alter was Doc Kelly with her face completely expressionless, staring straight ahead into oblivion. Evidently still under the Petrovich mind whammy.

Despite the circumstances, I was elated to lay eyes on her again. After all, I still owed her a beer.

As I slowly wrapped my head around the scene in attempt to process what I was looking at, the harrowing voice of my executioner sent a distinct chill down my spine. Crossing my line of sight, Petrovich strode purposefully toward the alter paying me no attention. Seemed logical as he just finished unloading a shotgun into my chest a mere few seconds earlier.

"You know, *Priest*, it is unfathomable to me that you find humor in this situation," he condescendingly said glaring at Father Watson. Reaching the alter he stopped and loomed over the Padre. "Clearly, I will never understand the human mind. Such a curious, deluded construct."

Digging deep within his suit jacket, he produced what appeared to be a small scythe. He held it out to his front, in admiration, as it gleamed malevolently within the flickering candlelight. A series of Enochian glyphs, inscribed throughout the curvature of the honed blade, glowed a spectral crimson.

"I'm afraid our business is concluded," he said definitively. "Much to do. Much to do. Exciting times these are indeed. The time of harvest is upon us. Your soul will make a marvelous contribution to the future of mankind as I remake it in my worthy image. Rest assured."

"My soul belongs to the Father, and warded through my oath to the Guild," Father Watson confidently replied with a satisfied smile on his face. "There is nothing more you can do to me, you fool. Your ignorance is your undoing. Through your arrogance a Deacon has emerged. Called to existence by your very hand." In a sober tone he gazed across the room in my direction. "Prepare yourself, Azazel, the Wrath is upon you."

"Your delusions fail you," Petrovich snapped in a bitter tone. "*Deacons. The Guild.* Father's precious attack dogs. *Do not insult.* They hold no authority over me. So terribly predictable."

Lowering the scythe, he sarcastically looked around the sanctuary and said, "But perhaps your right, Priest. Perhaps the *mighty* Deacons — *the Seven lines of Seven* — and their flock of minions are lurking in the shadows of this very church, at this very moment. Waiting for the opportune moment to flaunt their tawdry cloaks and *smite* my poor children with their precious hell fire and blades of barzel. Frothing at the mouth to *cast* me back into Father's cage for all eternity." Pausing momentarily he mockingly placed a hand to his ear to listen. "Then again. Perhaps not."

With that, he raised the scythe above the Padre and muttered something under his breath in Enochian.

It was time.

Feeling a sense of controlled vengeance, I rose to my feet with my head bowed. Willing the cloak into being, my tattered uniform was restored to perfection in a spectral flash, and the standard camouflage pattern gave way to solid black — Johnny Cash meets Johnny Rambo. Thinking that was a nice touch, my lips curled into a dark grin.

The raw power of the cloak pulsed through my body like an electric current. It was our gift and our curse. The ever present source of our abilities. The wrath of God incarnate in physical form. A divine means to an end. The cloak flowed about my shoulders for a split second then vanished as I willed it into retreat. Didn't want to go 'full cloak' on Petrovich. Not yet. Reaching down I grabbed Bertha and rested her against my right shoulder.

"It's been too long, baby", I muttered to myself.

Now granted, a shotgun wouldn't do shit to an angel but damn if it didn't make me feel better. As a stern grin stretched across my face, I looked up and focused on Petrovich.

"Hey, handsome. Got a sec?" I shouted confidently striding toward him.

Spinning around in a state of absolute shock, Petrovich lowered the scythe to his side and stared at me with a look of total bewilderment. Tilting his head to the right he started to say something, but abruptly stopped. Apparently he was at a loss for words. That's a first.

"So, Wanted to let you know that I've had a good bit of time to give your employment opportunity some serious thought," I said pulling to a halt within a step or two from him. "As luck would have it, there's a competing offer on the table. So, after careful consideration, I regret to inform that — *You* can piss up a rope."

"*Interesting*," he said with a smug grin apparently over his momentary speech impediment. "A wonderful trick indeed. Something's different about you, Captain. Is that a touch of sorcery I sense? Didn't figure you for the type. It matters not. Unfortunately, I lack the time to entertain your amateurish arcane abilities."

Taking a step toward me, he raised the scythe to his side and admired it once again. Shifting his focus from the shimmering blade to me, he mockingly said, "Do you mean to *shoot me*?"

Slowly curling my hand into tight fists, I willed the ethereal gauntlets into being. Subtly manifesting with the signature spectral flash, they perfectly encased my hands and forearms in a rough-hewn ashen stone. His smug grin instantly vanished.

"I may shoot you later," I said as I winked at him. "Figured I'd hit you a couple times first."

"A Deacon," he muttered with a look of pure disbelief strewn across his male model-like face. "Not possible."

Willing the cloak into being, it instantly manifested and forbiddingly billowed about my shoulders.

"Didn't see that coming, eh?" I muttered feeling its dark power cascade through me. "Bit of a surprise to me as well."

In a flash of movement, I closed the short distance between us, and threw all my force into a menacing right handed cross that landed squarely in his washboard-like stomach. The sheer impact of the devastating punch, bolstered by my supernatural strength and the unbreakable hellstone covering my hands, instantly doubled him over in grimacing pain. The look of complete confusion on his face was absolutely priceless. A true polaroid moment. Instant classic. I'm talking — Christmas card quality — good.

With his entirely too good-looking face now conveniently at fist level, I quickly relished the moment and followed the cross with a left hook to the chin. The arc of my fist ripped through the air in a blur of motion and struck him like a sledgehammer. In what felt like complete slow motion, his face violently swiveled to the side as I geared up for the knockout blow. Totally amped up and having way too much fun, I instinctively reset my hips and sunk all my weight into a heavy handed right cross directly to the side of his exposed head.

The blunt impact of my stone fist took, the completely befuddled, Petrovich clear off his feet and launched him a solid ten feet backward. Slamming into a tall pile of discarded pews, he crashed to a most ungraceful halt amidst a heap of wooden carnage. Lamely sprawled out on the sanctuary floor in a most unangel-like position, he was apparently down for the count.

"Oooh. That had to hurt. I mean — like *really* hurt."

Not sure whether it was my spiked adrenaline level or the dark power pouring into me from the cloak, but I felt good. It was euphoric. Dangerously intoxicating.

Carefully leaning Bertha against the altar, I systemically grasped the mighty spikes impaled in Father Watson's limbs with the gauntlets. Upon my touch they simply dematerialized leaving gaping, gruesome holes in his flesh. Willing the ashen stone into retreat, I called for the healing fire. As the ethereal whitish blue flame replaced the course stone, I placed my hands on each of his open wounds and watched in wonderment as they unnaturally closed upon themselves. Unfortunately he was still in rough shape. I'd barely scratched the surface on how to employ the healing capabilities of my power. The Padre needed medical attention. Quickly.

"Hang in there, Father," I said, willing the gauntlets into retreat. "Have you out of here in a minute."

Lying perfectly still on the altar, he softly glared at me with empty eye sockets. With a placid smile, he said, "You have released me. Thank you, Dean. I believe my work here is now finished. Your work, however, is just beginning. Please continue with the task at hand and kindly leave me to my providence."

Crossing his arms over his chest, he shut his eyelids, and a look of consummate serenity washed over his battered face.

"Balance, Dean," he muttered in a subdued whisper-like voice.

As he exhaled his final breath, a delicate mist of incorporeal purple radiance ascended from the Padre's now lifeless body, and hovered inimitably in the still air. As I stood awestruck by the inexpressible grandeur of his disembodied soul, it elegantly drifted upward and vanished in a swirling vortex of celestial light.

The Padre had evidently left the building.

"Hell of an exit," I muttered to myself thinking that he was clearly going to be disappointed by the lack of 'holy water' where he was heading.

Maybe they'd make an exception. He'd earned it after all. At the very least I hope he filled up his flask.

Sliding my hands under his limp and broken body, I lifted him off the forsaken blood stained altar and turned toward the vestibule. No way I was leaving his body there. I'd make sure the boys gave him a proper burial at some point. Focusing on the doorway at the far side of the sanctuary, I took three bold steps, and within a brief second found myself standing in the vestibule by the main entrance to the church. Laying the Padre's corpse carefully against the interior wall, I reversed the process, and found myself back in the sanctuary standing over Doc Kelly.

Apparently angels had some serious mind control mojo because the Doc was still hunkered against the wall to the rear of the altar, gazing emptily at nothing particular. Briefly pausing to admire her stunning features — and making the mental note that only Erin could still look amazing in the midst of a shit storm like this — I carefully lifted her from the floor and cradled her petite body in my arms.

Although I was pretty sure she wouldn't hear me, I muttered, "Time to get you out of here, Doc. Hope you don't mind an IOU on that beer."

Again focusing my will, I turned, took three steps, and faded from the sanctuary only to manifest again in the vestibule. Quickly finding a safe place to stash Erin until I could call in for the evac, I delicately lowered her to the floor in back of an antique wooden desk against the far wall. As I began to slowly pull my arms away, I felt her hands reach out and tightly grasp my right bicep. A bit startled I abruptly raised my head only to find her staring directly at me with a somewhat vacant look.

"Hello," she said sounding like she'd had a few too many margaritas during a prolonged happy hour. Clumsily looking around the dimly lit room with glazed eyes, she started to uncharacteristically giggle like a small child. "What happened here? This place is a wreck."

"Kind of a long story-"

"Oh my," she said not giving me a chance to get a word in edgewise as she squeezed my bicep again, "Very firm. Do you work out?"

"Take it easy, Doc," I replied, chuckling a bit despite the circumstances. "You're not quite yourself at the moment-"

"Is that a cape?" She asked inquisitively gawking at the otherworldly cloak hanging about my shoulders.

"Ah, No — it's a cloak. Big difference-"

"Wait!" She said in a tone slightly more sober yet very un-Erin like. "You sound just like Dean. I think he's here somewhere. *Have you seen him?* He came to find me. I was in trouble."

"It's Ok, Doc. I'm here-"

"Am I still in trouble?" She asked as her eyes widened in fear.

"No, No. You're Ok. Just relax a bit. You'll be out of here and back to your old self soon enough."

"Oh, good. Thank You," she murmured visibly relaxing. "Please tell Dean that I'm here. He'll be worried. He works out too, you know. He's my favorite. Don't tell him though. He thinks he's a tough guy."

Upon completing her thought, Erin's eyes faded shut and she drifted into a deep sleep from what I assumed was an after-effect of the angelic mind whammy. Thinking it a bit odd that she didn't recognize me, I shrugged it off to the same factor.

"Thinks he's a tough guy?" I muttered to myself gently removing her hands from my arm, and placing them on her lap. "Clearly she's confused. I am her favorite though. That's gotta count for something."

With Erin momentarily out of harm's way, I focused again on the sanctuary, and within three steps found myself back at the altar. It was time to finish the job. Restore the Balance. As I started confidently walking toward the hot mess on the floor, also known as Goran Petrovich, I was stopped dead in my tracks by a thunderous growl emanating from the far side of the sanctuary. I turned just in time to see a large silhouette emerge from the oversized gopher hole in the church floor.

Tiny. And he looked pissed.

Chapter 11

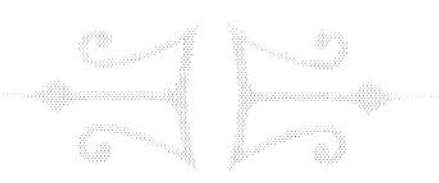

Slowly emerging from the darkness and into the dim lighting of the sanctuary, the giant determinedly stomped toward me. His mouth was curled into a wicked scowl, showing off his wolf-manlike incisors. In his right hand he had a death grip on the handle of a big-ass medieval looking battle-axe that he carelessly dragged behind him. The enormous axe head carved a visible path through the wooden floor of the church as he lumbered to meet me. Slumped over his left shoulder was what appeared to be a lifeless body. I could vaguely make out a pair of legs dangling limply about his massive torso. Legs with combat boots. The First Sergeant.

Son of a bitch.

Barreling through the labyrinth of makeshift hospital beds, he effortlessly batted them from his path as cot after cot soared through the air in various pieces and parts — recently deceased occupants and all. It was quite the spectacle. Abruptly stopping within ten feet of me, he glared hatefully through his black, soulless eyes. Reaching up with his left hand, he grabbed the First Sergeant's limp body and flung him to the ground in defiance as he shot me a mocking smile.

Turning his head and spitting a truly disgusting looking substance on Tony's corpse, he looked directly at me and said, "He was weak. Now it is your turn."

"You should not have fucking done that," I instantly replied through gritted teeth.

Overcome with rage, I curled my hands into tight fists and felt the wrathful power of the cloak roar to life as it amplified my anger to a near unrestrained level. Almost like it was feeding off my pain. Egging me on. Pushing me beyond my level of control.

In a blinding streak, Tiny placed both hands on the hilt of his mighty axe and raised it far above his head as he charged at me with breakneck speed. Closing the distance in a fraction of a second, I stood firmly and watched as he swung it, with every ounce of his unbound supernatural strength, directly at my head. A heart-stopping howl boomed from his mouth as his eyes tightly squinted with focused fury in anticipation of the kill. As his fifteen-foot frame loomed over me, and the blood-crusted blade of his axe swung to within inches of my neck, I couldn't help but smile.

"Tiny, You stupid Son of a Bitch," I muttered still standing firm.

Focusing on my hands, still clutched into fists by my side, I instantly felt the presence of the gauntlets as they manifested in the form of rough hewn, ashen hellstone. Taking half a step to my left, I sunk all my force into a perfectly executed right hook that squarely connected with Tiny's kneecap, which was conveniently at eye level. His manly battle cry quickly downgraded to a bitch-like squeal as my stone shielded fist completely obliterated his knee, dropping his sorry ass straight to the floor. Momentarily in shock, I couldn't help but snicker as he dumbfoundedly gawked at the fact that his thighbone was no longer connected to his shinbone.

"Might have blown an ACL there, asshole. Hurts — Don't it?"

Sprawled out in a giant mound on the church floor, he looked up at me in a state of complete and utter confusion. As he began to open his mouth to say something I instantly cocked my right arm back, dropped to my knees, and squarely delivered a stiff right to his face. His eyes shot wide open for a split second as the impact of my gauntlet bashed his oversized nose and slammed his big ass head into the floor. The violent collision resulted in the splitting of several floorboards as the foundation of the church groaned in protest.

Surging with adrenaline, I jumped back to my feet and held out my hands, focusing on the gauntlets. In a spectral flash, the ashen stone was replaced with glinting, argent metal. Glaring at the downed behemoth with a dark, brooding scowl, I willed the spatha into being and instantly felt the presence of the leather scabbard on my back. As the strength of my will steadily yielded to the wrathful influence of the cloak, I wanted nothing more than to carve Tiny's wretched body into a bloody fucking stump. The anticipation of meticulously ripping my sword inch by inch through his goddamned neck was overpowering.

I could literally taste it.

Slowly and excruciatingly I would make him endure every fucking ounce of torment he deserved. Payback with interest for all the souls he devoured throughout the course of his unnatural, cursed existence. He would beg for mercy before I was finished. And none would be granted.

As my scowl stretched into a dark smile, I reached back and grasped the stout hilt of the otherworldly sword. Decisively drawing it from its sheath, I felt a ripple of energy release into the stagnant air with an ominous hum. Holding it out, my eyes drifted to the inscription boldly blazoned upon the argent blade.

'No me satues sin razon.'

"Do not draw me without reason," I muttered translating the Latin phrase.

As the spoken words registered with my brain, I instantly broke from the homicidal trance and sheathed the sword. Fighting to reestablish rational control of my thoughts, I affirmably declared, "No. Not like this."

Shaking my head and exhaling a steady breath, I focused on a memory of Stephen.

Awkwardly toppling to the ground while feebly attempting to parry a Stephen sword attack, I dropped my longsword in defeat and muttered, "Any chance of swapping this thing out for a gun?"

"For an accomplished pugilist your footwork is truly appalling," he stoically replied ignoring my request. Lowering the massive blade and extending his hand to help me up, he said, "You wield the longsword with the skill of a one armed blind man with two broken legs."

"Thanks for that," I grumbled accepting his aid.

Reaching over his shoulder, with his free hand he drew a second, smaller sword from a leather scabbard strapped tightly to his back. Flipping the blade downward and handing it to me hilt first, he said, "Perhaps a spatha is more suited to your talents. With a one-handed hilt, it's lighter, faster — a soldier's sword."

"I think I should be insulted," I shot back begrudgingly accepting the shorter weapon. "You do realize that swords went out of style with Braveheart, right?"

"I was not aware of that," he dryly replied. "Thank You so much for enlightening me."

"That's what I'm here for."

"Forged by the Seraphim," he said resting the hefty longsword against his shoulder, "the barzel blade of our weaponry is lethal to all beings — mortal, divine, or otherwise."

"Gotta be a better way to take down a giant. Perhaps a nice grenade launcher? Something with a trigger and large bullets."

"Nephilim are impervious to earthly attack, Dean. Despite their abhorred nature, they are spawn of angels. Only a weapon of the Realms will end them. Separate the head from the neck — they will heal from anything less definitive. While the judgment of Gehenna fire will furnish the same result, it will be many centuries before you acquire the requisite level of mastery to wield it effectively."

"Awesome," I grumbled letting out an exasperated sigh, while pulling the spatha from the ground. "Killing giants with swords. An entirely new spin on bringing a knife to a gunfight."

"The path of the Deacon is not to kill indiscriminately, Dean," he said with a stern look. "We are to cast final judgment. There can be no malice — no anger — in our deeds. Acts without reason and honor violate the very Balance we have vowed to maintain. There are consequences for such dereliction."

꧁

Hearing a stirring sound to my rear, I turned my head and was absolutely shocked to hear a familiar voice.

"Hey, little help over here?"

Tony? He's alive — Son of a Bitch.

Momentarily back in control, and feeling somewhat like my old self again, I willed the gauntlets into retreat. Quickly spinning around, I saw the First Sergeant gingerly sit up. His swollen face grimaced with deep-seated pain as one of his arms hung limp by his side. His face looked like a damn punching bag, covered in blood. Both his legs were visibly broken. Damn — that's one tough bastard.

"About time you showed up, Big Sarge," I said helping him up to a stable sitting position. "Beginning to think I'd have to take care of this mess on my own. You Ok?"

"Who the fuck are you?" He dryly grumbled as he squinted at me through blackened, distended eyes. "Where's Captain Robinson?"

My momentary joy was dashed as the impact of Tony's question hit me like a damn baseball bat to the jaw. He didn't recognize me either. The warning heeded by Stephen flashed through my thoughts.

"*Although Deacons live in the world of man they are no longer part of it. Your mortal life has ended. You are a mere ghost to those you once knew. A strange face in the crowd — only recognizable to those touched with the Sight. Feared by most and revered by others. But make no mistake, Dean, should you choose this path, the life you knew upon the Earth is forfeit.*"

It was official. I was dead.

My best friend and brother in arms didn't know me. That hurt. Bad. For a split second I thought it might have been his wounds affecting his sight. Or the fact that he smacked his head and wasn't thinking straight. But the realist in me knew it wasn't. First Erin. Now Tony. I'd made my choice and this was part of the deal.

"I'm a friend," I replied despondently. "Robinson fell."

"Fuck You," Tony grunted pushing my hands away. "Where is he? Where's Doc Kelly? Father Watson? Help me up, goddamn it!"

Willing the ethereal gauntlet into being around my left hand, I slowly raised it to Tony's head and called for the healing fire. With a heavy heart, I muttered, "Mission's over, old friend. Fight another day."

As I gently placed my flame veiled hand on Tony's temple, his eyes flashed with instant tranquility as his broken body relaxed and began to sink back to the floor. His eyes slowly closed into a deep, placid sleep. Scooping up his massive frame with ease, I quickly ushered him to the vestibule and propped him up against the wall adjacent a slumbering Doc Kelly.

Hoping like hell my voice still sounded enough like the old me, I reached down and grabbed the hand mic clipped to the First Sergeant's tac vest. Pressing the transmit button, I calmly said, "Red Bayonet — Two casualties prepped for evac — One KIA — Main breach — Objective is not secure — Say Again — Not Secure."

Almost instantly, the radio chirped with Luke's response. "Roger sir, Enroute — Acknowledge the OBJ's hot — Coming in the front door — Two minutes — Will evac to the rally point."

"Roger — Target's in flight — I'm pursuing — Don't wait — Robinson Out."

With the cavalry on their way to snatch Tony, Doc, and the remains of Father Watson, I dropped the hand mic. Despairingly staring at my friends, I felt waves of melancholy anger undulate through my body. Tony and Erin would be Ok. Me, on the other hand, I wasn't so sure. The jury was still out.

Evidently long overdue, the reality of my mortal death and newfound supernatural existence finally hit me. And it hit me hard. Dropping to a knee and apathetically lowering my head, I was overcome with an intense, dark depression. The rancorous thoughts I'd recently held at bay came back — one hundred fold — as the brooding influence of the cloak raced through my veins like wild fire. Repeated, undeniable, savage impulses slammed my consciousness. Pushing me into a state of vindictive fury — goading me into action.

Closing my eyes, my mind flooded with an incessant yearning need for retribution — blood of the enemy — good old fashion payback. The cloak was vengeance incarnate and I was its vessel — We shared the same goal.

Somebody had to pay. Right fucking now.

No longer feeling the need to resist, I opened my eyes and muttered, "Yes."

Despite knowing deep down it was a really fucking bad idea, I allowed the vindictive power to freely flow into me as I slowly rose to my feet. Fully relenting to the unbridled Wrath, I burned with nothing short of pure primal rage. With teeth gritted, I felt my hands clench into tight fists, and again snarled, "Yes."

Feeling the ethereal metal flow about my hands and forearms, I called for the spatha. My mouth curled into a vicious smile as the presence of the scabbard was evident on my back. In a blur of motion, I drew the otherworldly blade and held it tightly with my right hand in fervent anticipation of casting judgment, with extreme prejudice, upon the enemies of Heaven — my enemies.

With my mind racing and chest heaving with unrestrained power, I growled in an unfamiliar guttural voice, "Now."

Taking one last wanting look at my mortal friends, I focused on that son of a bitch Tiny, and took three heavy steps. Instantly appearing in the sanctuary, in a state of unadulterated fury, I ripped the sword in a deadly arc toward the loathsome neck of the downed nephilim.

Chapter 12

As the blade lashed into the bare wooden floor in the precise spot where Tiny's big-ass head should have been, I snapped out of my frenzied state and looked up in complete confusion. There was a slight problem.

The giant wasn't there.

Standing upright and forcefully yanking the blade from the floor, I slowly gazed around in mild astonishment.

The sanctuary was restored to a state of immaculate perfection. The horror movie scene was completely erased. The blood — the carnage — the cribs — the freakish junior giants — the hospital beds — the dead women — the mammoth hole in the floor — the pile of half devoured body parts — the thousands of creepy candles — gone.

Replaced by row upon row of perfectly aligned pews leading up to the pristine altar. What the hell? Spinning around in disbelief, I dropped the sword to my side in an attempt to rationalize what I was seeing. Hearing what sounded like the flutter of massive wings, I felt a brisk rush of air sweep against my back accompanied by a mocking voice.

"Ah, the power of the left hand. Such a fickle beast. And to bestow such greatness upon a tempestuous mind such as yours. How terribly irresponsible."

Slowly turning, I found myself face to face with a very content and clearly recovered Petrovich, grinning at me with a roguish smile. Fixing him with an intense squint, I growled, "What the hell happened?"

"That is quite simple. You proved your true nature — Unworthy," he quipped. "Wielding the Wrath with malice in your heart, Tsk, Tsk. *So much more* is expected from a *Deacon,* after all."

Circling to my rear he happily looked around the church, and declared, "Gaze upon the consequence of the Balance disrupted. Well done. Straying from the light, you have veiled the darkness. Or haven't you received that lesson yet?"

Spinning around to follow him, I felt my face curl into a brooding scowl. Shooting him a fervent glare, I snapped, "Shut Up, asshole."

Still thoroughly confused as to what was happening, I felt the unbridled Wrath rearing in the deep recess of my soul. It felt different now. Calculating. Like a shrewd predator — waiting in the dark shadows of a cage. Biding its time. To free itself.

As if he could also sense it, Petrovich continued with his smug commentary as he paced around me.

"You know, Captain, I must admit to being truly startled by your *ascension* to the ranks of Father's *noble* huntsmen. Perhaps I should have been a bit more persuasive in my offer of employ. Had I realized that your dark aura was in fact the Wrathful touch, I would have taken a completely different tact."

"I Said — Shut Up, asshole," I snarled feeling my grip tighten on the hilt of the spatha.

"Like the others, you are weak," he snidely replied truly enjoying my frustration. "It is your unfortunate nature. The great human condition. However, I realize now that your master must be of a truly dire circumstance with his ranks thinning so quickly."

Stopping and fixing me intently with his wretched crimson eyes, he coldly said, "*You* will be undone by the Wrath. It is corrupting. Unyielding. Wicked and marvelous. You *will* be crushed in its wake. It is only a matter of time. And when that time comes — You will become the very *abomination* you have vowed to smite."

So that did it.

As his taunting words struck my ears, I felt like a damn bomb detonated in my head. A primal scream bellowed from my mouth and my eyes narrowed into a predatory squint as I felt the Wrath take over. Like it was trying to rip free from my body, the cloak defiantly burst into white flame as Gehenna fire encased my barzel gauntlets and sword. As my back locked into an unnatural arch, steady streams of apocalyptic white flame poured out of me and slammed Petrovich like a continuous wave of molten lava. Falling to my knees under the otherworldly force, my entire body constricted as my vision blurred to the point of surreal obscurity.

I have no memory of how long this went on. The unbridled rage fed the unfathomable power until it was no more.

Gone.

All of it.

As I felt my mind slip back into active consciousness, I willed the cloak into retreat and it vanished in a spectral flash as did the gauntlets encasing my hands. Struggling to breathe, I dropped the sword and doubled over in pain. As my vision snapped back into focus, I realized that I'd set the entire church aflame. Horrific pillars of infernal white fire shot clear through the vaulted ceiling and uncontrollably ripped through the sanctuary devouring everything in their path.

Slowly raising my head, I viewed a very satisfied and clearly unsmited Petrovich strolling toward me through the raging firestorm.

"Well done," he casually said in passing. "We shall be the best of enemies. I just know it. And please do give my very best to your *brethren*. They should be along any moment now."

He then turned and vanished as a powerful whoosh of air passed over me, accompanied by the flutter of massive wings. I really fucking hate that guy.

Leveraging all my remaining strength, I pushed off the floor and awkwardly staggered to my feet. Turning toward the vestibule, I painfully gazed through the sea of fire for any sign that Erin and the First Sergeant had made it out. Not able to see a frigg'n thing, I launched into an immediate state of panic and instinctively started moving in their direction. I managed to get two clumsy steps underway when I was promptly jerked to a halt by a powerful hand on my right shoulder, accompanied by a burly voice speaking in what sounded like a thick Scottish brogue.

"Steady, laddie. Ye don't need to be going in there. The sergeant and the wee lassie are safe. Your men carried them away. Not to worry."

Not understanding a frigg'n thing he'd said, I spun around to see the hulking silhouette of a man standing opposite me amidst the towering flame. With a somewhat friendly smile on his face, he just stood there gawking at me with his right hand still wrapped around my shoulder. Confused as all hell as to where he came from and whether or not he was friend or foe, I made a feeble attempt to swat his hand away as I executed one of my less impressive combat rolls toward my sword, still lying where I'd dropped it earlier. As I plummeted to the floor in a pathetic heap, a solid three feet from the spatha, I realized I had nothing left. All my strength was gone. I didn't even get my hands out to brace the fall.

It was ugly. Adding insult to clear injury, I heard the Scottish ape start laughing. Goddamn it. This mission had effectively gone to shit. For the second time. A failure of epic proportions. The Greeks wrote poems about shit like this.

"He's a feisty one, Aye?" I heard him mutter, as I lay completely defenseless with my face planted firmly on a floorboard. "Bit daft - but feisty. I like him."

Feeling two meaty hands wrap around my torso, he effortlessly lifted me up to a standing position and placed one of my arms over his broad shoulder to keep me steady. Guessing at this point that he was more friend than foe, and recognizing that I wasn't in much of a position to do anything about it even if he wasn't, I painfully turned my head and muttered, "Are you … from the Guild?"

"Aye, lad. We are."

"Oh, that's nice," I managed to blurt out. "There's more than one of you?"

As the flames continued to rip through the church, a second figure stepped into my quickly blurring line of sight. While not quite as bulky as the steroid version of Sir William Wallace, he was almost as tall. Bit more on the lanky side though. Amidst the smoke and fiery carnage, the only thing I could really make out was his hair. It was red. Insanely red. Like a goddamn red crayon exploded on the poor bastard's head.

"New Guy!" He excitedly said holding out his hand. "Great to finally meet you. I'm Rooster."

"Rooster?" I scoffed, quickly starting to fade. "Really?"

Realizing I didn't have it in me to actually raise my arm in response, he reached down and awkwardly shook my limp hand.

"This is Abernethy," he said pointing at Braveheart. "You can call him Big A. He's Scottish."

"No shit? I would've guessed French."

Despite the circumstances, I couldn't help but chuckle to myself at that one. You can't beat the classics.

"What the hell did he say to me a minute ago?" I asked fighting to keep my eyes open.

"He said that your friends, First Sergeant Coates and Doctor Kelly, are quite safe. Your team pulled them out before you set off the fireworks display. And we took care of Father Watson's remains. Not to worry. He's one of us."

Turning his attention from me to the large, apparently Scottish, fellow holding me up, he said, "Time to go Big A. We need to get him back to the Quartermaster. He's fading fast."

As he finished speaking, a large door emblazoned with illuminated angelic glyphs manifested directly behind him. Sliding my free arm over one of his shoulders, he and 'Big A' proceeded to carry me to the portal. No longer able to keep my eyes open, I felt my head drop stiffly against my chest as they dragged me along.

"Where are we going?" I asked in a slurred speech.

"Home, laddie. We're going home. There's a storm coming."

As everything faded to black, I muttered, "Home?"

Chapter 13

Darkness yielded to a brief flash of swirling light followed by voices. Several voices. Unfamiliar. Except for the Scottish guy.

"What the hell was his name? He was a big son of a bitch. That's it — Big something or other. And his buddy Chicken. No, that's not right. Crazy fucking hair. Red. Wait — was it Rooster? Rooster — What the hell kind of name is that anyway?"

More light. Glimpse of people standing over me. Blurry. Darkness again. Chatter. Splash of water.

"Am I floating? Damn, this actually feels pretty good."

Sinking. Good feelings gone.

"Swim."

Under water.

"Can't swim. No strength."

Silence.

Emptiness.

Struggling to catch my breath, I determinedly stomped my way up a winding, narrow path carefully cut into the side of a mountain.

"Goddamn — it's cold."

At least a solid foot of heavy snow made every step a labored effort. A persistent burning ache in both of my legs indicated I was rapidly nearing muscle failure.

"Don't even think about stopping. Pick it up. You can move faster than this. Push yourself."

My face stung from the persistent pelting of wet snowflakes whipping about in the howling gusts of wind. I couldn't feel my hands. Frostbite was settling in.

"This is nothing. Step it out. Almost there. Move your ass."

Feeling that most unpleasant sensation of a muscle spasm flicker in my right leg, I very ungracefully stumbled, and subsequently plummeted to the frosty ground in a pathetic heap.

As my face made contact with the frozen tundra, my dreamlike trance abruptly ended and I instantly snapped back into the moment. Feeling like I ended up on the wrong end of an epic bar brawl, all I could muster was — "Frigg'n Ow."

Unfortunately, my face was buried in several inches of snow, and I was pretty sure no actual words made it out of my mouth.

Exhausted muscles and frozen body parts screamed in protest as I fought to push myself off the ground. Looking around in utter shock, I grumbled, "How the hell did I get here?"

As a well-timed gust of wind blasted me with a blanket of frigid air, I exasperatedly muttered, "And where the hell is *here*?"

Bringing myself to a full upright position, with thick snow piled around my knees, I was graced with another surge of agonizing pain. Just for good measure, I tossed in a second — "Frigg'n Ow."

Regaining consciousness in strange places seemed to be my new thing. Couldn't say that I enjoyed it all that much, but at least it was becoming rather familiar. This time was different though. Unlike the past few occurrences, there was nothing gradual about it. It was instantaneous. Almost violent.

How did I get here?

A second ago my sorry ass was being hauled out of the burning church by a Scottish hulk and his carrot-topped buddy.

Was I sleep walking? Was that even possible?

It was definitely a first. Even for me. Not particularly pleasant either. For the record.

"If this is home — I am so moving," I grumbled, while gathering myself to a somewhat functional state, as I wiped a thick layer of hoarfrost from my face. Letting out a long, deliberate sigh, I slowly turned to survey my latest set of surroundings. As fate would have it, I was indeed smack in the middle of a goddamned blizzard. Although I could barely see my hand as I held it up to my face, it seemed that I was on the side of a mountain. The towering wall of rock to my immediate left and the bottomless abyss shortly to my right gave it away.

It seemed I was steadily making my way up a narrow path that wound through the cliff face at a daunting grade. Despite the snow, it was barely wide enough to support travel by a single person. Exactly why I was performing this particular action and how I got here in the first place — still remained a complete and utter mystery. Making the mental note that I seriously needed to figure out why I never woke up on a nice beach somewhere with a cocktail, I figured it was best to keep moving. I was evidently in a hurry. Pulling the hood of the cloak over my snow dusted head, I begrudgingly started back on my peculiar trek.

As I started to move I felt a warming pulse emanate through my frozen and exhausted body, restoring me to a state of perfect health. The cloak — it was protecting me. Feeling a little better about the situation, I slugged my way through knee-high snow for what seemed like a solid hour, when I started to make out a faint glow of light in the near distance. Moving toward it with as much speed as I could possibly muster, I felt the trail start to level out as my quads applauded in gratitude.

Although I was pretty sure I wasn't at the peak, I'd evidently reached some sort of a plateau. Good thing because it felt like I was about to cough up a lung. The cloak might have been keeping me warm, but it certainly wasn't giving me the agility and endurance boost that I'd come to rely on. Thinking that couldn't necessarily be a good thing, I kept pushing forward.

Upon taking a few more painful steps, I abruptly, and quite unexpectedly stepped out of the winter wonderland and into a small cave-like tunnel. Just like that. It was tall enough that I could walk upright without ducking, and about twice as wide as the path. Medieval looking lanterns composed of tarnished metal hung sporadically throughout the jagged rock walls, casting a faint orange glow on the immediate floor and ceiling. The ominous motif of deep shadows and dim light revealed that the tunnel wound through the mountain for as long as the eye could see. The unnatural sound of grinding rock caused me to quickly spin around, just in time to see the opening that I stepped through, just seconds before, close upon itself.

"I didn't want to go back out there anyway," I muttered.

Figuring it was onward and outward, I started moving down the enigmatic tunnel. As quickly as I took the first step, the cloak retreated in a spectral flash, and I found myself clothed in a linen tunic and matching pants. And of course, I was barefoot. Again. Goddamit. Thinking that was completely unacceptable, I willed the cloak back into being. When absolutely nothing happened, I called for it again.

And nothing happened. Again.

"That can't be good," I grumbled.

Getting the sneaking suspicion that somehow Stephen was involved, I felt my stomach churn with looming dread. No doubt he was less than impressed with my performance during the second trial. It was piss poor. Perhaps even tragic. Petrovich and his freakish band of carnies escaped into the ether. And there was that small matter of torching the church with apocalyptic hellfire in the process. Not good. This was going to suck.

Inhaling a deep breath, I picked up the pace and began to purposefully stride through the passage. No sense in dragging it out. Although I was never one to back down from a well deserved ass chewing, I had the solid suspicion that this was probably going to be a bit more dramatic. Like eternal damnation in a flaming ball of judgment fire type dramatic. Lost in melancholy thought, I continued to make my way along the dimly lit path at a forced pace. And it just kept on a' coming. The longer I walked, the longer it seemed to get. Never any semblance of an endpoint. Just more tunnel. And unlike cowbell, I did not have a need for more tunnel.

As my sullen attitude gave way to frustration, I abruptly pulled to a halt and it hit me. The mountains. The frigg'n mountains that I could never reach from the green hilltop where I first met Stephen. That must be where I am. The frigg'n irony. Classic Cloakboy.

"Ok," I muttered while nodding my head. "I get it."

Closing my eyes, I attempted to clear my mind of the dark aggravation and accept that which I could not change. Within a few short moments a serene focus slowly replaced my clouded thoughts, and the sound of grinding rock to my immediate front snapped me from my momentary trance. I opened my eyes just in time to see an opening slowly form in the solid rock wall. A wave of welcoming warm air gracefully rolled over me from the cavern within. Knowing, without a doubt, who was waiting for me, I stepped inside to take what I had coming. For the first time in my adult life I was about to be fired. Hopefully not literally — really bad choice of words, given the circumstances.

As I passed through the portal into the waiting cavern, I found myself standing, somewhat dumbfounded, in a massive rotunda lit only by the roaring fire ablaze in the pit-like hearth, located in the dead center. The smooth, almost shiny rock material making up the chamber wall glistened in the flickering light, which also cast a steady wraithlike glow throughout the vast domed ceiling. Standing on the perimeter of the fire-pit were two figures engaged in, what sounded like, a spirited conversation. I couldn't actually hear the words, but the tone was not exactly friendly — if you know what I'm saying.

Although they were a good fifty feet from where I stood, I instantly recognized one of the men to be Stephen. Dressed in his typical black suit, he stood opposite a larger man clothed all in white with a massive silver sword strapped to his back. Although I didn't know who he was, something about him sent a distinct chill down my spine. He was quite a bit taller than Stephen and exuded a presence that was practically tangible. You could almost see it outlining his powerful frame. He had to be an angel. Either that or an extra from one of the Conan movies. Sensing that the conversation was no longer private, they abruptly stopped talking and turned in my direction with a pair of intense scowls. It was an awkward moment. So incredibly awkward.

"Dean, I see you received my summons. Please, join us," said Stephen in a not unkind manner as the scowl effortlessly transitioned to his signature stoic mask. "Tell me, how are you feeling?"

"Ah, I'm well ... I guess," I awkwardly replied. "Little hazy. But well."

Gathering the requisite courage, I began the solemn walk toward the hearth. Trying to maintain eye contact with Stephen, I couldn't shake the soul-piercing gaze of his unidentified blonde buddy. He was looking right through me with his blazing blue eyes. Scanning. Probing. I could feel him sifting through my thoughts. Looking for something. Something he couldn't find. Although his regal, statuesque face maintained a neutral expression, I could sense his skepticism. Or perhaps it was contempt. Taking a bold yet graceful step in my direction, he squarely placed himself in front of Stephen, prompting me to pull to an abrupt halt.

"The Seventh of Seven," he said in a somewhat rhetorical fashion while continuing to gaze upon me with a scrutinizing stare. "Dean Robinson. The prodigal Son of Wrath. We have been anticipating your arrival for many centuries. I cannot say I am most pleased to make your acquaintance." Dismissively turning from me and facing Stephen, he solemnly said, "If the prophecy is credible — this marks the coming of the ascension. Are you prepared for what may follow?"

"I am," replied Stephen in a somber tone.

"Very well. Take heed, Deacon. Do not convey your trust without great caution. If what you say is true, you will find no solace outside of the Seven Realms. Mind your borders carefully. Scour the Earth. Find where the anakim are veiled. Time is no longer our ally."

Upon completing the statement, he walked directly into the towering flame of the hearth, and vanished amidst a powerful whoosh of air and a momentary flash of brilliant light. Feeling like a child that wandered into the middle of a movie, I turned to Stephen in a clear state of confusion.

"We have much to discuss," he said dismissing my look of befuddlement. "But first, allow me to properly welcome you to the First Realm, otherwise known as, Raven Spire — my home."

Completely awestruck, the first thing that came to mind was simply, "Your home? You live … Here?"

"In a manner of speaking," he replied. "From the Spire I am able to provide watch over all under my purview."

As he finished speaking, six large window-like openings formed throughout the circular wall of the rotunda, displaying a perfect panoramic view of the surrounding landscape. The blinding snow instantly gave way to a flawless blue sky as radiant sunshine flooded the room. It was nothing short of breathtaking. Almost too perfect for words. In complete wonderment, I carefully approached the edge of the closest opening, and gazed at what appeared to be a medieval castle built atop a formidable hill in the distant landscape. Surrounded by a small village, it was a scene straight out of a frigg'n movie.

"What is that place?" I muttered unable to pull my eyes from the surreal setting.

"That is Badencoch, the Seventh Realm. What you see before you is the home of the archdeacon and those in his charge," he replied while drawing my attention to the other openings. "Each window corresponds to a different Realm within the Guild of Deacons. They surround Raven Spire in a perfect six-pointed formation — aligned with the Earthly gates."

Speechless, I slowly made my way around the rotunda, taking in the various landscapes and the settlements contained within. Varying in setting, architecture, and time period, each Realm was a splendor in and of itself. Upon reaching the final window, I was dismayed to watch it slowly fade back into solid rock, and once again the room was cast in the dim lighting of the hearth.

"Guess the show's over," I muttered.

"You will understand all in due time. But now, join me for a cup of tea. We have precious little time," said Stephen as he walked past me toward a small wooden table on the perimeter wall of the rotunda.

"Tea?" I scoffed truly astonished at how this scene was unfolding. Firstly, some unidentified angel that evidently hated my guts, for some unknown reason, crawled around my head looking for something. I think that constitutes mind-rape. Not cool. And secondly, in lieu of a divine bitch slap from

Cloakboy, he invites me to a frigg'n tea party. What the hell was going on here? Reaching the table, I watched, in nervous anticipation, as Stephen carefully combined several obscure ingredients in, what appeared to be, humble stone goblets.

"Never underestimate the value of a well made cup of tea," he said while passing me one. "Settles the body as well as the mind. I believe you could benefit from both at the current moment. Yes?"

"That's a frigg'n understatement." I muttered while accepting the steaming drink. "You have anything stronger?"

As the slight hint of a smirk crept along his mouth, he replied, "I'm afraid not."

"Fair Enough," I said as my eyes drifted to the flickering light dancing across the dome ceiling. "To be honest, I have absolutely no idea what the hell is going on here. Wherever *here* actually is, for that matter."

Pensively watching me, Stephen said nothing. He simply stood there, observing.

Unable to hold back the barrage of deluded thoughts spinning through my head, I blurted out, "Ok, so, I fry the church — Petrovich bails — Enter Scotty and the Chickenman — I wake up half frozen with my face buried in snow on the side of a random mountain. That was unexpected. *Then*, I hoof it up said mountain in a blizzard — wander through an endless tunnel for hours — walk in on you going toe-to-toe with a sword-toting body builder who I presume to be an angel. Again with the unexpected. *And then*, the oversized Ken doll hits me with a mind whammy — goes on about seven somethings and prophecies — and makes one hell of an exit through the bonfire elevator. Unexpected? *Oh, Hells Yeah.* And just when I think the strange-meter is pegged — instead of being on the receiving end of an epic ass chewing for blowing the second trial — I get a cup of frigg'n tea. And just where the hell are my shoes?"

Casually sipping from his goblet, while tolerantly listening to my unfiltered tirade, Stephen calmly said, "Are you quite finished?"

"I think so," I grumbled.

"Good," he said pointing to a burly wooden chair to my immediate left that I swear wasn't there a second ago. "Please, sit then. Drink. It will help.

This particular brew is a concoction I've perfected over the course of a millennium, and I'm rather proud of it."

Taking a seat in a matching chair opposite mine, that I'm pretty sure wasn't there a second ago either, he said, "I understand your sentiment and will attempt to explain that which I am able. As I stated earlier — We have much to discuss."

Typical Cloakboy. All business.

Chapter 14

Feeling somewhat satisfied that I got that off my chest, I reluctantly took a seat and slurped some tea. And holy shit — It was amazing. A taste like I'd never experienced, matched only by the instant, almost overpowering, invigorating sensation that followed. It was happiness in a little stone cup.

"That was Gabriel," Stephen said getting the sense that I was ready to have a rational discussion. "I summoned you here as attestation that the Seventh of Seven was indeed incarnate. I apologize for the abrupt nature of the situation, but it was a necessity."

"Gabriel," I shot back while spitting out a mouth full of my new favorite beverage. "Gabriel — as in the archangel? You might have mentioned that earlier."

At the very least I would've held back on the Ken doll reference. To be fair, I probably wouldn't have. But at least I would've felt bad about it. For a short period of time anyway.

"What's the Seventh of Seven?" I blurted out trying to quickly move past the fact that I insulted perhaps the most badass angel to patrol the friendly skies.

"You, Dean. You are the Seventh of Seven," he said while gracefully lowering the goblet to his lap. "The Seventh Deacon of the Seventh line. For you see, the Father decreed that the power of his wrathful touch was to bestow upon humans of the line of David — seven by seven times. No more. No less. Throughout the course of history, Deacons have emerged in a time of Earthly need as dictated by the Balance. As I was the first — You are the last."

"The last?" I pensively asked while lowering my tea. "The last Deacon?"

"The last of forty-nine souls," he replied with a sobering look. "Never again will the Father's Wrath grace a son of man. The Guild is at full strength, so to speak. Nearly three centuries have past since the emergence of a Deacon prior to your arrival."

"But the trial," I said trying to wrap my head around what Stephen was going on about.

"Yes, the trial," he said stopping me in mid-sentence with a wave of his hand. "Tell me, Dean, what was the purpose of the second trial?"

"Petrovich — or Azazel rather," I replied feeling like that was one hell of a loaded question. "You sent me there to take him down. Eliminate the nephilim. Restore the Balance. Figured that was pretty obvious. I hit him with everything I had and still failed with flying colors."

"Failure is an earthly concept," he sagely replied while rising from his chair and placing his teacup back on the table. "Do you know why Azazel was unaffected by the judgment fire you cast upon him?"

"His really nice suit was fire proof?" I said with a smidge of sarcasm.

"No," Stephen replied with a look that made me instantly regret saying it. "You relented to the Wrath. There was no focus in your actions. They were driven purely by rage. Without reason — and without Balance."

"The Balance," I muttered. "That was the second trial."

"Correct," he replied. "The Balance within. The ability of the Deacon to exert his will and control the raw power of the Wrath. While you fell short, shall we say, in certain aspects, you succeeded in others. Despite the unyielding drive of the cloak, your first priority was to preserve the lives of three innocents — demonstrating the pureness of your heart. Furthermore, I must confess that the conditions of your trial were not exactly routine. I regret to tell you this, but I have not been completely honest with you."

"You don't say," I dryly grumbled in a perpetual state of confusion.

With what appeared to be a look of apprehension, Stephen seemed to be choosing his next words very carefully.

"In a time more — typical, a Deacon prepares for the second trial over the course of a century, under the mentorship of his archdeacon and support from a cleric. Unfortunately, the times we find ourselves in, at the present, are neither typical nor terribly optimistic."

Turning his gaze toward the roaring hearth, he said, "Truth be told — I'm afraid we are nothing short of desperate. It has been my belief, for some time now, that Azazel has somehow infiltrated the ranks of the Guild. We have lost several Deacons over the past decade. Simply vanished. Warded from our Sight. While my first inclination was that they had fallen at the hand of the enemy, I can still feel their presence. They are very much alive."

"You think they've gone rogue?"

"It is not possible for a Deacon to turn to the darkness," he said definitively. "The Wrath will not serve the enemies of Heaven."

"Then what the hell happened to them?"

"The truth continues to elude me. Although, your interaction with Azazel confirmed that he is undoubtedly connected. How and to what end — I cannot be sure."

"So basically ... you used me as bait," I said after pondering what Stephen just dropped on me. "You sent me in there half cocked on a damn fact-finding mission. You knew I'd go postal. It was a setup. I never had a chance."

"No. You did not," he replied with a somewhat uncomfortable sternness about him. "I trust that you will forgive my actions. The decision was not made lightly. You must understand, Dean, we had no other alternative. You presented us with a unique opportunity. Had we descended upon Azazel in full force, he would have sensed our presence and fled well before our arrival. But you afforded us the ability to gain insight into his motives. We were, in fact, ignorant of his presence in Bosnia until Father Watson conveyed his suspicions about the transgressions in Brezovo Polje. It was a literal needle in a haystack scenario."

Locking eyes with me, he said, "It was not by circumstance that your mortal path ended in that church. It was destined to be."

The resolute severity of Stephen's demeanor instantly shot down any feelings of trivial irritation I was momentarily harboring.

"Understood," I humbly replied.

"There is more," he said reluctantly. "I have contemplated how much of this to share with you, but given the dire nature of the situation I feel it would be unfair to not."

"Not sure I like where this is going," I muttered. "Is this where we get to the part why Gabe evidently hates my guts?"

"You are indeed wise beyond your years," he said with a dry smirk.

"What can I say? It's a curse."

"Indeed. I believe you and Abernethy will get along famously," he said while beginning to fix a second goblet of tea. "Despite the rather cold reception, Gabriel does not bear you any ill will. In fact, he is one of the few members of the Seraphim court that are tolerant of our kind. As you can imagine, the Deacon's very existence is rather offensive to the angelic, for the Father chose man over his divine sons to wield his judgment upon the nephilim. His less than friendly sentiment was a direct result of what you represent — The Son of Wrath — and that which follows."

"Fair enough. I've been called worse, I guess. Care to explain what the hell that means exactly?" I said while eagerly anticipating a second dose of the wonder tea. "Does this have anything to do with the prophecy he was going on about?"

With a pensive glare, he replied, "Amongst other things, the Son of Wrath prophecy foretells the incarnation of the last Deacon, the Seventh of Seven, as a prelude to the fallen Watchers liberation from their Earthly prison, and subsequent ascension to the Heavens resulting in a thousand years of darkness and unspeakable suffering."

"Awesome," I grumbled. "The prophecy doesn't by chance go into any detail about how that particular operation goes down, does it?"

"It does not," he said devoid of emotion. "Although there is little doubt that it will occur by the hand of Azazel, and result in the spilling of blood — angel and man alike. All indication is that he's building a force to the like we have not seen in a millennium. It is imperative we find the anakim — the nephilim giants. Destroy the anakim, and he is no match for the combined strength of the Guild. Even with our depleted ranks. Now that we have you."

"Me? How do you figure that? I couldn't even handle one frigg'n giant and his baby brothers. You just told me I had like a hundred years of training left."

"It is encouraging to hear you were actually listening to me," he said with perfect deadpan delivery while handing me a second goblet. "I had my doubts there for a good while."

Flashing him my 'piss up a rope' glare, I replied, "Now that's just hurtful."

"Hurtful?" He casually shot back while raising an eyebrow. "Like the moniker of 'Cloakboy?'"

Apprehensively accepting the cup while making the mental note to never, *ever, ever, ever* use that nickname again, I simply said, "Fair enough." And left it at that. "Hey, on an unrelated note, this tea is great. Ah, fabulous. I mean like *really* good."

"Yes, it is," Stephen said with his signature subtle to nonexistent smirk peeking out from the corner of his mouth. "Now back to business, shall we?"

"Yes, sir," I humbly said very eager to move off the topic. "With pleasure."

"Very well," he muttered while taking a modest sip. "You will soon realize that among the Deacons you are an anomaly. Within a period of months you have acquired abilities that typically require centuries. Albeit the use of a sword is not one of them."

Ignoring the last comment, I said, "How is that possible?"

"It is foretold. The power wielded by the Seventh Deacon of the Seventh line is legend — equal to only one other."

Solemnly matching his gaze, I muttered, "You."

"Correct. The first and the last. We share a unique bond. It's the very reason you were able to view my visions — my memories — in your dream. It's also the reason I was able to subconsciously summon you here from your state of sustained healing, perhaps prematurely. That, I imagine, would explain your 'sleep walking' experience. The full extent of our connection is still unclear to me, but I know its there. I can feel it. It is strong."

"Why me?" I asked somewhat floored by Stephen's commentary. "Why was I chosen for this?"

"Fair question. But I'm afraid not one I can answer. You were chosen by the Father and him alone. As is every Deacon."

"Chosen by God," I muttered under my breath thinking that I would've been better off not knowing that particular detail. Feeling the need to change the subject at the risk of becoming completely overwhelmed, I said, "Ok. So where do we go from here? Back to the trials?"

"Afraid not, Dean," he said somberly, "We are preparing for a war to which there has been no equal upon the Earth nor within the Heavens."

"What, like 'end of days' kind of bad?"

"No," he replied with the utmost sincerity. "Considerably worse, I'm afraid."

"Right," I muttered with a football size lump in my throat.

"Your place is on the battlefield. You are a Deacon of the Seventh Realm serving under Abernethy, your archdeacon. You must return to them."

"Return?" I asked. "Didn't realize I'd been there in the first place."

With a classic emotionless expression, he said, "Let us just say that you didn't make for very good company during your initial stay."

"Ah, Ok," I said making the mental note that I really needed to figure out what the hell that meant. "Orders?"

"Report to the Quartermaster — one of the Earthly gates of the Seventh Realm. Learn what you must of our ways. Abernethy will guide you. It is imperative we locate the anakim. The new generation has reached maturity. Time is more than precious, as you will quickly learn."

Placing his empty goblet on the table, he turned and walked toward the hearth. Abruptly stopping, he looked back and said, "Oh, and please inform John that I would be most appreciative if he prepared a batch of his orange butter scones for my next visit. They're quite good."

Absolutely dumbfounded, I muttered, "Ah, Ok — scones. John?"

"John O'Dargan," he said continuing toward the hearth. "You will know him as Rooster. Head cleric of the Seventh Realm. Unique fellow. Excellent cook. Bit of a temper."

Stepping headlong into the roaring fire, he simply vanished in a brilliant flash of white light. Completely unimpressed, I muttered, "Show Off."

Again left to my own devices, I stood there for a long second wondering just how the hell to get out of the rotunda. There were no doors, and there was no way in hell I was stepping into the bonfire elevator. Seemed like a really bad idea. Even for me. Luckily I didn't have much time to ponder on it because the sound of grinding rock was evident to my rear. Turning just in time to see a crude doorway morph in the solid rock wall, I figured it was exit stage left.

"Orange butter scones," I muttered as I stepped through the portal. "What the hell …"

There was a swirling vortex of blinding light followed by darkness, and just like that — I was somewhere else.

And it was cold.

Typical.

Chapter 15

"Hey! Pal! You can't be here!"

Stepping through the portal, I was met with a gust of bitter cold wind followed by a second wave of intense light — and some asshole with a thick New England accent screaming at me.

"You there! The park's closed! Get the hell outta' here before I call the cops!"

There's nothing quite like the Boston accent. Poetry and profanity all wrapped up in a steady stream of dropped syllables and alien inflection. Been a while since I'd heard it, having left when I was eighteen and never making the return trip. Always planned to go back for a baseball game. But the sting of growing up with the continued let down of the Red Sox sort of took the glamour out of it. Unfortunately, that never dissuaded me from being a die-hard fan. Something about misery and company.

Bastards.

"Relax, JFK, I heard you the first time," I grumbled squinting from the bright light pouring down from above. "Go *pahk a cah*' or something."

Rising to my feet, I brushed a thin layer of snow off my clothing. As my eyes slowly adjusted, I couldn't believe what I was looking at. Although the entire field was covered in snow it was unmistakable. The Green Monster looming in left field — the ginormous CITGO sign blazing in the night sky — the crazy triangle in center field — the sea of bleachers — the Pesky Pole.

I was at Fenway Park. Sitting directly behind home plate no less. In the very seat my Dad used to bring me to as a kid. Every spring. Some of my fondest memories. Never came back after he died. Wasn't the same.

Smirking to myself, I muttered, "Classic Cloakb — ah — Stephen. Classic Stephen."

Although it was nighttime, the stadium lights reflecting off the snow had the place lit up like it was mid-afternoon. An absolute spectacle. With exception, of course, to the portly night watchman angrily waddling his way toward my seat through the snow-tufted aisles. Gut proudly hanging over the belt of his rent-a-cop uniform, he relentlessly puffed on a cigarette as he pulled to a halt within a couple steps of me.

Short of breath and clearly pissed that I'd interrupted his routine of eating and smoking, he grumbled like only a true Bostonian could, "What a' you fuck'n deaf? I said, You — Can't — Be — Here."

As several smart-ass replies were about to fly from my mouth in rapid succession, I felt the cloak begin to stir. Then instantly, and without my summoning, it manifested and billowed about my shoulders in a vibrant show of force.

Before I had the chance to say anything, Mall Cop dropped his cigarette and jumped backward as a look of sheer panic washed over him. Arms flailing uncontrollably, he toppled over the row of seats to his immediate rear, sending his three hundred plus pounds of donut filled flab crashing to the waiting concrete below. As his tough guy demeanor vanished, he burst into tears and began to blabber nonsensically like a small child.

"No … no, no, no … Y-you … W-why are y-y-you h-here? I-I d-didn't br-break any rules," he repeatedly muttered as I watched in awe. Quickly scampering to his feet several steps from me, he threw both hands out to his front like he was trying to hold me at bay. "No. No, no, no. I've f-f-followed the rules. P-pl-please No."

"Take it easy there, Ponch," I said as delicately as possible trying to calm him down a bit. "Why don't you have another smoke. Maybe a Twinkie … or several. Sit down for a minute. Take a load off. If that's possible."

Now that he was up close and personal, there was something about him that I couldn't quite wrap my head around. It was off. Faint as hell, but it looked like a soft glow of reddish energy pulsing around his rotund body.

"You're not here to sm-smite me?" He apprehensively mumbled while lowering his hands and starting to calm down a bit.

"Smite you? I barely even know you," I said thinking that was one hell of an odd question. "Why the hell would I do that?"

"You wear the cloak," he said fumbling to light another cigarette with shaking hands. "You're a-a-a *Deacon*. I c-can See you." Successfully lighting his smoke, he sucked on it like it was the last cigarette on the face of the Earth. "When you guys show up it's game over. Everybody knows that."

"Ah, right. The whole game over thing," I replied having no frigg'n idea what he was going on about. Deacons don't render judgment on humans and, although one fat son of a bitch, this joker was no nephilim. So what the hell was I missing?

"But I've been good, bossman. Done everything the Guild guys told me. Minding my own business and all. Even got myself a job," he proudly said wiping the snow off his uniform.

Although I still had no clue what was happening, I figured it best to play along with Chubs. Evidently the Deacons had a rep to maintain. Giving him a stern look, I said, "Right. Well, tell you what, chief. Consider this a warning. Sort of like a courtesy call." Just for effect I willed the ashen stone gauntlets into being and with a spectral flash they formed on my hands and ignited with a fine layer of white flame. "Break the rules and I'll be back. Fry your sorry ass like a bacon double cheeseburger. We clear?"

Scared shitless, he dropped his second cigarette and stepped backward. "Yes … Yes, sir! We're clear. Whatever you say, bossman."

"Good," I said feeling rather satisfied. "Now get the hell out of here. And quit smoking. It's bad for you. In fact, do some damn sit-ups once in a while. And lay off the fast food."

In something between elation and absolutely fright, he abruptly turned and ran like hell. To be fair, it was more of a speedy waddle but the intent was clearly there. As he reached the end of the aisle and disappeared down one of the exit ramps, I stood in awe for a few seconds wondering what the hell just happened. Evidently, I had a few things to learn about Deacon operating procedures on Earth.

"First things first," I muttered while willing the cloak and gauntlets into retreat.

As the cloak faded from my shoulders, I found myself wearing a black, knee length peacoat and matching wool watch cap. By the grace of God, I was also sporting my favorite Levi's and brown leather work boots. Really, really happy that I had shoes on, I figured it best to get on with it. I needed to find the Quartermaster.

Thinking it would have been really nice if Stephen had actually sent me there instead of here, I started making my way down the snowy aisle to the ramp. Pausing to take one last look at the Green Monster in all its wondrous glory, I muttered, "That's funny. I don't remember there ever being seats on top of the Monster. Must've been added last season."

Making the mental note to look into that later, I turned down the ramp and started walking toward the exit. Reaching into my memories of visiting Fenway with my Father, I focused on some of our pre-game rituals. Getting a clear picture in my thoughts, I took three bold steps and found myself instantly outside the park, standing on the corner of Lansdowne and Brookline, staring at the Caskn' Flagon.

"Dad's favorite pre-game watering hole," I muttered somewhat fondly. "Still here. Too bad it's closed. I could go for some wings. And a beer. Make that several beers."

Thinking about food for the first time in who knows how long, I realized that I was really frigg'n hungry. My stroll down memory lane was rudely interrupted by a familiar whisper-like shriek accompanied with a blast of wind to the face.

"Ok … I'm going," I grumbled.

Although I still had no idea where it came from nor what caused it, I'd learned to take the hint. Keep moving. Turning right, I started walking down Lansdowne Street. For some reason it felt like the way to go.

Lit only by the neon signs from the various bars lining the street, it was completely deserted. Everything was closed. Must have been late. Persistent waves of howling, frigid air whipped through the buildings, creating an ominous series of mini-cyclones with the loose snow strewn about the sidewalks. Nasty weather. Felt like late winter in New England.

Pulling the peacoat collar up around my neck, I steadily moved down the empty street, mesmerized by the city lights in the distance. The familiar landmark of the Prudential building jutted far into the night, defining the skyline. Lit up like a beacon, it was a sight I remembered well. My Father always insisted on parking at the Prudential so he wouldn't have to deal with the traffic around Fenway. I could probably walk there in my frigg'n sleep from here.

Lost in thought, I longingly gazed at the building for a moment when I noticed something peculiar about the skyline to its immediate right. There was a distinct patch of sky that seemed to almost shimmer in the darkness. Sort of like the air above a hot fire. Stretching clear into the clouds, it was subtle but definitely there. Like a veil. As the whisper-like shriek buzzed my tower again, I figured that was probably where I needed to go. Judging by the location, it looked to be somewhere in the Back Bay area. With my stomach groaning with hunger pains, I hooked at right at the end of Lansdowne and moved down Ipswich.

Reaching into my memories, I focused on the park near the Boylston Street bridge that crossed the Muddy River where my Father and I used to stop occasionally. Getting a clear picture in my thoughts, I took three bold steps and instantly found myself standing there. Trying to pinpoint the obscurity in the sky, I moved down Boylston and hung a right on Hemenway. Maneuvering through the adjoining rows of Victorian brownstones, I reached the intersection at Westland Ave in a matter of minutes.

Catching a glimpse of a digital clock hung in the window of a convenience store on the corner, it read '3:32 Am.' That would explain why the streets were absolutely devoid of traffic. It also noted the date to be 'Sunday, 1/5.' Seemed it had only been a week since my departure from the land of the living. Looking to my left, the source of the shimmering veil was coming from the far end of Westland Ave near the Mass Ave intersection. Figuring I had nothing to lose, I started making my way down the deserted, snow laden street as chunks of ice crunched beneath my boots.

"Man this weather sucks," I grumbled.

Thinking it would have been nice if this Quartermaster joint was somewhere in the tropics or anywhere where it didn't snow for that matter, I kept moving. The street was lined with brownstone apartment buildings on either side, with the occasional laundry mat, pizza place, and convenience store sprinkled in. Within about a hundred feet of the intersection with Mass Ave and Symphony, I noticed an elderly gentleman, sitting on a foldout chair, casually puffing on a pipe directly outside an old, battered door to a would be apartment building.

Unlike the doors to the other buildings, which were set on stone stoops, this one was sitting squarely at street level. Thinking it rather odd that he be hanging out in the frigid weather at three thirty in the morning, I slowly approached him. Bundled in a burly black wool coat complete with thick scarf wrapped around his neck, tweed touring cap, and fingerless gloves, he simply sat there blowing smoke rings into the wintry air.

Getting to within a few steps from him I pulled to a halt, and noticed that he had one of those 'Hello, My Name Is' nametags stuck to the front of his coat. In red marker he'd written the name 'Fred' in capital letters. Not acknowledging my presence in the least, he continued to stare into the night sky sucking on his pipe.

"Ah, Hello, Fred," I finally said after standing there for a few awkward seconds.

"Hello, schmendrick," he replied without so much as looking in my direction, in what sounded like a harsh New York accent dripping of sarcasm. Knocking out the contents of his pipe against the chair, he turned and locked eyes with me. "About time you showed up. *So* glad you could make it. They're waiting for you inside."

Dismissively looking away he produced a bag of tobacco from inside his coat and very carefully repacked his pipe.

Although I wasn't sure what a 'schmendrick' was, I got the sense that it wasn't exactly a term of endearment. Seemed my man Fred wasn't a fan.

"Thanks, Fred," I muttered in a less than friendly tone. "Good talk."

As he mumbled something else of an unpleasant nature under his breath, I turned my attention toward the door. It was old. Really old. Rusted metal reinforced with several large rivets and laden with sporadic pronounced dents. Oddly, the doorknob was of perfectly polished bronze, which stood out like a sore thumb. Although there was no locking mechanism, a Chi-Rho was carefully etched into its center. Amidst the rust and dents there was also a series of Enochian glyphs faintly inlaid in the center of the door itself. In small, military-like typeface, the word 'QUARTERMASTER' was stamped neatly within the top of the wooden frame. Although subtle, there was a definite hum emanating from beyond the threshold.

"Ok, I'm going in," I affirmably said giving Fred another glance.

"Good for you, schmendrick," he snidely replied staring into the night sky while effortlessly blowing a perfect ring of smoke.

As my hand was about to grasp the doorknob, he said, "You know, they think you're a savior of some sort. The Seventh of Seven — *the one* that's going to *restore the Balance* once and for all. The turn of the tide. But I know the truth, schmendrick." Turning to look at me with an intense squint, he coldly grumbled, "They're wrong."

"Thanks for that," I awkwardly replied after a long moment. "Anymore pearls of wisdom before I go?"

Completely ignoring me, he rose to his feet and began to hobble down the empty street grumbling under his breath the whole time.

"Another time then," I called after him. "Great meeting you. I guess. Not so much."

Watching my disgruntled new buddy fade into the shadows, I figured it was time to check out the Quartermaster. Things clearly couldn't get any stranger. Again turning toward the door, I reached down and grasped the knob. As my hand made contact with the Chi-Rho, the door instantly swung open and I realized I was wrong.

The strange meter was not yet pegged.

Not even close.

Chapter 16

Boldly crossing the threshold to the otherworldly outpost, I felt a subtle wave of energy wash over me as I pierced the veil. Fully in the room, my initial impression of the surreal setting laid out before me was something to the effect of Middle Earth meets a Prohibition era Irish pub powered by a DeLorean with a flux capacitor.

It was insane. Almost too much for reality to accept and allow to exist.

The mouth watering aroma of delectable food sizzling on the massive stone hearth behind the mighty 'L shaped' bar was matched only by the incredible sound of acoustic blues and gravelly voice of the bearded dude in the far corner banging on a guitar. Oddly, I think a small feral pig was sitting on the stool next to him tapping a tiny hoof to the rhythm.

It was peculiar. Even for here.

Making the mental note to find out what in the hell that was all about, I continued with my observation. The place was packed despite the fact it was three thirty on a Sunday morning. And by packed I mean by hundreds of people. It was an absolutely massive expanse, which made no sense whatsoever. Gauging from the surrounding buildings on the street, it should have been a hole in the wall. It was like the laws of physics didn't apply. In fact, from where I stood I couldn't even see the end of the bar.

To be fair, that was probably due to the branches of the ginormous tree growing out of the floor obstructing my view. Easily the largest oak I'd ever laid eyes on, it was surrounded by a brilliant clear stream that flowed steadily toward the back of the room and out of sight.

"What in the hell," I dumbfoundedly muttered under my breath as I reluctantly shut the door behind me.

Making my way toward the bar amidst countless wooden tables filled with people happily clanking mugs and sucking down food, I was astonished at how such a place existed nonetheless tethered to the heart of Boston. Uneven pieces of multicolored slate lined the floor and the walls were constructed of aged rough cut wooden beams tacked together in various angles, melding into a mild arched ceiling. From which hung all manner of jugs, pots, and bottles of assorted color, material, and condition, forming a functional yet hobbit-like motif. The walls were completely covered with pictures, portraits, and random antique memorabilia dating back hundreds of years if not older. The uneven glow of oil lamps and torches randomly dispersed throughout the spacious room produced a mesmerizing effect of dancing light and shadows.

The dark wooden bar, built atop evenly spaced whiskey barrels, was shoulder to shoulder with yet more people in deep conversation. An impressive loft — proudly displaying a collection of ten or more colossal bronze vats complete with assorted pipes, hoses, and gauges — was built directly above it. Lining the wall to the rear of the bar, for as long as the eye could see, was a rack of tapped wooden barrels labeled of various brews. Probably the strangest thing in the whole damn place was the endless row of TV sets, fastened to the wall above the kegs, wrapping clear around the entire room. They actually looked more like mirrors set in antique wooden frames than TVs, but were clearly displaying scenes of random people performing various actions in a compilation of settings. Some in black and white and others in color. Something about the screens gave me pause. They shimmered like pools of water set vertically into the wall. I couldn't take my eyes off them.

My momentary fixation was broken by a figure briskly climbing down from the brew loft with a healthy keg barrel hoisted over his shoulder. Taking a closer look, I realized that I knew him. It was the Chickenman — ah, Rooster.

And damn, he was pretty spry for a lanky bastard.

Expertly maneuvering down the rickety ladder connecting the loft to the bar, he effortlessly tossed the wooden keg onto the rack with the others, and jammed an old fashioned looking tap into the side. Red hair flying all about his head in reckless abandon, he was sporting a purple 'Red Hot Chili Peppers' concert tee shirt, khaki shorts, and flip-flops. Pulling a white chef's apron with a pronounced red rooster logo over his head, he quickly fastened it around his waist and commenced to slinging a pair of formidable spatulas amidst the various assortment of sizzling delight he had scattered about his mighty stone hearth.

It was like watching a master craftsman at work wielding the spatulas of destiny — the forks of fury — the stuff of legend. Impressive. As my stomach made a groan loud enough to drown out all the surrounding noise, I decided to belly up to the bar. Hopefully he wasn't cooking chicken. That would just be awkward.

As I started to fight my way through the sea of patrons, I felt a distinct, almost uncomfortable hush start to pass through the crowd as people turned and looked at me only to immediately look away and make plenty of room for me to pass. It was almost like they knew who I was — and it frightened them. Figuring it was probably my imagination or the fact that I really needed a shower, I freely strolled to the bar to find one open stool.

"Perfect," I happily muttered while plopping my sorry ass down for a well needed respite. Without so much as turning around from his display of culinary combat, Rooster said, "Sorry. That's M's seat."

Not really giving much of a shit after the day I'd had, I shot back, "Yeah well, M can kiss ass. I'm sure he won't mind if I sit here for a couple minutes."

Upon hearing the sound of my voice he instantly turned in a state of pure astonishment. "Dean? You're awake … I don't believe it!"

Tossing his cooking instruments to the side he leapt over the bar, proceeded to wrap both arms around me, and squeezed with all his Chickenman might. To say it was awkward does not begin to give it justice.

Not stopping there, he bellowed, "You're awake! You look … you look great! I can't believe it! You're back!"

If it was remotely possible for the situation to become more awkward — it just happened. In fact, I'm pretty sure that all the cool points I'd accumulated during my entire mortal lifetime were just zero'd out. I may have actually gone negative.

"People are staring," I grumbled while trying to pry free from his stringy arms. "People — Are — Staring."

Finally letting go and resuming his post by the hearth, he said, "Oh, right, sorry. Might have got a bit carried away there."

"You think?" I said shooting him an intense glare. "It's only been a frigg'n week since I saw you guys. What the hell?"

"Wait — What?" He replied with a confused look. "A week?"

"Today's January 5th right?" I said removing my watch cap and stuffing it in my coat pocket. "It's been about a week since you dragged me out of the church."

"Oh, right," he awkwardly said. "A week. Yep."

Quickly moving off the topic, he grabbed a frosty mug from below the bar and held it under the keg he just tapped. Filling it to the brim, he then plopped a little umbrella on the top and slid it across the bar to me.

"Here you go, man. Welcome to the Quartermaster — provisioning for the mind, the body, and the soul. Plenty more where that came from. Brewed on the premises. I call it RoosterBragh."

I think he continued talking, but I didn't hear another word as I stared at the oversized mug like a desperate man dying of thirst. It was a thing of beauty.

Tall. Frosty. Beer.

Feeling like the Heavens had opened wide and shone a beam of divine light on me, I grabbed it with both hands and chugged it until there was nothing left.

"Holy shit that's good! Bar Keep, Uno mas cerveza, por favor," I said with great enthusiasm, in a horrible Spanish accent, as I slammed the empty mug on the bar. "Oh, that's *so* frigg'n good."

"Yeppers."

"You call it Rooster's bra?"

"No," he scoffed. "Rooster-*Bragh*. It's an Irish thing ..."

"Right," I muttered as my vision blurred for a quick second. "Got a bit of a punch to it, eh?"

"Yes. Yes it does," he said with a modest grin. "I was trying to explain that before you shot gunned the entire mug — in like three seconds. That's my Orange Honey Ale. More for sipping if you know what I mean."

"Noted," I replied while taking off my coat and draping it over the back of the stool. "Another please. And how about some chow? I'm starving."

Before he could answer, a hellaciously loud, prolonged chime rung out causing everyone in the joint to stop talking and take notice. It was followed by a second, then a third, and then a fourth. The source was evidently the mammoth grandfather clock sitting on the far wall next to the bearded bluesman. It was evidently four o'clock. As if they were expecting it, pretty much everyone in the joint stood up and started to make their way to the various doors. Some actually used them while others seemed to simply vanish mid-stride. It was a bit of a spectacle.

Pushing a tasty looking plate of sliders and another beer in front of me, Rooster said, "Four a.m. Duty calls."

"Who the hell are all those people?" I curiously asked while watching the crowd dwindle.

"Mostly clerics and acolytes," he answered matter of factly, "Members of the Guild. Final wave of the night. They're heading back to their posts." Reading the look of absolute confusion on my face, he said, "We have much to teach you of the Guild and our methods. Why don't you eat something first. Big A should be here any moment. He's no doubt aware of your presence by now."

"Fair enough," I muttered not really sure what else to say. "Thanks for the grub. I honestly couldn't tell you when the last time was that I ate something."

Stuffing one of the sliders into my mouth, I was overpowered by the indescribable explosion of tasty bliss. "Whoa, this is amazing. What is it?"

"That, my friend, is a genuine Rosemary and RoosterBragh Pork Sandwich. Made, of course, with house baked sweet potato rolls and garnished with bitter greens and Rooster salad dressing," he proudly announced.

"Incredible," I said slamming a second and a third into my already full mouth. "Any chance you have some barbecue sauce laying around here? It would be per-"

"Absolutely not," he scoffed as he cut me off mid-sentence. "That would ruin a perfectly balanced culinary masterpiece. Out of the question."

"Gotcha. Sorry. Not sure what I was thinking," I muttered popping a fourth and a fifth sammich into my waiting mouth. "Hey, speaking of pork … What's up with the piglet sitting next to the bearded wonder over there?"

"That's just Duncan. He's with Caveman. We don't ask."

With a blank look, I muttered, "You call the pig Duncan and the guy Caveman?"

"Yep. I'll make intros later. But, ah, Caveman's a bit on the hairy side. Better if you don't draw attention to it. Sensitive topic." As a somewhat serious look returned to his face, he said, "But seriously, Dean, you're sitting in M's seat. You should really move. Like now."

"For real? There's like a thousand empty seats in here. I'm sure this 'M' dude can use any one of them," I said while slugging back the remnants of my second man-sized beer.

Just as I placed the empty mug on the bar, I felt a healthy gust of wind belt me in the face followed by the familiar whisper-like shriek. Getting the distinct feeling that someone was behind me, I felt a hand on my shoulder followed by a woman's voice.

"M is most certainly *not* a man. Oy vez smear, Bubbala. I'm so meshuggina I could plotz," she said in a tone of scolding sarcasm with a distinct Brooklynesque inflection.

Quickly spinning around, while knocking the mug off the bar in the process, I found an attractive, petite woman with beehive piled dirty blonde hair, a sleek elegant face with pronounced nose, and more eye shadow than should be legal. She was all dolled up in a low-cut blue dress adorned with ruffles and sequins like something out of the nineteen sixties. In fact, if I didn't know better I'd swear it was a young Barbara Streisand. For a split second I swore that a glow of pure white light silhouetted her entire body. However, as I squinted and blinked my eyes it was gone.

"Oh man," I heard a nervous Rooster grumble from behind the bar. "I told ya."

"You — You're M?" I pensively asked while staring at her intently.

"Do you see anybody else standing here? Of course I'm M. Who else would be M?" She said matter of factly as her mouth curled into a wide smile. "Roosallah, Do you know any other Ms?"

As Rooster shook his head No, she turned back to me, and said, "See. I'm M. It's settled. Period — End of story. I'm M and you're in my seat, Bubbala. Move, move, move."

Feeling like I was just scolded by either my mother or my second grade teacher, I begrudgingly grabbed my coat and slid onto the next stool.

"How long have you been watching me?" I asked her thinking of all the random times I'd heard the curious shrieking sound since my arrival in the Realms.

"For longer than you know," she replied while reaching into her purse and pulling out a makeup kit. "It's my job," she added while adjusting her eye shadow.

Rooster brought over a steaming cup of black coffee and a plate with two bagel halves with cream cheese topped by what appeared to be thin slices of fish. Placing it in front of her, he said, "Here you go, M. Just how you like it."

Clapping her hands together in excitement, she happily gasped, "Ooh — Ooh. That's wonderful! Did you give them an extra little *schmear* of cream cheese?"

"Ah, yeah. Of course I did," he replied somewhat offended. "It's a hundred percent Kosher."

"Thank You, Roosallah darling. You are entirely too good to me!"

"What the hell is that?" I muttered giving the concoction a disgusted look. "It looks awful."

"Dean James Robinson! Shame on you. *That* is bagels and lox, and it is absolutely fabulous — like buttah'," M scoldingly replied while shooting me a look that would stop a train.

"Ok. Fair enough," was all I could sheepishly muster in response. She even pulled out my middle name. Ouch. "Ah, So care to explain why you've been following me around? Are you part of the Guild?"

Amidst dainty bites of her prized breakfast, she simply said, "No." And continued eating with a very content look about her.

"Great," I muttered under my breath signaling the Chickenman to hit me with another tall, frosty one. "You're about as helpful as my man Fred."

"Oh, don't you mind Frederick Binkowicz, Bubbala," she said finishing a sip of coffee. "He's a Brooklyn Jew. Always worked up over something or another. Bit of a nudnik, truth be told."

"Oh, well that clears it up," I said having not the faintest clue as to what she was talking about. "Why do you keep calling me Bubba?"

"Not 'Bubba' silly," she said between bites, "Bubbala." Giving me a very uncomfortable pat on the head, she said, "You're my little Bubbala. All grown up and on your destined path. I'm so proud!"

"What does that even mean?"

"Oy vey," she said holding a napkin to her face. "Give me a moment — I'm feeling verklempt."

"Ok," I muttered giving Rooster a 'check please' glance. Feeling more confused now than when I walked into the joint a couple minutes earlier, I happily embraced the new beer that had miraculously appeared before me. At least I had that going for me. Which was nice. Just as I grasped the handle, a burly hand appeared from over my right shoulder and covered the mug.

"Nae time for that, lad," came from behind me in a heavy Scottish brogue. "Yer be out yer face drinking the Rooster's ale. We have work to do."

Spinning around to see the massive frame of Abernethy, he slapped me on the shoulder, and said, "It's good to see ye, Dean. All healed up, Aye?"

Not sure if I was more taken back by the sheer size of his upper body, the meticulous braids throughout the burly beard hanging from his weathered face, or the fact he was bare footed and wearing a kilt. Actually, the whole package was a bit traumatic. Getting off my stool and standing face to face with the archdeacon, I found myself staring squarely into his oversized pectorals.

"Ah, all healed, sir," I awkwardly replied looking up to meet his gaze. "Ready for duty."

"Pure dead brilliant. Get yer wee bahooky out the chair and follow me. And call me Big A. All the lads do." Shifting his focus to Rooster, he said, "We'll be heading to the train'n pitch, Jackie. Join us when yer done in the scullery." Offering a gentlemanly bow to M, he said, "Awrite, Mariel, Pleasure to see ye. Thank ye for delivering Master Robinson." Shifting to a more serious demeanor, he asked, "Tell me, any news of the enemy?"

"Thank You, Abernethy. As always, it is simply wonderful to see you. I'm afraid I have nothing of substance to report," she replied taking a quick bite of fish bagel. "Although I was summoned rather abruptly by Ramiel upon my arrival at the Quartermaster. I will keep you abreast of any information he shares."

"Ramiel? A right scunner he is," grunted Abernethy in disgust. "Never understood why Gabriel puts his faith in a skelpit arse such as Ramiel. I don't trust him."

"Now, Abernethy," M said with a look of mild admonishment. "Ramiel is not our enemy. Despite what you may think of him." Flicking her hand at the large Scotsman, and with a pronounced inflection in her voice, she said, "Ferstay?"

"Aye," he grumbled in response lowering his head.

"Besides, to doubt him is to doubt Gabriel," she said turning her attention back to her breakfast.

"Aye," Abernethy replied like a scolded child unconvinced. "Very well. Be wary in yer travels, M." Raising his head and focusing on me, he said, "To the pitch then, Dean. Ye need to know what yer up against. This way."

As he turned and began to walk toward the back of the Quartermaster, the frustration of having absolutely no idea what the hell was going finally became too much to restrain. I lost it.

Defiantly grabbing my beer and taking a few steps toward the center of the room, I grumbled, "I'm not going anywhere until I get some frigg'n answers."

As everyone stopped what they were doing and stared at me, I took a man-size slug of beer. Wiping my mouth on my sleeve, I said, "First of all, I have no frigg'n idea what the two of you are talking about nor if you're using the English language. Second of all, within the past few hours I've woken up in a goddamn blizzard on the side of some random mountain, had tea with Stephen — it was good tea but still weird as hell, got mind jacked by an archangel that hates my guts, showed up in Fenway Park, and had one hell of a strange conversation with a plump security guard that begged me not to '*smite*' him."

In a full on rant mode I downed the rest of my beer, and said, "I'm not taking one step from this very spot until somebody explains what in the frig is going on."

As everyone continued to stare at me in bewilderment, I muttered, "I mean come on. I've only been out of commission for a week."

"A week? Bloody hell," Abernethy grumbled. "Yer off yer heid, lad. You've been simmering in the Water ay' Life for fourteen years. Dinnae ye ken?"

"What the hell did he say?" I barked at Rooster.

"I'm sorry, Dean," he reluctantly replied with a look of dreadful anticipation. "I wanted to tell you earlier but — you've been in the Water of Life, ah, in stasis — healing — for fourteen Earth years. We thought you knew. It's January 5th… 2012."

"What?"

Fourteen years.

2012.

What?

As the empty mug slid from my hand and tumbled to the floor in slow motion, I felt my vision blur and knees buckle. Well, at least the seats on top of the Green Monster now made sense. I wonder if the Red Sox had gotten any better since 1998. Crumbling to the floor in sensory overload, I heard Rooster say, "Oh great … He's passed out again."

Followed by the disgruntled Scotsman grumble, "Bloody hell. He's right blootered."

Chapter 17

Fading in and out of lucid thought, I was having one hell of a ridiculous dream. Giants. Angels. A cloaked society of sword wielding flamethrowers. Prophecies. A chef named after a farm animal. A monogramed Barbara Streisand look alike. A kilted highlander. Fourteen years in the future — and I was dead but not really.

It was the definition of insanity. Nonsensical. Laughable. And there was this tiny pig. Cute little bastard.

Good lord — I really needed to stop drinking. Good guys. Bad guys. Bullets. That's all there is to it. My life. A soldier's life. Simple.

The odd sensation of tiny teeth nipping on my ear coaxed me back into active consciousness. Slowly opening my eyes in a dimly lit, really large room, I found myself sprawled out on an oversized leather chair. That was odd. I should have been lying on my cot. Where the hell did this chair come from? As my eyes focused I realized that a brown spotted, miniature feral hog was sitting squarely on my lap. With tiny hoofs propped up on my chest, it was anxiously licking my face.

"Oh, Hi Duncan. What's up, little guy," I happily muttered in slurred speed while patting his little piggly head.

Wait. What the fuck? "Duncan?"

Throwing the piglet clear off my lap as it squealed in protest, I sat up in a state of pure panic and looked around. As the familiar scene registered with my half functioning brain, I once more accepted the peculiar reality of my situation. This was no dream.

"Aw, hell," I grumbled as I jumped to my feet, "It's real. Son of a bitch."

"Take it easy, bro," said the mellow mansquatch standing opposite me. "No need to be tossing Lil' D around. He was just trying to help, man."

"Oh, ah, my bad," I said now fully conscious and feeling rather badly about launching his pocket pet clear across the room. "Caught me off guard is all. You're, ah, Caveman, right? I'm Dean."

"Yeah, man. Everybody knows who you are," he said holding out his shaggy hand. "Been waiting for you to wake up — for like, ever. Things are getting bad, bro. Name's Mick. Mick Baskerville. But everybody calls me Caveman. Me and Lil' D handle entertainment around the QM. Do some other stuff too. You know, like odd jobs."

"Gotcha," was the only thing that came to mind as I did my very best not to stare at the dark mane of manscaped hair that covered pretty much all of his exposed skin.

Sporting a raggy yet stylish pair of faded jeans and an olive drab 'RoosterBragh, Get Crow'd - World Series 2004' tee shirt, he was an easy six-foot-two of furry muscle. The abundance of hair atop his formidable head was all schwooped up like a primal Elvis. His beard basically started right under his eye sockets and was like a well sculpted shrubbery covering the rest of his square-jawed face. His teen wolf-like arms were giving the constraints of his tee shirt a solid run for the money as they flexed and bulged with the slightest of movement. But his eyes were soft. Somewhat gentle even.

"Where'd you learn to play guitar like that?" I muttered feeling the need to say something else. "That was pretty incredible."

"Oh, thanks, man," he graciously replied. "Picked it up back in the fifties. Learned from the best, bro. Good times. Really bummed out when we had to send Elvis into lock down though. Played together all the time before I had to —"

"Hey, that's great. You're awake — again," said Rooster as he arrived at the scene purposely interrupting Caveman in mid-sentence while giving him a 'not now' glare. "You, ah, mind watching the bar for me, Mick? Big A and I need to talk with Dean."

"Sure, bro. No problemo." Giving me a furry nod, he said, "Take her easy, broseph. Good to meet you. Hope you, like, stop passing out and all that stuff." Turning as he curiously sniffed the air like a animal locked on a scent, he called out, "Lil' D! Time for breakfast, big guy. I smell scones."

As the sound of tiny hooves was heard scampering from under one of the tables, they casually strolled together toward the bar. A caveman and his piglet. Not sure there's any getting used to that.

Suspiciously looking at Rooster, I said, "He's not, ah, a *real* caveman, right?"

"A real caveman? No such thing, man. He's something else. A barghest to be specific."

"A what?"

"Hold that thought," Rooster said delicately. "We need to bring you up to speed on a few things. How about some coffee? And scones — you like scones? Just pulled them out of the oven."

"Just coffee. Not sure I'm sophisticated enough for scones."

"Suit yourself," he said while heading to a table next to the massive tree at the far end of the room, where a brooding Abernethy sat by himself sharpening his mighty claymore broadsword with an oversized whetstone. Pulling out a chair for me, Rooster said, "Make yourself comfortable. Be right back."

As he disappeared in the direction of the empty bar I reluctantly took a seat opposite the large Scotsman. After a few awkward seconds of watching him artfully run the stone up and down the other worldly blade, he looked up at me with a troubled expression.

"Seven hundred and nine years," he said solemnly. Not sure how to respond or if a response was warranted, I simply sat there and looked at him. Turning his attention back toward the sword, he muttered, "Ne'er have we seen a time like this, lad."

As Rooster appeared with a steaming pot of coffee and three stout mugs, Abernethy sheathed the longsword in the leather scabbard hanging from the back of his chair and fixed me with an intent gaze. Placing a mug in front of each us, Rooster dispensed some incredibly aromatic coffee, and enthusiastically said, "Ok, So let's talk."

Sipping my drink while giving him a sarcastic glare, I muttered, "Is this like a 'come to Jesus' meeting?"

"Jesus? Nae. He's not been to the Quartermaster in at least a century," said a pensive Abernethy completely missing the reference.

"Oh, good lord," Rooster grumbled while shaking his head and taking a swig of java.

As he was about to say something else, we were interrupted by an anxious looking Caveman striding toward the table with great haste.

"Sorry to bother, gents," he said sternly, "The Alpha's messenger is here. He needs to see you, Big A. Like now. Something's up."

"Aye, Mickie," said a solemn Abernethy rising to his feet and strapping the scabbard across his back. "Be right there, lad."

Turning to Rooster, he said, "Hold the fort, Jackie. Explain to Master Robinson what ye can. And do it quickly. The enemy's on the move. I can feel it."

"You got it, boss," Rooster replied.

"I know what yer feeling, Dean," Abernethy said firmly grasping my shoulder. "But there is nae time for doubt. These are dark times — none darker in my seven centuries of service. Ye are a Deacon. The Seventh of Seven. Clear yer mind, lad. Accept. Believe. Until ye do, ye are nae help to us — or yerself."

Turning toward the ancient door that subtly appeared to the rear of the table, his cloak manifested in a spectral flash around his massive frame. Stepping across the threshold, he called back, "And laddies, don't do anything daft in my absence."

As the door vanished in a flash of light I turned to Rooster.

"Daft?"

"Yeah, it's a Scottish thing," he replied while systematically glancing at the endless row of TV screens lining the walls. "You'll have to excuse Big A. These are rough times. In the past fourteen years we've lost more Deacons than in the past fourteen centuries. We've never seen anything like it. He's taking it hard. Especially hard."

"The Alpha. He's going to see Stephen isn't he?" I asked a somewhat distracted Rooster.

"Yes. Yes he is," he replied while shifting focus from screen to screen.

Studying his intense gaze, I asked, "So what's with the wall to wall TV sets?"

"Technically, they are TV sets but not quite in the sense you're thinking," he muttered. "Although we did watch the '04 and the '07 World Series on them. It was epic. Red Sox and RoosterBragh. Freak'n epic. We actually had tee-shirts made."

"Whoa, wait one. What was that?" I said feeling like somebody just shot my dog three times after kicking me square in the balls. "Are you telling me the Sox made it to *two* World Series while I was floating down the River Styx on a fourteen year involuntary hiatus?"

Still studying the various screens, he matter of factly replied, "Firstly, you were *floating* in the Water of Life which is fundamentally different from the River Styx. And secondly, the Sox *won* two World Series. First time in eighty-six years. It was epic."

"What? Seriously? They won — *twice*? And I missed it? That is wrong, man. So — incredibly — unbelievably — frigg'n wrong."

"Ah, right — forgot you were a huge Sox fan," he awkwardly said shifting his attention back to me and realizing he'd inadvertently stepped on a land mine. "So, ah, the TVs — they're scrying pools. Mirrors into the world, so to speak. Visions of things that are, things that were, and things that are destined to be. Unless, of course, a bit of divine intervention happens to supersede." Pausing for a nervous sip of coffee, he added, "It's a direct feed from Tenth Heaven — compliments of the all seeing eyes of the ophanim. This is how we monitor the Balance on our sector of Earth. We call it throneView. Or simply *tV*. Lowercase 't.' Capital 'V.'"

"tV, huh? That's cute." I said, still highly pissed that I missed not one - but two - Red Sox world series championships after a lifetime of heartbreaking let downs. "Bet you guys were up all night thinking of that one."

Shifting his attention back to me, he said, "The Alpha did warn us that your sense of humor was matched only by your prowess as a swordsman."

"Touché," I muttered with a droll glance.

Fixating on one screen in particular where a shady looking, portly security guard happily puffed on a cigarette while polishing off a bag of cheesy poofs and a six pack of beer, I said, "Hey, I know that guy. He was at Fenway — he mentioned the Guild. Knew I was a Deacon. He was scared shitless."

"Yeppers," Rooster said looking at the screen. "That's Uncle Skip."

"That asshole's your uncle?"

"No," he replied chuckling, "That's just what everybody calls him. Bit of a local fixture. We keep a close eye on him. He's a metamorph class nepher on the Guild's watch list. Straddles the line between light and dark. Never actually breaks the Rules but doesn't exactly abide by them either. But, to be fair, it's kind of in his nature. Metamorphs are shape shifters. Bit of a rarity, even in the nepher community. Been hanging around Boston for at least a couple centuries to the best of our knowledge. They say he's originally from Baton Rouge or something."

As Rooster's words somewhat registered with my befuddled brain, the slovenly figure on the screen morphed from a Jabba the Hut looking mall cop into a frail elderly Asian woman.

"What the hell?" I muttered in astonishment. "Did you see that?"

Putting on some ratty clothes and thick framed old lady glasses, he — or rather she — grabbed a cane and headed out the door of the apartment. As the scene transitioned to the street, the old woman stood hunched over on a busy corner hitting up passers-by for pocket change.

"And just like that, Uncle Skipper's your Aunt. The 'poor old blind woman' gag. Classic Skip. You should see him as a stripper. It's actually —."

"Oh, hell no," I blurted out, stopping Rooster in mid sentence. "That's a mental picture I can do without, thank you very much."

"Right," he replied amidst a subtle laugh. "Don't say I didn't warn you though."

"A *shapeshifter*? For real?" I said looking back at the row of people and images flittering about the various tVs. "Who the hell are the rest of these people?"

"Well, that's the rub, my friend. They're not exactly people. They're nephers."

"Heffers?" I asked. "Like fat chicks?"

"No, no. Not like fat chicks," he impatiently replied, "Nephers — nephil, as in nephilim. Angelic half-breeds. Hybrid beings."

"But — the nephilim are a race of giants," I said shaking my head in disagreement.

"Correct," he smugly replied sitting back in his chair.

"But these jokers are not giants," I said pointing at the screens.

"Also correct," he said with a satisfied grin.

"Ok, Yoda, cut the shit. Is it written somewhere in the Guild handbook that you guys have to be insufferable smart asses? Answer the damn question. What am I missing?"

"Well, somebody's grumpy," he mumbled. "I thought you might figure it out is all."

"And …" I grumbled while shooting him my very best 'piss up a rope' glare.

"Ok, it's like this," he said rising to his feet and waving his hands as he spoke. "As you know, the nephilim are a race of hybrid beings spawn from angel and human breeding. They nearly ate everything on the Earth … blah, blah, yadda, yadda … until God had enough of their shit. With *encouragement* from Gabriel they wiped each other out, and God sent the flood along just in case any of their sorry asses were still kicking around. You with me?"

"Yes," I impatiently replied.

"Ok. Now this is the part where it gets interesting. Angels shacking up with humans didn't just create giants — it created an aberration in the human genome, I.e. The nepher gene. A unique, recessive strand of DNA that spread through the human race like an STD gone viral, compliments of some old testament debauchery and associated acts of ill repute."

"That's just disturbing."

"Yeppers," he replied nodding. "Think about that for a second. Not the debauchery part but the other part. Imagine the limitless permutations of nepher genes passed through generation upon generation of humans over the course of thousands of years. The best and worst parts of divine beings at the molecular level weaving its way through the ancestry of humanity itself.

Evolving — mutating — crossing with other tainted strands — it's seriously mind boggling. I mean, mathematically speaking, that would equate to —"

"Ok, Einstein. I get the picture. So what next?" I grumbled looking around for some more coffee.

"Oh, right. Sorry, sometimes I get carried away. At any rate, it wasn't so good for the home team if you get my drift. The only way to preserve the human race was to take a big step back and start over — from scratch."

"And that's when God sent the great flood."

"Yeppers," he said taking a quick pause for some coffee. "So after binding the spirits of the slain giants to the Earth to forever plague mankind, and remind them that hooking up with angels was frowned upon in his establishment, God rebirthed the human race through Noah and his three sons, right?"

"Yep."

"Why Noah, you ask?"

"I didn't ask that."

"Well, that's an excellent question," he said ignoring me. "Aside from being one hell of a nice guy, good with animals, and a snappy dresser, was the fact that his lineage somehow remained 100% human, i.e. uncontaminated by the nepher gene. He and his three sons were the real dealio. So in theory, the flood should have cleansed the human race. Right?"

"Somehow I'm guessing the answer to that is, No," I dryly replied, wondering where the hell he was going with all this.

"Not bad for a guy that spent his entire mortal life jumping from airplanes and dodging bullets," he shot back with a modest grin.

"I'm really starting to not like you, Chickenman," I said with a stoic glare. "How does this story end?"

"Moving along then," he awkwardly muttered. Taking what appeared to be his last slug of coffee, he boldly declared, "It all comes down to Ham."

"Ham?"

"Yes. Ham."

"Not chicken?"

"Not ham as in *ham*," he said shaking his head while letting out an exasperated sigh. "Ham as in the second son of Noah."

"Oh, right. That Ham. Sorry. Please continue," I said rather satisfied that I was able to shut him up for two whole seconds.

"Ham's wife was a nepher," he said still shaking his head. "She carried the gene onto the ark and hence the cycle simply started over in the post flood world. But curiously, it seemed that the diluted gene was not capable of producing the big guys. The giants, or anakim as we've come to classify them, could only be created through direct angel and human breeding — first-gen offspring. Pure blood nephs, if you will. Named for Anak, the oldest nepher giant known to mankind, and one hell of a powerful being. But you already know that from first hand experience, don't you? That was totally sweet by the way — when you put the smack down on his big ass — epic."

"You saw that?"

"We watched the replay on throneView. Super cool in slow mo. I can play it if you want?"

"Thanks," I said with a disturbed glare. "But I'm good."

"Right. Probably some bad memories there. Anywho, since the fallen Watchers have been in the divine slam for the better part of six thousand years, there's only one angel still cranking out little Anaks."

"Azazel. Nice hair. Likes to run his mouth," I muttered while taking a seat and again cycling through the various tV screens. "So, all these people are not actual people. They're, ah, nephers. And nephers could be giants but could also be these shapeshifter things like Skippy the Rent-a-Cop slash the Little Old Chinese Lady from Southie."

"Well, sort of," he said joining me at the table. "But you're missing the big picture, man. Think about it like this. No two humans are exactly the same, right? Height, weight, build, eye color, skin color, hair color, strength, agility, intelligence level, etc. Now, despite what you may think, the same principle applies to angels, but the variations run the gamut of supernatural abilities and other worldly shit that would absolutely blow your mind. So, nephers are part human, part angel, and/or any variation of abnormality in between, resulting from millennia of cross breeding."

Pointing at the images on the hundreds of tV screens, he passionately said, "Nephers, my friend, are any number of sub-species within a species that's a sub-species of another two species which just so happen to originate from opposing dimensions of reality."

"Dude, you're killing me," I grumbled with a blank look. "Let's pretend I understood a fraction of what you just said. Just how many nephers are there running around out there?"

"Dean," he replied laughing out loud. "How many humans are running around out there is the better question. For *six thousand* years the nephilim DNA has been winding its way through the gene pool of humanity. Shit, nine times out of ten you wouldn't realize someone was a nepher if he was your best friend. And eight times out of ten he wouldn't realize it either."

"No, no, no," I grumbled while shaking my head. "So you're telling me that most *people* are *nephers* with these insane super human characteristics? No fucking way."

"Is it really that hard to believe? Think about it. Just to start, think about all the *exceptional* people you've ever known. Or ever even heard about. Like, for example, professional athletes. You think a human can *throw* a baseball a hundred miles an hour or *jump* from the damn free-throw line and dunk a basketball?"

"Yeah," I grumbled.

"Oh, Ok — what about running a mile in four minutes or bench pressing nine hundred pounds? How do you explain that?"

"Steroids," I replied matter of factly.

"Steroids," he scoffed. "Hell no. They're not human. They're nephers, man. Athletes, savants, artists, musicians, politicians, actors, business moguls, heads of state, the super rich, the super famous — society's elite and affluent. Safe bet, they're all nephers. God created humans equal, right? And yet some are not equal. They're so freak'n off the chart advanced in certain aspects, it's inconceivable. Unexplainable. So, how do you explain it?"

"Aliens," I offered thinking a response of steroids was clearly not going to work a second time.

"Yeah right," he said chuckling, "Although, that's a popular theory. Especially after the *Men in Black* movies."

"The what movie?"

"You know — *MIB*. They made like three movies. Will Smith. Tommy Lee Jones. Black suits. Sunglasses. Actually — really good."

With a blank look, I simply shrugged my shoulders.

"Right," he replied pensively. "Must've been after your time."

"After my time? Are you perhaps referring to the fourteen years you had me floating in a tank of frigg'n holy water after having my ass kicked for the second time by the same fallen angel?"

"Ah, possibly," he replied somewhat tentatively.

"Right," I grumbled. "Do me a favor and don't say that again. Like — as in ever again."

"Noted," he awkwardly replied. "But seriously, now that we've ruled out *aliens* … it's simple, man. Interwoven bits and pieces of twisted divinity flowing through the veins of humanity, compliments of the nepher gene. Some folks are gifted with superior size — strength — agility. Others with inexplicable intellect — an uncanny ability to control thoughts or read minds — unnatural long life — an influence over nature or events — extra sensory perception — dashing good looks, etc."

Pointing at the furry, muscle bound Caveman happily tending bar across the room, and then up at the tV screen displaying Uncle Skip, he said, "And yet some are gifted, or perhaps cursed, with other characteristics. More on the arcane side of the equation, if you know what I mean. The stuff of urban legends and bad reality shows."

Trying my damnedest to wrap my head around what Rooster just dropped on me, I poured myself another man-sized dose of java, and said, "But, unlike the giants —"

"The anakim," he said, correcting me.

"Anakim, right," I grumbled, "Unlike the anakim, these other nephers aren't subject to God's Wrath? Smite with extreme prejudice kind of protocol?"

"Well, that's the tricky part," he replied following my lead and pouring himself more coffee. "Bit of a loop hole really. While the big guys are still public enemy numero uno, the lesser nephs are allowed to coexist with man if they live within the Rules set forth by the Father and enforced by the Guild."

"This was so much easier when the bad guys were just giants … So, do all these nephers know they're, ah, nephers?"

"Some do. Some don't. We call those who know what they are 'the Conscious' and those who happily live their lives in ignorance 'the Blind.' Some nephers go their whole mortal life without a clue. Others are born into communities of Conscious and raised accordingly. Some are happy to operate within the Rules, masquerade as humans, and employ their talents to live a long, comfortable life. Others — not so much. Amongst other methods, we monitor them with throneView," he said while glancing back at the tV screens. "Conscious or Blind — breaking the Rules, and therefore disrupting the Balance, means a visit from a Deacon."

Thinking back to my encounter with a frantic Uncle Skipper, I muttered, "Game over."

"Yeppers," Rooster replied nodding his head. "Game over, man. Most nephers have the good fortune of laying eyes on a cloaked Deacon one time in their lives." Tipping his mug to me, he said, "At the end."

"That would make sense. Sort of," I said while taking a healthy swig. "So how is it that you can tell a human from a nepher? That is, if they're not covered in hair from head to toe, and have a pet piglet," I asked while dumbfoundedly glancing across the room at Mick, the happy caveman, throwing a Frisbee to Duncan, who was jumping an easy five feet in the air and catching it in his tiny mouth.

"Good question," he said nodding his head while giving me a little pointy hand gesture that he seemed to do when he got excited. "Most nephers look and act perfectly human. Except, of course, for the gothen which could look human until they take form or —," doing some exaggerated air quotes, "*Neph Out* — In which case they look like — well, we'll get to that later. Baby steps, right?"

"Please."

"Right. Ok, nephers have an inhuman aura about them. It's subtle but you, as with all Deacons, can See it once you know what you're looking for. Some are more pronounced than others, but once you develop your Sight nothing will be hidden from you."

"I actually did notice something 'off' about Uncle Skip when I saw his fat ass up close. Was like a faint glow around his rotund frame," I said, thinking out loud. Flashing back to the recurring words of Stephen, I muttered, "Open your eyes and See the evil in the world of man."

"Exactly," Rooster said nodding his head. "But, bear in mind that not all nephers are 'evil' per se. Some have renounced the inherent darkness that plagues their souls and turned to the light."

"Like Caveman."

"Like Caveman," he agreed. "And all the nephilim serving in the Guild. Including yours truly."

"You?" I blurted out. "You're a nepher?"

"I am," he said with a tinge of pride. "You'll find that most gingers are. Let's just say that red hair was not part of the Father's original design. It's a dead give away."

"Son of a bitch," I said reflecting on all the red heads that I'd known throughout my life. "That actually explains quite a bit."

"Yeah, man. Gives context to that insane girlfriend you had in high school right?"

"How the hell do you know about that?"

"We have files," he smugly replied with a shit-eating grin. "And, of course, it's all available for download on throneView."

Holding up a hand, I grumbled, "Before you ask, No, I don't want to see any replays. The occasional nightmares are enough …"

"Figured as much," he snickered under his breath. "But understand this, just as the Guild draws nephilim to the light, the Maradim pulls them in the other direction."

"The Maradim. Azazel's nepher army," I said, recollecting an earlier conversation with Stephen.

"Not so much an army," Rooster quickly replied. "More like a cult. A militant collection of miscreants. They see themselves as rebels fighting to liberate the Earth from the perceived persecution of Heaven — the *tyranny* of the Father. Strategically placed throughout humankind, they're hidden in plain sight — serving Azazel with absolute loyalty. Once a nepher bears the mark of the Maradim, they are bound to the darkness — for all of eternity."

"Awesome," I muttered, thinking about the endless ramifications of a nepher secret society unbound by the covenants of Heaven. Feeling a need to lighten the mood a bit, I said, "What about M? Is she a nepher posing as a cute Jewish broad from Brooklyn?"

Practically choking on the sip of coffee he was attempting to drink, he solemnly said, "M? A nepher? No, man. M is most certainly not a nepher."

"Well, she's clearly not human," I said matter of factly, "So, what's the deal?"

Placing his mug on the table, he said solemnly, "M is timeless. She's wind — light — hope — inspiration. Unbound wisdom and bestower of knowledge. The guardian of the western realm of Earth. A vigilant shepherd of humans and nephilim alike. She is Mariel — a principality class angel of the Third Triad. In all my years of service to the Guild I have yet to encounter a more powerful being."

"Well, that would have been good information to share a bit earlier. Guess I should get used to her calling me 'Bubba' then."

"Yes. Yes, you should. And it's Bubbala. Not Bubba," Rooster said coldly, as his eyes hardened and flashed a furious, blazing red for a quick second.

"Right," I said making the mental note that I'd evidently hit a nerve. "Bubba-lah. Got it." Trying to change the subject, I asked, "So, what's your particular nepher talent?"

With his demeanor returning to the jovial ginger that I'd come to know and somewhat like, he said, "Making really good beer."

"Amen, brother," I muttered, figuring there was a bit more to Rooster than meets the eye. Making the mental note to revisit the topic at a later time, I said, "Where did M go anyway?"

"M's a force of nature, man. No telling. She goes where she's needed. Although, I have a sneaking suspicion she ported to Seventh Heaven to meet with Ramiel."

"Ramiel," I said recalling the earlier dialogue. "The angel that Big A seems to slightly dislike? The 'skelpit arse' as he so Scottishly put it."

"Yeppers. That's the one. But he's no mere angel. He's an archangel - Gabriel's lieutenant. And trust me, *arse* is putting it mildly. Not a big fan of Deacons or the Guild. In fact, he pretty much hates our collective guts. Jealous, resentful, spiteful, you name it." Pouring himself a third cup of coffee, he added, "Which is not terribly uncommon for the angelic, but he's an exceptional prick. Bit of an asshole really."

"Didn't realize angels could be assholes."

"Man, you have no idea. Aside from Gabriel, M, and our *eyes in the sky* — the ophanim, we don't have many friends in the Heavenly Realms. Shit, we're more popular with demons, believe it or not."

"*Demons*, seriously?"

"Yeppers. They're out of our jurisdiction so to speak. But I digress, that's for another time," he replied. "Back to your crash course. You ready? More coffee? How about some scones and Rooster Orange Butter? They're sassy. You need to feed the machine, man. Your body is making up for not eating, for — well — fourteen years or so."

Although I didn't exactly know what a 'scone' was, the grumbling sensation emanating from the pit of my stomach made me want about fifty of them. "Fair enough. Scone me, Chickenman. Stephen did mention that they were the stuff of legend."

"Whoa, the Alpha said that? Serious? Sa-weet," said Rooster excitedly, while doing a little chickenman victory dance. "That's excellent. Be right back."

"Ok, sounds good. And please never do that again in my presence. It was disturbing. Feel like I need to wash my hands or something," I called after him while topping off my coffee mug and shaking my head.

Sitting back in the chair, I panned around the surreal setting in attempt to process the volumes of mind-blowing information I'd just received. Talk about a conspiracy theory. 'Humans — the minority race.'

Sort of gives some ominous context to *Planet of the Apes*. I knew that frigg'n movie creeped me out for good reason. Right about then I had a horrible thought.

Charlton Heston — a nepher?

"No frigg'n way," I affirmably grumbled to myself. "Not a chance."

As I wrestled with that particular dilemma for a quick moment, my attention was drawn to the far side of the room where the front door to the

Quartermaster boldly swung open and morning sunlight poured into the dimly lit bar. Tentatively standing at the threshold was the silhouette of a young man in his early twenties intently peering inside. Never actually stepping foot in the room, he simply stood there making visual sweeps back and forth like he was looking for something. Something he couldn't see. Rooster actually walked right past him with a mountainous tray of pastry on his way back to the table, and the guy didn't look twice at him. Nor did Rooster pay him any attention.

As he deposited the mound of delectable treats on the table, I pointed at the dude and asked, "Who the hell's that?"

Without so much as looking back, he simply replied, "I dunno. He's been by the past couple days. Evidently not quite ready."

"Not ready for what?" I impatiently asked. "What's he doing? It's like he can't see us."

"He can't," he said carefully placing scones on a couple of bronze plates. Opening a small mason jar of orange-tinted butter he began to methodically apply it. "He's drawn here. But he doesn't know why yet. He's a Gifted — a human with a divine purpose. You know, like prophets, seers, witnesses, healers, etc. If I had to guess, he's probably looking at an empty room at the moment. Searching for a glimpse of something to prove to himself that he's not completely losing his mind. Poor bastard."

Handing me a fully buttered scone, he added, "However, once he develops his Sight, the Quartermaster will be revealed and he'll be able to cross the threshold. Then we'll get him squared away. That's how it works."

"This just keeps getting better," I muttered while happily accepting the warm, buttery little piece of heaven.

Stuffing the flakey goodness into my watering mouth with extreme prejudice, I was not disappointed. Pointing at Rooster, I mumbled, "Holy shit. Scones are good."

Chuckling at the carnage of crumbs I'd spewed across the table, he replied, "Believe it or not, they're even better if you manage to keep a little bit *in* your mouth."

Casually flipping him off, I happily chomped on another one while slurping down some coffee. "So, you said when boy wonder over there gets 'his Sight' he'll be able to enter the Quartermaster — How's that work?"

"Ok. What I *said* was that he'll able to cross the threshold, and the Quartermaster will be revealed. The QM's a gateway to Badenoch — the Seventh Realm of Third Heaven. A world *between* worlds, so to speak. If you have reason to be inside — you are afforded the ability to cross the threshold. If not, the warding prevents it with an uber powerful veiling spell. You must have felt it when you walked in."

"I did feel it," I said thinking back to the wave of energy I experienced when entering the door from Westland Ave. "Did you say it's a spell? Like in magic?"

"One thing at a time, my friend. We'll get to that at some point. For now, just understand that thresholds have power. Wards and veils are used by us as well as those we hunt. You'll quickly learn that things are seldom as they appear. Make sure you use your Sight before storming through a door."

"Forbidden knowledge," I muttered, finally registering what he was talking about.

"Yep. You got it," he said shifting his focus to my unrelenting eating display. "Why don't you grab a couple scones to-go and follow me." Standing up and walking toward a large wooden door in the back of the room, he added, "Need to show you a few more things."

Somewhat disgruntled that my chow fest was being disturbed, I grabbed the entire tray and begrudgingly followed him.

Reaching the door, he stopped and said, "Ok, so as you've figured out, the QM is a bit more than just a place to get some kick-ass grub and incredible beer. Aside from being the earthly gate to the Seventh Realm and a refuge for Guild members, it's also our tactical command center, so to speak."

"Of course it is," I muttered.

"Behind this door is the Reliquary — the heart of the Quartermaster," he said pointing to the large doorway covered completely with Enochian glyphs and other sigils I didn't recognize. "It's our direct link to Tenth Heaven where the ophanim beam down their all seeing sight, and we translate it into battlefield intelligence, for lack of a better description." In a self congratulatory tone, he boasted, "Man, I've got tech in there that would make NASA shit themselves."

"A chef, a brew master, *and* a computer geek," I said stuffing another scone down my throat. "Didn't see that coming. I'm shocked. No, seriously. Shocked."

"Are you finished?"

"For the moment," I muttered, making the mental note that he wasn't appreciating the sarcasm so much.

"Great," he dryly replied. "Follow me. And Dean, what ever you do … *don't* touch anything. She needs to warm up to you first."

Thinking that was one hell of an odd thing to say, I simply replied, "She?"

Ignoring me, he placed his hands on the two glyphs in the center of the door, and I watched in wonderment as it swung open to reveal an intense, unyielding white radiance. Shielding my eyes in response, I struggled to keep Rooster in focus.

Turning his head toward me, he said, "Watch the first step," and quickly faded into the wall of light. Carefully guarding my scone stash like a running back carrying a football, I reluctantly followed him and stepped across the threshold, hoping the unnamed mystery women on the other side was not a fan of Rooster's scones.

Cause I wasn't frigg'n sharing.

Chapter 18

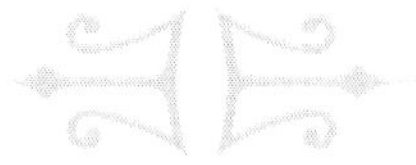

After a brief falling sensation I felt my feet firmly plant on the floor. As the blinding light slowly faded, a rotunda of pure white walls and arched ceiling came into focus. It was eerily similar to the rotunda at Raven Spire but completely sterile. Everything was white. No doors. No windows. No nothing. With exception to a bowling ball sized whitish orb slowly spinning atop a pedestal of dark rock in the middle of the peculiar room.

Upon closer inspection, the pedestal seemed to be set in the dead center of a large six-pointed star symbol, encased in a bold circle, inlaid perfectly into the pristine floor with a lustrous metal. From which, a nearly transparent force field of crackling energy formed a perfect cylinder that ran from the floor to the ceiling, seemingly guarding the odd structure. Before I had the opportunity to say anything, the booming sound of a female voice echoed through every inch of the circular space.

"Acknowledged — O'Dargan, John — Cleric — Seventh Realm. Acknowledged — Robinson, Dean — Seventh Deacon of the Seventh Line." With *her* tone changing to something more of a congenial nature, she said, *"Good Morning, Rooster. You are late. In your usual fashion."*

"Who the hell's that?" I asked Rooster under my breath as I awkwardly tried to pinpoint the source of the disembodied voice.

"*Welcome, Deacon Robinson,"* she said before Rooster could answer. *"We have been awaiting your arrival with great anticipation. I see you have recovered your strength."*

"Ah, Thank You," I muttered looking around the empty room. "I have … I think."

"Dean, I would like to introduce you to Skyphos — the sentient eye of the Guild," Rooster said with a content grin. "Amongst *other things*, Skyphos is the keeper of knowledge and centric to our operations on Earth. In addition to throneView, which you've already seen in action, she also powers the throneLink system, allowing the members of the Seven Realms to communicate across the boundaries of Heaven and Earth through various mediums. And with assistance from a humble yet brilliant cleric she's been fully integrated with the very cutting edge of technology."

"I did not require your assistance, Rooster. I simply became weary of your incessant badgering," Skyphos announced quite matter of factly.

"Is *Skyphos* the floating bowling ball?" I whispered leaning closer to Rooster.

In a lower whisper, he nervously replied, "Yeah, sort of, but —."

"So, the bowling ball is a divine super computer? Like an artificial intelligence?"

Before Rooster had the opportunity to answer, the incorporeal female voice boomed, *"I am neither a bowling ball nor an artificial intelligence, Deacon Robinson. I am Skyphos of Galgallin - An ophanim class angel."*

"Yes, Ma'am," I muttered jumping back from Rooster and thoroughly embarrassed. "Sorry for that. Apologies, ah, Skyphos."

"Apologies are not required, Deacon," she amenably replied.

Leaning over and whispering, "Real smooth," Rooster took a few steps toward the perimeter of the circle. Focusing his attention directly on the rotating orb, he said, "Skyphos, request permission to enter."

Turning back toward me, he said, "Now, watch this. Prepare to be blown away."

"Permission granted," she replied as the circular shield of near transparent energy, running from the ground to the ceiling around the pedestal, retreated into the shiny metal inlay on the floor with a distinct popping sound.

Approaching the orb, he gently placed his hand upon it, and boldly said, "Initiate Deacon Operations Command protocol."

When absolutely nothing happened, he determinedly said, "INITIATE — Deacon — Operations — Command — Protocol!"

When absolutely nothing happened for the second time, he sheepishly muttered under his breath, "*Please* … initiate Deacon Operations Command protocol."

"*Initiating Deacon Operations Command,*" boomed Skyphos with a detectable hint of satisfaction.

Making the mental note that I was really starting to like that bowling ball, I watched in amazement as the orb flashed a brilliant deep red and the sterile room morphed into an otherworldly command center. In a systematic yet graceful transformation, the blank facade gave way to an obscure mixture of technology, medieval style decor, and crude lightning. Although I'd never give Rooster the satisfaction, it was perhaps the coolest damn thing I'd ever laid eyes on.

A series of ginormous flat screen tVs blinking furiously with video feeds, streams of data, and assorted maps instantly manifested and covered all the available wall space from top to bottom, literally circling the room. The white, textureless ceiling and floor instantly morphed into a pattern of dark cobblestone, like something you'd see in a timeworn castle of the Middle Ages. Hanging from the ceiling appeared a series of iron, gothic-like chandeliers which housed countless small candles providing flickering, dim lighting throughout the daunting space. A number of ornate wooden desks, complete with old fashioned telephones and hovering tV monitors, formed a wide perimeter of workstations around the Skyphos orb.

Just when I thought the show was over, I turned to Rooster in complete and utter awe only to find him staring back at me with a full on shit-eating grin.

"Nice, huh? Now, for the grand finale."

Removing his hand from the orb, he raised both arms outward. Dramatically throwing his head back, he said, "Activate *the command bridge*." Although very faint, I also heard him mutter 'Please' under his breath right at the end.

What a putz.

Upon hearing the magic word, Skyphos boomed, *"Activating command bridge."*

Within a quick second, the sound of grinding rock emanated from the perimeter of the inner circle, and it inexplicably began to break free from the surrounding floor and rise steadily in the air, taking Rooster with it. As I stood at ground level watching the whole spectacle, I couldn't help but mutter, "Yep, that's pretty frigg'n cool," despite myself.

As the hovering stone platform reached height, roughly thirty feet above me, a spiral staircase of aged iron wound its way — step by deliberate step — toward the bottom. A dull thud echoed throughout the room as the final step manifested at floor level and I looked up at a beaming Rooster.

"Permission to come aboard *the bridge*, Admiral," I called up with just a smidgen of sarcasm.

"Permission granted, newbie," he smugly replied. "We usually make the rookies climb a rope the first couple hundred times. Consider yourself lucky."

Figuring that scones were probably not welcome on *the bridge*, I popped another couple in my mouth and carefully placed the tray on the nearest workstation for safekeeping. Reaching the hovering platform after a healthy climb up the narrow stairway, I found the Chickenman sitting rather comfortably in an oversized, leather captain's chair with his feet propped on a massive semicircular wooden desk — which had nothing on it but a black, rotary style telephone.

Statically hovering in the air around him were a series of holographic tiles, displaying various virtual images methodically organized in clustered groupings. Not having the faintest clue what to say, I simply stood there, speechless, watching the surreal display of otherworldly technology in action. Using his hands, he furiously plucked various translucent tiles from what looked to be a hovering, virtualized base console, and casually flipped them through the air into the correct cluster after a brief second of analysis.

Momentarily pausing on every third or fourth image, he used various finger gestures to artfully manipulate the virtual tile, creating a larger or clearer depiction before rendering disposition. The bits of information he deemed unimportant were virtually crumpled with a quick hand motion, and tossed backward over his shoulder where they simply faded into an imaginary trash-can and vanished. Feverishly muttering to himself, he did this for an intense five minutes as I stood there trying to process what in the hell was happening.

Just as I was about to say something, he abruptly jumped to his feet with a virtual stack of tiles in his left hand. Giving me a clever wink, he then proceeded to use his right hand to effortlessly sling them, like Frisbees, toward several of the gigantic tV screens lining the walls of the rotunda. As the tiles collided with their target, the information contained upon them instantly replaced whatever was currently displayed on the oversized monitors.

"Now you're just showing off," I said with a smirk.

"Yes. Yes I am," he replied while reaching down for a steaming mug of coffee that I swear wasn't there a second ago. "I'd say this was the latest in virtual technology, but it won't exist on Earth for at least another couple hundred years."

"What is it that you were doing there exactly?" I asked while slowly panning around the rotunda taking in the mind-blowing display of information.

"Sifting through the latest intel and updating our surveillance data. Had to collate the latest reports to prep the *DOC* for the incoming morning shift. They'll be firing up shortly. We're in between shifts at the moment." Pulling an antique-looking pocket watch from his khaki shorts, he added, "This place will be crawling with clerics and acolytes in exactly … six minutes."

"DOC?"

"Deacon Operations Command."

"Of course," I replied like it was common knowledge.

"This is how we track nepher activity on Earth — compliments of Skyphos. Over the years we've developed a pretty sophisticated process to monitor targets, and subsequently enforce the Rules. Kind of like a step program designed to keep the nephilim population on the right side of the line — with the final step being a visit from a Deacon for those who simply can't coexist with humanity."

"Like a nepher's anonymous? Are there weekly meetings? Coffee and cigarettes?"

"Not quite," he replied with a modest laugh. "But, it works. Aside from the anakim situation, we haven't had a serious threat to the Balance since the gothen flare up in the fifteenth century. Ironically, that was the foreshadowing to the whole '*Vampire/Werewolf*' craze. What a farce. It was a real mess. Story for another time though."

Pointing to the screen displaying a large map with several highlighted areas marked with concentric circles and various colored blinking dots, he said, "The Seventh Realm, our Realm, has oversight responsibility over North America."

"Impressive," I said nodding my head. "The big war room in the sky."

"Yeppers. Literally. From right here — we can dial up the past, the present, and — to some extent — the future. Nothing on Earth is hidden from the Sight of the ophanim. Well, almost nothing.

"Azazel," I said recalling an earlier conversation with Stephen.

"Yep. And the Maradim, to include the new generation of anakim," he muttered defeatedly. "For some inexplicable reason, they're able to operate completely off our radar. Veiled. Hidden. Like ghosts. Shouldn't be possible. Even for an angel. Azazel's either got some serious mojo we don't know about or — some serious help. Since your run in with him in Bosnia, we've been searching the globe for his bolt hole to no avail. Unfortunately, the signs of the anakim army are everywhere, man. The births, the feedings, the occasional sightings. We're always a step behind." Using hand motions, he zoomed the massive map to a section in northern Florida highlighted with a series of concentric circles. "You ever been to Tallahassee?"

"No. Too fucking hot. And I can't stand college football."

"Well, seems that a pack of anakim dropped in for a visit. Last week." With a flick of his hand, a collage of grisly, blood-smothered images appeared on the screen next to the map. "Took out a whole field of cattle on the outskirts of town. Devoured. We got there within an hour of the feeding and they were long gone. Nothing left but a collection of oversized footprints and fifty or so ravaged carcasses."

"Holy shit," I grumbled while studying the pictures. "No indication of where they went?"

"Nope. Smitty's been deployed there all week with a team of clerics. Shaking down the local nepher colonies. Looking for clues. He's due to report in this morning. Actually, any minute now," he said while glancing again at his pocket watch.

"Smitty?"

"Yeah, sorry. Henry Lee Smith III, aka 'Light-Horse' Henry. Or as most folks call him, Smitty. He's the sixth Deacon of the Seventh line. Your predecessor. You'll like him. Army guy — the Continental Army." With a flick of his hand, an image appeared on a virtual screen, hovering at eye level, in front of me. "There he is in all his glory. Tough bastard."

"Aha," I said not completely sure that I'd heard him correctly about the Continental Army but not really sure I wanted to ask for clarification. "Light Horse, eh?" I muttered, studying the animated picture of a modest looking man in his mid-thirties with shoulder length blonde hair, close cropped beard, and dark green eyes. His round face made him look somewhat jovial but his eyes were hard. The eyes of a soldier.

"Anywho, back to the feedings," Rooster said as the image faded. "At this point it's almost a damn daily occurrence. The anakim show up in the middle of the night in a random location, stuff their faces, and disappear into the ether. Mainly animals but we've seen a couple human buffets as well."

"After fourteen years of this shit, you haven't zero'd in on the target?"

"No," he grumbled shaking his head. "Not from lack of trying either. I've got Skyphos wired into every military, intelligence, and law enforcement data feed that exists. Not to mention the social networking sites and telecom companies I've hacked."

"Social networking?" I asked.

"Yeah, like Facebook and —" Realizing I had no idea what he was talking about, he stopped in mid-sentence.

"I know. I know. After my time ..." I grumbled.

"Yeah, I'll explain later. At any rate, we've got Guild members on twenty-four-hour patrols following leads around the country — and still nothing concrete. Azazel has clearly been able to create a heavily warded shadow realm without our knowing. Which again, should not be possible. The real kick in the balls is that we can't find the damn tether."

"A shadow realm? Like in Heaven?"

"Nope," he muttered while quickly pulling up and flipping several holographic tiles in the air around him. "Shadow realms are in the *between* space."

Reading my blank look, he said, "It's like this. Light — Dark — Shadow. The light realms are those of Heaven. The dark are those of Hell. Period. Although infinite in concept, they occupy discrete dimensional locations, so to speak, and were created by the Father's hand with a rigid admission policy — if you know what I'm saying."

"Ok," I said somewhat following the plot. "So these shadow realms are like purgatory?"

"Not so much," he quickly replied while flipping several of the floating virtual screens toward the large tV monitors. As several animated schematic-like images appeared on the screen, he pointed at them and said, "Although very difficult, *it is* possible for certain beings, whether it be angels, demons, powerful nephers, or a combination thereof, to literally punch a hole in the dimensional fabric and *create* a 'space between' that's off the grid. A limited scope alternate reality."

"What?" Was all I could muster, watching the virtual display of how such a mind boggling phenomenon of mysticism and physics was remotely possible. "That's insane."

"Well, it's actually quite sane if you think about it," he said while going into lecture mode. "The quantum mechanics of the dimensional —"

"Dude …," I grumbled, giving him a 'not now' glare.

"Right," he muttered clearly disappointed that I'd robbed him of his super geek moment.

Wiping the various images from the screens with a wave of his hand, he said, "Anywho, while shadow realms are allowed to *happen* — we do keep a close eye on them through Skyphos and the ophanim."

Flicking his hand again, a map of the world with several pulsating yellow dots appeared on the main screen occupying the wall to our front.

"These points indicate every tether across the Earth for each and every unique shadow realm. They *must be* tethered to a single, physical location on the Earth in order to exist. Some are as large as the entire United States while others are as small as a single structure."

Zooming the map to a section of Southern Europe, the island of Greece came into focus. Pointing to the pulsing dot hovering over a majestic mountain range, Rooster said, "Recognize that?"

"Mount Olympus. Seriously?" I said while glaring at the screen. "Come on, man. Olympus is real? And the Greek gods?"

"Actually, the Greek gods *are* real. They're nephers — ancient ones at that. And, Yes, Olympus is a shadow realm tethered to the mountain. Albeit a sin, the free will of mankind provides the choice to believe in pagan gods. Granted, we all know that particular path won't end well, but folks believe in what they will. And, for the most part — Zeus and his pantheon are harmless. The Guild pays them a personal visit every couple years. I've been once. Long time ago. That was enough. Togas, inflated egos, and raging hormones. Lot of grapes — literally and metaphorically. And Poseidon's a real asshole, for the record. But Athena on the other hand … she got it going on — Yep-pers …"

At a total loss for a response, I ignored the mental picture of the Chickenman rocking a toga while shamelessly drooling over a nepher goddess, and simply stared at the map in disbelief. Allowing me to stew on it for a moment, Rooster awkwardly said, "But back to my point, the ability to *create* a shadow realm without our knowing, and continue to keep it veiled from the Heavens takes some serious horsepower. Not something Azazel is able to do of his own accord."

Putting aside the latest revelation of mind blowing information, I asked, "But if the anakim are stashed away in a shadow realm, why do they keep coming back to chow down?"

"The anakim, unlike other nephers, are bound to the Earth. They can't live apart from it for extended periods of time," he replied matter of factly. "They require the flesh and blood of man. For them, there is no substitute."

Watching as I wearily rubbed my eyes, he said, "I know — it's a lot to take in. You with me?"

"Yeah, I'm with you."

"More coffee?" He said pointing to another mug on the desk that I swear wasn't there a second ago.

Graciously accepting, I took a powerful gulp, not caring in the least where the hell it came from.

"Thanks. Needed that," I muttered as my eyes started to feel incredibly heavy.

"Yep. You're running out of steam," he said with a look of concern. "Need some good old fashioned sleep. Despite all that you are — you're still somewhat human. Your body needs rest. Not to mention the load on your mind at the current moment. It'll take a while to adjust. Trust me. I know."

"Yeah well, seems we don't have a while do we?"

"Maybe not, but we'll need you at full strength, or as close to it as possible, when the fight comes. And it will come. Sooner than we'd like. Tell you what, why don't you get some rack before Big A gets back. A couple hours will make you feel like a new man — or at least a new Deacon … I set up a room up for you earlier."

Although I didn't particularly want to stop the indoctrination process, I knew I was smoked. I needed rest. Rooster was right.

"Ok," I reluctantly said, "An hour or two max."

"You got it. Follow me."

As we reached the bottom of the staircase and made our way through the labyrinth of workstations, the morning crew started to filter into the Reliquary and assume their various positions. Although everyone seemed to keep a cautious distance, I noticed that they all shot me a curios glance as they shuffled by, offering various good morning pleasantries.

"They'll get used to you," Rooster said as if he could sense what I was thinking. "Believe it or not, actually laying eyes on the Seventh of Seven is kind of like a human seeing Bigfoot. Ironically, you're a bit of an urban legend of the supernatural world."

"Awesome," I said letting out a sarcastic sigh. "Caveman is covered in hair and I'm the frigg'n sasquatch."

Making the mental note to ask him if Bigfoot was a nepher, I returned a cordial good morning nod to a young woman that passed me. Turning to Rooster, I asked, "Who are these folks?"

"Mostly acolytes — Gifted humans that have dedicated their lives to the Balance. They serve the Guild in countless capacities."

"Like Father Watson," I said.

"Yep. Like Father Watson."

"You said 'mostly' acolytes. Who are the others?"

"Clerics, like me. Nephilim who made the choice to serve the light in lieu of living in the shadows."

As we approached the door leading back to the Quartermaster, Rooster called out, "I'll be back, Sweetie. Don't miss me too much."

"Acknowledged, Rooster," the disembodied voice of Skyphos replied almost immediately. *"I will not. Rest assured. And as I have reminded you on more occasions that I care to assign number to — Do not refer to me as 'Sweetie.' It is upsetting."*

Chuckling to myself, I said, "So, I'm guessing the whole flaming red hair thing earned you the nickname Rooster?"

"Not exactly," he replied. "It's actually kind of a long story."

"Of course it is, "I muttered. "And probably one you're about to tell me now that I've asked."

"So there I was," he said ignoring my snide commentary as he continued walking. "It was July of 1453 and I was tracking a cell of rogue gothen across Europe with a team of clerics. And by a very unfortunate series of events we found ourselves in Gascony, France at the culmination of the Hundred Years' War. It was ugly. Real freak'n mess. We figured disguising ourselves as French soldiers would allow us to blend in and slip through all the chaos undetected. Didn't work out quite as planned."

"So you got the nickname in battle?"

"No. Not quite. When the French finally ran the English out of town at the Battle of Castillon the entire place went nuts. I'm talking a month long party of epic proportion. It was insane. And trust me — the old school French could throw down. Think I'm actually still hungover."

"Let me get this straight — you got your nickname partying in France — in the Middle Ages?"

"So, one thing leads to another — We swipe a cask of wine from some unsuspecting monks and next thing I know — I wake up sprawled out in a chicken coop in some random barnyard surrounded by a harem of local maidens who just happened to think I was the French artillery general and mastermind of the victory, Jean Bureau."

"And why exactly did they think that?"

"Probably because I stole one of his uniforms," he smugly replied. "And I might've insinuated I was him — in not so many words."

"So you got the name *Rooster* because you had a medieval orgy — in a chicken coop," I dryly muttered.

"*Oui Oui*," he quipped in a convincing French accent. "Best kind of nickname. Literal *and* figurative."

"You are so full of shit."

"God's honest truth," he said holding his right hand over his heart with a beaming smirk. "Ask Caveman. He was there."

"My ass," I grumbled. "And what about the gothen you were tracking? Did you find them?"

"They gave me the slip in France — but I did find them," he said pulling to an abrupt halt at the doorway as his demeanor instantly hardened and his eyes flashed a furious, blazing red for a quick second. "Some three hundred and twenty two years later. June of 1775."

Not really sure what to say to that, I just stood there gawking.

"Followed them to Boston," he said after a long pause. "Put them down at Bunker Hill. Been here ever since."

Speechless, I just stood there as he opened the door and faded into the white radiance. Making the mental note to lay off the Chickenman jokes, I started chuckling to myself as I crossed the threshold.

Adding '*Medieval French General*' and '*Minuteman*' to the arcane resume of my enigmatic ginger buddy who didn't look a day over twenty-five, I muttered, "To hell with the coffee, I need a beer."

Chapter 19

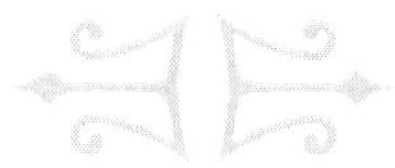

Ever heard the expression 'You'll get all the sleep you need when you're dead?' Well, I died and sleep is still a goddamn premium.

That expression is total bullshit.

Three solid knocks on the stout wooden door of my temporary lodgings rather abruptly roused me from a deep, powerful slumber. Instantly sitting up in the small bed, I instinctively threw the thin wool blanket off my body, swung my bare feet over the edge, and instinctively began to put my boots on.

One thing about spending your entire adult life in the Army Rangers, when it was time to get up — you got up. But this was a bit different. I wasn't waking up dog tired on the ground of a third world country amidst a barrage of bullets and mortar fire. I was waking up in the spare room of an other-worldly bar slash command center, which sat in a literal nether region between Heaven and Earth. And, I felt great. Incredible. Almost euphoric.

That was one hell of a power nap. Guess I really needed it after all. Just as I started to have a mild panic attack at the thought of inadvertently sleeping away another fourteen years, an unfamiliar male voice called out from the hallway.

"Good Afternoon, Deacon. Please pardon the intrusion but Rooster asked me to give you a wake up call."

"Ok, Thanks. Appreciate it," I called back while taking notice of the time on the antique looking analog clock hanging on the wall opposite the bed. It was almost 2 Pm. "Hey, ah, is it still Sunday, January 5th?"

"Yes, sir," the voice replied somewhat tentatively.

"Great, Thanks. And, ah, still 2012, right?"

"Ah, Yes, sir."

"Just checking," I awkwardly grumbled, "Be right down. Tell O'Dargan to cool his jets. And make some more damn scones. I'm hungry."

"Yes, sir," he replied amidst a few subtle chuckles. "Will do."

The creak of hurried footsteps moving down the hallway indicated he'd evidently had enough of my bizarre line of questioning. Exhaling a relieved sigh that I'd only slept for a couple hours and not another decade, I finished tying my boots while relishing in how absolutely refreshed I felt.

There is truly nothing like a good rack session. Alive, dead, or un-dead. Trust me on that one. Still wearing my favorite Levis, I quickly grabbed the black tee shirt Rooster had left for me and slipped it on. Making the mental note that it was incredibly tight on my chest, shoulders, and biceps I couldn't help but chuckle at the red Rooster logo and the slogan — *'Crow Like You Gotta Pair. RoosterBragh 2012.'*

Standing up and powerfully stretching my arms, I could literally feel every muscle in my upper body flex and flare up in response. For the first time in a long damn time I felt good. Like me — the old me — the human me. As I pondered that for a quick second I had another thought.

"The dream," I muttered out loud.

I didn't have the dream. The haunting, incessant dream that foreshadowed my mortal death and current supernatural condition. With an elated breath that I'd finally shaken free of that particular subconscious tether, I felt a wide smile stretch across my face. Feeling rather good about myself, I confidently opened the door and crossed the threshold into the dark hallway when the sudden onslaught of a splitting headache stopped me dead in my tracks.

The immediate and intense wave of crushing pain surging through my head felt like somebody was trying to drive an ice pick through one of my eye sockets and push it clear out the back of my skull. Instantly closing my eyes and dropping to a knee, I winced and grunted in complete agony, clutching my forehead with both hands in attempt to make it stop.

But it didn't stop. It got worse. A lot frigg'n worse. Unbearably worse.

Feeling like my head was about to pop under the unimaginable force, I started screaming. For the record — it was a manly, throaty scream. More of a yell than a scream actually. Just so you know. At any rate, just as I felt like I couldn't take anymore — it stopped. Rising to my feet and slowly opening my eyes, my befuddled brain struggled to process the unexpected scene laid out before me when the sound of a familiar voice sent a racing chill down my spine.

"Welcome, *Deacon*. It is as I foretold. The Wrath has brought you to your knees. *And here you are* — at my feet. Now, Henry — Are you prepared to serve a true master — a *just* master — or do you choose the unnecessary path of torment as did your misguided *brothers*?"

Dumbfounded and speechless, I stood motionless staring at the harrowing, crimson eyes of Azazel adorned in a white robed outfit and smugly pacing in front of a prisoner bound in heavy chains. Kneeling before him within a circle of purple-white flame in the center of a dark, musty room, the prisoner wore a cloak — a Deacons cloak.

Staring insolently at Azazel, he bellowed, "Fuck You," in a deep voice that rung with a heavy southern twang.

"False bravado and eloquence. How unfortunate," Azazel dryly replied, "Not unexpected however."

Motioning for one of his cronies to come forward, he whispered something to a man in a tactical uniform with a pair of swords strapped to his back in a crisscrossing pattern. Ironically, the guy looked a hell of a lot like Rooster except his blazing red hair was clipped tightly to his skull and a sharply cornered ginger goatee hung proudly from his chin.

"Yes, Dominus," Evil Rooster muttered offering Azazel a subservient bow. "I will see it done." And quickly exited the scene.

Still confused as all hell as to what was happening, I squinted in attempt to see anything beyond the dark shadows on the periphery of the flaming circle. As Azazel began to laugh, I was again drawn to his haunting silhouette as he further taunted the prisoner.

"Well, perhaps this will persuade you to reconsider."

With a casual flick of his hand, the chains binding the prisoner released and fell to the stone floor with an ominous thud.

"Arise, my dear Henry, and gaze upon the fallen *mighty*."

With a subsequent wave of his hand, a series of flaming circles began to ignite, one by one, around the floor of the peculiar room. Each circle contained a bound figure on their knees staring blankly into oblivion. Bound figures in cloaks. Deacons.

As the pattern completed and each circle glowed in fervent purple flame — only two were vacant.

"What have you done," muttered the now standing, unbound Henry as he slowly spun around in his flaming prison, gazing blankly in utter disbelief as the scene slowly unfolded before him. In a defeated voice barely above a whisper, he simply said, "No. That's — not possible," as a look of absolute horror washed over his face.

"Oh, Yes, Henry. *Yes* indeed. The possibilities are endless!" Azazel replied with a boastful smile. Pointing to one of the empty circles, he said, "Would you care to take your rightful place in my collection? Or — are you now prepared to discuss an *alternate* arrangement?"

As the scene started to blur, I felt the surging pain in my head again. Dropping to a knee and grasping my temple, I took one more determined look at the captive Deacon only to find him staring straight at me. As the chains rose from the floor with an unseen force and encased his hands and feet in the purplish-white flamed shackles, he took his place in the morbid collection and just blankly stared at me.

His face. It was familiar — round with a short-cropped blonde beard and brilliant green eyes.

Just as the scene completely faded to black and my eyes slid shut, it hit me. Henry. Henry Lee Smith III - Smitty.

Son of a bitch.

As the revelation hit me like a ton of bricks, my eyes shot open only to find Stephen standing opposite me in the hallway of the Quartermaster outside of my room.

"You saw him," he sternly said while fixing me with an intense, almost distraught gaze. Quickly helping me to my feet, he placed both hands on my shoulders. "Azazel. You saw him."

"Yeah — I saw him," I grunted between heavy breaths, still reeling from the surreal experience. "I was there — I think."

"Where? Where Dean?" He frantically asked. "What did you See?"

"I'm — not sure. A dungeon — maybe a cave," I forced out while struggling to breathe and stand up under my own power. "It's a prison. Circles — of purple fire."

"The holy flame. That — is not possible. A fallen angel cannot wield the holy flame," he muttered to himself while shaking his head.

"Smitty — He had Smitty. And the others. Deacons — shackled — bound. They were alive, but — something was wrong with them. They were out of it — like catatonic."

"How many?" He coldly asked as his grip tightened on my shoulders.

"I — I'm not sure. They circled the room —"

"How many?" He shouted as his eyes flashed with fury. "How many, Dean? How many did you see?"

"I don't know," I awkwardly replied completely taken aback by his uncharacteristic behavior. "Maybe Twenty? Maybe more. He called it his collection. There — there was only one circle left empty."

Releasing the violent grip he had on my shoulders, he stood momentarily speechless and stared at the floor as his eyes danced with rapid thought. With the signature stoic mask returning to his face, he looked me squarely in the eyes and said, "The reckoning is near. If I understand what is happening — You will have more visions. Speak of them to no one."

Turning and taking a few steps down the hallway, his cloak manifested around his shoulders in a spectral flash and he was gone. Although completely taken aback by the exchange, I was once again impressed, as all hell, by Stephen's ability to make an exit as I propped myself up against the wall, wondering what in the hell just happened. Hearing the sound of footsteps running down the hallway I looked up to see Rooster and another guy I didn't recognize bounding toward me at great speed with weapons drawn and looks of terror.

"Dean! You Ok? What's going on?" Rooster said reaching me within a matter of seconds, and looking exceptionally red from head to toe.

His unidentified buddy slid past me and entered my room with a pair of curved machetes at the ready like he was going to slay the first thing that moved.

"I'm fine," I muttered, trying to quickly recover from recent events. "Stubbed my toe. Hurt like hell." Unfortunately, that was the first thing that came to mind.

Lowering his sword as his skin instantly returned to a normal color, he dryly said, "You *stubbed* your toe?"

"Yeah, ah, guess I'm still getting my bearings back. I'm fine. Sorry for the commotion," I replied, trying to get off the topic as quickly as possible. "Hey, time for lunch?"

"I didn't realize the Seventh of Seven felt pain," said the new guy, skeptically, as he casually walked out of my room and sheathed his blades in twin scabbards concealed on his torso.

Offering a quick nod to the twenty-something newcomer, Rooster said, "Dean, this is Tiberius Jefferson."

"Tiberius, eh? Wow. Ok, *Tiberius*, try explaining that to my big toe. Probably never be the same. You guys ever considered painting the doorframe yellow? Maybe put a caution sign up? Damn thing came out of nowhere."

Chuckling a bit, new guy held out his hand, and said, "Call me Tango. It's a pleasure to meet you." Giving my tee shirt a curious glance, he added, "Nice shirt."

"Dean. The pleasure's mine. And, ah, thanks," I said amidst subtle laughter while firmly grasping his hand, and taking in his six foot frame of lean muscle, urban fashionista attire, and meticulously styled light brown hair. "I take it you're a cleric."

"You got it. I lead the surveillance and response teams for the Seventh Realm."

Enamored by his sea foam colored pants, intentionally faded blue polo shirt, and cool guy jean jacket, I said, "Surveillance, eh? That would explain why you look like you're about to crash a frat party."

"What do you mean?" He muttered while giving me a blank look and nonchalantly fixing his hair.

"Ah, never mind," I uncomfortably muttered. "Did someone say it's time for lunch?"

Before they had the chance to answer, the disembodied voice of Skyphos boomed, "*Deacon Robinson, You have an incoming teleLink from the archdeacon. Shall I connect you?*"

"Ah, Sure," I said not really knowing what the proper answer to such a question would be.

Within a brief second, a semi translucent virtual screen manifested at eye level, displaying a bulky Scotsman standing in the center of a colosseum-like structure holding a tree-sized log like it was a twig. As the picture zoomed to a close up of his weathered face, he said, "Good Morning, sunshine. Now that ye got yer beauty rest, bring yer wee self out to the train'n pitch, yeah? Jackie will show ye the way."

"Yes, sir," I replied while gazing into the otherworldly communications portal. "On my way."

As the screen faded, he grumbled, "Pure dead brilliant."

"So that's teleLink, eh?" I said turning to Rooster. "That was — neat."

"Yeppers," said Rooster matter of factly, "It's even smart phone compatible." Reading my blank look at the mention of an 'smart phone' he just said, "Yeah — Never mind. Mobile devices basically run society nowadays. Nepher technology. We'll get to that later though. Best to not keep Big A waiting."

Making the mental note to figure out what the hell that meant at a later time, I replied, "Ok. Let's go. Guess that means no lunch. Awesome." As we started down the hallway, I asked, "What exactly was he doing with that log?"

"Ever hear of the caber toss?"

"Nope."

"You're in for a treat, my friend. It was all the rage when Big A was a *lad*. Although, he's made a couple of extreme modifications to the spirit of the game. Just remember to duck." Rubbing the back of his head, he added, "Trust me on that one."

"Perfect," I grumbled. "Just how old is the big fella anyway?"

"Well," Rooster said with a devious smirk, "Let's just say that the kilt isn't a fashion statement."

Not having it in me to field a response, I walked in silence, reflecting on the dark prison and *collection* of mind whammied Deacons imprisoned within the holy flame. How was such a thing possible — And to what purpose? And Smitty — he looked right at me like he knew I was watching — knew I was there. In hindsight, I think I'd trade having my crazy dream every night for the rest of my un-dead life for this newfound voyeuristic ability.

"The reckoning is near," I grumbled under my breath as Stephen's words rung ominously in my head, and his atypical behavior still had me completely stunned.

"What'd you say?" Asked Tango walking to my side.

"Beer. I could use a beer."

Make that several.

Chapter 20

"So, where exactly are we now?" I asked Rooster as we crossed the threshold of yet another random door in the Quartermaster.

Finding myself on the wood line of a thick forest of ancient trees, I stared apprehensively at a colossus arena of white, ornamental stone sitting squarely in the center of an infinite green field and towering majestically into the blue sky. I couldn't help but smile as I envisioned Judah Ben-Hur cruising by on a pimped out chariot while casually beating down a Barbary lion with a pointy stick.

Yes — I went there again. It's a frigg'n classic.

Encouragingly slapping me on the back, he replied, "Where we are *exactly* — I've no idea. What I do know is that we're somewhere on the far northern border of Badenoch. We use it as our training grounds — or pitch as they say in *the Scottish.* The archdeacon comes out here to blow off steam. Oh, and as an aside, it's usually smart to be nowhere in the general vicinity when that happens."

"Noted," I said staring at the larger than life structure in the distance. "And the *Colosseum* looking joint over there — what the hell is that?"

"That's where you meet the enemy. It's actually a full scale replica of the actual Colosseum — as it looked in the second century of course."

"Of course," I dryly replied. As I stood momentarily entranced by the sheer size and grandeur of the Roman architectural marvel, I heard Rooster let out a subtle chuckle. "What?" I asked turning toward him.

"Oh, nothing. Just figured you were going to make some lame Ben-Hur reference is all."

Making the mental note that they certainly did have a ridiculously detailed file on me, I said, "Is it too late?"

"Yep. Moment's gone."

"Damn," I dryly muttered.

Shifting focus back to the structure, he said, "Anywho, Big A calls it the Dreghorn."

"Sounds lovely."

"Yeppers. Skyphos is able to construct live battle simulations, so you can't get anything closer to the *real* thing than the actual real thing."

"Simulations?"

"Yeah man, but trust me, it will still hurt. Good luck."

"You're not coming?" I said as he started to walk back toward the doorway.

"Nope. I have a project to finish in the armory. Been working on something for you. Something I think you may need in the very near future." Passing through the doorway, he called back, "Be back soon. Remember to duck."

"Wait — what?" I yelled as the door vanished in a brief flash of white light.

Per my usual confused state, I turned again to face the Dreghorn and felt the cloak start to manifest around my shoulders just as a ginormous, airborne log struck me squarely in the chest with the force of a wrecking ball. Taking me clear off my feet and launching me ten feet backward into the trunk of an mighty tree, the projectile like timber dematerialized as I slunk to the ground in a state of ineffable pain. Staring despondently into the brilliant blue sky, I was sprawled out and gasping for breath as a familiar female voice rung out.

"Deacon Robinson, You have an incoming teleLink from Cleric O'Dargan. Shall I connect you?"

"Yes ..." I halfheartedly mumbled.

As the semi translucent virtual screen manifested in front of my pain-ridden face, a shit-eating grin bearing Rooster appeared.

"You didn't duck did you?"

Swatting the image with my hand, I forced out, "You're an asshole."

As the screen quickly dissipated, I struggled to my feet and heard the trailing voice of Rooster call out, "Focus. Clear your mind. Balance."

Spitting out a healthy wad of blood and cradling my aching ribs, I determinedly glared at the stone arena. "Alright. Game — fucking — on."

Feeling the cloak ripple about my shoulders, a warm, almost electric sensation passed through my damaged body, instantly healing my injuries. Slowly pulling in a long, deliberate breath, I cleared my mind and focused my thoughts.

And I found the Balance — the perfect balance between wrath and clarity.

Flipping the mental switch, I instantly felt the boundless power well up in the deep recess of my soul, and an assertive smile stretch widely across my face. Willing the argent metal gauntlets into being, I felt them manifest with a spectral flash and pour seamlessly over my hands. Calling for the spatha, I felt the presence of the leather scabbard on my back as I reached back and grasped the stout handle. A distinct hum emanated through the surrounding air as I drew the otherworldly blade and began to boldly march toward the palatial stone structure in the distant expanse.

Pulling the hood of the cloak over my head, I took three bold steps and instantly found myself in the center of the faux Colosseum, standing opposite a fully cloaked archdeacon swinging a log like it was a stick directly at my midsection.

Please — like I didn't see that coming.

Reaching out with my left hand, I violently grasped the swinging timber in mid-arc, much to the chagrin of my supernatural superior, as my feet sunk a solid inch or two into the stone floor with the force of the impact. Just getting warmed up, I then cut the goddamn thing in half with a forceful swipe of my sword and finished it off with a powerful kick to the chest of the large Scotsman, sending him flying backward in a state of momentary shock.

"Reporting for duty, sir," I said removing my hood and sheathing the spatha. "Hit me with a tree once, shame on me. Twice? Not frigg'n happening."

"Not bad, laddie," said Big A amidst hearty laughter as he effortlessly rose to his feet while dusting himself off. "Aye. Not bad at all."

Taking a few steps toward me while drawing his claymore broadsword, his bearded face curled into a dark grin. "The cloak will protect ye from most attack. No weapon of man can penetrate its defense. When ye focus yer strength and balance yer thoughts, you are nigh unstoppable."

Firmly grasping the hilt, argent metal gauntlets instantly covered his hands as he swung the claymore at my neck with unnatural speed. In a blur of motion I drew the spatha and blocked his attack mere inches from being decapitated.

Amidst a shower of sparks resulting from the collision of the two otherworldly swords, he said, "But know this, Deanie, a blade of barzel will slice ye open like a wee fish and spill yer guts just the same. The cloak cannot protect ye from the metal of Heaven. Allow one to separate yer head from neck and yer be no more." Dropping the sword, he added, "Just as our weapons are made in the Seraphic forges, so be that of those loyal to Azazel. Never underestimate yer enemy. Drop yer guard — yer focus — and yer vulnerable."

"Understood," I said while lowering the spatha and cringing at the fact that he called me Deanie.

"Now, let's get down to it," he said looking around the arena. "This is the Dreghorn where we master the gifts bestowed upon us by the Father. Ye have power, lad. But it's blunt — ye must sharpen it, yeah?"

"Ah, Yes," I acknowledged while trying my damnedest to decipher his accent without the benefit of Rooster's translation. "Sharpen the skills. Got it."

"The enemies of Heaven take many forms. Ye need to learn them. Recognize what lurks beneath the skin. Understand their strengths and their weaknesses. Jackie schooled ye on the beasties, yeah?"

"Beasties — You mean the anakim?"

"Nae, lad," he said sheathing his broadsword. "The gothen — the right scunners of the nephil ranks. But, since you mentioned them, let's get started with the anakim. I believe you've met this particular foul bastart once before."

Hearing a subtle stirring of movement behind me mixed with the sound of heavy breathing, I turned just in time to see a familiar fifteen-foot behemoth hit me squarely in the jaw with an oversized fist. Soaring through the air in a state of confused shock, I crashed to a ungainly halt on the white stone floor of the arena. Quickly jumping to my feet and glaring at Tiny, I felt the cloak ripple aggressively about my shoulders.

"Tiny?" I shouted looking over at a smiling Abernethy. "Seriously? Where the hell'd he come from?"

"Where he came from matters not," he replied amidst laughter, "If I were you, I'd be more keen to make him leave, lad."

Fixing me with black, soulless eyes, the simulated Tiny clutched a mammoth battle-axe with both hands and cautiously circled me like a predator waiting to strike. Drawing the spatha, I focused on my strength and watched his every move.

"The anakim," said Abernethy as I readied for the impending attack, "Are the most powerful of the nephilim. Direct offspring of angels and humans. Impervious to weapons of man. Can heal from all wounds given enough time and human blood."

Circling each other in an intense stare down like the prelude to an epic boxing match, I sharply glared at Tiny watching for any indication of his next move. Continuing with his bizarre form of instruction, Abernethy said, "As with most of the beasties, ye have two options. Separate the head from the neck with a blade of barzel or wield the judgment of Gehenna fire. Either will do."

Raising his axe and charging me with blinding speed, Tiny belted out a truly horrible growl and fixed me with fury laden eyes. Focusing my will, I felt time slow to a dramatic crawl and watched expectantly as all his movement reduced to near slow motion. Casually stepping to the left and out of the downward arc of his axe, I boldly swung the spatha at his exposed knee cap in hopes of dropping his sorry ass to the ground so I could lop off his sputnik sized head and call it a day. Unfortunately, seemed that particular maneuver wasn't going to work so well a second time. Dropping the axe to parry my sword strike, he forcefully swatted me with a backhanded fist that sent me flying through the air in a cloaked heap as my sword sprung from my hand and went clear in the other direction. Not good.

"Agile growlers, the anakim are. Smart blighters. Ruthless warriors," bellowed Abernethy, "*And now* you've lost yer wee sword. Focus yerself, laddie."

"I — am — focusing," I angrily grumbled while quickly pushing myself off the dusty stone.

Hearing and feeling the rapid advance of giant footsteps, I instinctively rolled to my left just in time to see the honed edge of a massive axe sink a solid foot into the stone floor where my head was resting just seconds before. Yeah, that would've left a mark.

As Tiny began to violently pull his axe free, I figured it was high time to quit acting like a punching bag and put an end to this bullshit. From my impromptu prone position on the Dreghorn floor, I decisively whipped my legs around and took out his oversized, sandal wearing feet. As he grunted in protest and staggered backward, I spun to my feet in a blur of motion. Jumping several feet in the air and putting all my force into a devastating right cross, I traded out the argent metal gauntlets for the unbreakable ashen stone and with a spectral flash they covered my hands and ignited with subtle white flame in mid strike.

Catching him in a clumsy stumble, I drove my stone fist into his big ass, crusty beard wearing face that sent him hurling to the ground with a glorious boom. Eyes closed and body limp, I loomed over the downed giant with a dark smile. Victoriously waltzing to where my sword lay on the floor, I willed the stone gauntlets back to metal and picked it up.

Turning to Abernethy, I said, "What? No more commentary?"

"Not bad — but we're just getting started, laddie," he said with a devious grin.

"Fair enough," I grumbled while heading back toward Tiny and raising the spatha to close the deal.

As I readied to deliver the deathblow, I was halted by the exaggerated sound of Big A clearing his throat with a pronounced 'Ahem.'

"What?" I growled glaring back at him.

"Tricky thing about the anakim."

"What's that?"

"You'll seldom find one by itself. Bit of a pack hunter."

As his words registered with my adrenaline filled brain, I realized that Tiny was not the only bad guy in the near vicinity. Feeling the cloak ripple anxiously about my shoulders, I instinctively ducked and spun to the side as a mammoth sword ripped through the air, inches above my head. Trying to quickly get my bearings, I bobbed and weaved my way around a humongous razor tipped spear thrusting toward my mid-section from the opposite direction.

Reeling backward to establish a solid foothold, I laid eyes on, not one, but two additional colossal combatants standing on either side of the still downed Tiny. Equally as grotesque as their sidelined counterpart, they stood a healthy bit taller and appeared to be regulars at the local nepher gym as their hulking chests, shoulders, and arms absolutely bulged under their battle hardened armor.

"Howdy gents," I said catching my breath. "So, which one of you assholes is Hans and which one is Franz?"

Evidently not in the mood to entertain my questioning nor appreciating the reference, they dropped to a predatory crouch and methodically flanked me with weapons at the ready. Feeling a wave of turbo charged adrenaline, I focused on the gauntlets and apprehensively called for the fire. In response, a subtle layer of intense white flame covered my metal-shielded hands and flowed over the spatha like molten lava.

Although probably a hell of lot more efficient to hit these clowns with a blast of Gehenna fire, I wasn't exactly feeling 'firestorm capable' as my mind flashed with all the various and assorted apocalyptic fall out zones of ruinous devastation I'd inadvertently created in past attempts. Playing it safe — I figured I couldn't go wrong with the flaming sword gig.

As Hans, formerly known as Colossal Bad Guy Number One, thrust his mongo spear at my stomach and nearly turned me into a cloaked shish-kabob I sprung into action. With a single, blinding motion I ripped the spatha clear through the shaft of his giant skewer and fluidly cleaved his right leg off at the kneecap. As he awkwardly collapsed to the ground with a bloody stump for a leg and broke-ass spear, I kicked him squarely in the chest for good measure, and quickly shifted focus to Franz, formerly known as Colossal Bad Guy Number Two.

Just barely dodging his ridiculously large sword from removing my head, I spun to my right while lashing the spatha into his armored mid-section. The fire-smothered blade cut through the bronze plating like a hot knife through butter, as a macabre collection of oversized entrails poured from his lacerated torso and splattered a grisly crimson pattern across the white stone of the Dreghorn floor.

Roaring in primal pain that made my ears hurt, it dropped the mighty sword and grasped the open wound with both hands as I swung upward with all my force and removed its massive head with one strike. Collapsing to the ground like a felled tree, the giant carcass simply dematerialized and faded from being.

"Well done," patronizingly shouted a clapping Abernethy, "One out of three. At this pace, ye may even live long enough to see a fourth. May I offer a wee suggestion?"

Keeping a healthy distance from the incredibly pissed off, uni-legged giant bleeding out on the ground, I replied, "Does it involve you insulting my sword and/or my ability to use it properly?"

"Well, to be fair, it is a wee sword," he said while comparing the spatha to his claymore and chuckling. "But my point is this, Deanie. Ye have the strength of ten Deacons — that much is clear — but even you cannot defeat an army of anakim with just a sword, yer fists, and some puggled banter. And that's assuming yer swordsmanship was not the equivalent of a piece a' piss."

Making the mental note to ask him about that whole 'piece of piss' comment at a later time, I knew exactly what he was getting at.

"Gehenna fire," I muttered, somewhat rhetorically, while meeting his eyes.

"Aye. Unlike the rest of us, you've been graced with the ability to wield it well before yer time — with a force equal to that of the Alpha."

"I can't," I quickly replied. "Not yet."

"If yer afraid to try — you will ne'er succeed," he answered in a soft, fatherly tone.

"I can't control it," I shot back instantly overcome with unyielding doubt as the horrific image of the vindictive pillars of flame devouring the church in Brezovo Polje raced through my thoughts.

"Nae, you *can* control it. It's in yer heid."

"My heed?"

"Aye, yer heid." Reading my apparent blank look, he frustratingly added, "Yer heid, lad! The oof-lookin' thing sitting atop yer shoulders."

"My *head*," I muttered as a light bulb went off. "Right. Got it."

"Control the Wrath. Command the power," he stoically replied while tapping his sword on the arena floor. "Do not fear what you are." Slapping me forcefully on the shoulder, he added, "And don't think you'd be the first Deacon to set the Dreghorn alight."

Resting the claymore on his shoulder, he held out his left hand and the argent metal morphed into a translucent, ethereal material with a spectral flash. Holding out his palm, a perfect sphere of swirling white flame manifested and hovered for a quick second before launching from his hand and blasting Stumpy, until very recently known as Hans and formerly Colossal Bad Guy Number One, squarely in the chest. Poor bastard didn't even have a chance to scream before his massive, uni-legged frame flashed a brilliant white and dematerialized into nothing. Gone.

Completely dismissing the mind boggling, arcane feat like it was nothing more than blowing his nose, he said, "That's a wee drop in the bucket to what you're capable of. Find the Balance, lad. The fire will come."

"Understood," I said nodding acknowledgement.

"Pure dead brilliant," he muttered taking a few steps backward. "Because the anakim are not the only beasties ye need to concern yerself with."

"Awesome," I grumbled thinking that I was in for a long afternoon.

Chapter 21

Figuring it was a good idea to heed Abernethy's smug warning, I quickly turned to find faux-Tiny still laid up in a motionless heap on the arena floor. Picking up movement to my right, the cloak stirred uncomfortably about my shoulders as my latest opponent came into focus. But this time, it wasn't a giant.

It was a man of average height and weight casually dressed in khakis, a button down shirt, and tweed sport coat. Completing the look with some wire rimmed glasses and cute haircut sporting an abundance of gel, he looked like a frigg'n college professor. With a somewhat dry look about him, he slowly approached me, seemingly unarmed. Something was off about him though. His aura was wrong — wrought with a dark energy shadowed by claws and fangs. And death. Remembering Big A's earlier commentary and putting two and two together, I said, "So this is a gothen."

"One type, Aye. The gothen class nephilim are the dark creatures of legend and lore. The wretched things that go bump in the night. Beasties, lad. Aberrations of the hybrid breeding. Kin of the anakim, carried into the post flood world with a keen appetite for human flesh and souls that are black as the Earl of Hell's waistcoat. The heart and soul of the Maradim army."

"Awesome," I dryly said. "Beasties, eh? This guy looks pretty normal."

"Most will appear human until they take form. Others not so."

Meeting the intense gaze of Professor Snaggletooth, I said, "You said he's one type of gothen. How many are there?"

"All and all, there are five hundred and sixty-three primary species. The variations from cross breeding and mutations thereof are anybody's guess. The Guild stopped keeping track of the sub-classes some four centuries ago."

"What?" I blurted out. "Five hundred and sixty-three *species* — Fucking seriously?"

"Aye," he said amidst a chuckle. Nodding at the Professor slowly making a perimeter around us, he added, "This particular scunner is a draugr class — descended from the line of Nimrod — the cursed son of Ham. Feeding on the very life essence of man, the draugrs are a right nasty blight."

"The life essence of man," I muttered under my breath trying to process the information.

"Aye, but mostly they have a special thirst for blood. In Scottish lore they're called the Baobhan Sith. But you'll know them better as —"

"Vampires," I said cutting him off as it all started to make a semblance of sense. "Unbelievable. So, the whole 'they burst into flames in daylight' thing is bullshit, eh?"

"Aye," he replied laughing heartily. "Garlic, nor holy water, nor a wooden stake in the heart will do a wee bit of shite. Neither are they un-dead nor turn into bats nor slumber in coffins."

Completing his menacing circle and taking a post next to the still slumbering Tiny, the Professor simply stood there ominously as his aura fluctuated from that of a dark gray to a deep crimson red. Hearing footsteps to our rear, I turned to find a six foot something, burly looking character in jeans, a tight tee-shirt showing off his muscular torso, and a baseball cap strolling rather casually toward our location in the center of the Dreghorn. With a pronounced five o'clock shadow on his face, he took position adjacent the draugr and stared condescendingly at me with arms folded on his impressive chest.

"Another draugr?"

"Nae," Abernethy casually replied glancing at the newcomer. "A lycaon."

With an aura similar to the draugr, the lycaon seemed a bit more on the beastly end of the spectrum. A combination of ferocity, self-assurance, and primal strength emanated from his being. Without a doubt — something animalistic laid in wait beneath the skin.

"Fearless creatures they are," Big A said continuing with his explanation. "Carry the curse of the wolf. Their nature compels them to hunt — kill — devour. Foul gits. Fast healers. Short tempers."

"That's cute," I dryly muttered, "Vampires and werewolves. Feel like I'm in a bad eighties movie. What next ..."

Evidently not clear that it was more a rhetorical question, two additional dark aura'd cronies approached from our right and took position next to Teen Wolf Senior and the Professor of Applied Bloodletting. The first, a vertically challenged yet devilishly handsome gent sporting blue board shorts and a really obnoxious Hawaiian shirt. Not sure he could have looked any more non-threatening if he tried. Taking his position, he even offered me a polite bow and courteous nod.

And the second, a tall, slender blond bombshell with high cheek bones and brilliant blue eyes all dolled up in black leather pants, knee length biker boots, and a white tank top that was delightfully four sizes too small. Artfully decorating her sculpted arms were a series of interwoven black, glyph-like, tattoos that elegantly flowed from the back of her hands to the very peak of her shoulders and well into the crook of her neck.

"Let me guess," I said pointing at the latest edition to the Cirque de Neph. "He's the infamous Magnum PI of the Shire and she's the Wicked Swedish Bikini Model of the West."

"Nae," grumbled my Scottish mentor while shaking his head. Giving me an exasperated look, he said, "Ye truly are a daft lad."

"Thank You," I said snidely.

"Was not a compliment," he grumbled in return.

"Oh, well, no thank you then."

The icy stare followed by the thought of getting blind-sided by another log sized projectile in the chest wiped the smug look off my face rather quickly. Hanging his head and momentarily staring at the ground, he grunted under his breath, "Bloody hell, he's a daft one."

As he quickly composed himself and was about to school me on the latest editions to the gothen family reunion, yet another nepher strolled into the arena.

A nepher that I knew.

"Brought out the usual suspects I see," Rooster said to Big A as he walked toward us and glanced at Tiny, the draugr, the lycaon, and the yet unidentified Evil Hooters Girl. Upon seeing the dapper, Hawaiian shirt clad little fellow who may have stood five feet tall if wearing a pair of eight-inch heels — which he wasn't, he exclaimed, "Oh snap, you brought out a korrigan? Not holding back, eh?"

"Aye," Abernethy grunted seemingly very happy that he was no longer stuck alone with me in the Dreghorn. "Dean is about to talk him into submission with sage insight and dighted wit. Where ye been, Jackie?"

"Sorry, boss. Been in the armory. Had to finish up that special project for the newbie here."

"The thunder stick — Good timing. He may just need it after all. Does it work?"

"Absolutely," Rooster replied with an unconvinced look. "Well, I'm pretty sure. Actually didn't have time to run the full round of tests … but it should be fine."

"Thunder stick?" I said trying to break into the conversation.

"Yeppers," Rooster replied trading glances with Big A.

When no further information was offered I gave them both a glare of frustrated suspicion, and said, "Ok. Whatever. What the hell's a korrigan then?" Pointing at the pint-sized surfer, I asked, "Are you telling me Mr. Frodo over there's a gothen? Looks like more of a carny for Christ's sake. Small hands. Smells like cabbage."

Although I got a mild chuckle out of Rooster, Big A was evidently all set with my 'dighted wit' and didn't so much as crack a smile.

"Taking the form of wee humans, the korrigan class are forest dwellers at heart. Kin to a dwarf but stroppy as a hive of bees set aflame. Connivers, thieves, and knaves. Obsessed with wealth. Always looking to strike a deal. The wee blights thrive off the pain and suffering they inflict on the race of man. They'll be yer best friend until ye cross'em. Then their true form comes out. Ruthless bastarts — the korrigans. Vicious."

"Ruthless *and* vicious, eh? Ok, take your word for it," I muttered, completely unconvinced, as the little fellow waived congenially at me. "And Daisy Duke? What's her deal?" I asked while shifting focus to tall, blond, and leather.

Another inadvertent chuckle from Rooster earned him a stiff slap on the back of the 'heid' from the archdeacon.

"Aye, the best for last. *That* is no lassie, mate. It's a varangian. The berserkers of Norse legend — twisted with fury and spawn of wild rage. In days of old it was believed they wore the pelts of bears into battle, which gave them super human strength and speed."

Taking a closer look at the varangian, I was drawn to its aura. Similar to the others it was dark, but unlike the others it swirled and surged with madness. Like it was perpetually fighting itself to restrain the endless fury caged within.

"But lad," said Abernethy continuing with his lecture, "they were not covered in pelts. It was their true form. Hexed of the bear they are nigh unrivaled in strength, and averse to pain. Fiercely loyal to their master 'til death do part, they are. The ultimate blunt instrument in battle."

"So, the hot chick — is a bear monster. Didn't see that coming," I grumbled fixated on the indescribable violent nature of the varangian's aura lurching and lashing out with claw tipped tendrils. Looking around the Dreghorn for the next edition to the party, I said, "Ok. So, who's next?"

"This lot will do for now," said Abernethy, taking a few steps backward. "Clear yer mind, lad. And ne'er underestimate yer enemy, nor their fear and hatred of what ye represent. Prepare yerself. Ye have ten seconds before I let 'em loose."

Giving Abernethy a stern nod, I turned to face the Not So Fantastic Four and lowered my head to focus. As the serene sensation washed over me, I felt the Wrath welling in the deep recess of my soul, and raised my head as a mild grin stretched across my face.

For my right hand, I willed the argent metal gauntlet into being and felt it manifest with a spectral flash. Reaching back and drawing the spatha, I felt the distinct hum of energy as it released from the scabbard and readied for battle. For my left hand, I called for the ethereal gauntlet and watched with great anticipation as it manifested and covered my hand in shimmering, translucent energy.

Holding my palm toward the enemy, I called for the judgment — Gehenna fire. Painfully squinting in concentration, the gauntlet ignited with subtle flame, and a perfect sphere of wraithlike white fire carefully formed and slowly spun in my hand. Crackling and hissing with abstract heat and intangible power, it waited with perfect patience to be released upon my enemies.

"Well done, laddie," proudly bellowed a beaming Abernethy. Turning to Rooster, he muttered under his breath, "Maybe we won't need that wee thunder stick of yours after all." Focusing his attention back to me, he said, "Now focus."

With a wave of his hand, the odd collection of gothen sprang into action, and although I hate to admit it — I was not expecting what followed.

The first to act was the korrigan. And believe it or not, the son of a bitch shrunk a solid two feet. Within the blink of an eye he nephed out, and the kindly, vertically challenged little fellow was replaced by a gnome-like, squat creature of leathery dark brown skin with a ridiculously large head and pointy ears. As his grotesque face stretched into a devious smile, bearing two rows of unevenly spaced jagged teeth, he launched at me brandishing a small dagger he pulled from somewhere in his absurd outfit.

Covering the ten feet between us in the matter of a split second, I barely dodged its knife as the little bastard raked a clawed hand across my face as he streaked by my head in a blur of motion. Caught completely off guard, I awkwardly spun to the right and inadvertently launched the ball of Gehenna fire in the direction of Abernethy and Rooster. As they ducked and leapt to safety, I watched, in dismay, as the fire bolt sailed clear into the distant stadium seats of the Dreghorn and obliterated an entire section in a white-blazed mushroom cloud of rock and smoke. It would have been really frigg'n impressive if not a complete blunder.

"Oops," I muttered while shooting them a 'my bad' glance.

Jumping to their feet, they both took several more steps backward.

Turning to Rooster, Big A grumbled, "On second thought — Get the thunder stick ready."

Figuring my fire throwing exploits were still not quite ready for prime time, I called for the ashen hellstone and felt it encase my left hand as I swatted at the korrigan, who made a second pass at my face with blinding speed. Dodging his blade at the last second, I caught the little fucker in the ribcage with my gauntlet and sent him hurling through the air like a gremlin-sized football until he crashed to a halt on the Dreghorn floor behind his pals. As a drop of blood trickled onto my lips, I willed the stone gauntlet into momentary retreat and placed my bare hand on the sizable gash running down the side of my face.

"Focus! Stay in Balance or bleed at the hands of yer opponent," called out Abernethy from the peanut gallery. "Know yer enemy. *See* their attack."

Nodding acknowledgement, I quickly cleared my thoughts as a stiff electric like jolt of energy passed through me and the wound instantly healed upon itself. Getting back on his feet, which actually looked more like hooves, the korrigan produced a second dagger and readied for another assault. Taking the creepy little bastards flank, the lycaon and varangian joined the fray and fixed me with a pair of predatory glares.

"Awe, Yer in fer it now, laddie," bellowed Abernethy chuckling.

Muttering something under his breath to Rooster, they both took a few more steps backward. Highly pissed that I just let Nepher Smurf get the better of me, I set my feet into a bold offensive stance and tightened the grip on the spatha as wave after wave of surging adrenaline pumped through my system. Covering my left hand with the ethereal gauntlet, I held my palm toward my attackers and called for the fire.

This time though, I didn't conjure a well formed sphere of flaming destruction — it was more of a volcano-like column of fiery apocalypse. And it immediately hurled itself from my gauntlet like a poorly aimed scatter shot and blasted erratically through the formation of gothen, not really doing much of anything except piss them off. Not exactly the desired effect.

"Son of a bitch," I muttered as they gave me a collective snide glance.

Not waiting around for me to figure out how in the hell to actually wield the Gehenna fire, the varangian nephed out first. And damn — it was a frigg'n spectacle. The six-foot Norse goddess of tits and leather morphed into a nightmarish eight-foot beast with the head of a rabies stricken black grisly and the humanoid furry body to go along with it. Standing rather intimidatingly on two ginormous, clawed feet, she held out her powerful arms, which were a creepy mixture of flesh and animal pelt as she let out a roar that literally shook the ground of the arena. Dropping to all fours, her claw tipped, paw-like hands ripped into the stone floor, and her mouth foamed with unbound rage as she continued to growl at me like a frigg'n — well, like a frigg'n supernatural bear creature. Not entirely sure why the whole thing surprised me actually.

"And here I was thinking the wet tee-shirt contest was about to start," I muttered while taking in the whole beastly package.

Taking a few predatory steps in my direction, she was joined by a really frigg'n pissed off evil midget, wielding a couple of daggers and primed for round two. Not wanting to miss out on the melee nor take second hat to his beastly buddies, the lycaon started sprinting at me with unnatural speed. Literally taking form in mid-stride, the son of bitch's face morphed into a menacing maw bearing super-sized canine fangs, quickly followed by the rest of its head going full-on wolf. With eyes as black as pools of oil and thirsting for the kill, it charged at me in a blur of motion. Dropping to all fours within about five feet from me, his clothes ripped from his body in tattered fragments. Fully morphed into a steroid infused super wolf, the four hundred pounds of fangs, claws, and hybrid mutation then made one hell of a ferocious strike at my jugular with his gaping maw stretched out like a shark about to inhale a seal.

Ironically, if I wasn't expecting the stupid bastard to do exactly that, I would've probably been up shit's creek. Fortunately for me that wasn't the case.

Feeling the mental switch flip to the on position and the calmative awareness pass over me, I casually drifted to my right as the mutant wolf glided past my head in extreme slow motion, snapping his mighty jaws shut where my neck should have been. Tightening the grip on the spatha, I then simply lopped the shaggy fucker's head clean off the rest of its super sized canine body in a single stroke. As Wonder Mutt dematerialized in mid air with a flash of light, I immediately felt the cloak ripple violently about my shoulders, and instinctively spun away from a swiping razor tipped paw followed by the bum rush of the eight-foot biker bitch bear monster attached to it.

Quickly reestablishing my footing and gaining some standoff distance from mama bear, I felt the lawn gnome creeping in on me from my six o'clock. Fixing the varangian with a stern glare, I let the korrigan continue his advance on me from the rear as I covered my left hand in ashen hellstone. Curling my hand into a tight fist, I felt the little fucker launch his strike and casually side stepped to my right while swinging my stone fisted hand back to meet his big-eared face with a bone splitting clack. Spinning backward in a blur of motion, I then ripped the spatha through his grotesque, leathery torso cutting the wee bastard clear in half. Screaming and cursing at me as his various and assorted body parts plummeted to the Dreghorn floor with a series of thuds, I planted a boot square in its face, instantly ending the chatter.

Turning again to face the varangian, she was back on two feet and slowly circling me in a state of pissed off fury. Reaching back over her mammoth shoulders, she produced a honed double-edged battle-axe from somewhere amidst her bearish human backside.

It was awkward for a second or two as I wondered exactly where she'd been hiding it this whole time. Figuring that particular detail was rather insignificant at the current moment, I got back to business.

Hissing and growling at me through a snarled, teeth filled maw she readied for her next move as Professor Snaggletooth finally decided to join the party. Casually removing his tweed sport coat and carefully laying it on the floor next to the still slumbering Tiny, the draugr then proceeded to nonchalantly roll up his sleeves and remove his glasses. Producing a sleek scabbard he'd cleverly concealed in his khakis, he unsheathed one of those samurai looking Japanese swords.

Evidently he wasn't happy to see me after all — it actually was a sword in his pants. Never seen that particular maneuver before.

Feeling rather assured about my manhood, I watched suspiciously as he flicked the nimble blade through the air a few times in a presumptuous show of force and joined the varangian apparently ready to actually start fighting.

Half expecting him to sprout wings or bust out a red cravat and a ruffled white shirt, I was rather disappointed by the fact that the only indication he wasn't human was a whitish silver sheen overtaking his eyes. It was certainly creepy as all hell, but not remotely as extreme as I was anticipating. Not sure if that was actually a good thing I readied for the coming onslaught nonetheless.

Offering the varangian a friendly 'after you' nod, the draugr flashed me a dark smile as the eight foot, frothing at the mouth bear beastie tossed the battle axe into the air and dropped to all fours. Holding her mammoth head upward, she caught the axe handle effortlessly between her outstretched jaws and charged me head on, as muscle rippled beneath the fur and pelt of her freakish extremities. Setting my feet and focusing my will, I raised the spatha in my right hand while clenching my left hand into a stone covered fist. Within a few steps from me, she then did something I wasn't remotely prepared for. Flipping the axe in the air with her snarling mouth, she fluidly transitioned back to two feet while wrapping both hands, or rather gnarly paws, around the tarnished hilt, and brought it straight into my midsection in a blinding flash.

As the cloak violently rippled, I reeled backward and to the left, trying to avoid certain evisceration. Only partially succeeding I grunted in intense, burning pain as the honed blade ripped through the cloak and got a couple inches of my right abdomen in the process, opening a nasty slit. Barely swinging the spatha in time to parry the full brunt of the strike, I defensively jabbed at the varangian with my stone fist and landed a lucky punch square in her big-ass nose. As her eyes instantly crossed, and I knew from experience her vision blurred, I got the couple seconds I needed to regroup. Taking advantage of the situation, I threw a stiff elbow in the bitch's furry throat, and followed it with a stone bolstered left to the gut sending her staggering backward.

"Hurts don't it," I snarled while grabbing my bloody side.

Again setting my feet and feeling a steady stream of blood seep from the impressive laceration on my stomach, I caught a glimpse of movement from above and realized the draugr was taking the opportunity to come in for the kill.

And damn, that fucker had some serious ups.

Not getting a real fix on him, I instinctively raised the spatha above my head just in time to meet his other worldly ginsu knife swinging with supernatural strength straight down at my head like he was planning to slice me down the middle. Momentarily shell shocked and completely taken aback by his speed, I watched in awe as he nimbly landed on his feet directly opposite me and blasted me square in the face with the sword hilt before I even knew what was happening. Letting out a pissed off grunt, I took an awkward step backward with blood pouring from my nose like a damn faucet as Abernethy yelled, "Strength and anger won't get you outta this mess, lad! Clear yer mind! See their attack!"

With the draugr mere steps away and methodically charging me while waving his sword around like some shit out of a Bruce Lee movie, I lowered the spatha and closed my eyes.

Released the anger.

Cleared my mind.

Found the Balance.

As the raw power raced through me like a bolt of electricity, I felt my wounds instantly heal themselves, and sensed the draugr's sword swinging toward my neck like a free falling guillotine blade. Opening my eyes and shooting him a droll glance, I casually reached upward with my stone covered left hand and caught his blade inches from lashing into my neck. Ripping the sword from his hand and effortlessly throwing it clear out of the Dreghorn, I then shattered his nose with a healthy head-butt and followed it with a kick to the chest, sending his blood sucking ass hurling a solid twenty feet backward.

"Didn't see that shit on the Lost Boys, eh?" I muttered giving him a victorious glare.

Feeling pretty good about myself and clearly back in control of the situation, I heard Rooster frantically yell, "Dean! Look out!"

It was right about then that the eight foot, five-hundred pounds of super humanoid bear nepher tackled me from the blind side like LT taking down a quarterback after an eighties bender of cocaine and hookers. I didn't even have a chance to say 'friggn owe' before the varangian absolutely leveled me like a furry projectile. It was textbook.

As my body hit the stone floor with the force of a plane crash, the spatha flew from my hand and I found myself on the wrong end of an epic bear fight. Pinning me down with her massive girth, she proceeded to literally beat the ever living shit out of me as I quickly lost count of how many razor tipped paws pummeled my face and upper body. By the grace of God, quite literally, I was able to cover my face with my arms and the cloak and gauntlets prevented any serious damage.

Absorbing blow after blow in a very un-Deacon like position on the Dreghorn floor, I heard an approaching Abernethy say, "Gotta say, lad. I'm impressed ye lasted this long."

"Thanks for that," I grunted while shielding my face as the varangian feverishly ripped, lashed, and struck at me in a relentless state of maddened fury while keeping me pinned to the ground.

"May I offer ye a wee suggestion?"

"All ears!"

"Well," he said patiently, "It may be a keen time to call fer the fire, yeah?"

"Because that worked so well the first two times? Not really sure I can concentrate at the moment," I yelled as a paw landed squarely in my mid-section causing me to groan. "Little busy here!"

"Aye," he said letting out a hearty chuckle at my situation. "Perhaps the Rooster can help ye with yer ability to focus. I had high hopes we wouldn't need to use it but unless yer plan is to wait there until the beastie tires of hitting yer face I think we're right out of options." Pausing for a moment, he yelled out, "Jackie! Bring the wee thunder stick over. Let Dean have a go at it."

Raising my arms slightly off my face to take a peek at Big A, I saw Rooster tentatively approaching me while carefully avoiding the flailing paws of the perpetual varangian pummel fest. Dropping to knee a safe distance away, he said, "Hey buddy, How's it going?"

"Fucking great," I grunted catching a furry fist in the gut. "How are you?"

"Brought you a present," he said producing a dark leather, scabbard-sized holster.

"Is it a bear trap?" I said while quickly lowering my arms over my face again as I felt a horrendous claw scraping against my metal gauntlet.

"Sort of," he snidely replied while pulling an antique looking lever action shotgun with a sawed off barrel and wooden pistol grip stock out of the large holster. "This, my friend, is a genuine hero model 1897 Winchester. Fully customized, of course, with some nifty bells and whistles." Gazing at the impressive weapon like it was his child, he added, "Made for you and you only. First of its kind."

"That's great," I grumbled between grunts, "but last I checked — guns didn't do shit to nephers."

"Ah, but *this* gun is different. With a barrel forged of barzel, it shoots Gehenna fire rounds. You see, through years of experimentation and —"

"Skip to the end goddamit! How do I operate the fucking thing?" I yelled, cutting him off in mid-pontification as a solid swat to my sternum made me yelp in pain.

"Oh — ah, right — Sorry. Ah, the gun acts as a foci, allowing you to instantly concentrate your ability to wield the judgment. As you call for the fire, simply charge the lever and you've loaded a round. You can figure out the rest."

Raising my arms to look him in the eye, I yelled, "On three. Toss it."

As Rooster nodded acknowledgement, I channeled all my remaining strength, and yelled, "One!"

Reaching out with my gauntlet covered hands, I firmly grasped the incoming paws of fury and violently yanked downward bringing the mammoth head of the varangian lurching toward me. "Two!"

Putting all my force into a powerful sit-up, I lurched my torso upward and head butted that fucker as hard as I possible could. "Three!"

Whether it was the mere shock factor of the unexpected maneuver or the fact that I'd actually hurt the supernatural bear beastie, I couldn't be sure — but as it let out an ear splitting howl and flared backward covering its face, I reached out and caught the gun with my right hand. Calling for the fire, I then cocked the lever, jammed the stout barrel of the Holy Shotgun of Antioch squarely in the varangian's wooly chest, and very happily squeezed the trigger. And, although it most certainly was no Bertha, it was pretty fucking impressive.

As my hand blew backward from the recoil, I watched in gleeful wonderment as a devastating blast of judgment fire exited the muzzle and blew clear through the unnatural upper body of my over zealous opponent as the reek of incinerated furry flesh overpowered my nostrils. Letting out a ferocious, yet very short-lived, human-like scream the varangian slumped backward to the arena floor and quickly took the form of a naked, very hot blonde chick before dematerializing in a brilliant flash of white radiance. Still a bit stunned by the whole experience, I simply sat there for a second or two staring at the uncanny Winchester.

"You done good Chickenman," I muttered looking up at a beaming Rooster. "Real good."

Turning to Abernethy, Rooster said, "I told you it would work!"

"Aye. Well done, lad," replied the Scotsman, bending over and offering me a hand. "On yer feet, Dean. And watch where yer pointing that pop-gun." Pulling me up, he glanced at the approaching draugr, and said, "So, Now that ye have yer new toy — you care to finish things up here?"

Feeling the warm sensation pulse through my body restoring me to a state of perfection, I rolled my head back on my shoulders, and said, "Hells Yes," as I made a determined beeline for the Count.

Evidently all set with his aerial display of acrobatics and ninja-like sword twirling, the draugr boldly marched straight toward me with a rather intimidating scowl plastered across his pretty face. With each deliberate step, his whitish silver eyes steadily grew in intensity until they almost glowed like car headlights. Within about ten feet from me they flashed and turned solid black and he gracefully nephed out in mid-stride. Growing easily a foot in height, his unimpressive frame morphed into that of a body builder cut from stone and evidently on a very high protein diet. His skin instantly shifted from a Caucasian spray tanned orange to that of a leathery dark gray, and quite repulsive. And, of course, he smiled to reveal some rather imposing fang like incisors of a deep yellowish sheen, and honestly pretty frigg'n gross.

I think he was actually about to say something to me when I casually called for the fire, cocked the shotgun lever, and put a round through his throat. Sizzle of flesh — flash of light — no more draugr.

"Yep. Not sure we had anything meaningful to talk about, asshole," I muttered while turning and strolling back toward Big A and Rooster.

Passing a now stirring faux-Tiny with the shotgun propped on my shoulder, I placed a boot in the side of his jumbo head just for good measure. I didn't even slow down as he scornfully grunted and started to awkwardly push himself off the stone floor and stagger to his feet in a drunken like haze.

With my back to the giant, I joined my otherworldly colleagues within a few steps as Rooster tossed me the leather holster for the Winchester. "Thanks, Pilgrim," I said with my very best John Wayne impersonation while catching it and sheathing the shotgun.

"My pleasure," he replied still beaming at the effectiveness of his handy work. Pointing at the holster, he said, "You'll find that it sits very nicely on your back. I had fourteen years to get the measurements right."

Ignoring the mental image that came to mind of Rooster taking my 'measurements' while all sprawled out in a decade plus of stasis, I turned to Big A, and said, "So, we all set here, boss?"

Opening his mouth to reply, he abruptly stopped and took a step backward as his gaze drifted upward with widened eyes. Hearing the pounding of giant footsteps behind me, I casually unsheathed the Winchester, flipped him the holster, and focused for a quick second. Not bothering to turn around, I then cocked the lever, reached backward with the barrel, and squeezed the trigger.

Following the intangible blast that roared from the muzzle was the expected flop of a colossal body on the arena floor by my feet. As fake Tiny's massive axe flew from his lifeless hands and noisily tumbled along the white stone toward Rooster, a flash of brilliant white light signified that the giant had officially left the building. Giving Big A a self-assured glare, I grabbed the holster, again sheathed the shotgun, and said, "We done here?"

"Bloody hell," he muttered somewhat awestruck. "That'll do for now, lad. Aye, That'll do."

Chapter 22

As six hellacious chimes rung out from the centuries old grandfather clock in the corner of the dimly lit room, the dinner crowd took their collective cue and began to vacate the Quartermaster. The spectacle of hundreds of people systemically dispersing through the various arcane doorways or simply vanishing in mid stride was absolutely nothing in comparison to the spectacle of the asshole sitting on the stool next to me systematically devouring a mound of extra crispy bacon while relentlessly puffing on a pipe. Not acknowledging my presence in the least, he'd occasionally pause to take a healthy swig from a bottle of aged scotch.

"So, How you been, Fred?" I dryly asked the frail, crusty old bastard without much enthusiasm after a few painful minutes of silence.

"Better than you, schmendrick," he replied between voracious bites and plumes of smoke.

"That's some clean living," I said giving his dinner a curious glance. "Must be the secret to your youthful veneer."

Continuing to stuff the heart attack on a plate in his mouth like he was afraid somebody was going to take it away from him, he patronizingly stared at me with blood shot, beady eyes, and grumbled, "I like bacon. What's it to you? O'Dargan's a schmuck but he knows how to smoke a pig. I'll give'em that."

"Can I get you a bag of chips and a side of mayo? Really round out the food groups?"

"Where is O'Dargan anyway?" He grumbled completely ignoring my commentary.

Knocking back the remnants of the frosty beer Rooster poured me before he and Big A were rather abruptly summoned to the Reliquary, I muttered, "Busy."

"I would imagine so," he replied snidely. "The reckoning is near. Isn't it, schmendrick?"

Hearing Stephen's words played back to me sent an immediate chill down my spine. As the magnitude of the statement registered with my brain, I carefully placed the empty mug on the bar, and said, "What did you say?"

"You heard me," he replied while taking a healthy swig of booze. Momentarily at a loss for words, I fixed him with an intent stare. Slipping into a trancelike state, his gaze fell toward the bar and he methodically muttered,

"*The giants of old will grow legion upon the Earth,*
When Wrath comes upon the Seventh of the line of Seven.
The fallen Sons will shed their earthly bond,
And the screams of man will deafen the Realms of Heaven."

Returning to his normal, crotchety demeanor, he smiled and smugly said, "You really don't know, do you?"

"Know what?" I sternly asked glaring at him taken aback by his recitation of what I presumed to be the Son of Wrath prophecy.

"Know what ...," he mockingly muttered to himself shaking his head. Placing his lit pipe on the bar, he looked me squarely in the eye and barked, "The prophecy, you schmendrick! The rebirth of the anakim, the ascension of the fallen Watchers — all the other crazy shit going on." Aggressively leaning toward me, he said with marked conviction, "I've seen it! Fire. Blood. Rage. *It* will burn."

Jumping to his feet and sticking a boney finger in my chest, he growled with gritted teeth, "By *your* hand — *it* will burn."

"What are you talking about?" I said pushing his hand away. "What'll burn?"

"All of it," he blankly replied while slumping back on the stool and grabbing the bottle. "Everything."

As I sat in silence contemplating what in the hell he was going on about, the intensity of the moment was broken by a familiar whisper-like shriek and a blast of wind on my back.

"Frederick Binkowicz! Oy gavalt," exclaimed Mariel as she appeared on the stool next to Fred and glared disgustingly at the half eaten plate of bacon. "You certainly *are not* keeping kosher."

In a flash of light, his plate of prized pig evaporated from the bar and the bottle of liquor vanished from his hand.

Not reacting in the least, Fred shot her a dirty look and despondently grumbled, "What the hell do you care, M? A couple slices of bacon never killed a Jew the last I checked. Get over it already!" Getting to his feet in a drunken haze, he threw on his overcoat, grabbed his pipe, and faced me with a strangely genuine look on his face. "There's one more thing."

"Ok."

"That which binds," he muttered in a somewhat sober tone. "You are not beholden to it."

"Come again?"

"You are not beholden to it," he repeated ignoring my question. "Its power — is yours to command."

Returning to his crotchety self, he then staggered toward the door and disappeared into the wintry, Boston night. Not really sure what else to say, I just sat there for a long moment looking at M with a blank look.

"Poor Frederick. He's a terrible, terrible nudnik. It's not his fault, Bubbala," she said, shaking her head with a look of solemn concern. "To be a prophet of the Father is to shoulder a grave burden."

"A prophet," I muttered. "*Fred* — is a prophet?"

"Of course he is," she quickly replied while folding her hands on the bar. "Not a particularly bad one either. But, like all prophets — he doesn't know bupkes. They only See shreds of things to come. One drop in a sea of possibilities."

Thinking back to the conversation with Stephen during the 'tea party' at Raven Spire, I stared at my empty mug and asked, "What else does the Son of Wrath prophecy foretell — about me?"

"Why do you concern yourself with such things, Bubbala?" She said with a somewhat solemn look that seemed a bit atypical for Mariel. "Prophecies are simply words on a parchment." With a swift hand gesture, she added, "Nothing more. Bupkes."

"Fred just told me 'it would burn.' *By my hand*, it would burn," I said meeting her soft yet pensive gaze. "And what the hell was he going on about before he walked out? What does any of it mean?"

"Well, it could mean that Frederick had an incredibly powerful vision of your path," she said earnestly. "But more than likely — it's an indication the poor shlep drank too much. Are you not listening to me? It's bupkes, fersthay? Period — End of story."

With intense consternation I simply sat there stewing on the fact that M was clearly not telling me something. As if reading my thoughts, she gracefully transitioned to the stool next me, in a fluid flash of light, and placed her hand on my forearm.

"Don't confuse the words of prophets with your chosen path, Bubbala," she said with a warm smile. "It's not good for the digestion."

Upon her touch I felt a serene sensation wash over me and couldn't help but chuckle a bit as I muttered, "Fair enough."

Feeling the need for another frosty beverage, I looked around the massive room to find it completely empty with exception to the two of us. Figuring it was just bad business to leave the bar untended, I casually hopped to the other side and held my mug under a wooden keg labeled *RoosterBragh Red Ale.*

"Care to join me for a drink?" I called back to M as I grabbed a second mug and began pouring. When she didn't answer I turned my head back toward the bar only to find an empty stool where she sat mere seconds earlier.

"Like the wind," I grumbled under my breath. "More for me."

Jumping back to my stool with two man sized beers and a strong desire to rapidly consume both of them, the booming disembodied voice of my favorite divine bowling ball echoed through the massive room scaring the ever living shit of me.

"Deacon Robinson, the archdeacon requests your presence in the Reliquary."

Awkwardly juggling the mug that nearly flew from my hands, I grumbled, "Seriously? Can't it wait a minute? I got a beverage here, Skyphos."

"*Would you like me to inform the archdeacon that you are indisposed?*"

Begrudgingly placing the RoosterBragh on the bar, I had a quick vision of catching a log in the side of the head and muttered, "Nope. On my way."

Quickly slugging back the first mug, I longingly looked at the second, and said, "Don't go anywhere. I'll be right back."

⁂

Unlike the last time I was in the Reliquary, it was crammed full of people and hopping like a Night at the Roxbury minus the disco ball, thumping music, and two dudes bobbing their heads to the beat. Every desk surrounding the floating command bridge was occupied by at least three Guild members furiously working the virtual screens and talking loudly on old-fashioned telephones while scribbling notes.

The larger than life tV monitors lining the walls flitted with various streams of data, maps pulsing with countless dots and concentric circles, and live teleLink feeds from dozens of field operatives in undisclosed locations. Although I'd seen several military war rooms in action, I'd never seen anything quite like this. It was like Captain Jean-Luc Picard and Number One were having a frigg'n party with Dr. Strangelove on the holodeck. Looking around in complete sensory overload I was snapped back into the moment by a bellowing Scotsman yell, "Dean! Up here. Hurry, lad!"

Racing up the thirty feet of spiral staircase in a matter of seconds, I reached the command bridge to find Abernethy, Rooster, and Tango huddled around a large floating screen displaying a wiry gent with a cleanly shaven head sporting a faded, and somewhat tattered, crimson hoodie with the sleeves cut off at the shoulders. His rather impressive, and heavily tattooed biceps, combined with intense brown eyes, scraggly red goatee, and cheek full of chewing tobacco gave him some pretty legit '*He might be a Red Neck*' credibility. It also appeared he had a stout longbow and quiver of curious looking broad-head arrows slung across his back.

Reaching the group, I heard him say with a thick southern drawl, "Don't know what to tell Y'all. We were chasing our tails trying to figure out how that anakim pack ported to Tallahassee right under our noses when Smitty showed up." Pausing to spit some tobacco juice, he said, "He wanted to see the farm on the outskirts of town where the biggins chowed down on the fifty-some-odd cattle. Kept saying we were missing something. Truth be told, he was dagum obsessed over it. Once we got there, he started acting all squirly. Got real anxious. Drew his sword and walked off into the wood line. Told us to wait for him."

"Was that the last you saw of him, Coop?" Asked a clearly troubled Abernethy.

"Yessir, that was last night. Haven't seen 'em since. He ain't answering teleLink either." With a look of sincere concern, he asked, "Has he checked in with Y'all?"

"Nae," Big A muttered after a prolonged sigh. "We've not heard from him in near three days now. Nor is he visible to Skyphos." Frustratingly sighing again, he tentatively asked, "Did he say anything else? Mention — a coin, perhaps?"

"Nossir," Coop replied, very southernly, while shaking his head. "That was it. He just up and left."

"Damn it all," grumbled Abernethy under his breath averting his gaze from the screen. Focusing again on the unidentified arrow toting country boy, he said, "Mind yerself, Cooper. Stay in close contact. Trust no one without good reason."

"Durn skippy, boss. I'll be aw'ite. Y'all watch your back."

As the screen faded, Rooster leaned over to me with a grave look and said, "That was Cooper Rayfield — the cleric that oversees the southern region of the US." Pausing to compose himself, he said, "Smitty's gone, Dean. It's happened again."

As the vision of the flaming prison and collection of shackled Deacons flashed through my thoughts, I felt a lump form in my throat as I stood in uncomfortable silence. Desperately wanting to tell them what I'd seen — what I knew, I said nothing.

Turning to the face the group, Abernethy loomed in brooding defeat with his head hung low for a few awkward moments.

"Henry's fallen, lads," he said in a dejected tone. "The black souled bastarts ended him. May this be the last bloody time the Maradim robs us of a kinsman." Turning to Rooster and Tango, he grumbled, "I need to see the Alpha."

As his cloak manifested upon his massive shoulders in a spectral flash, he barked, "We will morn for Henry when the ground runs red with the bastarts blood! Find them, lads! Find where they skulk. The fight's at our very doorstep."

With a deep scowl plastered across his face, he turned and faded into the doorway that instantly manifested to his rear and was gone in a brief flash of white light.

"Sorry about Smitty, man," Tango said turning to Rooster and grasping him on the shoulder. "Never thought anything could take him down. Toughest son of a bitch I've ever known."

Momentarily at a loss for words, Rooster's skin turned exceptionally red as he blankly stared at the giant tV monitor covering the wall to his front while shaking his head. Figuring it was best to leave him be, Tango again patted him on the shoulder, and said, "I'm gonna port to Tallahassee and go through the throneView feed again with Coop. Smitty's right. We're missing something here. Call you in fifteen."

Giving me a humble nod, he disappeared through a doorway that subtly manifested near the stairway of the command bridge and faded across the threshold.

Not acknowledging my presence in the least, a sullen Rooster stared at the screen in deep thought while occasionally muttering something to himself. After what seemed like an eternity, his skin returned to a normal shade as he turned to me, and said, "Doesn't make any sense. Smitty represents the fifth Deacon in five years that the Seventh Realm has lost. It's always the same. One minute they're fine. The next — gone. Off the grid. Vanished. Ended. Dead. Shouldn't be possible."

"Five Deacons," I muttered. "That would mean —"

“That’s right, Dean. Only two remain in the Seventh Realm. Abernethy — and you.”

“What about the other Realms?” I said picturing the circle of Azazel’s captives. “How many Deacons are left of the forty nine?”

“Don’t know,” he replied shifting his attention back to the mass of tV monitors covering the wall. “That’s not exactly common knowledge. The archdeacons play stuff like that pretty close to the vest. I mean, there’s been rumors of losses across the Seven Realms but nothing definitive.” Reaching into the floating virtual base console, he began to flip some semi translucent tiles of data through the air to his front. “It’s been consistent for the past fourteen years — Azazel and his Maradim get stronger and we get weaker. He’s systemically decimating us. Don’t know how — but he is.”

“Attrition strategy,” I said somewhat under my breath.

“Seems it. Leveling the playing field for an all out assault on Tartarus with a shit ton of anakim and rogue gothen. Azazel won’t stop until the fallen Watchers, his twisted brothers, are freed. He’ll raze the Earth with a smile on his face to make it happen. And without the Deacons to stop him, he might actually pull it off this time.”

“What do you know of the holy flame?” I inadvertently asked while contemplating the doomsday scenario.

“Not much,” he replied while giving me an inquisitive glance. “Old Testament stuff. Powerful. Sort of like Gehenna fire but worse. According to lore it can literally strip angels of their grace. Far as I know, it can only be summoned by two beings. The Father himself — and the archangels. Why do you ask?”

As I fumbled for an answer that wouldn’t seem any more suspicious than asking the question in the first place, we were interrupted by Skyphos.

“Pardon me, Rooster, There is an incoming teleLink from Cleric Jefferson. Would you like me to connect you?”

““That was quick. Yes Please,” he replied immediately shifting his attention from me to the translucent screen manifesting to our front. As a vision of Tango standing next to the previously identified Cooper Rayfield came into focus, he said, “Please tell me you got something.”

"I got something," Tango said with a mixture of excitement and intensity. "The fucking Skipper. He was here — in Tallahassee, the day before the anakim showed up."

"Wait — what? You sure?" Asked Rooster as his skin again started to glow with a pronounced red sheen.

"It was him aw'ite," said Coop while messing around with a hand held computer looking device. "Didn't put two and two together the first time we watched the download. Sending it your way now."

As a second holographic screen materialized, a video of a little old Chinese lady getting out of a rusted, piece of shit pick-up truck in the middle of a field of cows came into perfect view. Hobbling around the dirt road for a minute or two, she got back in the truck and drove off. Whole thing was over in about thirty seconds.

"Now, watch this," Coop said while swiping his hand over the screen of his wizbang gadget. "This happened about five hours later."

A scene of the same dirt road appeared but now displayed a farmer atop a big-ass tractor towing a trailer full of hay bails. Just as he was about to pull out of the frame, a metallic blue Jaguar XK convertible, with the top down, pulled up next to him. Behind the wheel was a smoking hot brunette in a yellow bikini top that didn't leave much to the imagination. After a brief conversation that mostly involved the farmer ogling her tits and smiling profusely, she drove off in a cloud of dust waving at him.

"Please tell me that Uncle Skip was the farmer and not the chick," I muttered to Rooster. Ignoring me, he continued to intently focus on the screen.

"And finally, give this a look see. Two hours later. Right before nightfall," Coop said while sending over the last video clip. Waltzing down the same country road was the familiar slovenly Boston security guard dressed in faded overalls and a straw hat. Toting a sixer of beer and a box of fried chicken he casually strolled into the field and disappeared into the surrounding wood line.

"Son of a bitch. Skip's with the Maradim. I don't fucking believe it. I'm gonna rip his head off with my bare hands," growled Rooster in an unfamiliar guttural voice as he turned unnaturally red from head to toe and clenched his fists.

Giving him a triple take, I swore his tee shirt got tighter as he literally grew in height and girth for a quick second. Somewhat startled, I blurted out, "Are you OK?"

Letting out a deep sigh, he replied in his normal demeanor, "Yeah, I'm fine," and instantly returned to normal. Shifting his attention to Tango and Coop, he said, "Good work. We'll take it from here. Keep digging. Call me if you find anything else." As the screen faded, Rooster said, "Skyphos, Please give me a location on Uncle Skip —"

"*One step ahead of you, Cleric,*" Skyphos boomed cutting him off in mid-sentence. "*Philbert Amoury Pothier. Alias: Skipper or Uncle Skip. Classification: Metamorph. Current Location: 650 Columbus Avenue - Apartment Number 263, Boston, Massachusetts. There appears to be significant warding about his dwelling.*"

"Got it. Thanks, Sweetie," muttered a focused Rooster while zooming the large screen map to the apartment building on Columbus Ave and pulling out a mini-computer looking device, similar to Coop's, from the pocket of his shorts.

"*You're welcome. And do not refer to me as Sweetie.*"

Giving Skyphos a sarcastic nod, he held the device to his ear like a phone, and said, "Hey, it's me. Need your help taking down some wards. Where you at?" Pausing to listen for a quick second, he replied, "Ok, good. Bring the Magic Bus." Pausing again, he said, "Perfect. Twenty minutes. I'll send the address."

Ending the call and flipping his hand at the map on the gigantic tV monitor, it literally jumped from the large screen and dove into his pocket computer. Again stunned by the surreal technology, I inquisitively asked, "Is that one of those 'smart phone' things you were talking about earlier?"

"Nope. This is a whole new level of nepher tech," he said while casually sliding the James Bond contraption back in his pocket and starting toward the command bridge stairs.

"Do I get one?"

"Not a chance," he quickly replied while producing a much lower tech, plastic device from his pocket and tossing it to me. With a snide smirk, he said, "Baby steps … I made you this nice flip phone to compliment your twentieth century outlook on life."

Quickly reaching the staircase, he abruptly stopped and fixed me with a hard gaze before taking the first step downward. With his demeanor completely changed, he solemnly said, "It's go time. You ready for this?"

"Hell yeah, I'm ready," I said matching his gaze with one of my own. "We got a plan?"

"Still working out the finer details, but at a high level, it goes something like — We go to Skip's place, disable the wards, and kick the fucking door in."

"That's a good start," I muttered taking a couple steps in his direction. "And then?"

As his skin flashed a deep, brilliant red, he muttered, "We beat the piss out of him until he tells us something." As his skin instantly returned to a normal shade, he disappeared down the spiral staircase in a Chickenman flash.

"Good plan," I muttered with my face stretched into a wolfish grin. "Simple. Easy to remember."

Chapter 23

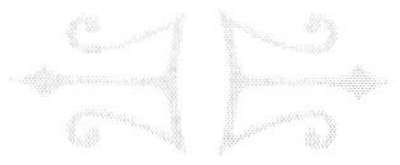

As my boots crunched through the thick layer of snow blanketing the sidewalk, I pulled the collar of my peacoat up around my neck as we briskly waltzed past Symphony Hall and waited to cross Mass Ave in the ridiculous rush hour traffic. Despite the fact we were a week into the new year, remnants of the holiday spirit lingered throughout the streets of Boston's Back Bay as oversized wreaths were draped on all the lamp posts, and the various storefronts were still decorated with obnoxious Christmas and New Years greetings.

Squinting at Rooster in the late afternoon sun, I made the mental note that if society in general had any inkling of the insane happenings that I'd recently become privy to they'd be holed up in fall out shelters eating Spam, pissing in plastic bottles, and saying Hail Mary's with a Bible in close proximity.

"Why is it that we're not using one of those fancy doors to get where we're going like everybody else does? It's not exactly walking weather out here."

Intently staring at his nepher phone while starting to cross the bustling street, completely oblivious to the honking cars and various Boston'esque obscenities directed at him, he muttered, "Firstly, we're only a couple blocks from Columbus Ave. Secondly, porting anywhere in the vicinity of Skip's apartment will most likely trigger his wards and tip our hand."

Looking up at me as we hoofed past the Symphony Station T-stop, he added, "And thirdly, I didn't think a battle hardened Army Ranger would bat an eyelash at a little stroll in the brisk weather."

"Yeah well, I had my fair share of frozen misery when I was alive," I grumbled as my breath was visible in the wintry air. "Should be some kind of proviso for that shit when you're dead — or undead as it were." Shielding my eyes from the intense afternoon sun bouncing off the snow, I muttered, "I'd give my kingdom for some sunglasses right now."

"Inside left pocket of your coat," he instantly responded.

Knowing damn well that there was nothing in the inside left pocket of my coat, I skeptically reached in, and was quite surprised to pull out a pair of classic RayBan Aviators. With the silver trim no less. My sunglass of choice. Thinking that was a pretty slick maneuver, I happily slid them on my face while giving him a droll glance.

"Thanks."

"Don't mention it. Figured you'd want those relics sooner or later. *You do* realize they've been out of style for the better part of twenty years, right".

"You can't beat the classics," I muttered casually flipping him off. "Good enough for Maverick — good enough for me. Chicks dig'em."

Pointing to the right, he said, "This way."

Hooking onto Huntington Avenue, we methodically weaved our way through the afternoon crowd of business people, street beggars, and assorted collection of local Massholes. The whole time I couldn't shake the acute feeling that people were either staring straight at me or conversely, looking straight through me — like I wasn't even there. As three random street-goers made a deliberate effort to get as far away from me as physically possible, I had to literally jump to safety before a thirty something woman nearly steamrolled me with a baby stroller. Looking to Rooster for explanation, I quickly dodged a slick haired, older guy in a suit and overcoat just before he walked straight into me without batting an eyelash.

"What the hell's wrong with these frigg'n people," I muttered as Rooster chuckled at my fancy footwork with his face buried in his pocket computer — which was really starting to annoy me by the way.

"Why do you ask?" He muttered, half paying attention.

"Are you not seeing this?" I muttered avoiding another near collision with a group of young women that didn't look twice at me. "It's like I'm frigg'n invisible — and the few that can see me are bolting across the street."

"Oh, right," he said looking up from his gadget. "Should've mention this before we left the QM."

"Mention what?" I said impatiently as we reached the New England Conservatory of Music and hung a left onto Gainsborough Street.

"Well, by virtue of what you are and what you represent — your presence on Earth is not exactly *natural* anymore. You've been touched by the left hand of God, Dean. You crossed into the Heavenly Realms — and came back."

"So, that makes me invisible?"

"No, no," he said chuckling, "it makes you — *different*."

"Different," I grumbled, dodging another group of people that were bee lining straight toward me while pouring out of a parking garage on the Northeastern University campus.

"You emanate divinity. Somewhat dark divinity, but divinity nonetheless. The average human will pay you absolutely no attention unless you address them directly or have some form of physical contact with them. It's like you don't exist on their plane of reality anymore. You're a face in the crowd, man. Except for those rare few with a powerful Sight, nobody will even remember your face the second you walk away. Your interactions with humans will be a foggy memory for them if they remember anything at all."

Recollecting the words of Stephen during the endless days of my initial training in the Realms, I muttered, "Feared by most. Revered by others."

"Correct. Now, nephers on the other hand, will be scared shitless once they See you. Although they may not know exactly what they're looking at, to cast Sight upon your aura is a major emotional event."

"How so?"

Momentarily stopping at the bottom of the footbridge that traversed a set of train tracks leading to NU's Matthews Arena, he looked me squarely in the eye, and said, "Well, to See a Deacon — *to actually cast Sight upon one* — is to catch a glimpse of the physical embodiment of the Wrath of God. It's like staring at the sun — that is, if the sun was a faceless swirling nightmare of walking hellfire tucked ominously in a black cloak and swinging a sword at your neck. Not something you do on purpose, if you know what I'm saying."

"Then why do it at all?"

"Well, sometimes nephers have an ultra-sensitivity to it. And other times," pausing to pick his words carefully, "Other times, the power of the Wrath is so intense — you just See it. It just happens. And it's something you can't un-see. Despite how many times you try."

"Got it," I blankly muttered as he started walking up the concrete stairs with his face again buried in his phone. Leaving me standing there alone for a quick second, I called up to him, "You ever See a Deacon?"

Reaching the top of the stairs and pulling to an abrupt halt, he looked down at me and stoically said, "Twice. The first time was many centuries ago. When I was turned from the darkness. And the second time — December of 1998 — In a church."

Speechless, I watched him dart across the bridge and start down the stairs on the other side. Reaching the bottom, he yelled back, "Let's go. Stoner's already here. The Magic Bus is up ahead."

Making the mental note that *a stoner* in a 'Magic Bus' was probably the last guy I'd be expecting us to link up with at the current moment, I hoofed it up the stairs and over the bridge to catch up with Rooster.

The footbridge deposited us onto Camden Street, where we climbed over a ginormous mound of packed snow speckled with brown and black remnants of winter road debris, to reach a vacant cul-de-sac. Parked about halfway up the street on the side of a snow-tufted basketball court was a curiously out of place seventies model Volkswagen van. Despite the thick layering of salt and slushy winter grime, a truly hellacious canary yellow paint job complete with the vintage white trim was clearly visible on the Mystery Machine-like vehicle. With black-rimmed wheels and tinted windows, it sat suspiciously idle with the motor running as a steady flow of exhaust poured from the tail pipe. The muffled rhythm of a Guns N' Roses song that I couldn't quite place thumped from inside the cabin as the entire van subtly jostled to the beat like the driver was playing some mean air guitar.

"Ok, so Skyphos still shows the Skipper in his apartment," Rooster said slowly approaching the purported Magic Bus while glancing at his phone. "That's Columbus Ave straight ahead. That building to the right is our target." Quickly pulling up a building schematic on his phone, he added, "Skip's apartment is on the north wall near the emergency stairwell. Second floor. Here's the plan, Stoner blows a hole in his wards —"

"Whoa, slow down, chief," I said stopping a few steps from the van. "Is *Stoner* the dude driving the banana mobile over here? Looks like that thing should be parked at Woodstock for Christ's sake. Who the hell is this guy?"

"He's a magus," he said also pulling to a halt. "One of the best we have."

"A magus?"

"Yeah," he said impatiently. "Nephers versed in the Forbidden Knowledge that can manipulate the elements … like a sorcerer, or a wizard, or a witch."

"So, a *stoner* who's also a *wizard* is going to get us into Skip's joint. What kind of Cheech and Chong, Monty Python bullshit is that? That's our frigg'n plan?"

"Ok, so he's not *a* stoner. He's *the Stoner.* And, he's not a wizard, he's a magus. There's a difference," he grumbled while repeatedly shifting focus from his phone to the apartment building across the street. "But basically, Yes. He's going to get us in. Here's the short story. Couple ways to disable some hefty warding. If you don't want to fry yourself or take down a city block in the process, you need a magus. They can basically deconstruct the spells holding the wards in place. But, it's time consuming and requires a hell of a lot of skill. You with me?"

Making a mental note that a response of 'Are you fucking kidding me?' was probably not appropriate, I grumbled, "Yes."

"Ok, so while the Guild has a ton of magi on the payroll, we don't always have the luxury of time for them to do their thing."

"Ok," I anxiously muttered waiting for the punch line.

"So, over the years, we," pausing to point at the yellow shagg'n wagon, "actually he — *Stoner*, developed a technique he calls ward breaching. Using a Skyphos powered super computer on wheels and a series of complex algorithms, Enochian counter spells, and sonic wave technology he's able to remotely punch a hole in the beefiest of wards with near pinpoint accuracy."

Not having a clue what to say to all that, I simply asked, "Near pinpoint accuracy?"

"Yeah … There's usually a little collateral damage. More of an art than a science. But it's effective. And fast."

"Awesome," I grumbled walking toward the mirth mobile. "We're off to see the wizard …"

As we approached the driver's side door of the van, the tinted window rolled down to reveal a burly dude with short dark hair, meticulously manicured silver highlighted goatee, and a huge pair of dark sunglasses that looked more like goggles. Sporting a real tree camo hunting jacket and an OD green turtle neck, he happily slurped on a fountain drink from a mega-sized styrofoam cup. Turning the blaring symphony of eighties hair metal to a normal volume, he barked in an irritated tone, "Where you ladies been? Thought we were in a hurry here."

"Sorry, man," said Rooster firmly grasping his outstretched hand, and giving him an awkward bro-hug through the open window. "Still breaking in the newbie here."

"So you're Robinson, eh?" Stoner said giving me a quick once over as he extended his hand. "Thought you'd be taller. And, ah, nice glasses."

Not in the mood to take any shit from a neo-Gandalf wannabe sitting in an ambiguously gay superhero van, I muttered, "Go fuck yourself," and gave his hand an obligatory shake.

Chuckling a hearty, yet very short-lived laugh, he said to Rooster, "Alright. I like him."

With the pleasantries over as quickly as they started, he barked, "So what are we doing here, girls?" Staring at a sleek laptop computer fastened to the dashboard, he said, "I'm picking up some healthy defensive spells from the north corner of that building. Somebody's pretty serious about their privacy and what have you. What's the target? Anakim? Gothen?"

"Metamorph," Rooster quickly replied while sliding his phone in the pocket of his wool overcoat.

"Seriously? You made me drag the bus all the way out here in this shit weather for a damn shifter? Come on, man," Stoner barked, in a generally pissed off demeanor, while taking a big gulp of his gas station super soda.

"He's with the Maradim," Rooster said sternly. "I wouldn't have called if it wasn't important."

"Alright," he muttered somewhat unconvinced. "I'll be wanting some of that Rooster beer when this is over. On the house."

Turning again to his laptop, his hands flew across the keys in a blinding flash as several virtual screens started popping up all over the inside of the van. As I heard the whirring sound of an electric motor, I took a couple steps backward to see a small satellite dish contraption raise from the van's roof on a telescoping rod and swing toward the apartment building in the distance. Shifting his focus back to us, Stoner grumbled, "Alright, I've got a lock on the source." Pointing at a schematic on one of the screens, he said, "It's the threshold of this apartment on the north wall."

"Yeppers," Rooster confirmed. "That's the place."

"Hot damn," Stoner said flipping through the various charts and graphs on the floating translucent screens. "These readings are off the chart. Whoever set those babies up is a goddamn artist. Something that intricate takes some serious fucking mojo. But, nothing the Magic Bus can't handle." Finished typing, he smugly muttered, "Ok, I'm ready. Gimme the word and the wards are toast."

"We're on," Rooster said with a hard gaze. Giving our computer savvy magus a quick glance, he said, "Thanks, man. I'll call when we're set."

As we started the short walk across Columbus Avenue to the apartment building, I heard Stoner yell, "Alrighty, man. Probably a bad idea to be standing in front of the door when I blow the wards. May want to shield yourself with that Deacon ... Just in case."

Looking back and casually flipping him off, I turned to Rooster and muttered, "I kind of like that guy."

"He's a good shit. Just don't piss him off. He may turn you into a newt."

"A newt? He can do that?"

Chuckling while giving me a quick 'You are a dumb ass' glance, Rooster all of a sudden looked like he forgot his lunch money and apprehensively switched topics as we crossed the street. Approaching the front door of the apartment complex, he said, "So in retrospect we probably should've worked this out before we got here but — this is Boston. Not Bosnia."

"Thanks for breaking that down, Professor. Very helpful," I muttered getting ready to give the revolving doors leading into the lobby a hefty push.

"No, I'm serious, man," he said firmly grabbing my shoulder to stop me. "We can't just bust in there and storm the lobby like this is some third world country." Pointing through the glass doors, he said, "Last thing we need right now is Rent-a-Cop over there freaking out and calling the real cops. On top of potentially tipping off the Skipper, it'll result in a hell of a lot of unneeded attention that we don't have time to deal with right now. This needs to be done with finesse. Subtle."

"Ok. Point taken," I replied. "So, what's the plan?"

"Well, *you're* the plan," he tentatively said. "All you need to do is employ your divine power of persuasion over the human mind and get us past the security guy without setting off any red flags. Once we get upstairs — it's game on." Giving me a look like he was making this up as he went along, he affirmably added, "Piece of cake."

"You're telling me this *now*?" I grumbled shooting him a frustrated glare. "Is this how you guys run an op?"

"No," he sheepishly replied. "We usually have air tight cover stories and very authentic fake credentials to handle this kind of stuff. In my haste to get over here, I might've overlooked that particular, somewhat small detail ..."

"Awesome," I grumbled still glaring at him. Shifting focus to the lobby, I muttered, "So what the hell am I supposed to tell this guy?"

"I dunno. You're the Deacon. Make something up. Tell him we're here to, ah, clean the pipes."

Making a mental note that Rooster seriously needed to lay off the eighties porn and get out of the Quartermaster a bit more often, I muttered, "You, my friend, are a real asshole."

"Just tell him something — anything," he quickly replied. "I think you'll be surprised at just how convincing you can be nowadays."

"Alright, I'm on it."

Giving the revolving door a solid push and holding his arm out in an 'after you' manner, he said, "Remember — subtle. I'll wait here. Go get 'em. And, ah, make it quick. We're on the clock."

Shaking my head and calling him an asshole again for good measure, I waltzed into the rather impressive lobby like I owned the joint. Hunched behind an oversized, ornate desk on the far side of the highly decorated room was a crack-skinny dude in his early forties staring disinterestedly at a computer monitor while sucking on a designer iced coffee from a green straw.

Dressed in a really cheap suit and loosely knotted tie, he lazily looked up and glanced in my direction like he was expecting somebody to walk in. Not seeing anyone and evidently satisfied that his eyes were playing tricks on him, he quickly drifted back to his afternoon excitement of mindless internet browsing — because that's evidently what people did in 2012. Crossing the lobby in a few steps, I pulled to a halt in front of his large desk and took note of the white plastic nametag pinned to the stalwart security guard's navy blue blazer. Placing my hands forcefully on the desktop and making a rather loud banging noise in the process, I said, "Hello Raymond, How are you this fine afternoon?"

Startled that I'd unknowingly walked up on him, he jumped backward and excitedly rolled his seat away from the desk. As his sluggish eyes shot wide open, he tentatively stood upright and gawked at me for a long second or two. He wasn't afraid — just completely awestruck. Like he was trying to figure out if I was really there — or not. It was an interesting reaction, to say the very least.

Unable to divert his eyes from me, he inadvertently dropped his venti sized plastic cup on the floor and mumbled in a clearly confused, monotoned voice, "I, ah, didn't see you come in. Ah, can I, ah, help you?"

"Yep, I believe you can, Ray," I replied shaking my head at the waste of a good latte. "You don't mind if I call you Ray, do you?"

Offering no response, he simply shook his head 'No' and continued to gawk. Getting the sense that perhaps Rooster was actually right and I could say just about anything to this poor bastard and he'd hand me his wallet and car keys, I said, "Ok, that's great, Ray. Really feel like we're having a moment here. But, I digress. Let me cut to the chase."

Pointing at the Chickenman suspiciously loitering on the sidewalk outside the door, I said with a slightly vindictive smirk, "You see that red headed whack job out there? Well, believe it or not, he's one of those professional *escorts*. Bit of an *exotic* dancer, if you will. While not an exceptionally good one, he's got a rather discreet, and very wealthy, *client* upstairs that really likes her some ginger." Giving Raymond a slap on the shoulder, I said, "You know what I'm saying here, Ray? She's gotta have that ginger."

Giving me an affirmative nod, my new friend continued to say nothing.

"And just so you know — he promised me there'd be none of that Pulp Fiction crap going on this time. Should be quiet — er," I convincingly said while trying to keep a straight face and still in somewhat disbelief this was actually working. "Ok, good talk. So we'll be heading upstairs now if you don't mind."

"Oh, Ok. Sure thing. Go right up, pal. I'll buzz you in," he vacantly muttered while reaching under the desk to unlock the glass door leading to the elevators. "Can I, ah, help you with anything else?"

"You know what, I feel very badly that you dropped your beverage," I said giving the pool of spilled iced coffee a quick glance. "How about you go pick yourself up another one. Maybe a nice mochaccino. Take your time."

"Yeah, that sounds really good. I think I'll do that," he muttered still staring at me dumbfoundedly. Walking past the desk in a trance-like state, he strolled out the front door and awkwardly gawked at the Chickenman as he passed him in transit. Making his way into the lobby, Rooster curiously looked back at Raymond the Security Guy purposefully moving down the sidewalk in the freezing afternoon weather.

"What the hell did you say to him?" He asked.

Opening the now unlocked door to the elevator bay, I smugly said, "I told him that my ginger colleague and I were friendly neighborhood supernatural crime fighters that needed to pay a visit to a resident shape shifter who's most likely sitting on a piece of vital information that could potentially save the world as we know it from certain apocalyptic demise at the hands of a well dressed fallen angel and an inconceivable horde of giants. Oh, and I also told him you would clean his pipes when he gets back. And … might've insinuated that you're an exotic dancer."

"Real nice," he grumbled shaking his head as he walked by me and pressed the button for the elevator. "Is that your idea of being subtle? Where the hell is he going?"

"Sent him on a beer run," I said with a dark grin.

"A beer run. Seriously?"

Willing the otherworldly shotgun into being, I said, "Yep." Feeling the presence of the scabbard-like holster manifest on my back, I pulled the Winchester free, and muttered, "Figured it'd be flat out wrong to have a bonfire without beer."

As the elevator doors opened with the signature dinging sound, Rooster's demeanor hardened and his eyes flashed a deep red for a quick second. As we both stepped in and the doors shut behind us, he muttered, "Good call. Let's go see Skip."

"Sounds like a plan."

"And just so we're clear … if it was Caveman that told you I was a dancer, he's full of shit. Never happened."

"Ah, Ok," I uncomfortably muttered.

Without making eye contact, he tossed in, "And if it did — I was drunk for three months straight and don't remember. Long, long time ago."

"That's awkward," I grumbled to myself staring at the floor and waiting anxiously for the elevator door to open.

After what felt like an eternity, the dinging sound indicated we'd reached the second floor and I happily barreled into the foyer with great haste trying desperately to erase the last thirty seconds from my memory banks. Making our way down the labyrinth of small apartments, we turned the corner to find a grandiose hallway leading to Skip's place, and it was fairly apparent that the nepher career path of nighttime security, stripping, and street hustling was surprisingly lucrative.

Either that or he had a mysterious benefactor.

The entrance to his sizable suite was very artfully tucked into the far corner of an isolated wing and tastefully decorated with a rather impressive heap of fast food bags, pizza boxes, and empty cases of beer. Classic Skip.

"He's still in there," Rooster said in a solemn whisper while studying his phone as we purposely strolled down the hall. Reaching into his coat pocket, he pulled out a tiny earpiece, turned it on, and casually slid it into his ear.

Giving the impressive trash pile a disgusted glance, I pointed to it and muttered, "If this is any indication of what he's been up too … I'd be surprised if he's still breathing."

Pulling to a halt about ten feet from the frat party like carnage, Rooster put his phone away and glared at me with intense eyes. His typical jovial demeanor was steadily giving way to a brooding alter ego that I was about to meet for the first time.

Tapping the earpiece, he waited a quick second, and muttered, "We're here. Blow the wards in sixty seconds." Waiting on the response, he said, "Yep. I'm gonna need a veil on this side of the building too." Pausing again, he grumbled, "Perfect."

Concluding his conversation he quickly snatched the earpiece and put it away. Pulling the antique pocket watch from his jeans, he looked at me and said, "Time to suit up. Fifty seconds."

Giving him a stern nod, I willed the cloak into being and welcomed the electric-like sensation as it manifested with a spectral flash and billowed about my shoulders. Removing his overcoat and casually tossing it on the floor, it was fairly apparent that the Chickenman came to party.

Sitting neatly over top of his black RoosterBragh tee shirt, complete with signature logo and slogan '*Want Some? Get Some!*', was a leather tactical harness with enough weaponry to launch a frontal assault on the gates of hell. Dueling semi-automatic pistols in a pair of shoulder holsters dangled ominously under each of his stringy arms and a literal collection of throwing knives were tucked into a dozen or more pockets lining the straps. Hanging from his waist, amidst several ammo pouches filled with extra clips, was a hunting knife that would give John J. Rambo himself a raging hard-on.

Strapped to his back, and completing the nepher commando motif, was a leather scabbard housing what appeared to be a cavalry sabre with a pearl hilt.

Not really sure what to say, I gawked at him for a second or two as he pulled out each pistol, slammed home a clip, and chambered a round. Sliding them back in their respective holsters, he muttered, "Forty-five seconds."

"You sure you got enough firepower there, Chuck Norris?" I asked with a hint of sarcasm.

"Go big or go home."

"Are those Glocks?"

"Yep. Glock 31's. I make the custom .357 rounds out of barzel. Won't take down an anakim — but they'll do some damage." Glancing at his watch, he coldly said, "Thirty-five seconds."

Making the mental note to revisit that particular topic at a later time, I said, "So, this being my first 'ward breaching' experience — what exactly do I have to look forward to?"

"If Stoner's on his game, it won't be anything more dramatic than a popping sound."

"And if not?"

"Let's just say I'll be standing behind you. Just in case," he said matter of factly. "Twenty-five seconds."

"Awesome," I grumbled. "And, ah, won't an otherworldly explosion on the second floor of an apartment complex bring some folks a' running?"

"Nope. Stoner's running a veil on the building. Nobody will see or hear a thing."

"Damn, he can do that?"

"Magus," he grumbled giving me another 'you're a dumb ass' glance. "Ten seconds."

Pulling the hood of the cloak over my head while making the mental note to seriously lay off the wizard jokes, I momentarily holstered the shotgun and willed the ashen stone gauntlets into being. Feeling them instantly cover my hands with a spectral flash, I quickly cleared my mind and focused my strength — focused on the Balance.

Drawing his gansta-like gats, Rooster's eyes flashed red as he grumbled, "Five seconds."

"Go time," I muttered feeling the mental switch flip to the on-position and the calmative awareness wash over me. Giving him a stern nod, I clenched my fists and started my advance on the garbage littered doorway to Casa del Skip.

Taking immediate position on my six and lowering himself in a predatory crouch, Rooster called out, "Three. Two. One."

Chapter 24

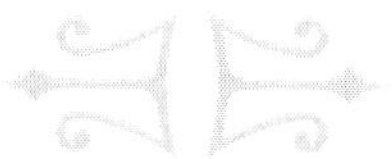

Quickly dropping to a knee and lowering my head, I braced for an explosion of epic proportion only to hear a faint fizzling sound followed by a subtle pulse of tangible, warm energy gently wash over us and roll harmlessly down the hallway to our rear. Bit of a let down to be honest.

"Wards are down," Rooster muttered in a whispered voice from behind me. "Game on."

"Roger that," I grumbled while rising to my feet and cocking my right arm back to put a hellstone bolstered punch into Skip's front door. Not really sure it'd be as effective as blowing the doorknob out with a shotgun blast, but there's just something about having stone covered fists that makes you want to punch shit.

And of course, I figured it would be downright rude not to knock.

Just as I was about to slug my way into Skip's not so humble abode, the doorknob started to jostle, causing me to momentarily hold back. Before I knew what was happening, the frigg'n door swung open to reveal a slovenly fat bastard in a pair of boxer shorts and fuzzy slippers with a cigarette lazily hanging from his mouth. Holding a stack of empty pizza boxes and struggling to keep his eyes open, it was pretty clear that the Skipper had just woken up from his latest bender and was doing a bit of house cleaning.

Somewhat realizing that he wasn't alone, he started to incoherently grumble something as his sleep-ridden eyes struggled to focus. Quickly coming to the very unfortunate realization that he was standing toe to toe with a cloaked Deacon, a priceless look of complete and utter panic overtook his face as his eyes almost popped out of his fat-ass head. As his mouth dropped open and the cigarette fell to the floor, I gave him a friendly smile, and said, "Hello Philbert. Nice place you got here. Remember me?"

And punched him square in the fucking chest.

Flying backward from the brute force of the impact and crashing to an ungainly halt amidst the rather nice furniture decorating his lavish dwelling, the Skipper scampered to his feet and made a deliberate break for a door toward the back of the spacious suite. Pushing past me with pistols at the ready, Rooster entered the room in a Chickenman flash and fired two quick rounds that ripped clear through Skip's kneecaps and dropped his sorry ass to the floor like a really obese sack of potatoes.

Screaming like a wounded animal, the Skipper then commenced to frantically crawling toward the back room with all the strength he could possibly muster. Closing the distance in a blur of motion, Rooster blocked his apparent escape route and violently slammed a pistol butt into the back of his head, sending the infamous Skipper into a instant state of unconsciousness.

Although impressed as hell by Rooster's commando-like prowess, I was somewhat taken aback by the sheer violence of his actions. It was cold precision. A side of him that I didn't know existed — until now.

Holstering his six guns and producing a pair of hand cuffs from his belt, Rooster then wrenched Skip's flabby arms behind his bare back and slapped them on like he'd done it once or twice before. Looking at me with an emotionless gaze of fiery red eyes, he barked, "Give me a hand getting this piece of shit on his feet."

"Yep. Sure thing," I muttered as I quickly willed the gauntlets into retreat and pulled the hood of the cloak off my head.

Throwing the scantily clad, grotesque body of our shape shifting captive, on the oversized leather couch to our immediate rear, I noticed that the handcuffs were inlaid with an interesting combination of Enochian glyphs.

"What's with the cuffs?"

"They're blessed," he muttered. "Negates the abilities of whoever or whatever they bind. So Skip can't shift on us. He's virtually powerless until they come off. *If* they come off."

"Hmm," I muttered ready to lose my lunch at the sight of Skip's saggy man tits and jiggling torso spread out all over the couch like a beached whale. "Just a thought here, but perhaps we have him shift into a bikini model and *then* put them on," I said, only somewhat jokingly, in attempt to coax Rooster's steely demeanor back to that of the jovial ginger that I'd come to know and somewhat like.

"No time," he grumbled while turning and gazing at the door in the rear of the apartment that the Skipper was so desperately trying to reach.

Following suit, I said, "What's behind door number two over there?"

"Not what," he grumbled. "Where. It's a portal. He was evidently trying to escape."

Concentrating on the door, I quickly realized that Rooster was right. Although it looked like any other door in the apartment, I could See a steady pulse of energy buzzing from the threshold and a faint glow of white radiance outlining the frame.

"A portal to where?"

"That's what we're about to find out," he replied removing his hunting knife from the leather sheath hanging from his waist. "Skip's been playing us. We need answers. Now."

Grabbing a can of beer from one of the many cases stacked on the rather nice coffee table, Rooster punched a hole in the top with his manly blade and proceeded to empty it on the Skipper's head. Shaking back to immediate consciousness, Skip's eyes shot wide open, and he frantically tugged on his handcuffs as a look of panic returned to his chubby face. Alternating anxious glares between Rooster and me, he started to hyperventilate as he realized that he'd rapidly departed from his happy place of alcohol induced comas and arrived in a world of shit.

Pulling up a chair opposite the cuffed and stuffed, underwear clad mound of cellulite, Rooster's skin turned a harrowing deep red as he maliciously said, "Skippy, you got some 'splaining to do."

Twirling the oversized hunting knife in his right hand like something out of a bad western, he glanced at Skip's bullet riddled, bleeding knees, and asked, "Bet that hurts, huh?"

"Y-you sh-shot me. I didn't do any-th-thing," Skip blurted out in a stuttering, incredibly pathetic voice.

Curling his left hand into a fist, Rooster then proceeded to break the Skipper's nose wide open with a forceful jab that sent his head blowing backward into the sofa cushion. As he grunted in pain, Rooster growled, "Don't lie to me, asshole. Drop the act. In case you don't know who I am — This isn't my first rodeo."

"St-stop … Please stop. I f-follow the R-rules," he mumbled with watering eyes and a hefty stream of blood pouring from his nose.

"Maybe you didn't hear me. I said — Don't fucking lie to me!" Rooster snarled as his eyes turned solid red, matching the color of his skin.

Flipping his knife into a reverse grip, he proceeded to sink it hilt deep into Skip's thigh in a flash of movement. As the Skipper let out a blood curdling scream that made my stomach churn, Rooster continued to apply pressure driving it deeper and deeper into his leg until a very interesting thing happened.

Skip started laughing.

Not like a '*He's lost his frigg'n mind*' kind of laugh. More of a maniacal, '*I know something you don't*' kind of laugh.

It was unexpected. And somewhat creepy. Just saying.

"Now then, that's more like it," Rooster said ripping the blade from his leg and forcefully burying it a solid three inches into the wooden coffee table. "You ready to have a somewhat civilized conversation now?"

Not having any clue what the hell was going on, I continued to intently watch as Skip's demeanor changed from that of a scared child to that of a really smug asshole.

"The Rooster, right?" He said while smiling a wicked grin and seemingly no longer phased by the fact he was shot, stabbed, and pummeled in a matter of two minutes. "I know who you are. Heard the stories over the years. Never seen a liderc before. Rumor has it — *you're* the last one still topside."

Curiously studying Rooster's reddish hue and fiery gaze, he snidely added, "Love the eyes. Terrifying."

Fixing him with an intent glare, Rooster said nothing.

"Tell you what, pal," Skip continued like he was haggling over the price of a used car, "Why don't we do this like gentlemen, eh? Take these cuffs off and I'll tell you anything you want to know. I got nothin' to hide from the Guild. I'm clean."

Making the mental note to ask Rooster what in the hell a liderc was at a later time, I intently watched as he ominously rose to his feet and loomed over the captive Skipper. Clearly holding back a pending out-lash of Chickenman fury, he said in a very controlled tone, with eyes glowing like orbs of fire, "You *haven't* seen a liderc, Skip. Not yet. Would you like to?"

"Easy now, pal," Skip apprehensively mumbled with a nervous laugh as he squirmed uncomfortably on the leather cushions. "No need for all that." Tugging on his handcuffs, he said, "Take these things off and we'll talk. You guys want a drink? Help yourselves. What's mine is yours."

"I got a better idea," Rooster said without any hint of emotion. "How about we leave the cuffs on and you still tell me what I want to know."

"Nah. Don't think so, pal," the Skipper shot back with a smug grin. "You guys ain't here to smite me. You would've already done that. So I evidently got something you need." Shifting his focus to me and smiling ear to ear, he said, "Don't I, *Deacon*?"

As Rooster took a step backward, I politely smiled back at Skipper the Hut and said, "Feel like we got off on the wrong foot here, Philbert. Please allow me to take a moment and bring some clarity to the rules of engagement."

Willing an argent metal gauntlet into being, I closed the distance between us in a blinding flash and wrapped my barzel covered hand around his meaty neck. Fueled with a turbo shot of adrenaline, I locked eyes with that fat son of a bitch as a subtle layer of white flame manifested along my forearm and steadily slithered down the gauntlet toward his head. Plucking the Johnny Rambo knife from the coffee table with my left hand, I buried it into Skip's good thigh, shattering his femur bone in the process. As he let out a squeal that would make Duncan proud, I snarled, "The only thing I *need* to do is to separate your fat head from your shoulders." As the intangible heat from the otherworldly flame crept to within inches of his neck, his eyes opened wide with primal fear as he attempted to squirm to safety. "So this is how it's gonna go. My friend here is going to ask the questions. And you — are going to fucking answer them."

Attempting to nod his head, despite the death grip I had on his neck, he mumbled, "Ok, Ok."

"I'm not done, asshole," I coldly said with a dark smile. As the skin on his neck and shoulders began to sizzle, I wrenched the knife deeper into his thigh. "You play ball and shoot us straight — I let you walk. Or at this point — crawl. You try and bullshit us again — I get medieval on your ass." Releasing him, I took a step backward and willed the gauntlet into retreat. As he gasped for breath, I said, "We got a deal, Phil?"

"Yeah, yeah. We gotta deal," he mumbled. "Whatever you say, bossman."

Giving Rooster an 'All yours' nod, I ripped the knife free and helped myself to a beer from Skip's sizable stash. Popping the top and taking a healthy gulp, I then pulled up a seat to enjoy the rest of the show. Returning my nod, Rooster exhaled a deliberate sigh and his skin instantly returned to a normal shade. Blinking his eyes a few times, they also returned to their usual blue.

Turning to Skip in a more rational state of mind, he said, "Alright. From the top. How long you been doing the Maradim's dirty work?"

"The Maradim?" Skip replied letting out a genuine chuckle. "Is this what this is about? I ain't mixed up with those sick fucks. That militant bullshit ain't my style. You know that. I like the world just the way it is. Besides … I'm a lover not a —"

"I thought we just had a fairly animated conversation about you telling the goddamn truth," Rooster said taking a step in his direction. "We already know you're working with them. Ah, Dean."

"Yes, Rooster."

"I'm not sure that Skip fully embraced the rules of engagement you so eloquently laid out a minute ago. You mind giving him another —"

"Whoa, whoa, hold on," Skip anxiously blurted out. "I mean — think about it, guys. If I'd sworn allegiance to Azazel would I be hanging around

Boston waiting to get pinched by the Guild?" Shooting us an endearing, nervous grin he added, "That'd be fuck'n suicide. Right? And I ain't got no death wish. You believe me. Right, bossman?"

"Of course we do, Skip. Absolutely," Rooster sarcastically replied. "In fact, I'm now feeling rather badly about shooting you. And stabbing you. Oh, and breaking your nose. So I guess the fact that you showed up in Tallahassee, Florida within hours of a pack of anakim in the *exact* spot where they chowed down on a herd of cattle is just an uncanny fucking coincidence."

"Yeah, that's right," Skip replied nodding his head in agreement. As Rooster's words registered with his panic stricken brain, he said, "Whoa, hold on … *anakim* — In Tallahassee? No shit?" As the ramification of that particular coincidence sunk in, he quickly said, "Don't know nothing about that."

"But you *were* in Tallahassee last week?" Rooster said continuing to pace.

"Yeah, sure I was," Skip replied. "I was there on business."

"*Business*," Rooster said raising an eyebrow. "What kind of business?"

Glaring at Rooster, a somewhat offended Skipper boldly replied, "Real estate."

"Come again?"

"Real estate," Skip proudly repeated. "Land acquisition to be precise. My *colleagues* sent me to check out some farm land they're interested in buying on the north end of town. I was supposed to give the property a good once over and, ah, get to know the farmer. You know, persuade him to sell." Pausing to give Rooster a seductive wink, he added, "If you know what I'm saying."

Fairly disgusted at the mental image of Skip the she-male nepher and the smitten farmer we'd seen in the video feed sharing some quality time together, I suppressed the urge to projectile vomit and put down the beer. Unfazed yet clearly losing his patience, Rooster grumbled, "Who sent you there?"

"My colleagues," Skip smugly replied.

"Yes, we're all very impressed that you have *colleagues*," Rooster grumbled. "Who are they?"

"I dunno. We don't use names. They're draugrs. No way in hell these guys are mixed up with the Maradim. They're businessmen. Real sophisticated.

Smart bastards. Bankers or lawyers … something like that. Got a lot of money."

"Draugrs?"

Apparently getting the feeling that Rooster wasn't remotely buying his story, Skip nervously said, "Look, they've had me scouting properties for a couple months now. Send me all over the place. They give me a location. I go look at it … maybe do a little *negotiating* with the land owner … come back and tell them what I've found out. Nobody gets hurt. No questions asked. They pay me and that's the end of it. Pay me real good."

"Quite a cinderella story, Skip. You got that going for you," Rooster said jeeringly. "So these anonymous draugr real estate tycoons you supposedly *work* for that are definitely not part of the Maradim … How do they contact you?"

Inadvertently diverting his gaze to the door at the rear of the apartment for a split second, the Skipper quickly looked away and said, "They, ah, leave me instructions."

"Where?"

"Look, I gotta good thing going here," Skip said going back into used car salesman mode. "I mean, can't you give a guy a break and —"

"Where?" Rooster growled evidently done playing Mr. Nice Chickenman.

Taking another hard look at the portal, I butted in and asked, "What's behind the door, Philbert?"

"What door?" He asked like a child caught with his hand in the cookie jar.

Rising to my feet to join Rooster and pointing at the portal, I said sternly, "What's behind the door, asshole?"

"Oh, *that* door? That's nothing," he replied with a nervous laugh. "It's, ah, my guest room. Go check it out if you want."

As Rooster backed away and gave me an 'All you' nod, I said, "You right handed, Phil?"

"What?" He grunted.

In the blink of an eye, I willed an argent gauntlet into being and lowered my metal fist like a sledgehammer on Skip's left hand. It was basically the equivalent of dropping an anvil on a bag of grapes. Pretty gross.

As his eyes shot open and he was about to let loose with an agonizing scream, I punched him square in the grill. To be fair, it was more of a love tap. Just enough to make him stop yelling. At this point it was getting old.

"Now, Phil, While you're still in possession of one good hand. I'm going to ask you one — more — time. What's behind the fucking door?"

"Alright … alright," he gasped amidst a deep grimace, trying not to look at the bloody pulp that used to be his fingers. "It's a portal."

"No shit it's a portal. A portal to where?" I snarled.

"Look, you guys gotta believe me," he said with a half hearted shyster-like grin. "I didn't know anything about this whole anakim situation. Hell, I didn't even know the anakim were still around for Christ's sake … Seems that my, ah, colleagues may be up to some questionable type of business transactions that I wasn't *privy* to. I'm just trying to turn a buck, you know?"

"Turn a buck," I muttered giving that sorry son of a bitch my very best scowl.

"Ah, hold on — I got an idea," he said. "Why don't we work together here? I hand over the draugrs and, ah, you guys let me walk. That's fair, right?"

Giving him the silent treatment, I willed the spatha into being and felt its presence on my back as it manifested in a spectral flash. Pulling it free, I took a step closer to our friend Philbert.

"This ain't looking so good for the home team here, Skip," Rooster said giving the Skipper a friendly pat on the head. "The sword's out … He's got that crazy look in his eye … Wish I could say it's been a pleasure knowing you but — it really hasn't. In fact, it's been a generally horrible experience. The world will be a better place without you in it."

Whatever remained of Skip's smug facade suddenly gave way to sheer and utter panic as he blurted out, "Hold on now. Let's talk about this, guys. I didn't know, Ok? They gave me jobs and I did 'em. Nobody got hurt. I didn't break the Rules."

"Good Bye, Philbert," I said tapping the flat edge of the otherworldly blade on his shoulder a couple times.

"It's … it's a vault," he blurted out. "Ah, like a safe house — in a shadow realm. The draugrs set it up. It only opens for me."

"Well then, on your feet, Philbert," I said sheathing the sword and smiling. "Let's go have us a look."

"Ok, yeah sure," he replied starting to breath normal. "But, you're gonna let me go right? I open the portal and, ah, you let me go. Right? That's the deal. Right, bossman?"

"Philbert, you have my solemn word," I replied placing my hand over my heart. "You open the portal and I will let you go."

"Ok, Ok. Deal," he quickly replied with a nervous, endearing grin. Leaning forward and pulling on the handcuffs, he said, "And the cuffs?"

Shooting him a generally pissed off glare, Rooster produced the key from his pocket and begrudgingly unlocked them. Taking them off Skip's hands, he coldly muttered, "Next time there won't be any cuffs. Because you'll be dead. We clear?"

"Sure thing. Sure thing, bossman," Skip mumbled. "I'm on your side, remember? We're, ah, partners."

Exchanging suspicious glances, Rooster and I grabbed a flabby arm and pulled the naked man-blob off the couch. Amazingly, within seconds of removing the holy handcuffs each of the wounds he'd received from the red hands of fury and my best rendition of supernatural 'bad cop' instantly healed right before my eyes.

Completely taken aback, I shot Rooster an astonished look that he acknowledged and said, "Metamorphs are legendary healers. Averse to pain. That's why I had to shoot his kneecaps out. Nothing else would've stopped him. All that screaming and crying was bullshit. A well rehearsed act." Slapping the Skipper on the shoulder, he said, "Ain't that right, Skip. Always putting on a show."

Smiling uneasily, the now standing Skip replied, "Can't fault a guy for trying, right?" Giving him a friendly yet encouraging push in the direction of the curious inter-dimensional doorway, Rooster grabbed an oversized bathrobe hanging on a nearby chair and tossed it at him.

"Shut Up, asshole. It was a rhetorical question."

As Skip donned the rob and fumbled to light a cigarette from the pack he'd conveniently stashed in one of the pockets, Rooster leaned toward me and muttered under his breath, "An entrance to an off the books shadow realm mere blocks from the Quartermaster … that takes some serious balls. And some serious mojo."

"What do you think we're dealing with here?"

"This has Maradim written all over it. I'm just wondering how deep the rabbit hole goes," he replied as he pulled his knife out of the coffee table and effortlessly tucked it into the sheath on his belt.

"You think the Skipper knows more than he's letting on."

"Definitely," he replied pulling one of his pistols from the holster. "But at the moment, he seems to be more afraid of *them* than he is of us."

Concluding our conversation, we turned our attention back to Skip and found him thankfully covered in the bathrobe and happily puffing on a cigarette. Grabbing him by the shoulder, Rooster said, "Let's go," and escorted him to the threshold of the portal.

Reaching the doorway within a few steps, Rooster stood for a moment studying it as Skip exhaled a plume of smoke and said, "Just like we agreed, right? I open the door — you let me go. Fair is fair."

"Cool your jets, Phil," I said taking position to his side and trading the spatha out for the shotgun. "Barging through doors is a dangerous proposition. What if some bad guys just so happen to waiting for us on the other side? Now, I can't imagine you'd be slimy enough to walk us into an ambush but just in case — you'll be going through first."

Swallowing the golf ball sized lump in his throat, he took another drag from his smoke and nervously said, "Ah, sure thing. Happy to."

"Awesome," I dryly muttered as I turned my attention to Rooster, "You ready?"

Still fixated on the door, he pointed and muttered, "Look at this. You ever seen anything like it?"

Following the path of his pointed finger, I momentarily studied the Enochian glyph faintly inlaid into the door panel.

Not able to read it either, I replied, "Nope." Turning to Skip for explanation he simply shrugged his shoulders in a 'no idea' fashion.

"Fuck it. We're going," Rooster grumbled raising his drawn pistol to the ready position and taking a step to Skip's rear. "Open it."

Putting out his cigarette and dropping the butt on the floor, Skip reluctantly placed his right hand over the glyph and muttered the activation phrase under his breath. As a glow of spectral blue light emitted from under his hand and instantly silhouetted the doorframe, the distinct thud of a lock disengaging was heard from deep within the panel.

Removing his hand from the glyph and grasping the doorknob, Skip apprehensively gave it a turn and the door propped open. Not giving him the opportunity to pull a fast one on us, I firmly grasped the back of his bathrobe and lowered a shoulder into his back pushing him squarely through the peculiar gateway as he began to yell at the top of his Skipper lungs something to the effect of, "It's me - It's me! Don't shoot — Don't shoot!"

If you haven't put it together by now, Skip's a real asshole.

Chapter 25

Using Skip as a screaming 'not so human' shield, Rooster took immediate position on my six as we dramatically, and quite ungracefully, barreled through the gateway. Fully expecting to be met with a barrage of bullets, swords, spears, knives, arrows, or countless variations of other supernatural type shit that I was pleasantly ignorant of at the current moment, I was rather pleased to find us standing alone in a small room.

"Room clear," I grumbled completing my hasty scan with shotgun at the ready. "You done good, Philbert. Feel free to unpucker your asshole now. Guess you're buddies stepped out for a smoke."

Holstering his pistol, Rooster methodically made his way around the 'safe house' as Skip fumbled for another cigarette while giving me a sheepish grin. The entire space was maybe ten feet by ten feet with the walls, floor, and ceiling constructed of near seamless metal. It had the appearance of an otherworldly bank vault dimly lit by several glowing orbs of reddish light inexplicably set into the ceiling and floor. The room was completely sterile with no additional doorways and was furnished by a simple metal desk and three humble chairs set squarely in the center. Set upon the desk were two large, unmarked manila envelopes like something you'd see in an office building.

"This is it?" I said turning to Skip.

Tensely nodding and starting to sweat, he replied, "This is it, bossman. Just like I told you."

Standing at the desk, Rooster picked up one of the envelopes and said, "What's the deal with these?"

"Those are the instructions for my next job," Skip replied while lighting a fresh cigarette from the one hanging out of his mouth. "I pick them up on Monday and have to finish the job by Friday."

Opening the envelope, Rooster emptied the contents onto the desk and started to methodically sift through a stack of documents. Holding up various sheets of paper, he said, "Picture of an industrial warehouse on the side of a lake, plot surveys, tax records, aerial photos, information on the land owner," pausing on one item in particular, he said surprisingly, "Here's the address of the warehouse and a town map. Looks like the latest acquisition is in Liverpool."

"Liverpool — in the UK?" I asked.

"Nope," he said dryly with his face buried in the map. "Liverpool, New York. Near Syracuse. Evidently the salt capital of the US. Looks lovely. Whopping population of twenty-three hundred people."

Pulling out another sheet of paper, he squinted at it and said, "Not sure what this is … ten digit number with a two letter prefix. Mean anything thing to you?"

"That's a grid coordinate," I said glancing at it for a quick second. "The letters are the designator and the numbers are the position in the military grid reference system. A ten digit coordinate will put you right on top of whatever you're looking for."

Turning to Skip, I asked, "Why would you need a grid coordinate if you already had a property address? What's this for?"

"Oh, right," he said looking like somebody just shot his dog. "Forgot about that part …"

"Forgot about what?" Rooster said taking a few steps in his direction.

Lighting his umpteenth cigarette, Skip anxiously said, "So, these jobs … there's one more little thing that I may have neglected to mention earlier."

"Do tell," Rooster said with an impatient glare.

"This is gonna sound weird, but the coordinates — they're for, ah, burial sites."

"Burial sites," Rooster said skeptically while ominously tapping a finger on the hilt of his hunting knife.

"Yeah, that's what they told me," Skip replied looking exceptionally nervous. "Of their ancestors, ah, ancient draugr colonies and such. The burial sites are within the property limits of all the places they're buying up. Usually out in the woods somewhere."

"Are you telling us you've been traveling the country digging up dead vampires?" I said. "What the fuck, Skip?"

"No, no," he blurted out. "It's not like that. All I have to do is find the tree with the special mark on it. Then I wedge the coin in it. It's, ah, supposed to be some kind of tradition or something."

"You put a *coin* in a *tree*," I muttered. "Seriously?"

"Yeah, I'm telling you the truth, bossman," he said pointing at the open envelope. "Look inside. There's probably a coin taped to the bottom. Always is."

Grabbing the envelope from the desk, Rooster dug around inside and pulled out an ancient looking coin fastened to the bottom. Giving it a quick once over, he flipped it to me and said, "Looks Roman. Maybe first century. Check out the backside. Got a glyph on it. Similar marking as the one on the door."

Catching the peculiar coin, I felt an immediate surge of energy pass through my hand like a jolt of electricity. It buzzed with power. Dark power. The bust of an ancient god of some sort was cast into one side. The flip side bore the image of an eagle with the mysterious glyph weaved into the backdrop.

Turning to Skip, Rooster asked, "Is the *special mark* on the tree the same one on the coin?"

"Yeah, some kind of draugr symbol. Supposed to mean 'Rest in Peace' or something like that," he replied now profusely sweating.

As Rooster's eye danced with rapid thought, like he was connecting a series of dots, he coldly said, "So couple things here, Skipper. You're either the dumbest mother fucker on the face of the goddamn planet *or* you know a hell of lot more than you're telling us. That's not some *draugr symbol*, asshole. It's Enochian. And you know what that means? Your *colleagues* are working for the Maradim."

"What?" Skip grunted lowering his smoke. "No, no — You gotta believe me here. I didn't know, bossman."

Still fixing him with an intense glare, Rooster said, "When exactly are your draugr pals expecting you to complete the job in Liverpool?"

"Ah, Friday … Friday," Skip said awkwardly lighting yet another cigarette. "I have until midnight on Friday."

"And you have no scheduled contact with them between now and then?"

"No," he replied between puffs. "They only want to hear from me if I run into any issues."

With his wheels clearly turning, Rooster turned and gave me an ominous wink. With a dark smile stretching across his face, he said, "You know what, Dean? I think we're done here. Time to let the Skipper *go*." Pulling out his nepher phone, he swiped his fingers over the screen and subsequently tapped it a few times. "However, in light of recent developments, I feel it would be simply irresponsible to let him walk the streets unprotected. Once the draugrs figure out that he helped us, he's as good as dead."

"I could not agree more," I said playing into whatever scheme he was cooking up. "Downright irresponsible."

Chuckling rather smugly, Rooster put down the phone and said to Skip, "I mean, you potentially just double-crossed the Maradim. That's some heavy duty shit. There's nowhere on Earth you'll be able to hide once that gets out. Now clearly, we're not going to say anything, but you know how these things work. Word's *going* to get out. Just a matter of time. You're fucked, Skip. And I can't have that on my conscious."

"Hold on — We had a deal," Skip said backing toward the door in panic. "I get you in here and you let me go. We had a deal."

"I did say that I'd let you go," I said matter of factly. "What I failed to clarify in the terms of our negotiation was where you'd be going, nor exactly how long you'd be there."

In a flash of bathrobe and blubbery thighs, Skip plucked the cigarette from his mouth and broke into a full on sprint toward the door leading back to the perceived safety of his apartment. Not even stopping to say goodbye, he disappeared through the portal in a brief flash of white light and was gone.

No sooner did he break the threshold did the booming, disembodied voice of Skyphos declare, "*I was able to successfully reroute the destination of the portal as you requested, Rooster. Philbert Pothier is now positively contained in Ward Nine of the Reliquary. Is there anything else I can assist you with?*"

"Portal high jacking. An oldie but a goodie. Can't beat the classics," Rooster said smiling ear to ear. "Well done, Sweetie. One more thing. I'm sending you a picture of an old coin. Looks Roman. See if you can figure out what it is."

"*Will do. And do not refer to me as 'Sweetie.' It continues to upset me.*"

"That was pretty slick," I said to Rooster with a shit eating grin. "Not sure if you're more dangerous with those pistols or that computer phone. What's Ward Nine?"

"Ward Nine makes the depths of Hell look like summer camp," he replied matching my grin. "Let's just say the next time we see Skip he'll be more than willing to tell us anything else that he may have *neglected* to mention."

Tossing him the peculiar coin, I said, "So, I'm assuming you don't believe that Skip's simply been paying homage to dead draugrs amidst his misadventures in land acquisition, eh?"

"No. I don't," he replied casually snatching it from the air and stuffing in his pocket. Giving me a pensive look, he asked, "Back in the Reliquary, do you remember when Coop told us that Smitty wandered off in the woods obsessing over the fact that they were 'missing' something?"

"Yep," I replied curious as to where he was going with this.

"Well, Big A asked Coop if Smitty said anything before he walked off."

Thinking back on the conversation, I felt a light bulb go off in my head, and muttered, "Yep … He asked specifically if Smitty said anything about — a coin." Curiously glaring at Rooster, I said, "He knew."

"Or at least he suspected," Rooster replied nodding his head. "Which means he probably knows what we're dealing with. There's clearly a link between the coins and the ability of the Maradim to open gateways. And it seems we have until midnight on Friday to figure out what it is."

Nodding, I said, "You ever been to the salt capitol of the United States?"

"Nope. But it sounds like a good place for an ambush."

"Roger that," I replied holstering the otherworldly shotgun on my back. "Almost like we planned it."

As Rooster began to collect the various documents strewn across the metal desk, I spotted the unopened, second manila envelope which was covered up by the map. Grabbing it and prying open the clasps, I pulled out a single sheet of paper.

"Forgot about that one," Rooster said looking up at me. "What's in it?"

"It's a list. Names and addresses," I muttered, studying the handwritten roster crudely scratched onto the folded legal sized paper. "Looks like a hundred people or so. You think it's a target list of some sort?"

"Dunno, maybe," he replied preoccupied with stuffing the various documents back into the first envelope. "We'll have Skyphos run the names through the database when we get back — figure out the correlation. We need to get out of here."

"Roger," I muttered tucking the sheet back into the envelope.

Accidentally dropping it on the metal floor in the process, I bent down to pick it up and happened to focus on a single name circled on the lower right hand corner of the document. As my brain processed what I was looking at, I slowly stood upright as an intangible chill raced up and down my spine. Without the ability to speak, I was slammed by wave after wave of deep rooted emotion from my mortal past.

Human emotion. Emotion long since suppressed. Buried. Forgotten — until now.

Realizing something wasn't quite right, Rooster said, "You Ok?"

Without making eye contact, I placed the paper on the desk and pointed to the name 'ERIN KELLY' scribbled in block letters and circled in red ink.

No. I was not Ok. Far fucking from it.

Chapter 26

QRF Compound, Bosnia
5 July 1998 - 08:15 Hours
14 Years Earlier

"Got something to tell you, sir. And you're not gonna like it," grumbled First Sergeant Coates making his way into the mess tent as I sat alone at one of the several makeshift wooden tables studying our first mission brief since arriving in Bosnia three days earlier.

"You planning on making another pot of joe?" I muttered with my face buried in a stack of satellite photos. Still contemplating whether or not I had the balls to drink the first cup of Tony's morning brew I'd been staring at for the past hour, I said, "If that's the case — you're right. I'm not going to like it."

"Oh, apologies your highness," Tony drolly replied with his signature scowl. "We're fresh out of quadruple mocha-kateeno lattes this morning." Nodding at the nineteen-eighties vintage industrial percolator sitting ominously in the corner, he said, "Nothing wrong with that coffee. Hell, you've been drinking it for ten years for Christ's sake. Quit acting like such a woman."

"Quadruple mocha-kateenos, eh?" I rhetorically muttered, highly impressed with his deliberate butchery of my favorite gourmet java when stateside. Putting down the stack of documents, I gave him a stoic glare, and said, "Tell me something, Big Sarge."

"What's that?" He replied with a shit eating grin.

"Is being that funny a full time fucking job or just something you dabble in on the side?"

"What can I say?" He replied taking a seat opposite me at the table. "It's an unfortunate side effect of putting up with your sorry ass day in and day out."

"Fair enough," I said smirking. "So, you here to actually tell me something or just stopping by to give me shit?"

Taking a healthy swig from his Green Bay Packers coffee mug, he muttered, "I just got off the radio with Task Force. They're sending in a humanitarian team. Should be here any minute. A priest and a doctor. They evidently need an escort to the northern sector."

"Escort duty?" I grumbled with a highly pissed off glare. "What the hell do they think we are? The goddamn National Guard? Who sent the orders?"

Rising to my feet and incredibly chapped at the thought of some pencil pushing dickhead having the balls to relegate my team of elite shooters to a squad of babysitters, I barked, "Actually, never mind. I'll call the Colonel right now and get this squared away. No frigg'n way we're carting a couple of limp-dick civilians around the goddamn Bosnian countryside. That's what those weekend warriors at Task Force are for. This is total bull—"

"You Captain Robinson?" A female voice boldly called out from the entrance to the tent.

Spinning around with a deep scowl to find myself completely awestruck by a striking vision of olive skin, brown eyes, and flowing chestnut hair tied into a tight ponytail I very awkwardly replied, "Ah, who are you?"

Taking a few steps toward me while forcefully extending her hand, she smugly replied with the cutest damn smirk I'd ever seen, "Doctor Limp-Dick Civilian. It's a *real pleasure* to meet one of America's *finest*."

And that was how I met Erin Kelly. Or more appropriately, insulted her in our first meeting. Regardless, it took me all of about five seconds to realize that in the most unlikely of places and under the most unlikely of circumstances, I'd met the woman I fully intended to spend the rest of my life with.

Now granted, at the time I wasn't counting on the fact that within the next six months I'd see the rest of my life run its natural course. Bit of cosmic irony there. My timing always did suck when it came to women.

⁂

"Got to be times like this when you ask yourself what the hell you were thinking," I said meeting Doc Kelly at her Humvee and handing her a canteen as we trudged through the mud toward the command shack in a wave of staggering humid heat following an epic rain storm.

"What do you mean?" She replied taking a quick drink and handing it back to me, seemingly unfazed by the weather and subhuman living conditions.

"What do I mean?" I rhetorically asked glancing around the compound. "You traded the life of a *highfalutin* Boston surgeon for *this*."

"What's your point?"

"My point? For the past two months you've been living like a frigg'n gypsy in a war-torn circle of hell trying to *help* people that really don't want your damn help. And you're more than likely going to get yourself killed in the process if you keep it up. I mean seriously — What the hell are you doing here, Doc?"

Pulling to an abrupt halt, she said with a hard gaze, "Not that it's any of you're business, Captain, but maybe — maybe I'm looking for something."

"Looking for what?" I asked noting the intensity in her voice. "Something you lost?"

"No," she replied softly with her brown eyes burning with empathy. "Something I took. That I need to give back."

And left me standing alone in the mud thinking there was a hell of a lot more to Erin Kelly than met the eye.

My men and I weren't the only ones here on a mission. That much was clear.

⁂

"That's good enough, Doc," I muttered as the needle penetrated my skin for the umpteenth time, nearly completing the lengthy row of stitches. "You getting paid by the stitch here or what? Put an amen to it already."

Without diverting her attention in the least from closing the sizable gash running from my right shoulder clear down the length of my arm, she frustratingly murmured, "This would go a hell of a lot faster if you'd simply — Shut your freaking mouth for two seconds and let me concentrate."

"Anybody ever tell you that your bedside manner really sucks," I said with a wide grin, finding it damn near impossible not to stare at her.

As the stinging-sharp pain of a deliberate needle jab made me yelp, Erin said, "Oh, my hand slipped. Sorry about that."

"That was completely uncalled for," I said with a stern yet playful glare.

Chuckling to herself while putting in the final stitch, and tying off the thread with a pair of tiny tweezers, she said, "All set, tough guy. Probably want to lay off the pushups for a couple days … You're going to have one hell of a scar when this heals."

"Chicks did scars," I muttered admiring her handy work.

"Is that a fact?" She asked fixing me with her mesmerizing brown eyes.

"Don't they?"

"Well, *they* must — if you say so," she said quickly packing up her medical instruments.

"What about you, Doc? You dig scars?"

"No," she replied walking out of the med tent with her bag in hand. "But I have been known to make exceptions."

⁂

"Good evening, Dean," said Father Watson as he and Doc Kelly pulled their Humvee into the compound and the final minutes of daylight faded from the remote countryside. A hard chill rolled through the air as the Bosnian autumn was quickly giving way to the renowned harsh winter. "Apologies for our unannounced arrival, however, it appears that our radio has shit the proverbial bed."

"Shit the bed, eh? Pretty sure there's a more priestly way to put that, Padre," I said chuckling. "You know that you and the Doc are always welcome to a room in the Ranger Hotel. The accommodations are notably less than accommodating, and the continental breakfast consists of a stale MRE and some really shitty coffee, but the price is right. In the meantime, Luke will get your comms squared away."

"If I wasn't such a tired old man, I'd say something else of an unpreistly nature," he wearily replied. "In lieu of that, I'll simply say Thank You. If you'll excuse me for a moment, I need to make Task Force aware of our situation before they start wondering what the hell happened to us." And he stumbled off in the direction of the command shack, amidst Lieutenant McCormick and his team prepping for evening patrol.

Walking to the rear of the hummer to find an equally weary Doc Kelly unloading their gear, I said, "Long day?"

"Long day," she confirmed. "Don't suppose there's any chance of getting a hot shower in this joint?"

"Define what you mean by hot."

"That's what I figured," she grumbled. "How about a beer?"

"Actually, you may be in luck in that department. Willis smuggled a few cases in yesterday." Grabbing her gear, I said, "Follow me. I'll show you to the *VIP* suite. We can hit the armory on the way."

"The armory?"

"Where else would we keep our beer stash? One could make a compelling argument that on multiple fronts, beer is more valuable than bullets out here."

Shaking her head and subtly laughing as we traversed the dimly lit compound, she said, "The Armory Pub, huh? That is so *you*."

"Not sure if I should be flattered or offended," I muttered with a smirk. "Tell you what, you ever get tired of playing doctor — we may even have an opening for a bartender. Pay sucks but you'd have some high quality clientele. And you wouldn't even have to shower regularly. I mean this is a real win-win proposition here."

"Yeah, that sounds really great. I didn't realize such a visionary entrepreneur lurked beneath that battle hardened solider facade," she replied dripping of sarcasm.

"You laugh now but watch — before you know it, armory pubs will be popping up in third world countries all over the globe. Don't say I never gave you an opportunity to get in on the ground floor. This could be big, Doc."

"Well, I guess it couldn't be any worse than tending bar at the Irish Rose," she said with a hint of pride.

"Whoa, The bar in Boston — Irish Rose? You worked there?"

"Yep. How the hell do you think I paid for medical school?"

"Damn," I muttered adding yet another reason why my Erin infatuation was well founded. "That's impressive."

With her demeanor slipping toward something like a veiled remorse, she said, "In retrospect — probably should have just stayed with bartending."

"What do you mean?" I asked unsure whether or not she was joking. "Not sure slinging Guinness at drunk Bostonians is quite as noble as being a heart surgeon."

Looking me straight in the eye she softly said, "Maybe not. But it's easier on the soul. That much I'm sure of." Snapping back to her jovial self, she added, "Who knows? Maybe they'll take me back when I finish up over here. New beginnings, right?"

"New beginnings," I solemnly echoed as I watched her disappear into the tent, "I'll drink to that."

Chapter 27

The sound of screeching brakes followed by a rapid succession of horn blasts snapped me from my moment of melancholy reflection and back into my peculiar reality. Wondering what happened to Rooster, and thoroughly confused as to why there was a taxi in the miniature shadow realm tethered to Skip's apartment, I turned my gaze to the irate cab driver enthusiastically waving his hands while shouting various obscenities at me in a foreign language. Backing out of the street and onto the nearby sidewalk, I watched my new friend stomp on the gas pedal and speed off down the side street like a middle eastern Vin Diesel.

As a stiff gust of wintry air howled through the towering buildings surrounding me, I pulled the collar of my peacoat around my neck and started moving toward the nearby intersection which was dimly lit by a series of frost covered street lamps. Reaching it within a few hurried steps, I looked up at the sign and muttered, "State Street. Son of a bitch."

As my brain registered where I was, I slowly turned to my right to find a familiar Boston landmark on the nearby corner.

Blankly staring at the contrast of glossy red doors, signature green exterior, and pointed arched windows decorated with more whiskey signs than should be legal, I said, "New beginnings."

And boldly crossed the street to see a bartender that I used to know.

⁂

Taking at seat at the rather empty bar, with absolutely nobody paying me any attention, I couldn't help but think that the Irish Rose in all its old-world charm and lustrous dark wood didn't hold a frigg'n candle to the Quartermaster. I bet they didn't even serve RoosterBragh. Damn that ginger bastard for turning me into a bar snob. Glancing at the clock hanging next to the rather impressive collection of liquor stacked on the wall behind a manly row of taps, I noted it was almost midnight.

"It's always dead on Tuesday nights, bro," said a rather large dude wearing a gray hoodie as he took a seat on the stool next to me. "They said I'd find you here. Rooster was kind of freaked out when you up and ported from Skip's place like that. How'd you do that, by the way?"

Pulling the hood back to reveal a rather handsome, rugged looking gent with some seriously gelled hair and impressive mutton chops, I did a triple take before saying, "Mick?"

"Yeah, bro."

"You — you shaved. You getting married or something?"

Chuckling, he replied, "No way, hommie. This is just my 'Caveman about town' look. Don't really dig it to be honest. Feel naked." Running a comb down his sideburns, he said, "Although the chops are epic."

Not really sure what to say to all that, I asked, "What are you doing here?"

"I'd ask you the same question," he replied giving me a somewhat concerned look. "Not sure you're going to like what you find here, bro."

Before I had a chance to respond, the sound of a familiar voice just about made my damn heart stop.

"Hey, Mick. You want the usual?"

Turning in disbelief to see none other than Doc Kelly standing behind the bar in a tight green tee-shirt bearing a big white shamrock and jeans that hugged her petite frame flawlessly, I felt all the air instantly leave my lungs and a blast of adrenaline race uncontrollably through my entire body. Amazingly, she didn't look a day older than when I last saw her fourteen years earlier.

"You know it. Thanks, Erin," Caveman happily replied. Turning her attention from Mick and looking me square in the eye, she just stared for a long second or two. Wishing like hell she could see me but knowing damn well she couldn't, I sat perfectly still lost in her brown eyes until something very unexpected happened. She said, "And how about you?"

"Ah, me?"

"You," she said smirking. "Tall, dark, and brooding. You want a drink or just plan on staring at me all night like a creep?"

"Oh, sorry. I'll have whatever he's having."

Giving me a casual nod, she turned and strolled to the far end of the lengthy bar to pour a couple beers. Turning to Caveman, in a state of astonishment, I blankly said, "She can see me. Why can she see me?"

"She was touched by an angel," he replied leaning on the bar looking rather pensive. "It leaves a mark, bro. Same reason she hasn't aged since the last time you've seen her."

"You're talking about when Azazel put the mind whammy on her."

"Yeah, man. Fourteen years ago."

With my mind swimming with questions, I gave him a stern glare and said, "So explain to me how she knows what your 'usual' is."

"Whoa, easy there, big guy. It's not like that," he said grinning. "Ever since that throw down in Bosnia, the Guild has kept a close eye on the Doc. I'm here most nights during her shift. Truth be told, she never goes anywhere without one of our folks in close proximity." Pointing to the very far end of the bar, he said, "See that dude down there?"

Casually turning my head, I spotted an burly guy in his mid-fifties with dark shoulder length hair and well groomed mustache softly playing piano in the corner. Sporting a leather biker jacket and designer sunglasses, he very casually scanned the crowd while doing one hell of a nice rendition of an eighties song I couldn't quite place. Somewhat perplexed by the peculiar faux beret looking thing on his head, I said, "Yeah, what's his deal?"

"That's Grayson," he replied. "He's Erin's shadow tonight."

"Is he wearing a beret?"

"Yeah, bro. Legit, right?"

"So, Erin's under surveillance," I grumbled without further commentary. "Why?"

"More like she's under protection. Our protection."

"Why the hell does she need protection?"

"We figured it was only a matter of time before the Maradim tried to snatch her up after Bosnia. Doctors are primo targets. And she's had success."

Thinking back to the church where Erin was forced to deliver the junior giants, I said, "With the anakim births."

"Yup. We're guessing they've left her alone all this time because she kind of dropped off the grid for a while after you exited stage left. Although that list you found seems to suggest she's back on the radar."

Walking back and sliding two pint glasses of Black and Tans in front of us, Erin said, "You guys want anything to eat? Kitchen's open for another half hour."

"No, thanks," Caveman replied. "I'm just swinging through."

"Ok, See you tomorrow then?"

"You know it," he said raising his glass. "Best Black and Tan in town."

"Damn straight," she agreed. "I hope you bring Duncan by. I need my beagle fix." Shooting me a curious glance, she walked off and disappeared into the kitchen area adjacent the bar.

"Beagle?" I said giving Caveman a confused look.

"Yeah, bro. Lil' D's a creature of many disguises. The ladies love the beagle," he said shotgunning his beer in about two seconds flat. "I gotta bounce. Got rounds to make. Big A wanted me to tell you to get your bahooky back to the Quartermaster pronto. Wouldn't keep him waiting too much longer. Uncle Skip's been spilling his guts since you guys stuck him in Ward Nine."

"Think I'll hang here for another few minutes," I said as my gaze noticeably drifted toward the kitchen door. "Got some catching up to do."

"Careful, broseph. You're treading in dangerous water. Erin's had a rough few years trying to cope with what happened in that church. She's been upside down, man. A woman apart. After a couple months of some serious depression, she walked away from her life and been working right here ever since.

Nothing good can come from you hanging around." Throwing a few bucks on the bar for a tip, he asked, "How'd you know she'd be here anyway?"

"Hunch," I muttered still trying to process what he'd said.

"Well, you're not going to like this, but — Deacons are not part of the world of the living, bro. Erin's human. And you're — not so much. All you can do for her at this point is cause more damage. Especially if she realizes that you're — *You*."

Although I knew he was probably right, it pissed me off to hear it, just the same. Giving him an unfriendly glare, I reluctantly nodded and said nothing. Taking the hint that it was one hell of a sensitive topic, he gave me a rather heavy handed yet encouraging slap on the back and gracefully left. Staring at my untouched pint, I just sat there stewing. This was not a scenario that I was remotely prepared for. Thinking Big A and the rest of the Guild could collectively kiss my ass for the next few hours, I took off my coat to reveal the black RoosterBragh tee-shirt I was still wearing and made myself comfortable. It was time to get drunk. Really frigg'n drunk. Epically drunk. Not sure how much alcohol was required to get an undead, semi-divine super solider liquor'd up, but I was hell bent to find out. Slamming my glass of beer like it was a shot, I slid the empty pint across the bar.

"You drinking to remember — or forget?" Erin asked appearing unnoticed from the kitchen area.

"Ah, not sure yet," I awkwardly said somewhat taken aback. "Maybe another drink will help me work it out."

"Spoken like a true drunkard," she said while grabbing the glass and smiling at me. "Another Black and Tan?"

"Please. And a double shot of Jager. Actually, just bring the bottle if you'd be so kind."

"Man on a mission," she said as she turned and pulled a bottle of Jäegermeister from the liquor collection lining the wall to the rear of the bar. "That bad, huh?" Putting a shot glass in front of me, she proceeded to pour a healthy dose. "So what *are* you drinking to?"

Raising the glass, I looked her squarely in the eye and said, "To old friends — and new beginnings."

Downing the burning liquid, I placed the glass on the bar as she gave me an intrigued glance and poured another one. As I reached out to grab it, I noticed her eyes drift to the sizable scar running down the length of my right arm. Although it had long since healed, it was still more than noticeable. Fixated on it, she began to say something and abruptly stopped.

As her pensive gaze shifted to my face, she studied me for a long second and softly said, “Chicks dig scars.”

Longingly meeting her gaze, I was about to say something very witty, when the moment was broken by the manifestation of a floating, translucent screen to my immediate left. As an image of my otherworldly ginger colleague appeared, my pocket started to violently vibrate.

“Hey, buddy. Firstly, nobody beside you can see or hear me. Secondly, that vibrating sensation in your pocket is your phone. Take it out and answer it so it doesn’t look like you’re talking to yourself.”

Thinking that his timing seriously sucked, I dug around in my pocket and pulled out the small plastic device he’d given me earlier in the day. Flipping it open, I asked Erin to please excuse me for a moment and grumbled, “This had better be important.”

“You need to get back here,” Rooster quickly said. “We figured out the link between the coins and the anakim raiding parties. The Alpha’s called for a Gathering. First time — ever. This is big. We’re going on the offensive.”

“Understood,” I muttered as the intensity of Rooster’s words snapped me back into a somewhat rational mindset. Although I wanted nothing more than to stay here with Erin and fill in the blanks of the last fourteen years, I knew it was futile. The situation had changed.

I had changed.

As the screen began to dissipate, Rooster said, “Don’t worry about Erin, man. She’s well protected. Oh, and there’s some cash in the pocket of your coat. Leave a tip. Hurry Up.”

Snapping the phone shut and begrudgingly stuffing it in my jeans, I grabbed my peacoat and found a wad of hundred dollar bills in the pocket that I’m pretty sure wasn’t there earlier.

"I, ah, gotta go. Thanks for the drink," I reluctantly said to Erin as I dropped the entire stack of money on the bar.

Still staring at me with a somewhat blank look, she said, "This may sound really strange, but — do I *know you*?"

Feeling like my heart was being pulled from my throat with a pair of pliers, I took a deep breath and lowered my head. Burying all the things I wanted to say to her in a dark place in the back of my mind, I looked into those big brown eyes and muttered, "I never did find out if chicks dig scars. I'll be seeing you, Doc."

Turning to give Grayson a nod, I abruptly left the Irish Rose with a lump in my throat and a scowl that would stop an anakim dead in its tracks.

Chapter 28

Raven Spire was just as creepy as the last time I'd been there. Fortunately though, in lieu of having to make the repeat trip up the frozen trail of tears to Stephen's bolt hole atop the First Realm, all I had to do was step through a nifty portal Rooster opened from the Quartermaster. Sometimes it was the little things in afterlife that put a smile on my face.

What can I say? I am but a humble dirt soldier.

"Everyone's assembled," Rooster said as we entered the dark rotunda lit only by the roaring hearth blazing in the center. "We need to take our post with Abernethy. This way."

"Who are all these folks?" I asked with a whispered voice following him around the perimeter of the medieval-like room.

"I'll explain later," he replied with a hushed tone. "We're late."

Surrounding the pit-like hearth in a semicircle were seven distinct groupings of humble stone seats occupied by what appeared to be Deacons in the first row and what I presumed to be clerics in the second. Regardless of who they were, everyone was sitting like solemn statues with their heads bowed in perfect silence. And if we were the last to arrive as Rooster alluded, several seats were ominously vacant. Quietly making our way to where Abernethy sat alone on the end of a row of six empty seats, we took our respective places to his side and back.

As if they were awaiting our arrival to get started, the towering flames subsided and a pedestal-like podium formed in the center of the hearth. Rising to his feet, Stephen humbly stepped onto the platform and removed the hood of his cloak to reveal his signature stoic gaze, complimented by eyes burning with intensity. As if on command, each Deacon amidst the circle slowly raised their heads and followed suit. Focused solely on the Alpha, they continued to sit in reverent silence in clear anticipation of his message.

A quick scan of the faces revealed an eclectic group of men spanning all variations of ethnic composition and physical stature spread across all known periods of history. Ironically, no one looked a day older than forty. Although each man vastly different, their eyes were the same. Not in color or shape — but in spirit. They were the eyes of warriors. Cold — with a hint of compassion.

As I settled in, I suddenly felt an inexplicable prickling sensation on the nape of my neck. It was like somebody was watching me. Staring at me. Eavesdropping. Somebody that wasn't — *here*. Quickly looking around the room in attempt to locate the source, I came up empty. It was weird as hell.

Turning quickly, I whispered to Rooster, "Do you feel that?"

"Feel what?"

"This is a call to arms," Stephen said somberly not giving us the opportunity to finish the conversation. His voice echoed in a surreal manner throughout the circular structure. "The likes of which, there has been no equal."

Pausing and slowly turning on the pedestal to meet the intent gazes of his followers, he said, "For two millennia we have stood upon the brink of the delicate Balance between the light of mankind and the abhorred beings that draw the Earth into darkness. Beyond the call of our mortal existence we have sacrificed, bled, and upheld our solemn oath without flaw or falter. But our task is not complete. It begins — Now."

With his voice steadily increasing in volume and intensity, he said, "Sitting amongst you is the Seventh of Seven. The *last* of forty-nine souls bestowed with the mantle of Deacon. The *last* of which to join our humble ranks. The Lines of Seven are complete — hence by definition, the Balance lies in the greatest of jeopardy."

Stephen spoke with a fervent eloquence to which I'd never heard an equal. The energy in the room was indescribable. Almost electric. Whether it was the combined presence of all the Deacons congregated in a single place or something else entirely, I couldn't be sure, but it was intense. Rippling, surging waves of intangible forces billowed through the crowd as Stephen continued in a more reserved tone.

"Never before have we gathered our ranks as we do now. For never before has the Guild been compromised in the manner we find ourselves in at the present moment." Stepping down from the stone platform and slowly making his way through the crowd, he paused at an empty seat. "What I am about to tell you will be difficult to comprehend. But you deserve to know — for the totality of the situation will either strengthen our collective resolve or subsequently solidify our ruin. And with it — the ruin of the Father's great creation."

Scanning the faces of the seated Deacons, he boldly said, "As in the days of old — The anakim are reborn in, what we believe to be, staggering numbers. Azazel and the Maradim have grown to a strength that is, quite candidly, incomprehensible. And if the Prophecy is to be believed — the liberation of the fallen Watchers is imminent." Pausing, he added, "The reckoning is upon us."

As his stoic mask returned, he boldly declared, "While the source of this resurgence remains unclear, the consequence to the Lines of Seven is shockingly definitive. We have suffered loss — unparalleled loss. Where the strength of forty-nine Deacons will be required to combat the greatest challenge put upon us since our very inception — we are but twenty-five strong." As a roll of astonishment slowly overtook the crowd to hear this staggering admission, Stephen slowly stepped upon the pedestal once again. "The dark forces of our enemy have claimed the lives of nearly half our brothers across the Seven Realms."

Making direct eye contact with me, he solemnly said, "Twenty-four Deacons — erased from existence. A fate more than unworthy of their testament."

With my mind again flashing back to Azazel and the captive Deacons entrapped in holy flame, I broke eye contact with Stephen and gazed at the stone floor. They weren't dead and he damn well knew it. He was lying. To what point or purpose was yet to be determined.

Scanning the room, he said with conviction, "For too long have the Maradim operated in the shadows of our Sight — Praying upon the very flesh and will of mankind. I've gathered you here because we now have an opportunity to end it. Once and for all."

As confused whispers began to emanate from within the ranks of the gathered Deacons, Abernethy boldly rose to his feet and addressed the group.

"It is as we've suspected, lads. They've a shadow realm. A shadow realm with a network of tethers that shift throughout the Earth. That's how the anakim have been moving about undetected."

"That is simply not possible," sternly said a wide shouldered, dark skinned gent with a deep African inflection in his booming voice. Quickly standing, he locked eyes with Big A from across the hearth with an intense pensive gaze. "Such a thing is not possible, Abernethy. You know this."

Leaning forward, Rooster whispered, "That's Berko. Archdeacon of the Third Realm. He scares the crap out of me."

"Aye. But it is possible," replied Abernethy. "It's been done before. Long ago. It requires an object of power."

"What object could perform such a feat?" Berko scoffed.

Flipping him what I presumed to be the coin we lifted from the Skipper, Abernethy said, "An Instrument of the Passion."

Casually snatching it, Berko's face hardened as he gave it a scrutinizing glare. "A Tyrian shekel — The Thirty Pieces? Can this be?"

"Aye, the Judas pennies. The cursed blood money paid for the betrayal of Jesus Christ himself. It's the key."

"Even with an Instrument, this action would require a level of power and mastery well beyond that which Azazel could summon of his own accord," Berko said will conviction. Turning to Stephen, he said, "This is proof. He is receiving aid from within the Heavens."

Without the slightest waiver to his stoic mask, Stephen replied, "I will not dispute these claims, Berko. There are forces at work here that we cannot begin to comprehend. But it matters not. We have an opportunity to act. An opportunity that has not presented itself until now." Turning and nodding at Rooster, he said, "Please enlighten our brothers as to your discovery."

Jumping to his feet, Rooster stood aside Big A and produced his gadget phone from the pocket of the black leather bomber jacket he was sporting for the meeting. Feverishly working the screen with his fingers for a quick second, a virtual semi-translucent monitor jumped from the phone and grew in size hovering in mid-air over the hearth. Displaying a series of images to include one of the curious coin and a map of the United States with several flashing dots, he faced the group in a lecturing fashion.

Clearing his throat like he was a bit nervous, he said, "Ok, here's the short story. Last week an anakim pack showed up in Tallahassee, Florida and went to town on a field of cattle. No different than we've seen them do countless times before across the globe. Although, this time we caught a break. In the course of the investigation, we realized that a metamorph on the Guild's watch list was conspicuously in Tallahassee at the very site of the feeding — mere hours before it happened."

As interested murmurs were heard throughout the intent audience, Rooster started to pace around the hearth while flipping various images onto the floating monitor. "So we paid him a friendly visit, and it was pretty clear he'd been operating under orders from the Maradim."

Pointing at the coin, Berko still had clutched tightly in his hand, Rooster said, "That's when we found the shekel. Amongst other tasks, the metamorph was given precise instructions to place it in a 'special tree' to which he was given a set of grid coordinates."

Pulling up an enlarged image of the coin, he said, "A Skyphos analysis indicated that it is, in fact, one of the Thirty Pieces of Silver — a dark Instrument we thought to be long since destroyed. While we have no idea how the coins ended up in the hands of the Maradim, they've evidently been doctored up with an unidentified glyph, providing some extra horsepower."

Pulling up another picture of a tree amidst a thick forest with a section clearly highlighted, he said, "We located this tree at the Tallahassee site. Note the circular mark burned into the trunk. It's a similar glyph as imprinted on the coin."

As the images faded and were replaced by overlapping depictions of the two symbols, Rooster said, "The way we figure it, the mating of a glyph on the coin with its counterpart inscribed in a tree — a hemlock tree to be specific — creates a tether. A temporary yet incredibly powerful tether. Best we can tell, it only lasts an hour — maybe two. Once established, a portal can be opened from within the shadow realm, and we all know the rest of the story."

Pausing to survey the attentive faces hanging on each and every word, he added, "It's a well coordinated, precise operation. The locations, times, and dates are predesignated." Pointing to the map as it zoomed in on a small town in central New York, he said, "According to the information we intercepted, the next portal will open here — Liverpool, New York. Friday — at midnight."

"Thank You, John. Well done," declared Stephen giving Rooster a grateful nod while stepping onto the pedestal. "Gentleman, this is the breakthrough that's eluded us for the better part of two decades. We can only assume that Azazel is concealing his entire legion of anakim within this very realm until which time they come to the Earth to feed."

"Rats in a cage," Berko said rising to his feet again with a fervent look of anticipation. "Their salvation will be their tomb. The fires of judgment shall rain upon them as we storm the gate with the combined force of the Guild."

"They will be shown no mercy, Berko," Stephen replied with a calculated gaze. "However, the combined force of the Guild may not be required." Shooting me a solemn glare, he said, "For we need not storm the gate. We must simply close it."

As muddled whispers echoed throughout the crowd, Stephen casually pulled the hood of his cloak over his head. Stepping down from the pedestal, he said, "Now please return to your stations, brothers. I must consult with the archdeacons."

Following suit, the archdeacons donned their hoods and faded from sight through a doorway that formed within the solid rock wall to the rear of the hearth. The remaining Deacons and clerics filed through a series of other doors that I presumed led back to their respective Realms. Some of them gave

Rooster and I a nod as they passed. Others, not so much. After a quick minute or two, we found ourselves alone in the rotunda.

As the flame resumed its normal raging level, I stood staring into the void while trying my damnedest to piece together what in the hell I'd just witnessed.

Then it hit me like a ton of bricks. I knew what Stephen intended to do. He was going to bring down the shadow realm — and with it, sacrifice the trapped Deacons.

Son of a Bitch.

Chapter 29

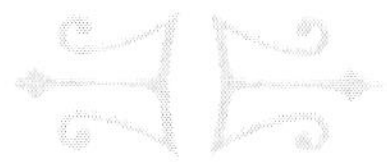

With my thoughts clouded with uncertainty, we abruptly returned to the Quartermaster as I determinedly followed Rooster through a thick crowd of people buzzing with nervous excitement. Although no one knew exactly what was going on, rumors that the Deacons and head clerics from across the Seven Realms were summoned to Raven Spire was fairly conclusive evidence that some serious shit was about to go down.

Stopping at the bar, Rooster casually hopped to the other side and grabbed a couple of coffee mugs. Grabbing a seat and casually gazing around the vast expanse of the QM to find hundreds of people stuffing their faces and slurping down various drinks from copper mugs and pint glasses, I asked, "Just where the hell does all this food come from anyway? I never see anybody cooking."

With a smug grin, Rooster said, "Five loaves and two fish."

Figuring I didn't really want to know anything more, I switched topics and grumbled, "So those were all the remaining Deacons?"

"Yeppers," he replied preoccupied while feverishly sliding his fingers over the screen of his phone. Looking up at me with a sullen squint, he added, "Still can't believe that twenty four have fallen. That just doesn't compute, man. Deacons are a freak'n force of nature."

"Yeah," was all I could muster knowing damn well that they had indeed *not fallen* and were currently a part of Azazel's *collection* in the shadow realm we were evidently about to light up. In an attempt to lighten the mood, I said, "Not an exceptionally talkative bunch, eh?"

"Well, Deacons aren't typically known for their adept conversation skills and butter knife-like wit," he dryly replied as he slid me a tall mug of coffee. "You're a bit of one off in that regard."

"Touché," I muttered taking a healthy swig. Attempting to fill in some blanks from the Gathering, I asked, "So how exactly do you 'close the door' to a shadow realm."

"Well," he replied taking a sip of coffee, "You basically have to unmake the fabric of existence that binds it together. Collapse it on itself. Implode it."

"With a magus?" I asked.

"Maybe with a thousand or so of them, Sure," he replied. "But it would take time. Months. Maybe even years to take down something as large as what we suspect Azazel has constructed." Putting his mug down, he said, "Nope. For a job like this we need something special. Something with juice. Hellfire and brimstone to an order of magnitude that would make an archangel piss himself type of juice. Gotta be quick — decisive. Leave no window for escape."

"And where does one acquire such a doomsday device?"

"Well," he replied, "Theoretically speaking of course, a brilliant yet misunderstood cleric may have developed just such a contraption several centuries ago."

"You don't say?" I muttered.

"It's never been fully tested of course," he said matter of factly.

"I don't even know what to say to that."

"Pretty sure it works though."

"That's great," I dryly grumbled. "Please tell me you don't keep it behind the bar."

"Behind the bar? Hell no," he scoffed. "Nope. That puppy's in my bedroom."

"That's not weird at all," I said as one of the throneVision screens, lining the wall atop the bar, caught my eye. It looked like a heated shouting match between a gaggle of people trying to jockey to the front of a line in an airport terminal. More than happy to get off the topic of the otherworldly suitcase nuke that Rooster evidently had stashed in his underwear drawer, I asked, "Is that an airport?"

Taking a step forward and looking up so he could see the screen, he said, "Yeppers. Looks like Atlanta. Airports in general are nepher havens. We keep an eye on all the big ones."

"Seriously?"

"Hell Yeah. Think about it. Where else can you find thousands of pissed off humans cooped up in a single place for twelve hours a day — every day. It's an uninterrupted current of highly concentrated frustration, anxiety, and self-centeredness. Human nature at its absolute worst. Nephers love it. They feed off the negative energy like it's candy. Airports, man. Bad, bad places. Only one thing worse than an airport."

"Yeah, what's that?" I asked fairly convinced that his whole airport commentary made a hell of a lot of sense.

"Piano bars," he replied blankly as his demeanor subtly hardened.

Thinking that was pretty damn funny, I broke into laughter when something about the look on his face made me quickly come to the realization that he wasn't joking. It was awkward.

Making a poor, yet valiant, attempt to mask my chuckle by faking a cough, I made the mental note to revisit that particular topic at a later time. Fortunately for me, the general awkwardness of the moment was quickly diffused as the booming disembodied voice of Skyphos blared through the ether like my high school principal.

"*Cleric O'Dargan and Deacon Robinson, Your presence is required in the Reliquary.*"

Tossing a scone at me, Rooster grumbled, "Let's go."

Winding our way through the labyrinth of people and hanging a hard left at the giant oak, we crossed the threshold into the Reliquary. Amidst the feverish activity of the DOC staff preparing for what appeared to be World War III, we quickly proceeded up the stairs to the command bridge where my gaze was drawn to a gigantic digital clock sitting atop the massive monitor on the circular wall of the rotunda. Boldly displaying the date, time, and a foreboding countdown timer, it read — '07:32 Wednesday, 1/8/12, T Minus 34 Hours - 28 Minutes.'

Reaching the top of the spiral staircase, we found Caveman, Tango, and Cooper Rayfield talking to an assortment of field agents thru several live tele-Link feeds while taking turns updating a virtual map hovering in midair to their front. And somehow in the mere hours since I'd last seen him, Caveman managed to regrow his fury manscape. Impressive.

Spitting some tobacco juice into a plastic cup, Coop gave Rooster a hearty bro hug and turned to me with an extended hand. "Howdy, hoss. Cooper Rayfield. At your service," he said with a thick drawl and intense eyes.

"Dean," I said exchanging a firm shake. "Good to meet you."

Finishing his conversation with a field agent who appeared to be wearing an impressive ghillie suit, Tango waved his hand over the virtual screen and it quickly faded from sight. Turning to Rooster and me with an exhausted yet resolute look in his eye, he said, "Hey, guys — here's the situation. Thirty-four hours and change until the window opens."

Gesturing to the map floating to our front, he pointed to a section of woods highlighted with a pulsing red circle. "This is ground zero in Liverpool. Using the grid coordinate you lifted from the Skipper, Crockett and his guys located the hemlock tree marked with the glyph."

"Is Crockett the dude in the ghillie suit?" I asked.

"Yeah, bro," Caveman replied. "But that wasn't a suit."

"Right," I muttered wondering why the hell I even bothered to ask. Shifting back to Tango, I said, "And you were saying."

"At the moment, I've got a total of four teams on the ground. Two tactical squads in an overwatch of the target location itself. And two surveillance teams canvassing the surrounding town trying to pick up some passive intel from the locals."

"Nicely done," I muttered admiring the uncanny mixture of good old fashioned reconnaissance tactics and otherworldly technology that would make the CIA piss themselves. "Any movement thus far on the target?"

"No. It's been quiet. Nothing's been within a couple miles of the hemlock tree since we arrived on site twelve hours ago."

"How about the town?" Rooster asked waving his fingers over a virtual screen displaying a map of the Village of Liverpool. "Anything suspicious?"

"Well, aside from the distinct possibly that nobody told these guys that it's not 1983 anymore and they have a museum dedicated to *salt*," Tango said dryly, "It all seems fairly normal." Pulling up what appeared to be a pie chart on a separate screen, he added, "Although, there is one curious demographic to note."

Studying the graph for a quick second, Rooster said, "No freaking way. Is that accurate?"

"Yeah, bro," said Caveman. "It's a nepherville."

"And they're all Blind? I don't believe it," Rooster said skeptically.

"*It is accurate, Rooster*," said Skyphos jumping into the conversation. "*The entire population of the Village of Liverpool, New York — two thousand, three hundred and forty two souls have definitive levels of nephilim DNA. None of which are Conscious of their condition.*"

"Are you sure?" Rooster blurted out shaking his head in disbelief.

After a very deliberate pause, Skyphos replied, "*Yes, Cleric. I am always sure. I am Skyphos.*"

Figuring I needed to interject before Rooster caught a divine bowling in the side of the head, I asked, "Someone want to break this down for the Guild impaired? What, pray tell, is a nepherville?"

"Yeah. Sorry," Tango said casually smirking. "It's what we call places with a concentrated nephilim population. Typically, they're smaller pockets within towns or cities. Places where the Conscious tend to set down some roots and colonize. Or — in the case of Phoenix, Arizona — it's pretty much the whole damn place. Nevertheless, it's pretty rare to see a town like this — where everyone's Blind."

"Got it," I muttered somewhat following the plot. "And by 'Blind' you mean they don't realize they're nephers."

"Durn skippy," said Cooper. "Blind as a Texas salamander on a sunny day."

"Right," I muttered making the bold assumption that whatever Coop just said was Redneck for 'Yes.' "And, out of pure curiosity — why hasn't anyone told them that they're not quite human?"

"*They have broken no Rules nor have displayed any inclination to gaining Consciousness of their condition, Deacon Robinson. Per our covenants, we simply allow them to continue with their existence unhindered.*" Answered Skyphos.

"Ok," grumbled Rooster impatiently. "So we have a whole town of Blind nephers who have an affinity for Eighties hair, a proud history of mining salt, and are otherwise seemingly harmless. Let's move on."

"Yep," said Tango, snapping back into mission mode. "To that point, Stoner and his crew have established a five mile perimeter around the target, watching for any indication of portals, veils, or wards. So we're pretty confident that between our boots on the ground and the magi dragnet we'll be able to pick up any Maradim attempts to infiltrate the area of operations."

"Well done," said Rooster quickly analyzing the floating map displaying the tactical grid around the hemlock tree. Giving me a stern look, he added, "Now all we need is a plan."

"We don't have a plan?" Asked Caveman raising a bushy eyebrow. "Then what went down at Raven Spire, bro?"

As Rooster and I took turns exchanging the details of what was discussed at the Gathering, the crew stood in perfect silence taking in the unfiltered report on the compromised state of the Guild and the believed strength of the Maradim. Although they asked no questions, the solemn looks made it pretty clear that the dire magnitude of our current situation was more than well understood.

Completing the brief, Rooster said, "So, we're in a holding pattern until Big A gets back. I suggest we all try and grab a couple hours of sleep."

Looking like he was about to pass out from exhaustion, Tango emptied what appeared to be his fourth or fifth can of Redbull and muttered, "I'll take the first shift. Any change to the situation — I'll send word."

"Not a chance, pard," said Coop assuming position at the captain's chair behind the wooden desk. "You look like death on a cracker. I've hung buck heads on my wall with more life in 'em than you. I'll take the first shift. Anything happens — I'll holler. Y'all get some shut eye."

"Let's go, Tiberious," I said giving Tango a slap on the back. "I've never seen a stuffed deer with pastel pants and cute hair, but Coop has a point. You look like three bags of shit."

"Back in three hours," Rooster said to the group. Turning to Coop, he muttered, "If Big A shows up in the meantime —"

"I'll let Y'all know — Count on it. Now, go on. Git."

⁂

Breaking free from the crowd and making the short trek to my humble room within the bowels of the Quartermaster, I felt the adrenaline rush of the past eighteen hours quickly fade, and was instantly overcome with total mental and physical exhaustion. I barely managed to get my peacoat off before the primal need for sleep took over, and I collapsed onto the small bed. Although my mind was still a maelstrom of confusion and anxious thought, I fell into a deep slumber as quickly as my head hit the pillow. Right before everything went completely blank, the question 'How did it come to this?' repeated in my head like a broken record.

And then something rather unexpected happened. Somebody answered me.

"Destiny," said a familiar voice. "If you believe in such things."

Opening my eyes to find myself atop the familiar green hillside staring into the majestic mountain range on the far horizon, I said, "What if I don't?"

"I'm afraid it matters not, Dean. Even someone as strong willed as you cannot change that which is destined to be."

Barefoot and dressed in a linen tunic, I turned to my right to find Stephen clad in similar attire and gazing mournfully into the perfect blue sky.

"Am I dreaming?"

"Yes," he replied without averting his eyes from the horizon.

"So you've reverted to high jacking my dreams again, eh? Thought we'd cleared that particular hurdle."

"You can't beat the classics," he casually said matching my snideness.

"Touché."

"At the moment, it's the safest way for us to communicate," he said slowly turning his head to look at me. "And we have much to discuss."

"Ok. Let's start with why you're lying to everyone about the fallen Deacons. They're not dead."

"No — they are not," he replied with no hint of emotion. "And I have chosen to conceal that fact from our brethren."

"And you think Azazel has them locked up somewhere in that shadow realm, don't you?"

"I do."

"And it's your intention to leave them there when we take the place down, isn't it? To abandon them — to let them die."

"It is," he said definitively.

"Well, we can't frigg'n do that!" I barked as the memory of Smitty's paralyzed gaze sent a surge of anger through me. "Don't you want to save them?"

"A fair question," he said shifting his gaze to the mountainside. "What I want — what any of us *want* — is irrelevant. Our responsibility is to the Balance — to the preservation of mankind. Nothing can deter us from that objective. It is our charge. Our purpose. And if my suspicions are correct, we are already too late to help them. A timely end to their torturous state of existence will be a welcomed mercy."

"I don't get it," I grumbled.

"I do not believe they are simply imprisoned, Dean. I believe they are being systematically stripped of their mantle. The Father's Wrath ripped from the very fiber of their souls to which it was joined by His very hand."

"What?" I scoffed. "How is that even possible?"

"I cannot be sure," he replied starting to slowly pace along the hilltop and shaking his head. "But the fact you witnessed our brothers encased in holy flame was my first clue. The ability to summon such power is only held by two types of beings. The Father himself —"

"And the archangels," I said completing his sentence.

"Correct," he muttered giving me a sage glance. "In simplistic terms, the holy flame is an angel trap. Created for the express purpose of removing the grace of a rogue angel when they've fallen to the darkness."

"So you think one of the archangels is using holy flame to strip Deacons of their Wrath?"

"That is my theory," he replied as the stoic mask returned to his face. "A theory that Gabriel does not share. Such an act of treason would shake the very foundations of the seraphic court and divide the Heavens in the process."

"So the traitor's an archangel," I muttered.

"Or someone very close to their ranks. The truth of the matter continues to elude me."

"You said the holy flame was your first clue. What was the second?"

"The mantle of power bestowed upon each Deacon represents an equal share of the Father's Wrath. A divine energy that freely shifts between our ranks based on the active number of Deacons. Hence when a Deacon's term has ended or they perish — their mantle is returned to the collective source."

"But that hasn't happened — because they're still alive," I muttered.

"Yes," he said frowning. "Or at least being *kept* alive in some form of sedated stasis. In Azazel's 'collection' as you witnessed in your vision."

"So, their mantles are not just being stripped from them," I said connecting the dots. "They're being stolen."

"Stolen," he said rhetorically with his frown deepening. "For what purpose? That is the question."

Dialing back an earlier conversation, I said, "But you said it yourself — the Wrath will turn upon itself before serving the enemies of Heaven."

"The Wrath is restrained by the free will of the Deacon," he said dryly. "And when that control is compromised. What then?"

When I offered nothing but an empty look in response, he said, "And now you understand my position." He sighed. "This is a sacrifice each and every one of them would gladly make for the sake of mankind."

Closing the distance between us, he gently put his hands on my shoulders and said, "Our time is short, Dean. It is very likely that Azazel and his traitorous *ally* have already harvested the power of twenty four Deacons. By your own account — there is but one vacancy left in his prison. Should *one more* of our brothers fall before we destroy the shadow realm — the scale will forever be tipped in favor of the darkness. The very Wrath of the Deacons will be turned upon us. Should that happen," he lowered his hands from my shoulders, "I cannot begin to fathom the consequence. The world will not be enough. This — must be done."

Three stout knocks on my door instantly snapped me from the dream state and back to the present moment. Instinctively looking at the clock hanging on the wall, I took note that it was nearly ten-thirty in the morning. I'd been asleep for almost three hours.

"Pardon me, Deacon Robinson," a young voice called from the hallway. "The archdeacon has returned. He requests your presence in the Reliquary as soon as possible."

"On my way," I grumbled, already on my feet and putting on a fresh RoosterBragh tee-shirt from the stack on the bureau. Someone had also taken the liberty of dropping off a pair of black tactical fatigues, which I happily threw on as well. Throwing the peacoat over my shoulder and heading out the door, I muttered under my breath, "There'd better be some frigg'n scones waiting for me."

Chapter 30

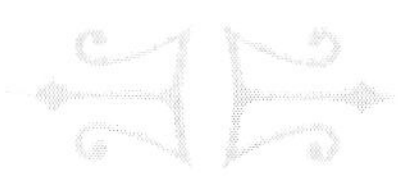

"Gather round, lads," said Abernethy with a fiery edge as the usual suspects gathered on the command bridge amidst the hive of activity occurring on the Reliquary floor below. "Time is against us so I'm going make this brief. We have much to do in the way of preparation."

Waving his hand in the air, a virtual tactical map appeared and hovered to our front. Upon closer inspection, it depicted the location to the portal entrance in Liverpool and a detailed rendition of the surrounding area. Facing the group, Big A said, "Let's start with what we know. According to the blethering shapeshifter occupying a cell in Ward Nine, the Maradim will activate the portal precisely at five minutes after midnight on Friday." Pausing to glance at the countdown timer, he added, "Thirty-one hours from now."

Leaning closer to Rooster, I whispered, "Is he talking about Skip?"

"Aye," Rooster smugly replied thoroughly enjoying the fact I still couldn't understand a damn thing Abernethy said.

As Big A waived his hand for a second time, several dots appeared on the hovering virtual battlefield. "The metamorph was also kind enough to share with us that a security team of beasties will be the first to pass through the gateway."

"Gothen?" Tango asked.

"Aye. Most likely varangian," Abernethy replied. "Although I wouldn't rule out any combination of other nasties. Regardless, he said to expect at least four of them. Two of the scunners will guard the portal. The rest will conduct a sweep of the immediate area. Only after they're satisfied that the location is secured will they bring the anakim pack through. At which time, two guards will remain at the gateway, and the rest of the lot will carry on to the feeding site."

"How many anakim are we talking about?" Asked Caveman.

"According to Skip — between ten and twenty," Rooster replied. "The more rural the area, the more they let out to play."

Casually hawking a wad of tobacco juice into his trusty plastic spittoon, Coop said, "We gonna ambush the biggins as soon as they clear the gate?"

"Nae," Big A replied. "The raiding party will be allowed to continue to the feeding site." Pointing to the map, he said, "Which we believe to be this farm — two miles northeast of the portal."

"We're going to let them go?" Asked Tango sharply.

"Aye, we are. For they're not our objective," said Big A with conviction. "Berko and his Deacons will deal with the bastarts."

"Because we're going into the shadow realm," I muttered somewhat rhetorically putting two and two together.

A wolfish grin stretched across Abernethy's face. "We're going to pay Azazel and his lads a wee visit. A visit he'll not likely forget. It's a job for a thousand —"

"Or a job for a few," Rooster said completing the thought. He squinted pensively. "We're gonna need the Dragonfly."

"Aye, Jackie. We're gonna need the Dragonfly. You've less than thirty-one hours to make the bloody thing work."

As his eyes flashed a blazing red for a quick second, Rooster assuredly replied, "That's thirty more hours than I need."

⊰⊱

"Coffee? Food?" Rooster asked as I plopped down on what was coming to be known as 'The New Guy's' stool at the Quartermaster bar. Decked out in a black tactical uniform similar to mine, he was sporting his full compliment of firearms and cutlery. Although he was amicable, there was a noticeable sternness about him.

"Hells Yes," I grunted glancing at the small antique clock hanging next to the row of wooden kegs lining the wall to Rooster's back. It was closing in on eleven P.M.

"We've got ten minutes to be in the Reliquary for final prep and deployment," Rooster reminded me as he slid a plate of tasty morsels across the bar. "You and Big A been in the Dreghorn this whole time?"

Making the mental note that I truly hoped never to lay eyes on the otherworldly training facility again for the rest of my undead life, I grumbled, "Yep. Time really flies when a centuries old Scotsman is all up in your grill."

As the rest of the crew spent the past thirty-odd hours prepping for Operation Trap Door, I had the pleasure of spending some quality time with Abernethy being schooled on some of the finer points of the Deacon's mantle. Although I was still somewhat of a blunt instrument, I had a couple new tricks up my sleeve — or cloak as it were.

He chuckled. "So you good to go?"

"Good as I'm gonna be. Let's hope it's good enough. The big guy seems to be satisfied that I'm mission capable … Or at the very least — he's satisfied that I'm not going to accidentally fry him with a ball of fire."

"So you made some progress then?"

"If you measure progress by how many times I reduced the Dreghorn to ash — then Yes — I made some progress," I muttered. "Let's just say it's a good thing I have the thunder stick."

"Gotcha," he said realizing it was a touchy subject. "You'll be fine. Trust in your ability. We do."

Shooting him a grateful nod, I turned attention to my plate as my mouth watered like a faucet from the overpowering aroma hitting my nostrils. "Thanks for the steak. Think I could eat a whole cow at the moment."

Scoffing, he quickly replied, "Not just a mere steak, my friend. That's an aged filet mignon garnished with asparagus drizzled in Rooster hollandaise sauce. Cooked a perfect medium rare. Which, if I'm not mistaken, is your preference."

Still amazed at just how much these guys knew about me, I said, "In my file?"

"In your file."

Shrugging it off, I cut a man-sized chunk and happily tossed it in my mouth. "How about you? The *realm buster* all squared away?"

"Yes. Yes, it is," he replied glancing at what appeared to be a jumbled Rubik's Cube sitting on top of the bar to my immediate right. "The Dragonfly's ready for action."

Thinking it was so incredibly 'Roosteresque' to create a weapon of mass destruction out of a toy, I reached out to grab it and take a closer look.

Grabbing my hand, he said, "Yeah … Might be better to look and not touch."

"Is that a frigg'n Rubik's Cube?" I asked pulling my hand back.

"Maybe."

"You turned a kid's toy into an apocalyptic bomb? Really?"

"Of course not," he scoffed. "I turned a kid's toy into a complex arming and trigger device. Actually thought it was pretty clever."

"So the bomb's inside?"

"Yeppers," he replied. "And it's not a bomb. It's a quantum destabilizer mechanism fueled by concentrated Gehenna fire and a smidge of nonbaryonic dark matter. The whole system's no bigger than a marble."

As I stood gawking, he added, "And for the record — a Rubik's Cube is not a kid's toy. It's an engineering marvel of logic and reason."

"Right," I muttered. "Why can't I touch it?"

"Technically you can touch it. But an intense blast of Gehenna fire could inadvertently trigger the Dragonfly, and you're not exactly known for your —"

"Fair enough," I grunted. "Say no more."

Snatching my coffee and glancing at the clock, I said, "Grab your stocking stuffer and let's go. The others will be waiting. It's go-time."

⁂

This time when we rolled up on the Reliquary the typical chaotic bustle was replaced by a palpable calm. There was a nervous excitement in the air, but the clerics and acolytes manning the various battle stations circling the rotunda were all about business. Cool professionals. The plan was set. It was time to execute.

"Bout time you girls showed up," barked Stoner looking down on us from the Command Bridge looming high above the floor.

"Who invited Mr. Wizard?"

"We need a magus," Rooster said heading up the spiral stairs.

"Didn't realize we'd be breaching any wards," I said chasing after him.

"Hopefully we're not."

"Oh, good."

"It'll all make sense in a minute," he affirmed.

"Lovely," I grunted.

Reaching the top of the platform, the entire crew was gathered with exception of Abernethy. Tango and Caveman were huddled in front of a virtual teleLink monitor while Coop and Stoner were diligently prepping their gear. And oddly, Duncan was happily sitting on the captain's chair lapping some coffee from an oversized mug. Nonchalantly looking up at me, he casually waived a tiny hoof and continued to enjoy his beverage.

That was unexpected.

Everyone was decked out in varying versions of black fatigues and bearing an interesting array of weapons and assault packs. Taking post next to Tango, I got a good look at Crockett, the ghillie suited cleric, on the other end of the teleLink feed.

And damn — I kind of wish I didn't know that he wasn't wearing a ghillie suit.

Perched like an apex predator in some form of a tree stand, he blended almost perfectly into the backdrop of branches and steadily falling light snow. His intense green eyes were the only real thing I could lock on to. The rest of his silhouette seemed to shimmer in a perpetually morphing camouflage pattern.

"What's the latest?" I asked trying my damnedest not to stare.

"Calm before the storm," Tango replied. "According to Crockett here, it's all quiet on the western front."

"With exception to a shit ton of snow and an occasional deer — there's been nothing inside the perimeter," Crockett grumbled in a subdued, gravelly tone.

"Looks cold," I said.

"It is," he confirmed without emotion. His eyes hardened as his flowing shape became increasingly difficult to differentiate from the surroundings. "Cold doesn't bother me, never has. It's the wind that gets me."

"Call you back when we're about to port," Tango said as Crockett's animal-like gaze continued to sweep the area below his stoop. "Let me know if the situation changes."

"Will do," he grunted and faded from sight.

Giving Tango a curious look, he said, "Crockett's a bit of an outdoorsman. King of the wild frontier — so to speak."

"You don't say?" I said dryly.

"Yeah," he replied, "He's not stepped foot indoors in over a hundred and fifty years."

"Why's that?" I asked.

"Still pissed about the Alamo."

"Right," I muttered not exactly sure how to take that. Making the mental note to address that particular topic at a later time, I turned to find Abernethy standing behind us.

"It's time," he said with a dark gleam in his eye and signature claymore broadsword resting on a shoulder. "Let's review the plan."

As the team gathered around the floating, virtual map, he said, "Our primary objective, lads, is to enter the shadow realm, deposit the Dragonfly, then get the bloody hell out of there before we become permanent residents. Once back on Earth, we destroy the tether thus keeping all the beasties inside."

"Simple — Easy to remember," I muttered.

"From the top then, yeah? Once we port to Liverpool, Dean will activate the tether prior to midnight just as the Maradim are expecting."

Turning to Stoner, he said, "The rest of us will hold fast in Mr. Stoner's veil, and wait for the bastarts to open the door."

"Got it," Stoner said nodding and pointing at the map using a peculiar walking stick inlaid with an interesting collection of sigils and glyphs. "I'll set our hunting blind up here — a few hundred yards upwind of the target — to the north. Should keep us well out of range of any recon party they send through."

"What if they get closer?" I asked. "You gonna beat 'em down with that cane?"

"It's a staff," he casually and somewhat condescendingly replied. "And they could be standing right on top of us and not realize it. My veils are a work of art."

"Then we wait," Tango said moving on with the plan.

"Aye," Abernethy grunted. "Then we wait. When the portal opens — the clock starts ticking, lads. We've one hour to be in and out. One hour. Jackie will have his eye on the time."

"Got it, boss," Rooster said tapping his antique pocket watch.

"Once the beasties come through and secure the area — they'll bring out the anakim pack and head south leaving two guards at the gateway. Once we get the word from Berko that they've cleared out of the immediate area, we'll make our move."

He turned to Coop. "Starting with the guards."

"Yessir," Coop replied holding out his otherworldly longbow. "I'll silence the guards while you and hoss creep in to close the deal."

"With arrows?" I asked skeptically. "From a couple hundred plus yards away — in the dark."

"Dagum right," he replied with an air of confidence.

"Coop starts it — we finish it. Quietly," Abernethy said shifting focus to me and putting a marked emphasis on the *quietly* part.

"Roger that," I said still unconvinced that an arrow launched from a football field's length away was going to do anything to a varangian beside piss them off. Even if it did hit them.

"With the guards disposed of, we cross the threshold into the shadow realm. Me and Dean first — then the rest of you lot. Mickie, You and Duncan will bring up the rear, yeah?"

"All over it, boss," Caveman said with his furry hands wrapped around the hilt of a double edged battle axe.

"Duncan is coming on the mission?" I asked.

"Yeah, bro," he replied glancing over at the pocket pig still happily slurping away on his coffee. "Lil' D's a hog of war. He's been throwing down with anakim for centuries. Old school, bro." Pausing to proudly gaze upon his little buddy, he added, "I don't go into battle without him."

"Right," I muttered not sure why I bothered to ask.

"Jackie, If you please," Big A said, handing over the remainder of the brief to Rooster.

"Yeppers," he replied nodding. "A realm can only be unmade from the very physical location that it was created. So, once inside we'll need to identify the point of origin." He glanced at Stoner.

"I've got the spell ready," Stoner barked. "The ley lines at the point of origin should be pumping out some serious juice. Won't take me long to get a lock on it."

"Once we figure out where we're going — it's an all out sprint to get there and deploy the Dragonfly. Tango will take point and scout the path."

"Got it," Tango chimed in.

"As with any realm," Rooster continued, "the point of origin won't be far from the Earthly tether. So, with any degree of luck — we'll be in and out."

"How long to we have once the armageddon cube goes thermonuclear?" I asked.

"Well, that's the tricky part," he replied.

"Tricky?" Tango asked raising an eyebrow.

"It's hard to tell," Rooster said. "Depending on the size of the realm and the amount of energy binding it together — five minutes. Maybe a little more."

"Maybe less?" Coop asked, with a hint of concern.

"It's possible," Rooster replied. "And once the devolution process starts — it's a runaway train. There's no stopping it. With exception, of course, to an act of divine intervention — which is highly unlikely. At any rate, I've rigged a timer on the arming mechanism to give us a head start back to the portal. But, trust me, we don't want to be in there when the Dragonfly kicks into gear."

"What exactly does this most Rubik of cubes do?" Asked Caveman with a look of mild consternation.

Choosing his next words very carefully, Rooster replied, "Picture a whirlpool. Now picture that same whirlpool but made of judgment fire tainted with dark matter. Now picture that swirling mass of fiery death expanding exponentially while violently sucking time and space into itself, like a voracious black hole, until there's nothing left."

"Epic," Caveman muttered seemingly impressed and terrified at the same time.

"So we'll be keen not to take in the scenery, lads. Once we're out, we destroy the tether trapping the rats on the burning ship," Abernethy said sheathing his sword. "Anymore questions?" Everyone sternly shook their heads. "It's sorted then."

"We get in, drop off the package, and get the hell out," Rooster said with conviction.

"Slap high-fives. Call it a day," I added.

"Anything gets in our way — We cut the bastarts down where they stand," grunted Abernethy. "We shall not fail. The Light shines upon us." His eyes squinted into an icy glare. "For our fallen brothers — For the Balance."

"The Balance," the group replied in unison.

As an otherworldly door subtly appeared to the rear of the command bridge, I willed the cloak into being and felt a warm jolt run through me as it manifested in a spectral flash around my shoulders. Almost immediately, a familiar prickling sensation on the back of my neck gave me the unequivocal feeling that somebody else was *here.*

Watching. Listening.

The same feeling I had at the Gathering.

What the hell?

Quickly convincing myself that I was just being paranoid, I shook it off and followed Big A across the threshold to begin perhaps the strangest tactical operation I'd ever embarked on. The ominous words of Stephen rung heavy in my thoughts.

The world will not be enough.

Failure was not an option.

Chapter 31

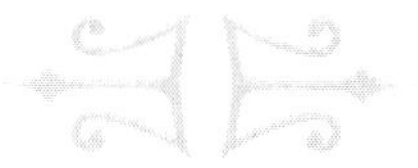

It was cold. Damn cold.

Of course it was. Evidently that's the only kind of place I had the pleasure of visiting in my humble not so afterlife. When this was over I was *so* renegotiating the terms of my immortal contract.

White sandy beaches — Palm trees — Fruity drinks with little umbrellas — Bikini clad super models — Ricardo Montalban and his vertically challenged buddy yelling 'Ze plane! Ze plane!' — Pamela Anderson diligently patrolling the shore line on a surf board. I would accept nothing less.

The brogue accentuated bark of my supernatural superior snapped me from my fleeting moment of happy delusion as my boots crunched through the snow in a small clearing bordering a heavily wooded area on the fringe of Liverpool, New York.

"This spot will do, lads," Abernethy said pulling to a halt. "The target is straight away."

It was quiet. Serene. A steady flurry of light snow gracefully drifted from the night sky adding a fresh layer to the already blanketed trees and surrounding landscape. A picturesque half moon sporadically peaked out from beyond the clouds, giving the scene an occasional opaque glow as the moonlight danced along the wintery setting.

"Jackie, Time check."

"Eleven forty-two, boss."

Big A flipped me the cursed coin. "You're on."

"Roger," I said snatching it from the frigid air and quickly tucking it away in a pocket. Instantly snapping into mission mode, I pulled the hood of the cloak over my head and willed the spatha and the otherworldly Winchester into being.

After all, showing up to a sword fight with just a sword was so incredibly first centuryish.

Feeling the presence of both the sheath and holster-like scabbard on my back, I focused my will for a quick second and just like that — I melted from sight.

Yep. I could turn myself invisible. Who knew, right?

Well, not exactly invisible but close enough. One of the nifty little tricks of the trade Abernethy had shared with me during our pre-game training session. The Deacon's cloak was full of all kinds of similar arcane pleasantries. Unfortunately, it didn't come with an owner's manual. Typical.

At any rate, now that I had my cloaking device activated — it was time to get the party started.

Cloak-*ing* device … Yes, I went there. Couldn't resist.

Finding the hemlock tree with my Sight was not a difficult task. Infused with power from the glyph, it shone like an otherworldly beacon on the far side of the clearing, roughly a hundred and fifty yards to the south. Leaving the rest of the team to set up shop in our temporary defilade position, I focused on the tree and took three bold steps.

Instantly arriving at the target location, I heard a rather curious bird call and turned my attention upward. Crouched within the tree tops was an ambiguous shape that was barely detectable even with my Sight. As what appeared to be a hand started to wave and form a peace sign, I realized it was Crockett. And he could evidently still see me despite my best attempt at veiling myself. Casually returning his wave, I watched in awe as he fluidly leapt through the treetops like a supernatural Tarzan until he was simply gone.

"Yep. That was cool."

Making the mental note that I really needed to figure out what that guy's deal was at some point in the future, I pulled the Judas penny from my pocket and carefully approached the tree.

Just as the first time I touched it, the shekel hummed with a dark energy. A cursed energy. As I reached up and placed it into the circular pattern burned into the trunk of the hemlock tree it was like placing a key into a lock. A perfect fit.

Upon the mating of the Instrument with the Earthly tether, a brilliant radiance of purple-white light flooded the surrounding forest. It was pure elegance. So much so that I had trouble watching it. Slowly swirling into the form of a sphere, it steadily ascended into the night sky. It was also familiar. I'd witnessed such a phenomenon before.

And that's when I heard the voice.

Free me.

It was the voice of a woman. She said it again.

Free me.

And then rather violently, the sphere was yanked downward and sucked back into the coin by an unseen force. The light abruptly vanished, like a candle was blown out. As the tether once again looked like nothing more than a simple tree in a moonlit forest, I heard another word spoken in a tone so desperate that it made me cringe.

Please.

And then there were only the sounds of the woods.

My face curled into a brooding scowl as the reality of what was happening became suddenly apparent. My mind flashed back to the Bosnian church and Azazel parading around with his glyph-laden scythe.

The unfathomable power required to punch a hole through the fabric of reality and create a temporary tether to a shadow realm was not provided by the coin. The coin was merely the conduit. The raw power to perform such a feat required something more. Something unquantifiable. Something precious.

A human soul.

A human soul brutally harvested by Azazel himself, just as he attempted to do to Father Watson as he lay on his deathbed. The mysterious glyph on the shekel was a binding spell — a soul trap.

Son of a bitch.

My mind instantly filled with harrowing images of the unspeakable torture inflicted on countless people to feed this dark purpose. The primal power of the cloak surged from deep within, and I found myself instinctively snarling. My hands were instantly covered in the ashen stone gauntlets, and the snow around me began to melt. I think I was about to do something incredibly stupid when the snapping of a branch from a nearby tree overloaded with snow broke me from the fury fueled trance.

Exhaling deeply and burying my rage, I turned and took three bold steps returning to the crew.

The passing of the next few minutes felt like hours — days — months. As I regained rational control over my emotions and briefed Abernethy and the team on my discovery, we waited anxiously in our veiled hiding spot for the Maradim to open the portal.

"Trapping souls," Rooster rhetorically muttered in a whisper. "Damn ..."

"Bloody hell," Abernethy grumbled.

Stoner was about to say something but never had the chance, for a floating virtual screen appeared, and a shimmering image of Crockett came into focus.

"The portal's manifesting," he whispered.

Snapping our combined attention across the clearing, we locked on to a definitive source of light steadily pulsing from the hemlock tree. Within a few seconds, the bluish-white silhouette of a large doorway formed on the edge of the wood line. And out stepped two figures. Although they were large framed and noticeably tall, even across the great distance, they were certainly not anakim. It also appeared they were naked. Awkward.

"Lycaon," muttered Crockett in a hushed tone as the picture on the screen shifted to an aerial view of the now open portal. The dark figures took a few steps into the clearing, and without speaking they dropped to all fours and took the shape of steroid infused super wolves. Immediately darting into the surrounding forest with their noses to the ground, they faded into the darkness of the trees, evidently looking for anybody that shouldn't be there. Like us.

"Keep still, lads," Abernethy whispered.

The occasional muted sounds of large paws tramping through the snow at a high rate of speed echoed through the woods, and it was fairly apparent that the lycaon sentries were systematically making their way around the perimeter. Within a few seconds, two more figures emerged from the dim lighting of the gateway. They were taller than their predecessors and all dolled up in snazzy looking body armor making their already formidable shapes look *just that much more* ominous. Despite the darkness, I was still able to make out an array of sharp and pointy instruments of death strapped throughout their torsos. And oddly, it actually looked like one of the jokers had an M-240 machine gun slung across his shoulders. That was new.

As the wonder mutts completed their patrol and met the newcomers at the entrance to the portal, Crockett's camouflaged face once again appeared on the screen.

"The new guys are varangian. One of them has a gun," he muttered. "A big one."

"Sweet," Tango said with just a hint of sarcasm from behind me.

Within another second or two, another shape passed through the portal. A massive shape. Boldly stepping into the woods like he owned the joint, there was no mistaking it — anakim. And a big frigg'n one at that. Like — easily twice as tall as the varangian and easily four times as wide — kind of big. Its muscles had muscles. Hell, I think its frigg'n hair had muscles. The cloak flared up around my shoulders as I clenched my teeth and pulled my hands into tight fists.

"The biggins are coming," muttered Coop pulling two broad head arrows from the quiver hanging from his shoulder.

"Aye. Steady now, lads," Abernethy said eagerly.

Exchanging a few quick words with the sentries, the Head Mother Frigg'n Anakim in Charge turned his mammoth head back toward the portal and grunted something undecipherable. Then he simply broke into a hefty jog heading north across the clearing.

Upon receiving the command, a parade of giants emerged from the portal like it was a frigg'n clown car. One after the other a single file of massive shapes, clad only in dark tunics, lumbered through the otherworldly gate and fell in formation behind their leader. The dark mass of behemoths glided through the clearing in lock step like a unit of highly disciplined soldiers, making no sound as they methodically moved through the woods. It was unnerving to put it mildly. Azazel had been busy.

If not for the up close and personal experience I'd already had with such creatures I think I would have shit myself. Instead, I slowly drew the spatha from its sheath and locked eyes with Big A.

"Steady," he said again.

When the entire horde of giants had passed through the gateway and faded into the darkness of the woods, the two lycaon scampered after them leaving the varangian sphincter twins alone at the entrance.

"I counted eighteen," Caveman whispered to the group.

"Yep," I grumbled. "Same here."

Duncan, who I'd actually forgot was there with us, let out a low growl-like squeal, which I presumed was pocket pig for 'Me too.'

"They were, ah, rather large," whispered Tango.

"I've seen bigger," Rooster said. Which earned him a jaw dropping gaze from the rest of the us.

"Aye," Abernethy grunted in agreement. "That was a wee lot."

A long silence followed as we waited for the green light to proceed to the next phase of the mission. At the rate the anakim were moving, it wouldn't be more than a few minutes before they reached the feeding site. They were on the clock, just like we were.

Meanwhile, at the portal entrance, the varangian sentries stood like statues. They neither moved nor spoke. If not for the occasional beam of moonlight silhouetting their armored frames, you wouldn't even know they were there.

In what felt like a damn eternity, but was probably no longer than a couple minutes later, a blurry image of Crockett appeared again on the teleLink screen and muttered, "Got word from Berko. They've picked up the raiding party. You're clear to proceed. Good hunting." As quickly as the screen appeared, it dissolved and faded from sight.

Rising to his feet and carefully drawing his broadsword, Big A said, "Cooper, if you'd be so kind."

"My pleasure, boss," Coop coldly replied as he slowly stood up. Fastening not one, but two arrows on the string of the mighty longbow, he effortlessly drew it back to his ear. "In the throat?"

"That'll do," Abernethy replied very businesslike. Shooting me an icy stare, he said, "I'll take the one on the left. The other beastie is yours."

"Bad Guy on the right," I confirmed. "Got it."

"Separate the head. The barzel arrows will confine them to their human form — but not for long."

"Roger that." I took my post on his side and willed the argent metal gauntlets into being. Wrapping my hand tightly around the hilt of the spatha, I raised it in an offensive position. "Ready."

Doing his very best impersonation of Legolas' red-neck elvish cousin, Coop raised the bow and muttered, "On Three."

"One."

His eyes hardened into a predatory squint as he locked on the targets.

"Two."

His arm slightly drew back on the already taut bowstring adding *just* the precise amount of tension to make the impossible shot.

"Three."

His mouth curled into a dark grin as his fingers released the arrows.

Game on.

Chapter 32

The barzel tipped bolts rocketed from Coop's bow and whirred like missiles across the clearing in a blur of motion. Despite the great distance and looming darkness, they impossibly plunged squarely into the neck of each varangian sentry before the poor bastards even had a chance to turn their heads.

It was rather impressive. The country boy got some dagum skills.

Making the mental note to never piss off Cooper Rayfield, I took three bold steps while focusing on the rightmost Bad Guy. Instantly manifesting opposite my heavily armed adversary, who was desperately trying to pull an arrow from his throat while attempting to morph into an unnatural bear creature, I muttered, "Let me help you with that."

And cleaved his head off with a single powerful stroke of the spatha.

As Abernethy did the same to the bogey on the left, our quarry evaporated in a flash of white radiance as the rest of the team joined us at the portal entrance.

"Jackie, time check," Abernethy said.

"Eleven minutes after midnight. Fifty-four minutes on the mission clock."

"On with it then. Remember, lads, Don't believe anything you see in there," Abernethy said in a hushed tone. "It's a shade of reality. Nothing more.

We'll be cut off from Skyphos — so stay close." He shifted attention to me. "Ready?"

"Ready," I confirmed.

He smirked and offered a courteous bow. "Then, by all means — after you."

Giving him a smug grin, I focused for a quick second and felt my veil snap into place around me. Trading the spatha out for the Winchester, I called for the fire and cocked the lever chambering an otherworldly round. Raising the gun to a reflexive firing position under my chin, I boldly approached the doorway as the calmative awareness washed over me.

With a cold gaze and a tad of reluctance, I crossed the dimensional threshold fully prepared to find a cavern of hellish nightmare or something inconceivably worse waiting on the other side. Quickly passing through the expected vortex of time and space, I felt my feet firmly plant on soft ground and was rather shocked by what I saw.

It was neither nightmarish nor horrible. Oddly enough, it was sunny — and warm — and breathtaking.

An unsurpassed marvel of majestic landscape unfettered by civilization was laid out before me. It was kind of like the golf course version of Jurassic Park without the dinosaurs. Finding myself on the perimeter of a dense redwood forest, I dumfoundedly gawked across a vast savanna carved with ravines and canyons that perfectly melded into countless mesa-like bluffs set against a pristine backdrop of reddish mountains. An intricate network of brilliant blue rivers and streams fed countless gardens that sporadically bloomed amidst the panorama.

And shockingly, there was not a bad guy in sight. Hell, there was no evidence that anybody nor anything even existed here.

The only real indication that this place was not quite Earth was a distinct heaviness to the air. It was off. Oppressive. Laced with a feeling of dread.

Quickly moving from the portal entrance to the cover of a ginormous tree on my immediate right, I took a knee and focused my Sight. Making another visual sweep of the area, I saw nothing out of sorts.

We were alone — for the moment.

Dropping my veil and sending a cautious 'All Clear' signal to Abernethy, the rest of the team advanced through the portal exhibiting similar awestruck expressions as they gazed upon the shadow realm. Everybody, that is, except for Duncan who was seemingly unimpressed. Bit of diva that piglet.

"Whoa," Rooster said panning around the countryside. "Not exactly what I was expecting."

Caveman shook his head. "Nah, this makes perfect sense, bro. Azazel sees himself as a god, right? He's not gonna have some ghetto shadow realm. Dude's gonna go all out." Scoffing, he added, "Probably got a club med with a wet bar out there."

"Where are all the biggins?" Asked Coop dropping the bow to his side while he scanned the landscape.

"Far side of those mountains maybe?" Rooster said looking rather perplexed. "Don't know."

Abernethy grunted. "It's quiet."

"It is," I confirmed. "Too quiet."

"Fifty-two minutes," Rooster muttered, stuffing his pocket-watch into his tac-vest. "Clock's ticking."

"Aye," Abernethy grumbled. "Keep a keen eye, laddies." Turning to the resident magus, he said, "Which way are we going, Mr. Stoner?"

"I'm on it," Stoner replied throwing his assault pack on the ground in a small clearing amidst the trees. Pulling out his sleek laptop, a small bronze bowl, and a series of mason jars filled with random shit, he quickly went to work on whatever voodoo he planned on using to locate the shadow realm's point of origin. Rooster immediately jumped in and started helping like they'd done this particular dance a time or two before.

As Big A stood watch over them with his broadsword drawn and scowl on his face, the rest of us fanned out in a tight perimeter securing the area. Taking the flanks, Coop raised his game and actually loaded three arrows on his bow while Tango produced a pair of obscure machete-looking things from opposing sheaths fastened to his chest.

"Those are cute," I muttered, taking a good look at the Aladdin-like blades.

"Kukri knives," he said. "The blades are coated in barzel. Picked them up in Nepal during the Gurkha War."

Although I was by no means a history buff, I was fairly certain that the Gurkha War was fought in the early eighteen hundreds. Finding myself at a real loss for a coherent reply, I simply grunted and made the mental note that he was a few years older than he looked.

Caveman secured our six o'clock with his oversized battle axe and hoglet of war while I drifted up on the edge of the tree line to cover our twelve with the holy shotgun of Antioch.

Glancing back over my shoulder to see a somewhat comical vision of Stoner and Rooster taking turns dumping ingredients from the various jars into the bronze container while Stoner repeatedly murmured something in Latin, I figured it best not to ask how much longer it would take. Roughly thirty excruciatingly long seconds later, there was a distinct whooshing sound followed by a flash of light. Hoping that was a good sign, I turned to confirm they both still had eyebrows. The no eyebrows thing always creeped me out.

"Found it," Stoner whispered as he shifted his attention from the bowl to his laptop and feverishly pounded away on the keys. As he, Big A, and Rooster studied what I presumed to be some kind of techno wizard GPS thingy on the computer screen, he said, "There it is. A mile and change to our nine o'clock."

Standing and pointing across the landscape, Stoner barked, "Over there. It's the top of that bluff."

Following their gazes past the border of the woodland, it was clear that the point of origin was on a mesa overhanging a picturesque blue pond in the not so far distance.

"Jackie," said Big A presumably wanting another time check.

"Forty-eight minutes, boss," Rooster replied.

"Brilliant. Looks like we can hug the tree line and stay out of the open until we reach that wee loch," Big A said as we congregated around him. "We'll need to move at a good clip, lads. Tango, Find us a path."

"On it, boss," he replied. Decisively sheathing his kukri knives, Tango broke into a full on sprint through the surrounding tree line in the general direction of the bluff. In mid-stride, his feet very suddenly, and without any hint of warning, stopped being feet and started being little tornado-like columns of misty smoke that sparked and flared with greenish white light.

Before he completed another step, the transformation fluidly crept up his legs and torso until — well, it was pretty much all of him. He basically turned into a man-sized cloud of swirling light and smoky haze. Like a surreal swarm of hornets, he then zipped through the air at a blinding pace until he faded from sight into the depths of the woods. Yep. It was weird as all hell. And slightly disturbing.

"Man, I love it when he does that," said Caveman getting a real kick out the fact I clearly had no idea what the hell just happened. "Pretty cool. Huh, bro?"

Before I had the opportunity to respond, Tango Storm Cloud was back. As the swirling mass of glinting fog morphed into the shape of a man, he said, "Follow me. We got a clear shot to objective." And he was Tango again. Just like that.

"Let's move," Abernethy barked.

Adding yet another mental note to my rapidly growing collection, I took point in back of Tango as the group fanned out behind us. As we started double timing through the woods toward the peculiar point of origin, I had the unyielding suspicion we were walking headlong into a fight.

Something here was off. Besides — of course — Rooster, Caveman, Tango, Stoner, Abernethy, Coop, and Duncan. Especially Duncan.

I think we've already established that premise.

Chapter 33

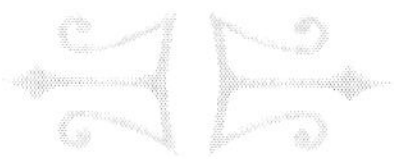

With Tango back in sparky smoke monster form, he drifted through the woods staying a solid fifty meters to our front. Following his lead, the rest of us hauled ass, with reckless abandon, through the plush forest at a superhuman pace. I'm talking like — Olympic sprinters all hopped up on crack cocaine and espresso shots — kind of fast. And with the primal power of the cloak surging through me like electricity, I wasn't even breaking a sweat.

Providing a bit of levity to the situation, Duncan was running step for step with Caveman despite the fact his little piggly legs were only four or five inches tall. Although it made no sense whatsoever, it was funny as hell to see in action.

Racing between a cluster of skyscraper sized redwoods and doing one of those parkour vaulting maneuvers over a car sized stump covered in spongy moss, I spotted a definitive patch of blue sky up ahead. We were rapidly approaching the edge of the forest. As I threw my hand up alerting the crew to slow down to a more cautious pace, the mini tornado cloud buzzed my tower and morphed back into Tango before I could say 'Negative Ghostrider.'

As I instinctively jumped backward a step or two, he smirked and said, "You Ok?"

"I'm good," I grumbled. "That whole smoke on the water thing is going to take some getting used to."

"Understood," he replied with a quick chuckle.

As the rest of the crew quickly huddled around us, Tango said, "Once we pop out of the trees up ahead it's about a half mile to the target. And unless anyone's in the mood for a swim, we need to skirt to the right, around the pond and come up the backside of the mesa. There's a path cut into the rock face."

"Well done, Tiberious," Abernethy said. "Did ye get a good look across the plain?"

"I did. Still no sign of life," Tango replied with a concerned look.

"Dagum strange," muttered Coop.

"Forty-one minutes," Rooster announced.

Turning to Stoner, I asked, "Can you run a veil over us while we get across the field?"

"Maybe," he grumbled. "It'll take all my reserves to pull it off though. No telling how effective it'll be. The energy here isn't like Earth."

"Never mind then," I said. "We'll move at a slower pace. Keep a good spread. Heads on a swivel."

"Aye," Abernethy grunted. "Any sign of trouble — we split up. Dean, You and Mick get Jackie to the bluff. The rest of us will hold the line, yeah?"

With no need for any further discussion, we each nodded and started pushing through the remaining stretch of woods with Tango and I leading the charge. Leaving the safety of the forest and stepping foot into the grassy lowlands made my stomach churn. It was a good half mile of wide open field without a hint of cover until we reached the bluff and surrounding rock formations. And it was broad daylight. Not exactly the ideal scenario for conducting a clandestine infiltration op.

If we were going to get ambushed, this was the place. It was the perfect kill box. Once we got halfway between the mesa and the forest there was nowhere to go — we'd be sitting ducks.

Keeping the pristine blue pond to our left, we carefully maneuvered through the field of knee-high grass on high alert, in a staggered file. It was eerily quiet. The only noises were that of the water steadily flowing from the occasional small creeks and the blades of grass brushing against our shins.

Reaching the halfway point without issue, Tango pointed to the bluff in the near distance and twirled his index finger. Within the blink of an eye he morphed into bedazzled smoke and zipped toward the rock formation like a flock of humming birds.

Reaching into my bag of new tricks, I focused for a quick second and extended my thoughts, creating a telepathic link with him. Feeling the connection snap into place, I used my inner voice, and said, *"Hey, Smoky. It's Dean. You hear me?"*

"Ah, yeah," he replied painfully. *"Feels like you're screaming through a megaphone wired straight to my eardrum."*

"Ah, Sorry. That better?"

"Not so much ..." he cognitively grumbled.

"Right, ah, How we looking up there?" I asked, trying my best to mentally whisper.

"I'm at the top of the mesa. Nobody's home. Got a clear view for miles."

"Roger. Stay where you are. See you in a couple."

"I think my brain's bleeding."

Dissolving the link and making the mental note that I really needed some work on my telepathy skills, I held my arm up in a pumping motion, announcing to the group that it was time to pick up the pace. Breaking into a steady trot, we reached the base of the rock formation within the next couple minutes without any fanfare. Although I was still fairly certain all hell was about to break loose at some point in the near future — it was so far, so good.

Taking the winding path up the three or four hundred foot mesa was not exactly pleasant, but it beat the hell out free climbing up the rock face. And although it didn't appear the path had been used very recently, there was clear indication that creatures of large proportions had traversed it in the past.

"Damn bro, those claw marks?" Asked Caveman pointing to a series of definitive gauges in the shape of extra large talons roughly six feet up on the rock wall to our right.

"Looks it," replied Coop. "And they ain't from no anakim."

"No. No they're not," Rooster muttered like he knew something we didn't.

"You thinking what I'm thinking?" Stoner asked in an unsettling tone.

"Liderc," Rooster said blankly with a thousand yard stare. "No mistaking it."

"Whoa — serious?" Caveman asked tightening the grip on his axe. "There's a liderc in here? But I thought you were the last —" Realizing he'd said something he probably shouldn't have, he cut himself off in mid sentence.

"Focus on the task at hand," Abernethy said, shutting down the conversation. "It matters not, lads."

Although I didn't exactly know what a liderc was, I assumed it was an especially nasty type of gothen. And based on Skip's reaction to Rooster during our 'visit' and now this, I was starting to realize that my ginger buddy was one of them. It also seemed to be a topic that wasn't openly discussed, for what I presumed to be good reason. Figuring it could wait, I continued to trek up the serpentine path on high alert.

A few tense minutes later, we reached the plateau atop the mesa, and there was no mistaking the point of origin was close. The entire place buzzed with a steady current of power — like static electricity only more potent. It actually made the hair on the back of my neck stand up.

"You feel that?" Stoner asked.

"Yeah," I solemnly replied. "Where's it coming from?"

"It's the electromagnetic field. Caused by the ley lines. They run right through the rock."

Reading the empty expression on my face, he added, "Ley lines — uninterrupted streams of elemental energy. Spiritual highways. They connect everything to — well, everything else. You know — ley lines."

Shrugging my shoulders in a 'no idea' fashion, he grumbled, "Damn, Robinson. You need to get out more."

Carefully making our way toward the center of the circular rock shelf, littered with a random collection of boulders, we found Tango crouched behind an outcropping. He was fixated on a group of reddish mountains defining the far horizon. Waiving his hands like we should stay down, we lowered our profiles and inched toward him.

"What is it?" I asked pulling up to his right.

"Not sure. Looks like movement at the base of that mountain. I couldn't see it from ground level. It's faint."

Following the direction of his pointed finger, I gazed across the five or six mile expanse separating us from the mountain range and couldn't see a damn thing.

"He's right," Abernethy confirmed in a hushed tone from behind me. "It's an encampment." Grabbing my shoulder, he muttered, "Project your Sight. Tell me what ye see."

Drawing on the power of the cloak, I shut my eyes for a quick second and focused on the mountains. As I opened them, my Sight raced across the plain like an otherworldly zoom lens locking onto a target. And unfortunately, once it reached the destination and the scene came into focus — I kind of wished I didn't look.

"Giants," I declared. "Hundreds of the them. It's a training area. Looks like that mountain's a barracks of some sort. There's a door cut into the base."

"Anakim HQ," Rooster muttered. "Time to spin up the Dragonfly and get out of dodge. Twenty-eight minutes until the portal closes. Let's be there in fifteen."

"Aye."

Reaching into the man purse slung across his shoulders that he insisted was a 'satchel', Rooster produced the armageddon cube. Creeping toward the center of the plateau, he said to Stoner, "Where do the ley lines intersect?"

Following suit, Stoner systemically tapped his staff on the rock surface until he reached a specific point that seemed to interest him. Muttering a few words in Latin, he tapped the stick again and every glyph carved into the handle instantly flared to life glowing a brilliant white.

"This is the spot," he announced. "Right here. Let her rip."

With a calculated look in his eye, Rooster took a knee at ground zero and made two quick twists of the cube.

"It's armed," he said. "Once activated, the timer will give us a ten minute head start before things get interesting. Then we have another five minutes — or roughly thereabouts — to get out of here. Everybody ready?"

Not really sure an answer of 'No' was appropriate, I nodded in the affirmative as did the rest of the crew.

"Do it," Abernethy grumbled.

Twisting the Dragonfly device into the final configuration, Rooster placed it squarely on the rock floor and took a cautious step backward. Almost immediately the individual squares began flashing an ominous red in a random yet somehow systematic pattern.

"Is it supposed to be doing that?" Caveman asked raising a bushy eyebrow.

"Yep. It's running through the timer sequence," Rooster replied as he turned toward the path to start the trek down the mesa.

"Some of the squares are turning white," Stoner abruptly pointed out with a hint of concern in his voice. "Why are they turning white?"

"It's fine," Rooster said assuredly and with a sharp edge. "One square turns white every ten seconds until the full sequence is completed."

As the entire crew gave him a skeptical look, he stopped walking and added, "Trust me. We're good." He glanced at his stopwatch. "Now, in exactly nine minutes and thirty eight seconds there'll be a hellaciously loud cracking sound followed by an ungodly plumage of black fire and molten ash. If we're still standing here when that happens — we have problems. I suggest we leave."

"Time to go, lads," Abernethy grumbled. "Let's move."

"Same drill back to the portal," I said. "Stay on high alert. Smoky, you got point."

"I'm on it," Tango replied morphing into mystical fog form before completing the sentence.

As the team quickly started to file down the path, we didn't make it ten feet before a distinct and rather definitive 'crack' ripped through the air like a clap of thunder.

"Ah, dudes …" Caveman yelled from the back of the formation with a noticeable quake in his voice. "Hellaciously loud cracking sound …"

Looking over my shoulder to see a raging pillar of black flame shoot hundreds of feet in the air like a really pissed off volcano, I casually muttered, "That was a fast nine minutes and thirty-eight seconds."

"Yes. Yes it was," Rooster drolly replied not bothering to look.

"We should probably run now," I added still gawking at the apocalyptic plume filling the sky.

"That would be a good idea," he blankly muttered.

"Awesome."

As an earthy gurgling noise bellowed from the top of the mesa, I broke into a dead sprint with the rest of the team on my heels.

It was right about then that I had the minor epiphany that the overall concept of deploying a world devouring weapon of mass destruction that was stashed in Rooster's junk drawer for the better part of four hundred years was probably not the best plan we could have come up with. But on the upside, I wasn't nearly as concerned about the horde of giants anymore.

So, I had that going for me.

Which was nice.

Chapter 34

By the time we'd reached the bottom of the mesa, the entire top portion was a swirling fiery maelstrom of rock and sky steadily twisting its way toward the ground. In the category of ridiculous things I'd witnessed, experienced, or even frigg'n heard about in my short lived supernatural existence — this took the frigg'n cake. No words prevailed to remotely describe what was happening in the backdrop of our miracle mile to the portal.

I actually take that back. The term 'Holy Fucking Shit' was probably good enough.

Aligned shoulder to shoulder in a surreal foot race, the crew moved with all the speed and agility we could physically muster. Nearly half way through the grasslands with the pond to our right, we rapidly approached the redwood forest with all hell breaking loose to our rear — quite literally.

"How long do we have, Jackie?" Big A shouted over the harrowing sucking sound of the doomsday vortex.

"Maybe five minutes," Rooster yelled looking over his shoulder and trying to gauge the progress of the devolution process. "Maybe less …"

Zipping through the formation, Tango transformed from smoky haze into metrosexual with cute hair and kept pace with our mad dash. Having returned from a quick recon of the remaining journey, the look on his face didn't exactly instill confidence.

"How we looking?" I asked hoping for a shred of good news.

"Couple things," he yelled. "The good news is that for the moment, we have a clear shot to the portal."

"What's the bad news, bro?" Caveman shouted with Little D galloping like a pint sized gazelle by his side.

"Seems we're not the only ones trying to get there."

"Anakim?"

"Yep." He replied.

Looking over my shoulder to find a dust cloud moving through the savannah at unnatural speed on the periphery of the sprawling fallout zone, I yelled, "How many?"

"Not sure," he shouted back. "All of them?"

"Dagummit," blurted Coop which I thought was an extremely tame explicative to use given the circumstances.

Reaching the edge of the wood line Abernethy pulled to an unexpected halt. With the mesa now completely obliterated and the earth churning whirlpool of death oozing like an oil slick across the landscape, we followed suit offering him a collective look of confusion.

"You lot keep moving to the portal," he said with a resolute calmness unsheathing his broadsword. "I'll be right behind ye."

"Where the hell are you going?" I yelled over the ear splitting calamity.

"To thin out the herd," he replied with his gaze fixed on the anakim in the distance.

"No," I protested. "I'll go."

"Nae, laddie. This calls for a more practiced hand."

Something about the tone of his voice and the hardness in his eyes made it fairly apparent that he planned on making a one way trip.

He was going to sacrifice himself — for the mission — for us.

As a distinct chill raced down my spine and a lump formed in the back of my throat, I held out my hand and said, "Give 'em hell, sir."

"Not to worry," he said in a fatherly tone. "I'll be giving the bastarts more than that."

Firmly grasping my forearm, he pulled me in close. Looking me squarely in the eye, he fervently muttered, "Get the lads home, Dean. And close the door behind ye. The anakim must not be granted passage to Earth."

I nodded.

Without further words, he turned toward the grasslands and faded from sight in three bold steps.

As everyone stood in shock for a quick second, I felt a warm blast of air on our backs accompanied by the violent sucking sound of the armageddon vortex closing in around us. A surge of anger pulsed through me, and I felt the cloak ripple about my shoulders in response.

"Big A doesn't stand a chance, bro," Caveman yelled shaking his head.

"He doesn't plan on coming back," Rooster coldly muttered as his eyes flashed a blazing red.

"Hell No," Tango defiantly shouted drawing his kukri knives. "We're not letting him do this alone."

"Yes we are," I sharply replied burying my emotions and focusing on the mission. "We have our orders."

Turning to the group with a resolute scowl, I coldly barked, "We complete the job. Blow the tether and seal the gate. The only way we're doing that is to get our sorry asses out of here. Big A's given us a chance to finish this. We dare not fail."

After a long second, the team responded with a collection of affirming nods marked with clenched teeth and steely gazes. Leaving Abernethy to a certain death was not something we were prepared to do but given the circumstances — there simply was no alternative.

We had a job to do.

Allowing the anakim army to escape onto the Earth would unleash a catastrophic series of events that would bring mankind to its collective knees.

The decision was easy to make. Despite how any of us felt about it.

This had to end. Now.

"Dean's right. We finish it," Rooster announced to the group with a melancholy sternness, lowering his head. "Let's go."

With the ground below our feet starting to tremble and the vacuum effect of the vortex steadily slithering to within a few hundred feet of us, we knew what had to be done. Without the need for anymore discussion, we resumed our well conceived plan of running like hell toward the one and only way out.

⁂

For the most part, the return trip through the redwood forest was just as uneventful as the first time through. With slight exception, of course, to the thundering sound of swirling fiery destruction and the associated apocalyptic nonsense that accompanied it. Adding to the pucker factor, the devolution process had generated a series of skyscraper-size tornado columns of nightmarish black flame that ominously bounced around the surreal landscape like pin balls ripping everything in their path to absolute shreds. And of course, there was the added pleasure of catching the occasional glimpse of the massive horde of rabid giants racing us to our destination.

Aside from all that, it was rather pleasant.

An excruciatingly long couple minutes later we busted out of the woods. As my eyes quickly scanned the clearing where we'd started this epic misadventure nearly an hour ago, I was elated to see the portal still intact despite the indescribable chaos enveloping its surroundings. The wood line on the far side of the once pristine meadow was a solid wall of black fire and clouds of putrid smoke billowed and swirled throughout the immediate area reducing visibility to almost nothing.

By the grace of God, perhaps literally, we'd arrived in the nick of time.

Realizing we had mere seconds before the gateway to Earth was swept into oblivion, I began to bark the order for everyone to get their sorry asses through the portal — when I felt it. A presence. A dark, dominating presence that made all my senses twitch and the cloak flare with anxious hostility.

We weren't alone.

As if on cue, the layer of smoke obscuring our view instantly dissipated to reveal two figures casually standing between us and the exit. And as the realization of who they were registered with my adrenaline filled brain, I was overcome with burning anger.

With a smug smile on his face that was clearly visible despite the distance, Azazel triumphantly stood in his white garments condescendingly clapping his hands in a slow, overly exaggerated manner. And next to him was the Skipper all dolled up in a very expensive pinstriped suit, looking like he'd just won the lottery.

"You," I snarled in a guttural growl fixated on Azazel.

My thoughts instinctively filled with rage. Boundless rage. My mind was dominated by a single, primal purpose — dispense the Wrath. Instantly losing all semblance of self-control, I felt the cloak roar to life and infuse me with a level of power that made every muscle in my body surge and spasm in response. The calmative awareness that I'd previously experienced was magnified a thousand fold, and I launched into uncompromising attack mode with blatant disregard for anything or anyone else around me.

Still clutching the otherworldly shotgun in my left hand, I willed the argent metal gauntlets into being and yanked the spatha from its sheath as I charged at my enemies with supernatural speed and predatory prowess. Covering half the distance in a fraction of a second, I gracefully leapt and impossibly glided through the air while raising the sword in a devastating death blow as I kept the shotgun carefully trained on Azazel's smarmy face. Before those two sons of bitches even had a chance to blink, I was milliseconds from ending their miserable existence with extreme prejudice.

I felt a dark grin stretch across my face. And it was right about then when it all went to shit. Typical.

Closing in on the unforeseen duo in my fury fueled death dive, I felt like a comet screaming through the atmosphere at the speed of sound. Just as I was about to slam Azazel with a shotgun propelled fireball while simultaneously ripping the sword through Skip's neck, something rather unexpected happened.

I stopped.

Literally stopped. In mid-air. Frozen. Like somebody hit the damn pause button. Sprawled out in a superman pose roughly six feet above the ground, I just hung there in suspended animation without the ability to move anything. I couldn't even blink. What the hell?

"Hello, Dean," said Azazel rather smugly as he stepped away from the tip of the shotgun muzzle mere inches from his face. "Impressive. You have grown stronger than I could have ever imagined. Such the quintessential warrior. So full of anger. And sadly, so incredibly predictable.

"Hey, bossman. Surprised to see me?" said the Skipper with an ear to ear grin. Pulling a sizable glyph-covered knife from the pocket of his jacket, he slowly ran the blade down my cheek, opening a nifty gash. "Funny thing about a good con. You never see it coming until it's too late."

Making the mental note to tell Skip to blow me when I regained the ability to speak, I just hung there fuming in a state of pissed off confusion.

Taking a casual look around the apocalypse that used to be his golf course like wonderland, Azazel muttered, "No, no. This simply will not do."

He snapped his fingers and the deafening sounds of the devolution process instantly ceased. The raging fires, the billowing smoke, the churning earth, the sucking vortex, the tornado columns — stopped. Leaving only pure, dead silence.

Offering me a satisfied wink, he snapped his fingers again and I plummeted to the ground with a healthy thud as he released the unseen force holding me in place.

Unable to break the fall, my face smacked into the charred earth and both the spatha and shotgun tumbled from my grasp. I suddenly felt a sharp pain in my head and my body instantly ached. Without my command, the gauntlets covering my hands and forearms retreated and as did the cloak. Everything went blurry. I could hear Azazel talking but I couldn't make out the words.

They were garbled.

Distorted.

Distant.

Pushing myself off the ground I tried to get to my feet but couldn't seem to get past my knees. I had no strength. My head felt heavy. So incredibly heavy. As my subdued gaze fell to the ground I realized why.

Despite my deteriorated sight, it was unmistakable. I was surrounded by a ring of purple-white fire. Holy flame.

The Deacon trap. I'd walked right into it.

Feeling myself steadily slipping into a complete state of void, I curled my hands into tight fists and tried my damnedest to focus my thoughts — focus my strength — focus on anything. My vision quickly degraded to nothing more than a psychedelic kaleidoscope of obscure colors and shapes. The only thing I could hear was a constant stream of white noise with occasional static mixed in.

It was a losing battle. I had nothing left.

Panic set in. Then anger. Then a string of mental obscenities that would have made a sailor cover his ears.

"No," I repeated to myself in inevitable defeat.

Goddamit it all.

It was over.

I'd blown it.

Chapter 35

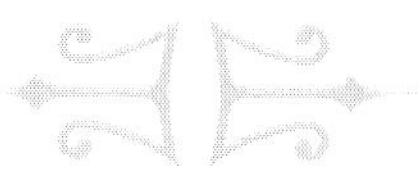

Lying powerless on the forest floor trying desperately to rationalize what was happening, I struggled to formulate a coherent thought. My mind was — jumbled. Random. Foggy. Trapped in a perpetual state of subdued consciousness.

Then, as if on cue, my hearing abruptly returned and my vision snapped back into focus.

"Arise and face your master," I heard Azazel say with a content heir of superiority.

Upon his command, I felt myself effortlessly push off the ground and rise to my feet. Like a mindless drone, I subserviently bowed my head and turned to face him.

What the hell?

"What you're experiencing is the divine affect of the holy flame," he said contently. "I'm told it's a rather strange sensation — to be imprisoned within your own body that is. And quite absolute I'm afraid. One of *Father's* more devious concepts."

Fleeting flashes of lucid thought raced through my head, but they vanished as quickly as they registered with my befuddled brain. The more I resisted, the more the purple flame lashed out and hissed like an implacable slave master forcing its supremacy upon me. Rewriting my thoughts. Beating me into submission.

Using all my remaining will, I called for the cloak but it didn't come. Although I could still sense its presence — it was locked away. Hidden far from my reach.

A prisoner — as was I.

"Resistance, Dean, is as much pointless as it is hopeless," Azazel said smugly. "But do not fret for it will soon be over. With the passing of each second, your conscious mind slips further under my control. Soon you will exist only to serve your master. Do you understand?"

"Yes, Dominus," I absently replied.

Dominus? What the hell?

"Excellent," he said with a content smile bearing his impossibly white teeth. "I was concerned that you'd pose more of a challenge to *break* than the others. It appears I was wrong."

With my gaze still emptily fixed on Azazel, the clamor of approaching footsteps was evident to my rear. Big footsteps. Presumably made by giant feet.

"How fortuitous," Azazel said as his grin widened. "The trail of bread crumbs so skillfully laid out by Mr. Pothier was designed to lure one Deacon of *great prominence* into my lair — and by my good graces, I have drawn two."

Gliding past me while triumphantly clasping his hands together, I mindlessly turned in my flaming prison to follow his movement like a puppet on a string. And despite my waning mental capacity, I felt a surge of anger pulse through my entire body at the sight of a badly beaten and completely catatonic Abernethy standing helplessly opposite me in his own circle of purple flame. Looming triumphantly behind him was none other than that son of a bitch Tiny, accompanied by the Evil Rooster character I'd seen in my vision. And forming a menacing skirmish line to their rear was a snarling brood of forty-or-so anakim brandishing all manner of medieval weaponry and dressed in nothing but sullied black tunics.

"The *great and mighty* Abernethy," Azazel gloated. "It's been too, too long. Seven hundred years if it's been a day. Rosslyn Chapel if memory serves."

"Aye, Dominus," Abernethy mumbled blankly in a heavy Scottish brogue.

Staring hatefully at Big A for a long moment, Azazel said, "Before your mind fully collapses — know this, *Deacon*. You and your petulant underling will serve as the crowning jewels in my collection of Father's *noble* assassins. And your gifts — *your precious gifts* — will be untimely ripped from the very fiber of your feeble human construct and rightfully bestowed upon a being worthy of their power. The reckoning is upon the race of man. My brothers will soon shed their bonds and vengeance will follow. *You — have — failed.*"

"It is as you say, Dominus," Abernethy again muttered staring into nothingness.

"Yes," Azazel delightfully snarled. "It is." Turning his attention to Evil Rooster, he said, "Well done, Carrick."

"Thank You, Dominus," he replied very businesslike with a noticeable Irish inflection. "I do regret the Scotsman's capture was not without loss. Many fell upon his sword before he relented to the holy flame."

"Regrettable," Azazel said with a slight hint of remorse. "But an acceptable sacrifice. Please see that our new additions take their proper place in the collection. Anak will accompany you as will Mr. Pothier. I shall join you in due time."

"As you wish," Carrick humbly replied with a clichéd bow. "And what of the others?"

"The others," Azazel said somewhat rhetorically, shifting his attention back toward the woodline. "How terribly rude. I'd nearly forgotten about the remainder of our esteemed guests from the Seventh Realm." Focusing specifically on Rooster, he said, "It appears fate has also brought your dear brother to our doorstep. Or do my eyes deceive?"

"It is he," Carrick replied coldly as his eyes flashed a deep, burning red. "Our blood is that of kinsman — but a brother to me he is not."

"Yes, Of course. A *cleric* of the Guild. A loathsome traitor to his race — his family," replied Azazel with a hint of satisfaction. "Consequently, the path of betrayal ends in judgment. And his *judgment*, as with the others, can be nothing less than that of death. Do you concur?"

"A just sentence," Carrick replied without emotion with his glowing eyes fixated on Rooster. "If I may be so bold, Domnius, I find it more than fitting these traitors be struck down by the very Deacon that led them into our humble sanctuary."

"A brilliant offering," Azazel said with a dark grin. "See it done, and conclude our business here." Locking eyes with me he commanded, "Execute them — beginning with the liderc." And casually strolled toward the Earthly portal until he faded from sight in a whooshing sound of unseen massive wings.

Upon his command, I again rotated within my flaming prison like a robot, and the harrowing sight of the team frozen in the obscure state of suspended animation made my stomach curl into a tight knot. They stood like surreal statues on the edge of the woodline completely powerless under the crushing force of Azazel's dark dominance.

Following me with his eyes, Rooster was in mid-motion of throwing his hunting knife while simultaneously squeezing off a round from one of his pistols. Tango had both kukri knives clutched in a fighting stance with his entire lower body stuck mid-transition in mystical smoke form. Caveman's mammoth battle axe was reared high above his head with Duncan frozen in a predatory lurch to his side. Coop had three broadheads drawn back on his bow while Stoner boldly held out his staff that pulsed with an orb of crackling blue energy.

Execute them.

Lowering my head, I felt my eyes squint into a piercing gaze and a spectral silhouette of pure white radiance form about my shoulders. Without my summoning, the cloak violently manifested and flared out like a caged animal, sending visible shock waves of light and heat through the surrounding air. The otherworldly metal flowed down my forearms and encased my hands in seamless gauntlets as I clenched them into tight fists. Turning my hands toward the sky, dueling spheres of Gehenna fire slowly formed in my open palms. Slowly spinning as they grew, the fireballs hissed and sparked with intangible power.

Execute them.

Raising my head, I locked gazes with Rooster. Unable to move or speak, he simply returned my stare. Something about his eyes gave me pause. Gave me clarity.

It wasn't fear.

Or regret.

Or anger.

It was more like sadness. Deep, resolute sadness.

But not for him.

For me.

⁂

"Oy vey, Bubbala. You look awful," came a familiar voice from somewhere in the nether regions of my mind.

"M?" I cognitively asked as my head instantly cleared like somebody threw a bucket of cold water on my face.

"Of course it's M," she said matter of factly, "Mach shnel! Mach shnel! We don't have all day here."

Upon blinking my eyes, I was, surprisingly, no longer in the shadow realm. I was seated in a bustling diner sharing a booth with an incredibly well dressed Principality class angel, sipping on a cup of steaming black coffee. No longer sporting the gaudy sequined dress she had on the first time I'd met her, she donned a perfectly cut navy blue blazer. The highly pressed hot pink shirt underneath was unbuttoned in a fashionable yet very businesslike manner adding the signature 'M' splash of pizazz to the ensemble. Her once hive-piled hair was tightly pulled back on her head and wrapped into a petit bun. Completing the uber executive look was a pair of sleek reading glasses with a leopard print frame like something you'd see on a naughty librarian.

"Where the hell are we?"

"I've no idea," she said looking around the diner in disgust. "But they could use a new cleaning crew. And this coffee is terrible. I could plotz. You hear me? Plotz!"

Having absolutely no idea what the hell was going on, I just stared at her waiting for the punch line.

"We're in your noggin, Bubbala. I just popped in for a quick chat." Looking around she added, "This *place* is bupkes. A figment of your imagination."

"Bupkes," I repeated rhetorically.

"*Bupkes*," she emphasized. "You know — like prophecies."

"Prophecies," I muttered as the gears started turning.

Her faced curled into a cunning grin.

"Now on the rare occasion when prophecies *are not bupkes* — they may actually be quite insightful. Perhaps even provide a glimmer of hope when all appears woefully lost. That is, of course, if you take stock in such things, Bubbala."

"Insightful?" I asked. "Wait — Are you telling me all that crap Fred was spouting off in the Quartermaster was true? And it was about *this* — Azazel's shadow realm?"

"I am telling you nothing of the sort," she replied dismissively. "*Although*, there does seem to be a rather discernible relevance in Frederick's prophetic commentary to your current set of circumstances. Is there not?"

"You told me he was drunk," I dryly muttered.

"Perhaps I was mistaken," she replied tilting her head forward and peering at me over the rim of her glasses. "It's been known to happen — on rare occasion mind you."

Sitting in silence for a couple seconds, I replayed the various and assorted nonsense dispelled upon me by my least favorite prophet amidst his barrage of condescending outbursts. Thinking out loud, I muttered, "Fire. Blood. Rage. It will burn. By my hand — it will burn. Not beholden to that which binds. Its power is mine to command."

"Son of a bitch," I grumbled as a light bulb, the size of a hot air balloon, went off in my head. Locking eyes with Mariel, I said, "I know what I have to do."

"Fabulous," she replied while placing her coffee on the table. "Now go do it."

Leaning across the table, she flicked me squarely in the forehead with her index finger, and yelled, "Mazeltov!"

As my eyes blinked, I was back in the shadow realm.

Or more appropriately, I was back in the shadow realm about to lob two soccer ball sized orbs of judgment fire at my friends while under the influence of a divine brainwashing. Rooster's eyes flashed a blazing red as the fireballs spun in my hand like macabre pinwheels ready to break free from their tether.

Although I still felt the crushing dominance of the holy flame incessantly forcing its will upon me, the situation had changed. I knew something it didn't.

Or at least I was pretty sure I did.

"Execute them, *Deacon*," impatiently grunted Carrick, taking a step in my direction while drawing a sword from the pair crisscrossed on his back. "Do it. Now!"

"No," I snarled forcing the words from my mouth with every ounce of will I could muster.

As a look of confusion mixed with intense aggravation formed on his face, the purple flame roared and thrashed in response to my defiance. Conversely, the cloak flared majestically about my shoulders sending waves of wrathful power cursing through my being.

It was protecting me — Aiding my resurgence.

As the battle for control of my mind raged within, my arms began to visibly shake. Every muscle in my body tensed. My head throbbed with wave after wave of acute, concentrated pain. I felt a stream of blood trickle from my nose and flow over my pursed lips. The very ground beneath me began to quake and fracture. And yet, my face curled into a defiant grin.

"Centurion! You will do as commanded," bellowed Tiny knocking Evil Rooster out of the way and looming over me with unspeakable hatred radiating from his soulless black eyes.

As the holy flame wrapped around my legs and began to slither its way up my body like a nightmarish anaconda planning to crawl down my throat, I closed my eyes. Its mind numbing influence slammed my subconscious with the force of an avalanche forged of the highest mountain — crushing me in its wake. Burying my thoughts in a limitless surge of delusion. Throwing all of its primal power at me.

And it was right about then I did something unexpected.

Opening my eyes, I stopped fighting and let it in.

All of it.

What? Its not like I bet the entire future of mankind on the drunken, slurred ramblings of Freddy Binkowicz or anything.

Well, when you say it like that …

Chapter 36

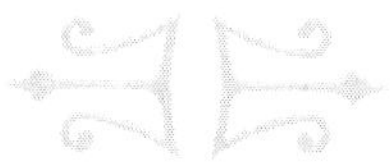

For the record — opening the flood gates to a raging torrent of otherworldly matter that was hell bent on turning me into a supernatural vegetable was not something I'd be in a hurry to do again. Some cliché about desperate times and desperate measures is probably more than appropriate.

But I digress.

Barely holding the spinning fireballs at bay, I threw back my arms, and the incensed tendrils of purple flame leapt from the confines of my circular prison and poured into my being like water into a sponge. And for a long horrible second, it felt like I'd just inhaled a radiation filled mushroom cloud. It was not pleasant. When the entire circle had dissolved and presumably now writhing around my innards like a caged serpent, I forced a smile.

"Gotcha."

Feeling the mental switch flip to the on-position and the calmative awareness wash over me, my perception of time slowed to a dramatic crawl until everything simply stopped.

Time — space — reality. Everything.

Except me. For I was no longer bound by the holy flame. At the moment — I owned its sorry ass. For better or for worse.

"My turn," I grumbled.

Feeling the cloak ripple about my shoulders, a warm, almost electric sensation passed through my damaged body instantly healing my injuries and restoring my strength. Slowly pulling in a long, deliberate breath I cleared my mind and focused my thoughts.

In a moment far removed from physical reality, I looked inward and drifted through the dark corners of my subconscious self — searching for it. Searching for the Balance. The perfect balance between wrath and clarity.

Amidst a plain of infinite darkness, I was drawn to a kernel of pure white light on the very edge of my perception. It was subtle as first, as if dwarfed by an unseen dominance. But as I latched onto its presence with every remaining ounce of my will — it responded.

Hurtling from the deep recess of my soul in an explosion of light, it ripped through the black void like a force of nature. The darkness cowered in its wake as the rippling shockwave of illumination devoured the shadows. For the briefest of moments, a spectral sheen of purple white fire silhouetted the cloak as the holy flame dwindled and became one with the Wrath.

Its power was now mine to command. The slave had become the master. Things were about to get interesting.

Reveling as the combined force of the two otherworldly powers raced through my veins, I slowly rolled my neck back on my shoulders. My eyes hardened into a predatory squint. As my mouth curled into a dark grin, I watched in super slow motion as Tiny swung his ridiculously large battle axe toward my head. Evil Rooster was backpedaling trying to figure out what the hell just happened, and Skip looked like he was about to shit himself. The horde of giants to their rear — well, they just looked big, stupid, and generally confused in a menacing sort of way.

Taking a glance at my team still frozen in mannequin mode, I locked eyes with Rooster and gave him a casual wink. His glowing eyes instantly responded by returning to their normal blue.

Game - fucking - on.

Time resumed with a thunderous clap accompanied by the ear splitting cacophony of giant vocal chords, screaming, "Centurion!"

Side stepping as Tiny buried his axe two solid feet in the ground where I was standing a second earlier, I muttered, "How many frigg'n times do I have to tell you to stop calling me that, asshole?"

I'm pretty sure that dumb bastard was about to call me 'Centurion' *yet again* when the holy flame infused fireballs launched from my hands and seared a couple Frisbee-sized holes through his oversized pectorals. The look on his mammoth face went instantly blank as he simply erupted in a flash of judgment fire and was gone. Like in — *gone gone.*

"See ya, Tiny," I grumbled as Carrick and the rest of his crew of miscreants stood momentarily dumbfounded by the unexpected turn of events. Unfortunately that only lasted for a brief moment before they got really pissed. Then, in typical fashion, they launched into all out attack mode and descended upon me like the Mongolian horde on steroids.

If I had a fan handy, I would have thrown some shit at it. Just saying.

Dodging the thrust of an oversized spear, I punched its large owner square in the kneecap with my metal fist. Willing the spatha into my hand, I then cleaved his head off with one mighty strike. Nimbly dodging and slashing at a few more overzealous assailants, Carrick, the malevolent ginger, threw himself at me with blazing red eyes and dueling swords raised in the strike position. I think he was about to say something witty when I reared back and punched his carrot topped ass square in the chest with the force of a wrecking ball. Blowing backward like he'd been hit by a train, he temporarily faded from sight amidst the incoming swarm of giant bad guys.

Glancing over my shoulder, I released Rooster and the boys from their state of suspended animation with a casual wave of my hand. Instantly snapping back into action and embracing the age old adage of 'the best defense is a good offense', they waded into the gaggle of oversized adversaries with supernatural prowess and a collective need for some pay back with extreme interest. Amidst the slugfest, I maneuvered to the perimeter of Abernethy's fiery prison and began to unbind the holy flame when I heard Cooper Rayfield very southernly yell, "Look out, hoss!"

Feeling the presence of several anakim bearing down on me, I spun to face them just as several arrows whirred past my head and plunged squarely into their eye sockets stopping them dead in their tracks. Still very much alive but evidently a bit flustered, they frantically struggled to pull the arrows out while howling in ineffable pain. Seizing the opportunity, I held out my barzel shielded hand and called for the fire. In response, a blinding circular burst of hissing white flame, highlighted with streaks of brilliant purple, erupted from my hand and literally obliterated the squad of giants leaving nothing but a sizzling minivan sized crater in the ground where they stood seconds earlier.

"Da-gum," blurted Coop taking post by my side while launching another series of barzel tipped arrows at the mind blowing onslaught.

"Well said," I muttered completely taken aback by the apparent new heights my capacity for destruction had reached. Making the mental note that I probably still needed a bit of work in the control department, I caught a glimpse of my inbound ginger buddy.

"Catch!" Rooster yelled throwing me the Winchester while fighting, shooting, and slashing his way through the melee like he'd done this once or twice before. "More focus."

"Roger," I replied cocking the shotgun lever and blowing away a hulking behemoth on his blindside who was seconds away from squashing him with a massive medieval looking sledgehammer.

"We need to grab Abernethy and get the hell out of here!" He yelled defending Big A's right flank. "Can you free him?"

"Working on it," I yelled back while loading another round and training the shotgun on the latest giant bad guy barreling toward with us with unnatural speed when a burst of crackling blue energy smacked him clear in the face.

"Blinded with sorcery!" The anakim grunted followed by an ear splitting growl.

Searching throughout the indescribable chaos, I spotted Stoner atop a small mound to our far right, launching a relentless bombardment of energy balls from his staff like it was a surreal pitching machine. It was rather impressive. Giving him an appreciative nod, I turned the muzzle on Stevie Wonder and put an abrupt end to the screaming.

It was getting old.

Flying past me in a complete blur of motion, a man-sized tornado column of greenish smoke bobbed and weaved through the mob of blinded giant combatants cleaving heads and various other body parts as it twirled about. Barely visible amidst the spinning cloud of death were two hands sticking out. Two hands with a pair of gleaming kukri knives clutched tightly in their grasp.

"Son of Bitch," I muttered. "Tango."

"Pretty cool, huh bro? That whole flying knife thing is epic," came a guttural animal-like voice from behind me. Coming into full view and taking position to my immediate left flank was, well — I wasn't exactly sure what the hell it was.

Standing on two feet, it was easily seven feet tall and covered in thick waves of jet black fur. Its head was a bizarre mixture of human and canine with a threatening, blood stained maw, boasting a ridiculously large set of razor-like choppers where its mouth should be. Clothed only in a pair of black fatigue pants, its wooly upper body rippled and swelled with layer upon layer of predatory muscle. In lieu of hands, it had colossal paws with claw-like nails that looked about twenty years overdue for a clipping. And oddly, it was holding a battle axe.

It was a dog. No — it was a man. No it was —

"Caveman!" Yelled Coop, launching a barrage of arrows over our heads at a incoming throng of massive assailants.

"Mick?" I blurted out, dumbstruck.

Without so much as flinching, the apparent nephed out Caveman let out a heart stopping snarl as he instinctually spun and lurched at the incoming anakim like a — well, like a supernatural dogman wielding a big-ass battle axe I suppose. A few short seconds and a couple tufts of fur later, several giant carcasses, sans heads, plummeted to the ground with a collection of thuds.

"You Ok?" I yelled.

"Yeah, man," he replied through gravelly canine vocal chords. "It was time to let the dog out."

"More biggins — Nine o'clock," Coop yelled before I had the chance to respond.

In a presumed last ditch effort to bullrush our improvised fighting position defending Abernethy, a phalanx of anakim donning what appeared to be oversized Kevlar body armor were stomping a determine beeline toward us chanting an ear splitting war cry.

"Yeah — I got this, fellas," Caveman growled, wiping the blood from his axe blade on a furry arm. "Lil' D! It's rhino time, buddy!"

As the ground starting to quake and the sound of large galloping hooves was heard from behind us, I turned just in time to see a pig the size of a pick-up truck barreling toward us in a cloud of dust. With two jagged, elephant sized tusks protruding from its elongated jaw, its massive body was a harrowing ivory white and covered in rhinoceros-like armor plating. Grisly streaks of crimson blood, that I was pretty sure belonged to somebody else, ran down the length of its massive hide. With complete and utter reckless abandon, the hog o'war was on a rapid collision course with the formation of giants. Like a runaway freight train, it didn't even slow down as it bolted by us. Winking at Rooster and me with a predatory yellow eye, Caveman simply grasped his axe with both paws and leapt on Duncan's meaty back like a surreal surfer catching a wave.

Amidst a barrage of grunts, squeals, and howls, the unlikely duo proceeded to bust through the center of the enemy formation like a bowling ball splitting the frame. It was insane. And ridiculous. And incredibly awesome. All at the same time.

"Didn't see that coming," I mumbled under my breath sending another few fireball rounds downrange while making the mental note to address the topic of Cavemanimal and Moby D at a later time.

"Dean! The portal!" Rooster yelled with blazing red eyes while pointing to our rear.

Spinning around to view the inter-dimensional doorway still intact a good twenty feet behind us, a surge of panic shot through me. While it seemed we were temporarily winning the battle, we were clearly losing the war. The portal was fading as was our hope of getting out of this shit show. I needed to do something.

Now.

"Yo! Mr. Wizard!" I yelled trying to get Stoner's attention.

"What's Up?" He yelled back still peppering the battlefield with blue energy blasts like a mystical machine gunner.

"Can you spread some mojo on the portal and keep the door open a little longer?"

"Maybe," he yelled. "I'll need to stabilize the tether on the Earth side. It's running out of juice."

"Do it," I barked while cocking the shotgun lever and casually blasting a hole through a rather nasty looking large fellow launching a frontal assault at us. "Now!"

"I'm on it," Stoner replied executing a wizardly combat roll and making a break toward the portal entrance.

"Coop, you go with him," I yelled dodging a humungous spear rocketing toward my torso. "We'll mop up here and be right behind you."

Spitting a wad of tobacco juice while shooting me a look that clearly indicated he wasn't too keen on leaving us behind, Coop lowered his bow and reluctantly said, "Aw'ite. Ya'll don't make me wait too long."

"Deal," I grunted giving him a stern nod. Catching glimpse of a familiar pear-shaped figure clad in a really nice pinstriped suit inconspicuously skulking toward the portal entrance amidst the chaos, I said, "Do me a favor on your way out and make sure Uncle Skipper sticks around. I have something for him."

Pulling two broad heads from his quiver, that somehow never needed replenishing, Coop drew back and launched them across the meadow like ballistic missiles. Offering me a satisfied grin as they slammed into Skip's flabby arms and forcefully impaled him on a mammoth redwood, he said, "Dun and dun. See you soon, pard."

Quickly joining Stoner at the flickering portal, they crossed the threshold and faded back to the Earth.

Making note of all the painful things I was going to do to Uncle Skipper when the time came, I scanned the combat zone taking stock of the situation. At first glance, it appeared we'd put down a good two thirds of the anakim horde, and I was fairly confident the rest were soon to follow at the hands, paws, and tusks of my erstwhile colleagues. But there was something else. Something stirring on the very edge of the far horizon.

Something bad.

Closing my eyes, I focused my Sight and projected it across the mangled landscape. Catapulting across the great distance like a powerful zoom lens, it slammed to a halt as my eyes shot open.

"What is it?" Rooster yelled while repeatedly squeezing off barzel tipped rounds from his pistols like it was the OK Corral. "What do you see?"

"More company on the way," I blankly muttered. "Time to go."

And by 'more company', I meant a seemingly infinite legion of giant creatures pouring from every crevice in the mountain range like a colony of pissed of ants.

Must of have been something about the look on my face that prompted him to hold all further questions and simply mutter, "Got it. You take care of Big A. I'll round up the rest of the crew. Meet at the portal in two minutes."

"Make it one."

Nodding affirmation, Rooster began to haul ass toward the twirling cloud of green smoke when a sword hurtled through the air like a bolt of lightning and sunk hilt deep in his chest. Without so much as a grunt, his eyes flashed a blazing red as he ripped it out and threw it to the ground with a single, fluid motion. Scanning the near vicinity for the source of the attack, a second sword rocketed toward his head. Before I could even yell 'Look Out,' Rooster's skin turned bright red as he casually batted the blade away like it was a twig.

"You'll have to do better than that," he snarled in a deep, very unRooster-like voice. "*Carrick.*"

Incredibly red from head to toe, Rooster's estranged brother slowly emerged from within a nearby grove of trees. Bare chested and bloodied, his eyes blazed with madness.

"Then *better* — I shall do, *brother*. You will not leave this place."

As Rooster stomped off like Achilles about to throw down with Hector outside the gates of Troy, I looked down at my catatonic archdeacon kneeling within his purple flamed prison, and grumbled, "So much for Plan A."

Chapter 37

So, the fact we were staring down permanent residency in this jacked-up bizzaro world, and literally within minutes from being trampled by a raging stampede of countless titanic beasties, was instantly lost on my man Rooster. He evidently had something more important to tend to. A debt to settle. One that was long overdue.

After all, Hell hath no fury like a ginger scorned. Everybody knows that.

As Rooster and Carrick hatefully circled each other in an ominous prelude to the imminent O'Dargan family slugfest, I turned my attention to Abernethy.

"First things first," I muttered focusing on the holy flame binding his thoughts. Placing both hands on the ground amidst the circle of purple fire, I concentrated my will in attempt to gain control of it. And after a few long seconds and a screaming headache later, it started working. Like dust to a supernatural vacuum cleaner, the divine matter began to slowly crawl into my gauntlets and simply dematerialize under the crushing force of the Wrath. Doing my damnedest to maintain focus on the tedious and incredibly painful task, the cloak flared on my shoulders and I felt the presence of something flying toward me at a high rate of speed. Looking up just in time to realize that the *something* was actually Rooster, I braced for impact as he slammed into me knocking the both of us ass over tea kettle.

"You have grown weak, brother," I heard Carrick bellow, laughing a deep throated, horrible cackle. "Face me in your true form, Eóin O'Deargáin. Or do you choose to die like a human? Slain like the pet you've become."

With Rooster temporarily down for the count, I pulled the shotgun from its sheath and spun to my feet in a blur of motion while cocking the lever. As I decisively swung the muzzle toward Carrick fully intending to blow a hole in his chest and call it a day, I found myself completely awestruck by what I saw standing opposite me. It was not a man. It was a thing.

A hulking, beastly thing that stood an easy ten feet tall with scaly, blotched red skin of chiseled muscle and veiny tissue. Its bony, deep recessed shoulders were three times too wide for its frame, making its already taut torso look *just* that much more sinister. Peering at me through eyes like orbs of blazing fire, its beaming face was a hellish compilation of spiny ears, barbed yellow teeth, and a hooked beak-like nose. Looming over me with sinewy, sculpted arms that hung ominously well past its double jointed kneecaps, its ghastly claws and ridiculously large razor tipped talons gleamed in the daylight. Yep, I said talons — like some shit you'd see on a frigg'n velociraptor.

And if all that wasn't enough, completing the traumatizing package was a fine layer of orange flame silhouetting its entire massive physique.

"Fuck me," I muttered to myself. "So that's a liderc."

"I do not fear you, Deacon," Carrick growled in a deep, very discomforting voice looking down at me. "I am fear."

"Yeah," I grumbled. "I'm frigg'n terrified. Can't you tell?"

Raising the Winchester to my shoulder, I trained the muzzle on his washboard stomach and blasted his sorry ass with a hissing fireball.

Fully expecting him to shrivel up and go poof, I was more than disappointed when he instead starting laughing, and effortlessly slugged me in the chest with a monstrous fist.

"I was conceived in the Fires of Gehenna," he bellowed as his face curled into a dark scowl. "You are powerless in my presence. Death is upon you, Deacon."

"Already tried death," I snarled picking myself off the ground as I willed the spatha into being. "It didn't agree with me."

In a spectral flash, the sword manifested in my metal covered hand as I leapt at the liderc with blinding speed while ripping the otherworldly blade at its wretched, gaunt neck.

Smiling a wicked grin, the beast simply batted it away and dismissively swatted me to the ground like an insect. Staggering to my feet with my head swimming, I struggled to get my bearings as the liderc circled me like a shrewd predator toying with its prey.

"You should not have come here," it said unequivocally and without any hint of emotion. "I am going to end you now."

And much to my chagrin, the situation degraded pretty quickly from that point forward.

Despite the fact I was running on uber overdrive with the cloak's full compliment of divine power surging through my system, I didn't so much as catch a glimpse of the next blurring strike from Carrick's gangly, talon tipped claw until it was inches from ripping my head off. As the solemn severity that somehow this infernal creature was completely out of my league hit me like a ton of bricks, I quickly came to an inevitable conclusion.

It *was* going to end me. And there wasn't a damn thing I could do to stop it. But, for some inexplicable reason — I knew it wasn't going to happen.

"No," I muttered assertively under my breath. My task wasn't finished. Not yet.

As my face curled into a defiant scowl and the razor tips of massive talons tore into my neck, something happened to prove me right.

As if on cue, another liderc stepped between us.

A bigger one.

And it winked at me as if to say 'I'll take it from here.'

"I am not weak, brother," growled a fully nephed out Rooster in a gravelly, guttural voice dripping of rage as he caught Carrick's arm in mid strike and squeezed it until bones started cracking. "I — Am — Angry!"

He then let out an ear splitting roar and proceeded to pop open a venti sized can of red hot whoop ass. The talons of fury went to quick work slashing and ripping scaly flesh as the twelve foot, hulking frame of the red Rooster moved with impossible grace and uncanny precision as he pummeled the ever living piss out of his brother. With blinding speed barely perceptible to the human eye, he delivered blow after epic blow, cleaving muscle from bone in a fury fueled trance. Slamming Carrick on the ground like a nightmarish rag doll, Rooster glared at me and growled, "Tend to Abernethy."

"Ah, Yeppers," I replied, snapping out of the temporary state of elated shock and quickly turning my attention back to Big A. As the battle raged between the Brothers O'Dargan, and the swarm of unnatural beasties poured from the mountains, I picked up where I'd left off with the holy flame liposuction treatment. Having momentarily run out of anakim to slay, Tango, Cavemanimal, and the Great White War Pig huddled around me taking in the spectacle.

"H-o-l-y shit," muttered Tango, back in human form and apparently as awestruck by the liderc battle royale as I was.

"Damn, bro," Caveman added through canine vocal chords. "Which one is Rooster?"

"He's the one kicking the other one's ass," I muttered, trying to coax as much speed into the process of unassembling Abernethy's flaming bonds as I possibly could.

"Should we help him?" Tango asked still gawking.

"Nah," Caveman muttered as Carrick hurtled by us in a bloody red heap and split the trunk of a ginormous tree wide open with his face. "I think Rooster's got this."

Moby D apparently agreed as he let loose with a booming grunt of approval.

"Hey!" Stoner yelled from behind us as he popped his head through the somewhat stabilized portal. "Let's go, girls! I can't hold it open for much longer!"

"Go," I said to the crew as the holy flame binding Abernethy was nearly diminished and the ground started to literally tremble with the force of the incoming legions crossing the plain at unnatural speed. "We'll be right behind you."

With absolutely no intent on leaving without us, the trio just stood there staring at me defiantly.

Even Duncan. What the hell?

"Do it!" I barked. "That's a goddamn order! We can't fight what's coming. Its over. Go. Now!"

Begrudgingly, Tango sheathed his kukri knives and sternly said, "Don't be late, Dean."

"If anyone but us comes through the portal after you — blow the tether. No hesitation."

"Like I said," Tango said. "Don't be late." Turning to Caveman, he grumbled, "Let's go."

As I watched them double-time to the inter-dimensional gateway and fade from sight as they crossed the threshold, I was pleasantly surprised to hear an unexpected voice.

"You look like shite, lad," muttered the archdeacon gazing at me through battered, swollen eyes.

"Hate to tell you this, boss," I said with a grin "But you've looked better yourself."

Grunting as he winced in pain, he asked, "Where are we?"

"Not in Kansas," I said quickly helping him to his feet. "Can you walk?"

"Aye," he halfheartedly mumbled as he staggered to his feet and immediately began to collapse under the power of his own weight.

"Easy, boss," said Rooster with his creepy liderc voice suddenly appearing in a blur of movement and gracefully catching Big A.

"Jackie —," Abernethy mumbled upon recognizing Rooster's 'Mr. Hyde' form just as he passed out from what I suspected was a combination of his injuries and the lingering after effect of the holy flame.

"Time to go," Rooster growled, looking down at me with flaming eyes while cradling Abernethy like a child in his massive red arms.

"Where's Carrick?" I asked.

"Where he's supposed to be," Rooster said definitively with an ever so slight hint of remorse as he plodded toward the portal entrance now steadily flickering in and out of existence.

"Right."

As the inconceivable force of anakim and assorted beastly creatures of twisted divine genetics were less than a kilometer out and closing fast, I followed the big red palooka to the gateway. And despite the absolute dire nature of the situation, I couldn't help but feel a momentary sense of relief. The mission was nearing completion, and the team would live to fight another day.

Me on the other hand — I still had one thing left to do to make all that possible.

"You first," Rooster growled stopping at the portal entrance now flashing erratically and seemingly within seconds of fading into the ether.

"Afraid not, my friend. The job's not finished," I replied with a cold demeanor glancing at the incoming barrage of unnatural beasties. "Not yet."

"There's nothing left to do here," he snarled understanding my intentions. "It's over. We're leaving."

But he didn't know what I knew. My destined path ended here. By my hand this place would burn.

All of it.

Rooster's Dragonfly device was never supposed to bring an end to this cursed realm and its inhabitants.

I was.

It was my purpose. A purpose I now understood.

Pausing for a long moment to take in his hulking red frame and generally nightmarish appearance, I smiled despite the situation.

"You know what, John?" I said with a shit-eating grin. "I think I like you better as a liderc."

"What?" He grunted in confusion. "Why?"

"Because if you didn't look like an oversized carny, I'd probably feel bad about this."

As his burning eyes flashed brighter, I channeled all my supernatural strength and punched him as hard as I could square in the bony kneecap. Buckling under the force of the devastating and unexpected blow while still doing his best to hold an unconscious Abernethy, Rooster momentarily lost his balance. Seizing the opportunity, I gave his big red ass a healthy shove and watched contently as he and Big A fell across the threshold.

The last thing I saw before the otherworldly gate snapped shut was his eyes. They instantly flashed from fiery orbs to their normal brilliant blue as he locked gazes with me. Then he was simply gone.

And I was alone.

"Sorry about that, buddy," I muttered out loud to no one in particular.

Slowly turning to face the horde of abominations racing across the landscape at me like a surreal swarm of locusts, I heard a faint whimpering sound to my immediate right. Quickly glancing toward the source, a familiar slovenly fat bastard in a jacked-up pinstripe suit was strung up like a side of beef on the trunk of a mighty redwood.

"Philbert!" I blurted out with the darkest of grins. "Always hanging around in the wrong places."

Yeah, I went there. Couldn't resist.

"Ah — Hey, bossman," said Uncle Skip as his chubby face drained a pure white.

"What was that you were saying about a good con?" I asked, stalking toward that smug son of bitch as I called for the fire and felt the presence of a flaming sphere form in my gauntlet.

As Skip's eyes widened with primal fear and his jaw dropped open, I blew a hole the size of a manhole cover through his goddamn chest in a sizzling flash.

Contently watching as he vaporized in an eruption of searing white fire leaving nothing behind but Coop's arrows, I grumbled, "Never mind."

The pounding of giant feet accompanied by a deafening clamor of grunts, howls, and throaty screams drew my attention back toward the meadow. Slowly turning to see a wall of dust practically blocking out the daylight, I found myself in the dead center of a horseshoe formation of infuriated aberrations. An eclectic collection of countless anakim, varangian, lycaon, and all kinds of other weird looking fuckers I hadn't had the pleasure of meeting yet stood before me. Eyes fuming. Fangs dripping. Chests heaving.

Willing the spatha into my hand, I wrapped my fingers tightly around its stout hilt as my face hardened into a predatory squint, and I met the multitude of loathing, soulless eyes glaring back at me.

"Listen up, assholes," I boldly declared pulling the hood of the cloak over my head. "My name is Dean Robinson. Seventh Deacon of the Seventh line."

The cloak flared and billowed about my shoulders like a caged animal as the Wrath welled like a seething maelstrom of infinite power within me. Silence swiftly spread through the monstrous formation like a surreal domino effect until you could literally hear a pin drop.

"I am my Father's Wrath. And I'm the last thing you sorry sons of bitches will ever lay eyes on."

As the words flowed from my mouth, they immediately boomed with a commanding echo throughout every corner of the wretched land. Holding the spatha high above my head, the legions descended upon me with ravenous fury.

And I simply let them come.

"Control the Wrath. Command the Power," I murmured as I closed my eyes. Drifting deep within myself as the calmative awareness washed over me, I felt no fear as I approached the blazing light of my divine mantle. There was only serenity and clarity and purpose. For this time when I untethered the Wrath from my being — it was without malice, without anger. It was with sacrifice.

A willing sacrifice to end this cursed realm in fire, in blood, and in rage. To set the divine judgment free upon the bane of mankind — the enemies of Heaven.

Focusing every ounce of my will on this sole purpose, I opened my eyes and called for the fire. In a spectral flash, a torrent of otherworldly flame erupted from my metal gauntlets and encased the sword in a pulsating glow. The air rippled with waves of searing heat and the brilliant glimmer of pure white light.

As the sword literally hummed with unfathomable power, I boldly raised it to the sky. Looking to the Heavens, I spoke the Words of Enoch.

"And when the Lord thy God shall deliver them before thee — thou shalt smite them, and utterly destroy them — thou shall make no covenant with them, nor show mercy unto them."

In a blur of movement, I then reversed the sword and thrust it with all my power into the ground before me. As it penetrated the surface, a boundless wall of infernal white fire erupted from the charred earth like a raging volcano. It stretched from left to right as far as the eye could see and subsequently raced forward with unbridled speed toward the charging legions. Reaching the front of the formation, the unbound Wrath mercilessly ripped through the unyielding multitudes until the unnatural creatures were nothing more than blazing silhouettes amidst the dust. Their inhuman screams were that of absolute horror and utterly deafening.

But that was not the end. Rippling across the expanse like a voracious shockwave, the raging wall of judgment fire reached the mountain range on the far horizon within mere seconds. Upon colliding with the majestic peaks, the fire catapulted into the sky and instantly formed an unthinkable funnel of swirling, fiery apocalypse that made the Dragonfly look like a flash in the pan.

Dropping the spatha and falling to my knees in absolute exhaustion, I watched with fading eyes as the firestorm ripped through the landscape — sucking time, space, and reality into its voracious vortex. My perception of time came to a screeching halt as my senses began to steadily dull. Mustering enough strength to pull the hood off my head, I collapsed to the ground in relief.

I'd done it.

The chain of events leading to the reckoning of mankind was broken. The new generation of anakim would not plague the Earth as in days of old. The divine mantles of the enslaved Deacons would return to the source upon their regrettable yet merciful death. The Balance was restored.

It was over.

And unfortunately, by consequence — so was I.

As my vision faded to black and I felt myself checking out for good, something quite unexpected happened. A strangely familiar prickling sensation tingled on the back of my neck. And just like the other times I'd experienced it, I instantly had the unequivocal feeling that I wasn't alone.

As I contemplated that for a quick second, a face appeared in my blurred vision. A face silhouetted in a wraithlike luminous sheen. Despite the fact my senses weren't exactly running on all eight cylinders at that particular moment, I could still discern that it wasn't the face of a giant nor a horrid beast — it was the face of a man. And he was leaning over me — smiling.

What the hell?

"Well done, Master Robinson. You've more than lived up to your reputation," he said in a garbled yet somewhat charming voice. "However, your part is not yet played out I'm afraid. This was but the first act."

As the shadow realm imploded in a literal blaze of infernal glory around me, I felt a hand forcefully grasp my chest accompanied by a powerful whoosh of air and the flutter of massive wings.

Angel wings.

Then there was only darkness.

Chapter 38

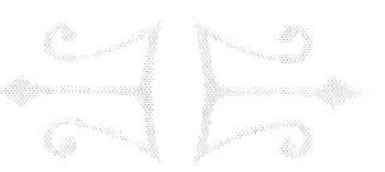

"You're an asshole," Rooster said waiting for me like he knew I was going to walk into the bar at that exact moment. Wincing in pain, he dismissively turned and began to hobble through the Quartermaster on a set of crutches with his right leg in a bulky cast.

Barely awake yet somehow fully dressed in a pair of jeans and yet another RoosterBragh tee-shirt, I muttered, "Nice to see you too."

"Thought we were friends," he grumbled glancing down at the cast.

"We are friends."

"You punched me," he said drolly. "Really fucking hard."

"I, ah, punched you *because* we're friends. It's a complex emotion. Heat of the moment kind of thing."

"Aha."

"If it makes you feel any better, I felt bad about it — For a couple seconds."

Remaining silent, he simply shot me a rather snide glare as his eyes blazed red for a quick second.

"Come on, man, it was for your own good. Get over it already. I said I was sorry."

"No — No, you didn't."

"Oh, right. Sorry?"

"You're an asshole," he repeated as his face curled into a mild grin.

"Look at it on the bright side. I could've shot you."

"Do I need to call you an asshole again?"

"Nope. I get it."

Still completely baffled as to how the hell I got back here, I was nonetheless tickled pink to be back in the QM with all its otherworldly charm. But as I meandered through the labyrinth of smooth wooden tables and benches following a gimpy Rooster, I couldn't help but wonder where everybody was. The place was a ghost town.

"How long was I out?" I asked.

"Three days," he replied. "But the topic du jour is how the hell you *got out*?"

"You mean from Azazel's funhouse?"

"Yeppers."

"You say it like you're not happy to see me."

"Not at all," he replied still inching along on his crutches. "I'm over frik'n joyed to see you. As was everyone else when we got back from Liverpool thinking you were toast only to find your sorry ass all laid up on the Reliquary floor. What none of us can wrap our heads around is — how the hell you did it?"

"Did what?"

Stopping in mid hobble, he spun around and shot me a pensive gaze prompting me to stop as well.

"Did *what*? For reals?" He asked rhetorically yet incredibly sarcastically. "Ok, so shortly after you shattered my kneecap and opted to go all lone gunman on the anakim militia — which was so incredibly not cool for the record, Skyphos registered a massive energy displacement where the shadow realm was located. *Curiously*, at precisely that same moment — *you* mysteriously ported into the Reliquary all jacked up and unconscious in your usual fashion."

"So," I grumbled.

"So? You single handedly obliterated *an entire realm* within a matter of seconds and somehow managed to port back here *without* a gateway. *Then* … three short days later, you're back on your feet and cracking bad jokes like it was nothing. And not to mention that whole dealio about inhaling a ring of holy flame. What the hell was that about? Nobody does that, Dean. Nobody."

Not sure it was prudent to tell Rooster that I based my entire Machiavellian scheme to save mankind on the prophetic ramblings of Freddy Binkowicz nor that I was evidently whisked from oblivion's doorstep by an unidentified angel whose motives were still in question, I simply shrugged.

"What I can say? Had to improvise. Seemed like a good idea at the time."

"You had to improvise," he said fully knowing I was holding something back. "That's what you're going with, eh?"

"Look, man, the last thing I remember before waking up in my bed ten minutes ago, surprisingly not dead — *again*, was going thermonuclear on the horde of friendly neighborhood creatures charging at me with bad intentions. And now I'm here. That's all there is to it."

"Fine," he said realizing the conversation had reached a momentary dead end. As he resumed his determined hobble toward a large stone door at the back of the massive room, he added, "But we're going to talk about this again — soon."

"Fair enough," I replied. "Right after you tell me all about fuzzy dogmen and smoke monsters — and lidercs."

He momentarily paused.

"Deal." Reaching the massive door within a couple more labored grunts, he said, "Alright, let's go. We're late."

"Late for what?"

"The feast."

"The what?"

"The feast — to end all feasts. The official 'Ding Dong the Giants are Dead' soirée. Not sure if you heard, but some lunatic managed to wipe every breathing anakim off the face of God's green earth in one fell swoop. Big A figured that called for a celebration of epic proportion."

"Medieval France epic?"

"Maybe not quite *that* epic."

"Will there be chicken coops?"

"No chicken coops," he replied smirking. "Everyone's gathered at the Dreghorn. Just waiting on the guest of honor to show his ugly mug."

"But, how'd you know —"

"When you'd wake up from your latest dirt nap?" He said finishing my sentence. "Stoner's been monitoring your healing process." Glancing at his pocket watch, he added, "He figured you'd be back on your feet exactly fifteen minutes ago."

"That's, ah, really disturbing."

"Magus."

"Right," I muttered. "Will there be RoosterBragh at this most fabled fiesta?"

He scoffed.

"Enough to probably kill you. And for good this time."

"Well then," I happily muttered. "Count me in."

Balancing on one crutch as he reached down and placed his hand on the Chi-Rho etched into the center of the massive door, he paused.

"Damn it. Forgot the batch of mead I promised Caveman. Must've left it on the bar. Be right back."

"Leave that to me, Hop Along. I'll catch up with you," I said turning around. "Won't be too difficult at the pace you're moving."

"Damn nice of you," he said with a smirk. "But don't think this gets you off the hook for bashing my knee. We're going to square that debt at some point."

"Looking forward to it," I grumbled.

As I walked away, he called out, "Hey, Dean."

"What now?" I groaned stopping in mid-stride and looking back.

With a sober, sincere gaze, he just stared at me for a long second or two like he was choosing his next words very carefully.

"What you did in the shadow realm — for us. All of us. I mean — there's no words for something like that. I never said thank you."

Nodding, I simply replied, "And you never should."

After a second healthy stroll, I arrived back at the bar to find two man sized ceramic growlers labeled '*Money Honey — for Caveman Use Only.*'

"Now that's just funny," I muttered shaking my head as I quickly grabbed the stout bottles. Glancing upward at one of the tV screens, a comical vision of several douchebags in tight suits and large guts elbowing their way to the front of a line in some random airport terminal made me chuckle.

"Probably some goddamn consultants," I joked to myself.

Just as I turned to walk away, the sound of an unexpected voice caught me off guard.

"Marvelous places — airports. I must confess, I take great pleasure in the engendered hostility. It's simply exceptional."

Stopping dead in my tracks, I spun back toward the bar to find a roguishly handsome character of medium build with slicked back silver hair and a pair of Buddy Holly spectacles. Dressed all in black with a pristine white apron covering his torso, he was taking great care to meticulously polish a pint glass with a piece of cloth.

"And you are?" I said glaring at him.

"No one of consequence," he casually replied as he finished the glass he was working on and carefully placed it on a shelf. "However, my friends call me Lew."

Without so much as looking up, he simply grabbed another one and went to work on it like I wasn't even there.

There was something about his voice. It was familiar.

"I haven't see you around. You new here?"

"Quite the contrary," he replied amidst a modest laugh. "I've been around for a long, long year."

"Well you're evidently missing the party of the millennium. Everyone's at the Dreghorn slugging back Rooster beer like it's free. Something about all the giants and their bean stalk going poof."

Finishing the second glass, he methodically placed it next to the first and boldly smiled at me.

"So I've heard," he replied in a fluid, charming voice with the ever so slightest hint of an accent I couldn't quite place. "But I'm afraid you'll find that particular celebration slightly premature. As I told you before, Master Robinson, that was the merely the first act."

As his words registered with my brain, I instantly felt the prickly sensation on the back of my neck.

"*You*," I blurted out putting the bottles down. "It was you — that's been eaves dropping. You pulled me out of the shadow realm."

"Quite correct," he replied folding his hands and placing them on the bar. "It was I."

"Why?"

"Because I am an enemy of your enemy. Which if I'm not mistaken, makes me your friend."

"My enemy? You mean Azazel."

He grinned.

"Azazel is a deluded child, Dean. A pawn. There is a greater being who threatens the integrity of the game. A being of power and influence. He and he alone is your true adversary."

"The traitor," I grumbled. "You know who it is."

"It is within my purview to know such things."

"But you're not going to tell me, are you?"

"I am not," he said removing the apron and draping it over the bar. "I'm afraid it would be very unsportsmanlike, shall we say."

"Awesome," I muttered. "You mentioned a game. What game?"

"Why the game of life, of course," he said smiling. "The great human choice — devotion or transgression. Sinner or saint. To rise — or to fall."

Still not following the plot, I just glared at him.

"For the rules are absolute. As they've been since the very beginning," he quipped. "It's a game of subterfuge — to be played in the shadows of mankind with the utmost of finesse. But there are forces at work that will undoubtedly change the nature of the contest with a brutish stratagem fueled by deluded concepts of *world order* and revenge. Something that I simply cannot tolerate. It's terribly bad for business, you see."

"*Business*," I grumbled still clueless as to what he was droning on about. "What business is that exactly?"

"*My* business," he replied very casually.

"Alright," I muttered losing my patience. "What the hell is it that you want?"

"The grand conspiracy is still very much afoot despite your valiant efforts in brother Azazel's paradise lost. I merely want you to finish that which you've started. Restore the Balance."

"Not sure where you're getting your news from Lewis, but it's over. The giants are toast. I've already done that."

"No — You have not," he said in a cordial yet stern manner. "But I believe you will. Given the proper *oversight*."

"Right, Ok," I muttered having had enough of this bullshit conversation. "This was fun. Appreciate you stopping by, and thanks for this incredibly insightful chat. It was great. Seriously. We should do it again. Actually — let's not."

Grabbing the bottles of mead, I said, "And thanks for saving my ass. Still not sure why the hell you did it, but at the moment — I really don't give much of a shit. On a cautionary note, *Lew* — I wouldn't recommend sneaking around here anymore. Especially behind the bar. Rooster doesn't like people touching his stuff. Got a nasty B side, if you know what I'm saying. You wouldn't like him when he's angry. Trust me on that one. At any rate — Keep it real."

As I started to walk away, I turned and asked, "And what the hell kind of angel name is *Lew* anyway?"

As his grin morphed into a beaming smile, a loud chime rung through the vacated Quartermaster, and I instinctively spun to find the centuries old grandfather clock in the far corner announcing the changing of the hour.

"You are a quick study, Master Robinson," he said with a modest chuckle. "However, it's been quite some time since *my* name has been associated with that of an angel. Fare thee well, my friend. We shall chat again - soon."

As quickly as I turned back toward the bar, my mysterious new pal was gone. Doing a quick scan to find myself completely alone, I suddenly had the gut wrenching feeling that 'Lew' was most likely an abbreviation for something else. Perhaps something with a couple more syllables and slightly more terrifying.

"Lucifer," I muttered to myself. "Didn't see that coming. Thought he'd be taller."

As I turned and started back toward the party, suddenly not feeling very party like anymore, the front door of the Quartermaster swung open and a gust of wintry air blasted through the empty bar. Spinning around to find the silhouette of a petit frame standing firmly against the Boston night, I felt a surge of adrenaline rip through me.

"Dean Robinson!" She barked crossing the threshold with her fists clenched. "You owe me a goddamn beer."

"Doc?"

And once again in my short lived supernatural existence, things had become interesting.

EPILOGUE

Everybody has dreams. Some include bikini clad super models and fruity cocktails with little umbrellas. Others include giant beings with poor hygiene habits and fallen angels with daddy issues. Either way, dreams are truly an interesting phenomenon.

In my mortal life, I operated under the premise that dreams were nothing more than a random offshoot of my subconscious mind. A haphazard collection of unfinished thoughts woven together and played back in a nonsensical loop when my brain needed a smoke break.

But after being on the flip side of things for a while — I knew otherwise. There was meaning. Purpose. Direction. Things that would cook your frigg'n noodle if you thought about it too much.

So I decided not to think about it. For the time being anyway. And as fate would have it, spending a rather enjoyable celebratory evening in the Dreghorn was just the distraction I needed to put things back in perspective. If such a thing still existed in the not-so afterlife that is.

There was just something about watching a miniature feral hog and his furry BFF moonwalk their way through a full scale replica of the second century Roman Colosseum that puts a whole new spin on the way you look at things.

I also came to the conclusion that being seven hundred years old and Scottish *does not* make you proficient at the bagpipes. Although I'm not sure

Big A would share the same sentiment as he serenaded the masses with a relentless cacophony of really bad music right up until his prized instrument curiously burst into flames.

It was an accident. I swear.

And believe it or not, before the festivities drew to a close I had yet another astounding revelation. With the precise application of RoosterBragh in mass quantities — It indeed *was possible* to get an undead, semi-divine super solider liquor'd up. Pretty sure I should have laid off those shots of glowing orange liquid at the end though. I think it might have been cleaning solvent. Hell of an aftertaste.

As a streaming replay of the unexpected reunion with Erin Kelly dominated my thoughts, I plummeted face first onto my humble bed in the bowels of the Quartermaster and quickly drifted into an intoxicated slumber. And right when I had the unequivocal feeling that everything was going to be OK, the onslaught of a splitting headache hit me like a force of nature.

Typical.

Feeling like my head was about to pop under the unimaginable force, I squeezed my eyes shut and grabbed my forehead with both hands. After an excruciating couple seconds, the pain subsided, and I coaxed my eyes open to find an unfamiliar scene laid out before me.

No longer lying in my bed, I was standing on a rocky ledge jutting out from what appeared to be the near top of a massive, snow laden mountain in the center of a desolate valley. It was approaching dusk with the sun steadily falling below the horizon. Blocking my view of the surrounding landscape stood two figures on either side of an oversized torch that blazed bright with a hearty flame. Inching closer, I came to the quick realization that one of them was my pal Azazel. His unidentified counterpart was at least a head taller and carefully concealed his face inside a leather praetorian helmet deep within the hood of a brilliant white cloak. An almost tangible aura of pure white light silhouetted his powerful frame. The aura of an angel. A traitorous angel.

"A minor set back at best, my Lord," Azazel said encouragingly. "Rest assured that our losses in the shadow realm are more than trivial. The plan is very much on schedule despite the unforeseen events."

The hooded figure scoffed. “Is it your intention to insult me — Or do you simply take me for a fool?”

“I do not understand, my Lord,” Azazel said uncomfortably.

“There is nothing *unforeseen* about the events in the shadow realm. Our *losses* are the result of gross negligence. *Your* negligence.”

“My Lord,” Azazel rebutted. “I simply did not anticipate —”

“It is not your place to *anticipate*,” the hooded figure snarled. “It is your place to follow instruction. And yet again you prove incapable of doing so. You had but one simple objective - capture the Seventh of Seven. An objective you failed to deliver upon.“

“I do apologize, my Lord,” Azazel subserviently replied as he knelt at the feet of his apparent better. “My actions were — regrettable. Please allow me the opportunity to correct them.”

“Your petty hubris betrays you, brother. You *reek* of them — the humans,” he said with a sharp edge. “Compromise our endeavors once more and that wretched pit from which I plucked you all those many centuries ago will seem like a paradise in comparison with the eternal torment that lies in wait. Are we quite clear?”

“Yes, my Lord,” Azazel muttered like a scolded child. “Abundantly.”

“Then let us try this again,” said the White Hood motioning for him to stand. “The collection — it is secure?”

“Of course. The enslaved Deacons remain safely concealed deep within the Earth.”

“And what of their *gifts*?”

“The extraction process is nearing completion, my Lord. Soon — the harnessed Wrath will be at your beckoning.”

“And due to your *indiscretion*, we remain one mantle shy of the majority. Without that of the alpha or the omega — I cannot wield the Wrath.”

“Regrettably, my Lord. However, please trust that I will soon rectify that dilemma.”

The White Hood broke into a harrowing, deep-throated laugh.

“I trust that you understand the consequence should you again fail to do so,” he said shifting his attention to the frozen plains. “It is possible, however, that your ineptitude has yielded a window of opportunity. With the fall of your precious realm, the resurgence of the anakim is undoubtedly perceived thwarted. We must strike while both the Guild and the seraphic court revel in this false victory. The hour of judgment approaches. Our children grow — hungry. Perhaps it is time they rise from the shadows and once again assert their dominance upon Father's precious creation."

"Understood," Azazel humbly muttered bowing his head as he spoke. "It shall be done."

As the vision started to blur, I reluctantly moved to the edge of the stone platform and gazed upon the valley below. Slowly taking in the scene, I was slammed with a wave of adrenaline as I came to the spine-chilling conclusion that I was wrong. The race of giants was not destroyed.

There was more. Thousands more. Tens of thousands. The anakim were not wiped from the Earth. They were legion upon it.

"No," I murmured in horror as my eyes flew open, and I jumped from the bed in a cold sweat to find Stephen intently standing over me.

"What did you See?" He asked.

"It's not over," I grumbled as my face curled into an intense scowl.

"And I'm gonna need a bigger gun."

ABOUT THE AUTHOR

Not much of substance is known of James MacGhil. According to popular theory, he fled his childhood home in rural New England to seek fame and fortune as an infantryman in the United States Army. Many years and misadventures later, he's purportedly surrendered to middle age and rocking the suburbs in Tallahassee, Florida with the love of his life, two amazing kiddos, and a pair of slothful canines.

ACKNOWLEDGEMENTS

If you'd told me ten years ago that at some point in the not so distant future I'd be writing a book — I would've told you to piss off. So as I sit in my study trying to coherently cobble together my humble thanks for the multitude of family, friends, and colleagues that helped me get here, I can't help but feel a bit surreal about the whole thing.

At any rate, here's my best shot at acknowledging all the folks with undeniable culpability in the creation of this story, which by the way, was written over a period of two years spanning five states, four houses, countless hotels rooms, and more airplanes/airports than I can honestly remember. And I'm pretty sure I never wrote a single word during hours of daylight. So here we go …

First and foremost, I'd like to express my undying gratitude to my beautiful wife, Sherrie — who not only put up with the ridiculous amounts of time, energy, and life force I poured into this effort over the past few years but consistently encouraged me to get after it. I would've quit long before I got started had she not given me the much needed boot in the arse it required to coax me into writing the first sentence. For that, I will forever be grateful.

Now that I've given my wife top bill, everyone else is in no particular order …

That being understood, I need to throw some serious props to my Ranger buddy on this mission, Hans Holland, for — well, for pretty much helping take this whack job idea I had and turning it into a story. Hans was there from the very beginning and has probably read this book about a thousand times over during the course of its unnatural conception. Beyond the call of duty, he endured countless late night plot discussions (emails, text messages, phone calls, etc.) and subjected to more than a few horrifically bad turns I took along the way. Can't thank him enough for walking every step of this epic journey by my side and for tuning down his Stephen Hawking-like intellect enough to work with me. Although he's got an SAT score that's higher than most alien life forms, I do take solace in the fact he's a ginger kid and everybody knows that ginger kids have no soul. So at the very least I have that leg up on him — which is nice.

Next on my list of no particular order is my first beta reader (and also my editor), Julie Gilmore. Julie was more than instrumental in this twisted production and supplied the undying enthusiasm that got this story over the finish line. I can't begin to quantify the amount of time and energy she poured into this project but I'm more than grateful for her encouraging spirit and relentless attention to detail. And there's the small fact that trying to edit the work of a 'control enthusiast' such as myself has to absolutely suck … that being understood — I'm really hoping she sticks around for the next couple books in the series. You rock, Jules! Fist bump …

I've read somewhere that it takes twenty people or something like that to write a novel. To that point, I'd like to both acknowledge and thank my Wednesday night 'Focus Group' hommies of Mike Mahan, TJ Fields, and Jake Galley for not only hanging out on Wednesday nights and drinking beer but more importantly helping to shape my harebrained concepts and ideas into somewhat more coherent harebrained concepts and ideas. Specifically, I'd like to call out Mike 'the Wonder Beard' Mahan for employing his otherworldly Ivy League education and superior intellect to provide sage counsel and incredibly insightful critique throughout the writing of this novel. Much appreciated and valued. It's Rhino Time!

Any of you have a mother that's an English teacher? Well, I do - and I'd like to give me mum, Marianne McMichael, a big shout for being gracious enough to not only say she *liked* the rough draft of my novel but holding back commentary on how much my grammar sucked! Thanks, Mom!

In the vein of old friends reunited — I'd like to thank my old Ranger buddy, Brian Shea, for creating the incredible artwork displayed on both my book cover and website. He captured my visions incredibly and put some serious blood, sweat, and tears into his work. Thanks, bro!

In the vein of friends made along the journey — I'd like to express my sincere gratitude to Donna Labermeier (author of the incredibly awesome The Healers Trilogy) for not only taking time out of her busy schedule to read my early drafts but providing the much needed validation I needed to keep going. She was an incredible inspiration and an author I aspire to be like when I eventually grow up ... whenever the hell that is. Thank You, Donna!

Lastly, I'd like to thank my dear friend and colleague, Ginny Levi, for recognizing the importance that writing this novel meant to me and providing the invaluable mystical influence to see it to fruition. Over many long trips up and down the east coast, Ginny also served as my chief Yiddish advisor ensuring that I never plotzed when I wanted to shlep. Mazeltov! Hells yeah!

In dire conclusion, I'd like to thank You - the reader. If you've got this far, I can only hope that you enjoyed the quirky escapades of Dean, Rooster, and the crew. And I sincerely hope this story put an occasional dark smile on your face and perhaps widened your perspective on this outlandish world we live in. Please check in with us at www.jamesmacghil.com for more absurd commentary on giants, nephers, evil clown guys, and the next phase in the epic adventure of our favorite supernatural strike team from the Seventh Realm.

For as *Lew* so eloquently put it — This was merely the first act.

Made in the USA
Middletown, DE
02 August 2015